Immortal Rising

"I'm sorry."

Thorne glanced up from his plate with surprise at those softly spoken words.

Stephanie grimaced and said, "I didn't mean to ruffle your feathers. I shouldn't have touched you without permission."

His eyes widened incredulously at the solemn apology. He'd thought she was disgusted by him, but she seemed to be suggesting she'd felt bad for . . . touching him? Without permission? He almost assured her that the apology was unnecessary and she could touch him anytime, anywhere and any way she'd like, but caught the words at the last moment as he realized how they would sound.

Not that he didn't mean it. Thorne would be happy for her to touch him again . . . anywhere and as often as she'd like . . .

By Lynsay Sands

LYNSAY SANDS

IMMORTAL RISING

AN ARGENEAU NOVEL

AVONBOOKS

An Imprint of HarperCollinsPublishers

Excerpt from *The Chase* copyright © 2004 by Lynsay Sands.

First Avon Books mass market printing: April 2022
First Avon Books hardcover printing: April 2022

Print Edition ISBN: 978-0-06-311154-7
Digital Edition ISBN: 978-0-06-309743-8

Cover design by Nadine Badalaty
Cover illustration by Larry Rostant
Cover images © Shutterstock

FIRST EDITION

Printed in Lithuania

22 23 24 25 26 SB 10 9 8 7 6 5 4 3 2 1

IMMORTAL RISING

Prologue

"How many?"

That question from Lucian Argeneau made Stephanie open her eyes. She'd closed them to concentrate on the many voices sounding in her head, but now glanced around at Lucian and the group of rogue hunters awaiting her answer. It was predawn on a warm fall evening, the sun sending streaks of orange and vermillion out to pierce the night sky ahead of its arrival. But it was still pitch-black in the copse of maples they stood in. Even so, she didn't have trouble making out the twelve people ranged around her, or the overgrown yard of the somewhat run-down seventies-style bungalow on the other side of the trees.

The benefits of night vision, Stephanie thought grimly, and ground her teeth as she tried to block the flow of thoughts and memories pouring through her head from the men and women around her, as well as the people in the house, and pretty much everyone else within a mile radius of her. Not that she was sure it was a mile. It could be that she was picking up the thoughts and memories of people as far away as two or ten miles for all she knew . . . So many voices in her head.

"Stephanie? How many?" Lucian repeated, sounding impatient now.

"There are thirty-two rogues in the house," she responded calmly, unconcerned by the grumpy man's irritation. "And one more somewhere behind the house."

"Behind it like in the backyard?" Mirabeau asked, moving closer to her side.

Stephanie glanced at the tall woman with fuchsia-tipped hair, and shook her head. "Farther away. Past the woods behind the backyard."

"Probably just a neighbor on the next street, then," Lucian said dismissively, and turned away to begin giving his orders to the others.

Stephanie scowled at his back, but waited until he finished with his orders before saying, "I don't think it's just a neighbor, Lucian. The feeling I get is the person is—"

"Your feelings do not matter. Whoever it is, it's not someone we need worry about now," Lucian interrupted. "We will check it out after we take care of this nest."

"But—" Stephanie began in protest, only for him to cut her off again.

"Stay here until we clear the house."

Stephanie turned to where Mirabeau had been a moment ago, intending to enlist her aid in getting Lucian to listen, but the other woman was gone. She'd already melted into the dark trees to head around the property to the spot where she was to take up position before the group closed in on the house.

All of them were now gone, Stephanie realized as she turned back to where Lucian had been, only to find empty space. She was alone in the woods.

Stephanie threw her hands up with an exasperated huff and then lodged her fists on her hips and surveyed the situation. Despite the darkness and trees, she could make out several different hunters moving through the woods around the house, finding their spots. After having worked with them for several years, she knew the routine. They'd basically surround the property, and then approach at a signal from Lucian, closing in like a net drawn tight around the house. Each person had their orders. Some would guard windows or sliding doors while others would charge through the back and front doors, the idea being that no one inside should evade capture once the house was breached.

Stephanie watched the group maneuver, but her mind was elsewhere. She could hear that other voice from beyond the woods behind the house. The owner was responding to a beeping sound, going into a small room to check—

"Cameras!" Stephanie barked the warning as the thought entered her mind, and then scanned the front of the house for the security cameras. She couldn't see them, but knew they were there. Fortunately, either Lucian could see them or he was just trusting her, because he immediately barked an order and the slow approach was abandoned in favor of a much swifter one.

Stephanie watched as Lucian led the rogue hunters Decker and Bricker through the front door. There was no sudden shrieking or sounds of chaos. The rogues in the house were all either already asleep, or settling down to sleep at this hour. It was why the hunters struck at dawn, so that they could catch the whole nest and not miss any inhabitants who might be out and about during the evening.

It was also always easier to take them by surprise, Stephanie thought, and then closed her eyes and focused on that lone voice again. She'd known about the cameras because this person had been checking them and had seen the hunters closing in on the house. He wasn't just a neighbor. He was connected somehow to this house. She'd gotten that feeling earlier, but hadn't been sure how exactly he was connected to it and the people inside. Now she tried to sort through the person's thoughts for an answer.

Stephanie sifted through the multitude of voices in her head until she zeroed in on the one she wanted again. The individual was in something of a controlled panic now, if there even was such a thing. His thoughts were urgent, but he had planned for the possibility of this raid, knew exactly what he had to do, and was doing it. He was gathering the things important to him and preparing to flee the area. He'd have to set up somewhere else. It was inconvenient, but not unexpected. It was always best to know your enemies, and he had plans in place. There were—

"Bombs!" Stephanie shrieked, her eyes shooting open as she began to move. Running for the house, she yelled, "Bombs! Get out! Get out! Get out!"

She spotted Mirabeau at one of the side windows, with Tiny at the next one over, and felt a moment's relief as they, along with the others who had remained outside, began to back warily away from the house. But only a moment's worth. Three men had entered through the front door, and three men had no doubt

entered the back as well. More importantly, Decker—
her brother-in-law—was one of those men at the front.
If anything happened to him, her sister, Dani, would—

A relieved sob slipped from her lips when she saw
Decker coming back out through the front door with
Bricker on his heels. Her brother-in-law was looking
toward her with a combination of confusion and question. Obviously, they'd heard her shouted warning from
inside the house, but weren't sure what to make of it.

Stephanie opened her mouth to tell him and everyone
else that the house was about to explode, but the words
never left her lips. Like lightning before thunder, the blast
hit her first. Stephanie experienced a jolting sensation
like nothing she'd heretofore known. She imagined it was
similar to how it would feel to be hit by a freight train.

Since it was the blast wind that picked her up and
threw her backward, the fact that there was suddenly
no oxygen for her lungs was a bit confusing. Stephanie
had no time to ponder that, and was sailing through the
air before her ears picked up the boom of the explosion.

She landed hard on her back in the overgrown grass,
and found herself briefly staring up at the brightening
sky before she could find the wherewithal to move.
But then Stephanie gathered herself enough to stumble
to her feet again. She was vaguely aware that she was
swaying as she scanned what she could see of the yard
and the people in it. Most of the hunters in her view
seemed only mildly injured. There were a few moans
and cries of pain from those who had suffered broken
bones, or head wounds, but more were on their feet and
checking the injured than were down.

Mirabeau and Tiny were among those up and about,
helping the others. Decker, she saw, was crouched over

Lucian. Obviously, the head of the North American Immortal Council and unofficial leader of the rogue hunters hadn't got out of the house before the explosion, but she presumed he'd been close enough to the door to be tossed out by the blast. Judging by the smoke wafting off him, he'd also caught fire, if only briefly, which suggested the bombs had been incendiary in nature.

Stephanie waited until she saw Lucian move before turning her gaze toward the woods in back of the house again. This time she didn't have to work hard to hear the thoughts of the lone man. He was a calm mind amid the pained and upset hunters in the yard, and the chaos and agony of the panicked rogues trapped in the now burning house. He was glued to the camera monitors, his focus on her as he wondered how she had known there were bombs.

Her brain not yet firing on all cylinders after the shaking it had taken, Stephanie burst into a run toward the back of the property. Her only thought was to catch the bastard before he made his escape.

The woods behind the house were much deeper than those at the front, but there was something of a path through it. Just a dirt trail wide enough for a person to slip through the densely growing trees. Stephanie took it at a dead run, using all the speed her body could give her. It made the trip much faster than it would have been for a mortal, so fast that she was caught a little by surprise when she suddenly burst out of the woods into a clearing around a second house.

This yard was no better kept than the other. What had probably been a beautifully manicured lawn at one time was now overgrown with waist-high grass and weeds.

Stephanie slowed as she approached, her gaze sliding over the light shining from the windows of the dilapidated old Victorian two-story house as she neared the dark wood door. It was solid, without a window to see inside. She was reaching for the door handle when the chaotic thoughts from the scene she'd just left faded enough for her to catch the thoughts of the man inside. He knew she was there. He was waiting.

Stephanie released the handle and retreated a couple steps as she reached around her back for the gun tucked into the waistband of her jeans. It was loaded with darts full of a drug that had been developed specifically for rogue hunters to use. It was the only thing that could take down a rogue immortal with any certainty.

"Steph?"

She jerked around in surprise to see Mirabeau sprinting out of the woods and hurrying toward her. The fact that she'd left the scene of the explosion rather than staying to help with the wounded had obviously not gone unnoticed. Neither had the fact that she now had her gun out. Mirabeau's expression was both surprised and concerned as she focused on the weapon. Which was completely understandable, Stephanie supposed. She usually left the actual capturing of rogues to the others. Her purpose at these hunts was generally to tell them how many rogues they had to deal with and where they were. She also helped with the questioning after, pulling the answers Lucian was looking for from the captured rogues' minds like plucking cat hair off a sweater. But despite her years of training alongside the hunters, she was always kept back from the actual takedowns.

"What—?" Mirabeau was halfway across the overgrown yard when she began to ask her question. The one word was all the woman managed to get out, though, before her gaze suddenly shifted past her. Mirabeau's eyes went wide with alarm a heartbeat before she suddenly stumbled and fell.

Stephanie instinctively started to move toward the other woman, but then just as quickly whirled back to the house. The door was now open; a man stood in the doorway, tall, blond, and attractive. He had a gun aimed at her, and even as she recognized it as one the hunters used, like the one she was holding, he pulled the trigger. She felt a sharp pain in her chest, and glanced down at the dart piercing the edge of her left breast just over her heart, then she too fell as a warm wave rushed through her and every muscle in her body suddenly abandoned her. Stephanie didn't lose consciousness, though, nor feeling, and would have winced if she could have as she slammed to the ground and her head bounced off the hard-packed dirt path.

She came to rest on her side with her eyes closed, but her mind still functioning. Stephanie heard movement and tried to open her eyes, but didn't seem to be able to manage that. All she could do was listen to the sounds he made as he approached. He must have squatted next to her, or bent over to reach her, but whatever the case, she felt his hand on her shoulder and then was turned onto her back.

"You knew about the bombs. How did you know about the bombs?" her attacker muttered as he took the gun from her lax fingers and then tugged at her clothing, no doubt to check for any more weapons. "And how did you know there was a house back here? Or that I was in it?"

Stephanie didn't even bother to try to answer. Not that

she thought he expected her to. She suspected he was muttering to himself, and might not know she was even conscious. She shouldn't be, and wasn't exactly sure why she was. Like the gun he held, the dart had been easily recognizable as rogue hunter paraphernalia. That dart should have knocked her out. Yet she hadn't lost consciousness and could feel a tingling in her fingers and toes that suggested the drug was already wearing off. This was unexpected.

"Steph."

She was so startled that he'd used her name that her eyes shot open, and for a moment Stephanie was sufficiently distracted by the fact that they actually would open, that she forgot what he'd said.

"That's what she called you: Steph."

Stephanie peered at him to see that he was looking off toward Mirabeau and not at her. Even as she noted that, he turned his gaze back to her. His eyes immediately widened when he saw hers were open.

"You shouldn't be awake," he said, sounding nonplussed. "The dose in that dart would have knocked an immortal out cold for at least twenty minutes."

Stephanie wanted to tell him to go to hell, but unlike her eyes, her mouth still wasn't working. She wasn't able to move her jaw, and her tongue was a useless thing in her mouth. Then he was suddenly leaning over her, his fingers forcing their way inside her mouth and pressing on her palate behind her canine teeth. Disgusted and furious, Stephanie tried to bite him then, but her mouth still wouldn't work.

"You have metallic-tinted eyes like immortals, but no fangs," he muttered, retracting his fingers and eyeing her with fascination. "And if the drug from the dart is wearing off this quickly, you obviously have a stronger constitution than immortals. What are you?"

Unable to punch him in the face or claw his eyes out as she would have liked to do, Stephanie just glared back at him.

"This is fascinating. Perhaps I should take you with me," he murmured thoughtfully, and glanced toward the open door to the house behind him as if considering the logistics of doing so.

"Beau? Steph?"

Stephanie instinctively tried to turn her head toward that shout in the distance, but unlike her eyelids, her neck muscles didn't suddenly start working and she was unable to.

"Damn," her attacker muttered with what sounded like frustration.

Shifting her gaze back to him, she saw him look briefly toward the woods and scowl in the direction the shout had come from. He then shook his head and stood. "It looks like I'll have to leave you behind. But I sincerely hope we meet again, Steph whoever-you-are. I should like to get you on my table and find out what makes you tick."

A cold smile of relish crossed his face at the thought, and then he turned and moved unhurriedly into the house and closed the door.

Stephanie stared at the oak panel, almost afraid it might open again and he'd return for her, after all. While her first response to this man had been fury and disgust, the emptiness in his eyes and that smile of his as he'd announced his desire to get her "on his table and find out what made her tick" had wiped out both emotions and sent an icy flood of fear through her veins.

She was more than relieved to hear a curse sound much closer just before Tiny raced into view as he rushed to Mirabeau's prone body.

"What the hell happened to them?"

Stephanie recognized Decker's voice before she saw him speeding toward her.

"Steph? What happened?" Decker repeated when he dropped to his knees at her side and saw that her eyes were open. Apparently finding her lack of response alarming, he reached toward her and then hesitated. She read the worry in his mind that he had no idea what her injuries were and didn't wish to aggravate them or hurt her.

"Mirabeau has a dart in her neck," Tiny growled, sounding seriously pissed.

"A dart?" Decker glanced toward the other man with amazement. "What kind of dart?"

"One of ours from the looks of it," the big man said grimly, and she saw him pluck the dart from Mirabeau's neck and examine it briefly before tossing it aside. Tiny peered down at his life mate briefly, and then looked toward her and Decker. "Steph must have been shot too. Look for the dart."

Decker turned back to Stephanie and she saw his eyes travel over her body before shifting to the ground around her. When he suddenly cursed and reached for something in the grass beside her, she knew it must be the dart before he picked it up to examine it more closely, moving it into her view. It must have been dislodged from her chest when she'd fallen, she thought.

"Damn. It is one of ours," Decker growled before slipping it into his pocket. He cast a quick, wary gaze toward the house, scanning the windows and door, and then turned his attention back to Stephanie. His expression was troubled as his gaze narrowed on her open eyes again, and she didn't have to be a mind reader to know he was concerned as to why they were open, and what that meant.

"Her eyes are open!"

Stephanie shifted her gaze over Decker's shoulder at that surprised exclamation to see that Tiny had scooped up Mirabeau and carried her over to join them.

"Yeah," Decker said unhappily. "But she can't seem to move or speak."

"The effects of the dart must be wearing off, then," Tiny said, sounding relieved as he peered down at Mirabeau, limp in his arms. "That means Beau should wake up soon too."

Decker grunted what sounded like agreement, but the way he was looking at her made Stephanie think he didn't really believe that. But then she could hardly blame him. She doubted more than five or six minutes had passed since she'd been shot and it certainly hadn't been twenty minutes since the explosion and her racing back here. With his life mate unconscious in his arms, Tiny was too upset to have taken note of that. However, she wasn't Decker's life mate, so his upset wasn't as extreme as Tiny's. Oh, she could hear Decker's thoughts and knew he was worried about her. Even if she hadn't been able to hear his thoughts, she would have known that. While Decker was legally her brother-in-law, in truth he'd become much more than that over the last nearly thirteen years since he'd rescued her and Dani from Leonius Livius, the no-fanger rogue who had turned them. Decker had become like a real brother to her, as well as a friend, and even a father figure at times. But that wasn't the same as a life mate, and Decker was still able to think much more clearly than Tiny at the moment.

"Take Beau back to the vehicles and send as many hunters as are able to help search the house," Decker said suddenly.

Tiny hesitated, his worried gaze sliding to the house. "I don't like the idea of leaving you alone here when there's someone running around with a dart gun. Besides, wouldn't it be smarter to check out the house right away? What if whoever shot Stephanie and Beau gets away before we can search the house?"

"What if whoever shot the girls gives us the slip and comes out and beheads the women while we're searching the house? Or what if they shoot us and behead all of us before anyone thinks to follow?" Decker countered, standing up now and turning to face the house, his gun at the ready. "Go. Quickly. I'll guard Stephanie and watch the house until help arrives."

Tiny didn't bother to respond to that. Decker's pointing out that they could all be shot and beheaded was enough to have the man moving at once. Stephanie watched him go until he was out of her line of vision, and then shifted her gaze to Decker. The tingling in her extremities had been moving inward as the minutes passed. From her fingers to her hands and wrists and beyond, and from her toes to her feet, ankles, and calves. Her jaw was also now tingling, as was the tip of her tongue. Stephanie tried to move her fingers, and this time was able to do it. The same was true of her toes. She couldn't talk yet, though, but should soon be able to.

"Can you blink?"

Stephanie shifted her gaze back to Decker and then closed and opened her eyes.

The sight made him nod grimly, but he cast another wary glance toward the house before looking at her again and asking, "Did you see who shot you? Blink once for yes, twice for no."

Stephanie blinked once.

"Was it a hunter?" he asked next.

She wasn't surprised by the question. She and Mirabeau had been shot with hunter darts, and the man had used a hunter's gun. It wasn't surprising Decker would worry they had a rogue who was also a hunter. Stephanie also wasn't surprised by his relief when she blinked twice to tell him that wasn't the case. But his relief was short-lived as he then began to worry about how the rogue had got their hands on a hunter's weapon. While she read that in his thoughts, he didn't bring it up, but instead asked, "Did you recognize the person who shot you?"

Stephanie hesitated. She hadn't recognized the man, but his thoughts had told her who he was. She couldn't convey that with a yes or no, though.

"Is there more than one?" Decker asked when she was slow to answer. He barely waited for her to blink twice before shifting his gaze back to the house for another wary look. It made her wish she could tell him there was no need for him to keep checking the house. The man was gone. His thoughts were getting fainter in her head as he moved away from the vicinity. He was on foot, taking a trail through the woods on the other side of this house to where a vehicle waited, stashed there for just such an event.

"So, one person," Decker murmured, and then glanced down at her again to ask, "Male or female?"

That made her raise her eyebrows, which caught her by surprise. The drug was wearing off quickly if she could raise her eyebrows. She was pretty sure she hadn't been able to do that when he'd first got here.

Realizing the mistake he'd made, and that she couldn't answer his question with a yes or no, Decker asked instead, "Male?"

Stephanie blinked once for yes, but a lot of her concentration was on her mouth now. Her tongue was tingling like crazy, like she'd had novocaine and it was wearing off. Most of her jaw and face were tingling madly now too. She tried moving her tongue in her mouth and was surprised to find she could. Stephanie tried her jaw next and was relieved to find she was able to move that too.

Decker had turned to look at the house again, but now peered back at her to ask, "Did this guy—"

"Dressler," Stephanie managed to spit out, although the word was somewhat garbled and with little air behind it.

Apparently able to understand her despite that, Decker was staring at her with horror when the sounds of people crashing through the woods sounded. The other hunters were coming. Too bad they were too late.

One

Seven months later

"What's happening? Where did you go?"

Stephanie turned away from the wall of windows at that call, and contemplated the computer at the far end of the kitchen. She'd been listening to Dani's rundown of how her life had gone over the week since they'd last spoke when she'd become aware that she was only hearing one voice. Dani's, and it was with her ears. The other voices usually crowding her head were absent. Used to hearing the voices of everyone within a mile radius, the utter lack of sound in her head had been staggering. Shocked and confused, she'd stumbled to her feet and walked out of view of her computer camera to peer out the windows as if that would somehow bring the voices back, or explain their absence.

"Steph? Where are you? Are you okay?"

It was the concern in Dani's voice that had her moving again. Stephanie walked quickly back into the kitchen and headed for the end of the island, but stopped to collect a can opener and a can of salmon along the way as she said, "I'm here. I'm just grabbing something."

Pausing in front of the laptop, she forced a smile and said, "I was just getting Felix's dinner."

Dani did not smile back. Instead, she scowled with exasperation. "Jeez, Steph. You're always flitting around like a butterfly when we video chat," the blonde complained as Stephanie dropped onto the high-backed bar stool she'd vacated just moments ago. "You're out of the screen more than you're in it."

"I can't help it if you choose to video chat with me at Felix and Trixie's dinnertime," Stephanie said mildly. "Besides, I can talk and prep Felix's salmon at the same time."

"How do you *prep* canned salmon?"

"I remove the bones," Stephanie explained, her gaze wandering back toward the wall of windows in the Muskoka room as she wondered why she couldn't hear anyone. Was it her? Was something wrong? Maybe there'd been a gas spill or something and everyone had evacuated or died.

"Why?" Dani asked with amazement.

"Why what?" Stephanie asked, forcing her attention back to the computer screen.

"Why would you remove the bones?" Dani asked with exasperation.

"Oh. Because he could choke on them, and apparently they can splinter and damage his throat or stomach," she explained, and wondered if she should tell Dani about the sudden dearth of voices in her head.

"You do know there's this thing out there called cat food, right? It comes in a can too and is made specifically for cats? It also costs a lot less than actual salmon and you don't have to take out any bones."

"Yeah, yeah," Stephanie said distractedly, and decided she'd keep the information about the silence in her head to herself. At least until she figured out what it was, or meant. It wasn't actually the first time it had happened, and the explanation had been simple enough then. Someone on the other end of the county had held a seventy-fifth anniversary party and opened it to the whole town. Absolutely everyone had gone but her, and she'd had silence in her head for a whole hour. It might be something like that again now, and she didn't want to worry Dani unnecessarily.

Focusing on the computer again, she noted her sister's expression and grimaced. She knew Dani was just being sarcastic with that bit about cat food, but still said, "Cat food stinks. I wouldn't eat it."

"Well, I would hope not. You're not a cat," Dani said, and then teased, "Just a cat lady."

"Cat ladies have lots of cats. I have one. I also have a dog. I am *not* a cat lady," Stephanie argued, her gaze sliding back to the wall of windows as she opened the can of salmon. She couldn't see the road from her house, but she didn't see signs of smoke or anything else that might have caused issues for the mortals living around her and sent them running.

"Well, you may not have a lot of cats *yet*, but you've only lived in your own place for a year, and you do spoil the one cat you have like a cat lady would," Dani pointed out, and then muttered, "Salmon, for God's sake."

"I don't always feed Felix salmon," Stephanie said defensively, forcing herself back to the conversation and trying to act as normal as possible. "It's just a Saturday treat kind of thing. Like Pizza Fridays used to be for us."

"Uh-huh," Dani said dubiously. "And what does he get the rest of the week?"

"Scrambled eggs, cottage cheese, and veggies for breakfast, tuna balls for lunch, and a special stew for supper," Stephanie murmured in a distracted voice, her gaze moving back to the windows.

"Seriously? Eggs and stews? You *cook* for that cat?"

The decided squawk to Dani's voice caught Stephanie's ear and had her glancing back to the computer screen. Seeing her sister's disgusted expression, Stephanie rolled her eyes. "Lots of people cook for their cats, Dani. And their dogs."

"Oh, please," her sister moaned. "Do not tell me that you cook for that boxer mutt you call your *soul sister*."

Shrugging, Stephanie glanced toward Trixie where she lay at her feet in front of her chair, and then ran one foot down the dark tan fur on her back, petting her as she said, "Okay. I won't."

"Oh my God, you *do*," Dani said with disgust.

"Cooking relaxes me," Stephanie said unapologetically. "Besides, I'm sure you'd cook for a pet if you had one."

"Sweetheart, I don't even cook for Decker," Dani said on a sigh.

"Only because you probably don't have the time now that you're back to work," Stephanie said mildly. Leaning to the side to open the cupboard under the island, she retrieved a soup bowl and a small plate. Straightening in her seat, she set them on the island. "Doctors are busy people."

"Yeah. Busy. That's it. It has nothing to do with the fact that I can't cook worth beans," Dani said unhappily.

A small grin tipped the ends of Stephanie's mouth at the whining complaint, and she nodded as she drained the salmon juice into the bowl and then dumped the meat itself onto the plate. "Yeah, you can't even make hot chocolate without breaking the teakettle."

"I was nine years old when that happened!" Dani protested, and shook her head. "I'm never gonna live it down."

"Sure, you will," Stephanie countered.

"No, I won't," Dani argued. "For heaven's sake, you weren't even born yet when I did that and still got to hear the tale *repeatedly*. I think it came up at almost every family gathering we had."

"Yeah, but we aren't with the family anymore, which means we won't hear that tale mixed in with our other siblings' blunders that are always recounted at family gatherings," she pointed out. "And I'm sure you now know better than to try to make hot chocolate by putting milk in an electric teakettle and won't do it again, so I'll forget about it eventually . . . in like a hundred years or so," Stephanie teased, forcing herself not to look out the windows and to concentrate on digging through the can-shaped clump of salmon meat to remove the bones. That was the only reason she wasn't more careful of what she said. It was also why it took a moment for her to notice that Dani had gone silent. Once that awareness sank through her distraction, she glanced up to see her sister regarding her with concern. Raising her eyebrows, she asked, "What?"

Dani hesitated, and then queried solemnly, "Are you good?"

Stephanie sighed, knowing exactly what her sister was asking. She hadn't taken it well when their lives had been turned upside down nearly thirteen years ago and she'd learned she'd have to leave their family behind. To be fair, though, she'd only been fourteen at the time. Well, fifteen, really, but she'd just had her birthday when her life had exploded around her, so often thought fourteen when she recalled it. Not that it mattered, fourteen or fifteen, Stephanie hadn't been ready to lose her mother and father and all the rest of their siblings. Their family had been a very large, very close, and very loving one. She'd been lucky that way, but it had made it harder to give it up.

"I'm fine," she said finally, and when Dani's concern didn't clear, she assured her, "Really, I'm good. I love my new home and living on my own. It's beautiful here and quiet. It has everything I need, and what I don't have, I order online and get delivered. It rocks."

"And the voices in your head? The headaches?" Dani asked with concern.

"Much better," she said, and for once didn't have to lie about it. Well, at least she wasn't lying if the lack of voices in her head this time didn't turn out to be a bad thing. It didn't really matter either way; she regularly lied to her sister and everyone else about how she was doing. If she didn't, they'd worry about her and she didn't want that. Besides, out here in the middle of nowhere, the "voices in her head," as Dani had called them, had been much reduced, which made the headaches come less often, and they'd been less severe when they did come.

"Thank God," Dani breathed, and then bit her lip and asked, "But you're okay, right? I mean you aren't lonely living out there in the middle of farm country by yourself?"

"How could I be lonely? I have Felix and Trixie here, and you call for an online chat every Saturday morning. Elvi does the same on Sundays, usually with Victor, Mabel, and DJ joining in. Then Tiny and Mirabeau, Dree and Harper, Sherry and Basil, and even Marguerite fill up the rest of the week with online chats. Honestly, I spend so much time on chats with everyone it's starting to interfere with my deadlines. Being lonely isn't a problem," Stephanie assured her, a true smile widening her lips as she thought of the people who had essentially become her family. Tiny McGraw and his wife, Mirabeau, or Beau as she called her, had both acted as an escort and basically bodyguards for her, delivering her to her new home in Port Henry when her life was disrupted nearly thirteen years ago. But they'd soon afterward become something like a sweet, protective older brother and a bossy big sister to her. From that point on until she'd moved here, she'd lived in the little town with Victor and his wife, Elvi, who had become surrogate parents to her, while their best friends, Mabel and DJ, were like an aunt and uncle to her. Essentially, she'd lost her birth family thirteen years ago, but gained a new one in all of these people who made it their business to check on her weekly and do whatever they could to help her.

"Yeah, it's hell being so popular," Dani said, relaxing enough to tease her.

Stephanie stuck out her tongue at her sister, and then changed the subject. "So? How are you enjoying having a family practice?"

"It's great," Dani assured her, and then chuckled softly as she added, "Really good."

"Oh?" Stephanie asked encouragingly. Dani had worked long and hard to specialize in gynecology and had been terribly upset when their lives had exploded and she'd had to give it up to go into hiding with Decker after the attack. Most people probably would have loved to travel the world and just hang out with the love of their life for a couple of years, but Stephanie supposed being forced to do so because a deranged madman was hunting you might have made it less enjoyable.

However, that situation had been handled a while back and Dani had been able to return to the career she'd worked so hard for. Recently, though, Dani had decided she wanted a change. She'd given up gynecology, and she and Decker had moved to Port Henry where she'd started a private practice as a family physician.

Stephanie found that a bit ironic. She herself had lived in Port Henry until a little over a year ago, when she'd moved out here to the new house she'd had built. Although her new home was only forty-five minutes southwest of Port Henry, so they were actually closer than they'd been while Dani was in Toronto and Stephanie was in Port Henry.

"Family practice is certainly a lot more interesting than gynecology was," Dani said now, drawing her from her thoughts.

Stephanie raised her eyebrows and asked, "Because instead of just women you have men and children for patients as well?"

"Well, yeah, that and the medical issues I encounter are a lot more varied. My patients come in with everything from ingrown toenails to boils on their butts," Dani said, and then laughed. "That reminds me of something that happened today. Well, yesterday, I guess, since it's morning now."

"Tell me," Stephanie demanded, scraping the now deboned salmon into the bowl with the juice and setting it aside.

"Well, I'm not sure if it's because I'm working in a small town rather than a big city, but the patients seem a lot more friendly and chatty here," she started.

"Or maybe it has to do with no one really wanting to chat with the doctor who spends most of their visit with her head between their legs, examining their cervix," Stephanie said dryly.

"Yeah, that could be," Dani agreed, looking somewhat surprised. It was almost as if she'd never considered that possibility.

Shaking her head, Stephanie said, "Anyway, back to your story."

"Right. Well, I have this one middle-aged patient, a real sweetheart. She came in last week with a hemorrhoid problem. So, after talking to her, I handed her an examination gown, told her she should change into it, and then lie on the table on her stomach and get comfortable while she waited for me to return. But she gives this snort as she takes the gown and says, "Doc, I have two road cones on my chest called boobs. You try lying on those and getting *comfortable*.""

Stephanie's eyes widened and a chuckle slipped from her lips before she shook her head and said, "I wish I had that problem."

"Nah," Dani assured her at once. "You don't need the backaches."

"The nanos wouldn't let us have backaches, sis," she pointed out.

"Yeah, well . . ." She shrugged helplessly.

"But it's sweet of you to try to make me feel better," Stephanie said, glancing down at her nearly flat chest in the loose, long-sleeved gray-and-blue jersey she was wearing. She'd been a little shorted in the breast department. She wasn't completely flat, but her B cups definitely looked tiny next to Dani's fuller figure. She also didn't have much in the way of hips either, unlike her older sister. Basically, she was as slim and long-limbed as a teenager compared to her sister's more curvaceous body. Which was something that used to bother her a lot when she was younger, especially when people were always saying they looked so much alike. The truth was, their faces were the only thing that was similar, and their hair. Both of them had long blond hair, straight little noses, and wide mouths in oval faces. They also both had large eyes, though Stephanie's were a silver-green to Dani's silver-blue.

When she was younger, Stephanie used to look forward to the day when she'd develop a curvy figure like her sister . . . She'd given up waiting.

"No problem," Dani said easily. "Although if I really wanted to make you feel better, I'd point out that you have the body of a model and can wear anything and look good, while the wrong clothes on me make me look fat when I know I'm not. However," she added wryly, "that's too hard on my own ego so I won't point that out."

Stephanie grinned at the words, and then stiffened, her head swiveling toward the security monitor as a high series of beeps sounded.

"What is it?" Dani asked, noting her expression.

"The driveway alarm just went off," Stephanie muttered, standing and moving to the far end of the long kitchen to look out the wall of two-story windows in the Muskoka room beyond it. It was six o'clock in the morning in late May. The sun had started to creep over the horizon half an hour ago, but the lightening sky didn't help her see anything. Two weeks ago at this hour, she'd have been able to see the driveway entrance fine through the naked tree branches. But the trees and flowered bushes everywhere on the property had not only budded, but burst into full bloom the last two weeks. Night vision was not X-ray vision. She couldn't see a damned thing.

A warm pressure against her leg drew her gaze down to find that Trixie had followed her. The irritation at her obscured view immediately slid out of her and Stephanie gave the pup an affectionate pat as she peered down into her sweet black-white-and-tan face. She then led her back across the kitchen to the security monitor with eight small images on it.

Stephanie was vaguely aware of the dog returning to her spot in front of her chair once she stopped at the monitor, but most of her attention was on the mouse she was using to enlarge the view of the front gate of the property.

The entire forty acres with two houses and a twenty-acre pond between them was surrounded with a seven-foot-high, black metal fence. But at the driveway, the fence gave way to a black metal electric gate that could be opened by remote, or by entering a passcode on the panel at the gate. Unfortunately, her delay in looking out the front first meant that she'd missed seeing who'd entered. There were no vehicles in view and the gates were already closing.

Stephanie quickly began to rotate through the other camera views, pausing when she caught movement on one. It was the camera that showed the garage doors of Drina and Harper's house at the other end of the property. The door to the side of the garage that Drina usually used was partially open. Actually, it was three-quarters closed and still lowering. She caught a glimpse of the lower half of a motorcycle, a pair of booted feet, and the bottom of what appeared to be a long coat before the door finished closing.

"I think someone on a motorcycle just parked in Drina and Harper's garage," she said with concern, clicking the mouse to return the screen to gallery mode where all eight camera views could be seen. With nothing of interest showing on any of them, she turned away and then hesitated, unsure what to do. Should she go find out who it was? Call Drina to ask if anyone was supposed to be there? Or maybe—

"Oh, shoot, yeah. That's Thorne," Dani said, drawing her from her thoughts.

Stephanie moved back to the end of the island. Careful to avoid kicking Trixie, she settled back on the chair, frowning slightly at the name Thorne. It sounded vaguely familiar for some reason, but she couldn't place where she'd heard it before.

"Sorry," Dani offered now. "Drina wanted to call you, but I told her I'd talk to you about it myself since we were having our usual Saturday chat today." Grimacing, she added, "I guess I should have brought it up first thing, but I didn't expect him to get there for another hour."

"Okaaay," Stephanie said, drawing out the word. "Well, we're talking about it now, so why is this Thorne guy at Drina and Harper's place?"

"Because he needs somewhere to stay for a while," Dani said apologetically, and when Stephanie stiffened, she rushed on to say, "If you have a problem with him being there, we'll of course arrange something else."

Stephanie's eyebrows had risen at the very suggestion that anyone might stay at Drina and Harper's house out here in the sticks. The couple never had anyone at their place without them there, and the number of times they'd actually brought someone with them could be counted on one hand. Well, actually, more like two fingers. They'd had Elvi and Victor out once, and Tiny and Beau another time. Harper and Drina, who were like a second pair of adoptive parents to Stephanie after Elvi and Victor, were really good about not "inflicting people on her," as Drina had once put it. Which made this sudden change noteworthy.

"But I'm really hoping you won't have a problem with it," Dani added, her voice both apologetic and pleading at the same time.

Stephanie suspected her eyebrows were probably somewhere up around her hairline by now. It was the pleading in her sister's voice and expression that caused that. It was obvious that this Thorne person's remaining at Drina and Harper's was important to Dani for some reason. She just had no idea why, so asked, "And this is important to you, because . . . ?"

"Because I really don't know anywhere more perfect for him to stay while he's in Canada," she admitted, sounding almost defeated. "Decker and I have considered all the options. Anywhere close to people is a hard no. It would force Thorne to stay stifled up inside for the weeks or months he's here and that wouldn't be good for his mental state, or fair to him. He needs to be somewhere away from people where he can go out without the fear of being seen. That didn't leave a lot of options," she pointed out. "I mean, Decker and I even looked into buying property somewhere, but there was nothing for sale that offered the privacy, seclusion, and beauty you guys have out there. At least, not any place with an inhabitable house on it. If we'd had more time, we maybe could have built something, but—" She shook her head helplessly. "I just—"

"Okay," Stephanie interrupted patiently, beginning to suspect her sister was just going to ramble on indefinitely without actually explaining the issue at this rate. "I get this is important to you. So why don't you tell me who Thorne is, and why he needs to stay someplace private and secluded in Canada? Obviously, he's not from here."

"Oh." Dani frowned and hesitated briefly. When she finally answered, she sounded reluctant and was obviously choosing her words with care. "Thorne is from Dressler's island."

Stephanie sat up abruptly on her stool. "Dressler? The crazy scientist guy who was kidnapping and experimenting on our people? *That* Dressler's island?" she asked with concern, unwilling to bring up her own encounter with the man just seven months ago. Dani had freaked out when she'd heard what had happened. The explosion that Decker had narrowly avoided, and the fact that Stephanie had been shot, had sent her into a panic that Stephanie and Decker had spent weeks talking her down from. They hadn't dared to tell her the man who had shot her was Dressler, and she wasn't about to do so now. There was no sense getting her upset all over again.

"Yes," Dani said quietly.

Stephanie bit her lip, knowing this was not a subject her sister would be happy discussing. Both Dani and Decker had been among the crew who had traveled down to Venezuela to try to help find the man and the missing immortals he'd kidnapped to experiment on. Dani had gone to offer any medical assistance that might be needed, while Decker had been among the hunters recruited to help search for Dr. Dressler's hidden lab. But things had quickly gone sideways during the hunt. Several hunters and nonhunters had been captured during the search efforts . . . including Decker.

Stephanie knew her sister hadn't fully recovered from the terror and loss she'd suffered when Decker had gone missing. Which meant Stephanie had to step lightly here. She was considering what would be the correct direction to take this conversation when Dani spoke again.

"Thorne was one of Dressler's genetic experiments."

"I see," Stephanie breathed, running through the things she'd heard about those experiments. Before discovering the existence of immortals and shifting his attention to kidnapping and tormenting the people with bioengineered nanos that basically turned their hosts into vampires, Dressler had been playing fast and loose with genetics. He'd spent decades splicing the DNA of various animals into human eggs or fetuses. Stephanie wasn't exactly sure which, and had never bothered to learn the science behind what he'd been doing, but the results had been some versions of old mythological creatures like mermaids, centaurs, and so on. Which made her wonder what this Thorne was a mix of. It must be something visibly different if they wanted him somewhere no one would see him.

"He wants his wings removed," Dani said.

Stephanie's head went back slightly, and her eyes widened as she suddenly recognized the name. "Thorne was the one who flew to the mainland and led Lucian and you guys to the island. He helped save Decker and the others."

"Yes," Dani breathed, her shoulders sagging a little. "Without him, I don't think we ever would have found the island and got Decker and the others back. They'd still be there suffering Dressler's torturous experiments."

Stephanie nodded, understanding a bit better now. Dani felt she owed Thorne, and she couldn't disagree with her. They all owed Thorne big-time, and not just for saving Decker. He wasn't the only immortal who had been captured while searching for Dressler's island. There had been several captives, but most important among them to Stephanie, aside from her brother-in-law Decker, had been Victor Argeneau and Mirabeau La Roche. While both were now family to her, Beau had also become something of a mentor to her when Stephanie had started working with the hunters to find rogue immortals who broke their laws. So had Beau's work partner, Eshe Argeneau, and she too had been among those captured by Dressler.

"Okay, of course he can stay. Thorne helped us, so now we help him," Stephanie said reassuringly, and didn't miss the relief that filled her sister's face. "You said he wants his wings removed?"

"Yes. He wants the chance at a normal life," Dani explained. "Having wings means he can't leave the island and live among people. If anyone saw him—"

"He'd end up spending the rest of his days in some government lab being poked and prodded and experimented on," Stephanie said grimly.

"Undoubtedly," Dani agreed.

Stephanie nodded. "So, will you be able to cut off his wings?"

"I don't know," Dani said, her expression troubled. "We took some preliminary X-rays and tests, but . . . His anatomy is much more complex than your average person. He has—" She paused abruptly, chagrin crossing her face, and shook her head. "I can't really talk about his case."

"Of course," Stephanie agreed, knowing doctors were never supposed to share such private information on their clients. The only reason she'd been able to share her tale of the lady with road cones on her chest was because no name had been mentioned. "But I'm guessing this won't be a quick fix?"

"No," Dani agreed. "We're trying to round up specialists in ornithology, veterinarian medicine, orthopedics, and a ton of other areas to see what can be done. But we're not even sure how anesthetic would affect him and . . ." She shrugged helplessly. "Basically, if it can be done at all without killing him, it could take a while. In the meantime, Marguerite was the one who pointed out that it would be best if he was somewhere that was away from people and secluded enough that he could walk the grounds and get exercise without the risk of being seen," Dani explained. "She suggested Harper and Drina's place right away, but the rest of us were concerned about infringing on your peace and quiet, so we looked into alternative solutions first."

"And couldn't find anywhere," Stephanie said for her.

"No," Dani agreed. "But we were still reluctant to have him stay out there so close to you until Marguerite pointed out that a lot of the hybrids on Dressler's island, including Thorne, are unreadable to most of us. She's hoping the same will be true for you. That you won't be able to hear Thorne's thoughts, so his presence wouldn't trouble you."

Stephanie merely nodded, wondering if that would be the case. She didn't trust that this sudden silence in her head was anything but a fluke where everyone nearby had left the area again or something. If so, she'd get to enjoy this silence for a bit, but knew that it would be hard when people began to trickle back home and into her thoughts again. Even with them coming back one or two at a time the last time, it had been harder to handle the voices in her head for a while after enjoying the silence she hadn't had since she was turned. If that was what was happening now, some weird fluke where everyone had left the area for whatever reason, it would definitely be wonderful to have someone around whose thoughts weren't invading her head.

But she'd learned from experience that just because everyone else couldn't read someone, it didn't mean she wouldn't have their thoughts intruding in her head. Maybe this time would be different, though. Or not. She wasn't often lucky, so wouldn't count on it. Still, it would be nice to be able to talk to someone without their thoughts pouring into her head, filling it like liquid in a bowl, and drowning out everything else.

"Can you hear his thoughts?" Dani asked suddenly.

Stephanie glanced at the computer screen with surprise and then turned to look toward the Muskoka room with its wall of windows and a view of the lake and the property on the other side of it. She tilted her head to search through the silence for even a whisper of a voice in her mind from Thorne . . . Only, it wasn't there. Not a thought, not an image, not a single word.

"Oh, right, you're inside and Harper had the house insulated with all that stuff to shield you from people's thoughts," Dani said now, drawing Stephanie's stunned gaze back to the computer screen as her sister suggested, "Go outside and see if you can hear his thoughts."

Stephanie almost told her then that the insulation no longer worked. Or perhaps the insulation in the walls worked, but the windows weren't insulated. Harper had had them triple-glazed, hoping that would do the trick, and Stephanie had lied and told everyone it had to ease their worries. But she'd still heard people's thoughts, though there were a lot less people out here to hear, which had made life better for her.

"Go on," Dani insisted. "Step outside and see if you hear him. I'll wait."

Nodding, Stephanie stood and headed for the door, unsurprised when Trixie immediately got up to trail after her. The dog was her constant shadow out here. Actually, the boxer was always at her side wherever she was. Trixie was a pack animal, and Stephanie was her pack. They went everywhere together. Felix, on the other hand, was a cat and not into packs, so Stephanie was a little surprised when the gray-and-white tabby joined them as well. They were a small parade of three as she led the way to the main entrance at the side of the house and unlocked it.

"Don't go far, Felix," Stephanie warned when she opened the door and the cat slid past her to rush into the night. "It's dinnertime."

The cat halted on the walkway to the driveway, briefly gazing longingly toward the front of the property, but then apparently decided to follow his stomach rather than whatever lure was out there. He came back to twine around her ankles as Stephanie stopped in the middle of the concrete pad of the covered porch and opened her mind to the voices out there. Not that she normally had to "open her mind." Usually she was trying to block the voices and thoughts coming at her and failing miserably. But now, with nothing but silence around her other than the occasional hoot of an owl, Stephanie tried to open herself to the thoughts of Thorne and any other people who might be in range.

Silence. There wasn't a single thought or voice in her head. The only thing she could hear was the rustle of nocturnal creatures in the trees and bushes, and the whisper of Trixie sniffing her way around the lawn in search of a good place to relieve herself. Sounds she couldn't normally hear over the voices in her head . . . and they were beautiful. So normal. Something she hadn't experienced but once in almost thirteen years . . . and had longed for desperately. She closed her eyes and savored it. But when she opened them again, Stephanie began to frown.

It was early enough that the sun was just creeping above the horizon, sending the first rays of light into the sky, but for the most part it was still dark. Was there anywhere that everyone could have gone at this hour? She didn't think it was likely. Which meant . . . Could the voices have stopped? Was she going to be free of them from now on? The possibility was a staggering one.

"Dear God," Stephanie breathed, unsure herself if it was just a shocked murmur, or the beginning of a prayer of thanks for this gift. For years she'd been bombarded with people's thoughts and memories. Some whispering, some screaming, but all just filling her mind to overwhelming levels that had left her wanting to clasp her head and scream madly to try to drown them out. It had made those she loved fear for her sanity.

Stephanie had done her best to reassure them, but the truth was, she too had feared for her sanity. At least, she had until moving here. With her home surrounded by farms, it meant there were only at most a dozen people's thoughts she had to contend with depending on the hour, which was much better than when she'd lived with Elvi and Victor in Port Henry where hundreds of voices and thoughts had constantly assaulted her, or the city where the number had reached the thousands.

Now, however, she had none of that. Not a murmur of a voice, a sigh of a thought, or even a whisper of a memory. It was bliss and, surprisingly enough, brought tears to her eyes. Which she didn't realize until Trixie came to lean against her leg with a soft, concerned whimper, and she glanced down through blurry eyes to look at her.

"Oh," Stephanie said on a slight laugh as she reached up to brush away the tears that were pooling in her eyes and drifting down her face. "Mommy's okay. She's just being silly," she said to the dog, and then reached down to pet her before turning to the door. "Come on. Let's go make your supper."

Mentioning the word *supper* was always a cue for

Trixie and Felix to go a little crazy. Trixie barked excitedly and nearly knocked her over trying to get through the door first when she opened it. But Felix was no better; he was just too small to unbalance her as he rushed into the house. Shaking her head, Stephanie followed them in. She automatically locked the door as she closed it, and then headed into the kitchen.

TWO

Dani's voice was coming from the computer at the far end of the room, sounding impatient. Ignoring it briefly, Stephanie stopped to collect Trixie's dog food from the fridge, and her bowl and a spoon from the drawers, before returning to her seat at the end of the island.

"There you are!" Dani said with relief when Stephanie sat down with her collection of items. "I was starting to worry."

"Nothing to worry about," Stephanie said lightly as she removed the lid from the glass container of dog food and began to spoon some into the dog dish. "I was just doing as you suggested and checking to see if I could hear Thorne."

"And?" Dani demanded anxiously.

"I heard nothing," Stephanie assured her with a brilliant grin.

"Oh, thank goodness. Then you wouldn't mind if he stayed out there until he can return home?" she asked.

Realizing Dani didn't understand what she was saying, Stephanie opened her mouth to explain that not only had she not heard a new voice in her head that could be Thorne's, she wasn't hearing *any voices at all*. But she changed her mind and simply said, "Of course. Happy to help."

"Thank you," Dani squealed. "I'll tell Drina and Harper you're okay with it."

"All right," Stephanie said easily.

"Also, I've arranged with that place that delivers your groceries to bring out some for Thorne too. I know it usually comes Saturday afternoons, but since Drina said there wasn't much out there at the moment, I arranged for them to bring it earlier than they normally would so he isn't left hungry until late this afternoon." Expression apologetic, she added, "Sorry to ask, but could you stay up and open the gate for them? They said they could deliver between ten and twelve."

"All right," Stephanie repeated, managing not to make a face at the idea of staying up four to six hours later than normal. She had become a night owl, sleeping during the day and working through the darkest hours, when most people were asleep and their voices in her head were reduced and less distracting. Dani, on the other hand, kept mortal hours. Running her family practice during the day and sleeping nights meant early to bed, early to rise for her. Although Dani didn't usually rise as early as this. She only got up at—as she called it, the god-awful hour of—5:30 A.M. on Saturday mornings to talk to Stephanie before she went to bed. They usually spent an hour or two online, and then Dani would head out about her day and Stephanie would feed Trixie and Felix, and then take them out for a last walk to relieve themselves before locking up and heading to bed. But Stephanie could survive staying up later. It would just mean consuming more blood.

The thought made her grimace and she ducked her head to hide it as her sister added, "They'll be delivering to both of you at the normal hour after today, though, and you'll still have to let them in then. Thorne doesn't know how to work the gate from inside the house."

"Of course. No problem," Stephanie assured her, and carried Trixie's now full bowl of food to the microwave to heat it up.

"Thank you!" Dani said happily. "Oh, and there is a benefit to Thorne's staying there too. It turns out he's really good with techie stuff. I guess it's something he's had to learn since Dressler took off and they got Wi-Fi and stuff on the island. He said his mother and her maid are pretty much addicted to the internet now that they've been introduced to it. Waiting for a tech guy to come out from the mainland when it drops out would be a nightmare for them, so he's learned all he can about it so he can get it back up and running when it acts up, which I gather happened a lot at first," she explained. "But anyway, when Harper warned him that you'd been having some issues with the internet out there, that it's been a bit unreliable, and he was having trouble booking someone to take care of it, Thorne said not to worry. He'd give it a look."

Stephanie turned from watching the bowl go around in the microwave to peer at her computer with surprise. She couldn't see her sister, though; the computer was sideways to her. And before she could respond, she heard a ringtone followed by Dani suddenly cursing.

"Oh, damn, it's the answering service. One of my patients must have an emergency to be calling at this hour. I'm going to have to take this, but I'll text you later to make sure the food got there and everything is okay. And, of course, we'll chat online again next week. Love you. Bye."

"Bye, love you too," Stephanie responded automatically, but didn't think Dani had heard her. She was pretty sure her sister had ended the chat between their byes. At least, that's when the soft music that had been playing in the background from Dani's end of the chat had ended.

Or maybe I'm going deaf, Stephanie thought wryly. *Can't hear the voices in my head anymore, can't hear music—*

She gave a start as the microwave blared out four beeps behind her, announcing that Trixie's food was done.

"So, not deaf," she muttered, turning to open the door and retrieve Trixie's bowl.

Stephanie grabbed Felix's deboned salmon off the island, and carried both bowls to the other end of the kitchen and out into the dining area. It was separated from the kitchen itself not by a wall, but by another counter that ran across all but four feet of that end of the room. The four feet had been left open as an entrance.

Pausing in the open space, Stephanie glanced at Trixie and Felix, who had followed her from the kitchen and were now hovering on either side of her. She raised her eyebrows.

"In your spots," she reminded them. Both the dog

and cat immediately moved out in front of her several feet apart and turned to face her, then sat down to wait. Stephanie smiled. It was rare that she didn't also have to remind them to sit, but they'd been getting better at it lately. Murmuring, "Good babies," she bent to set down the bowls, one in front of each of them. Stephanie then straightened, and eyed them for the count of ten before saying, "Okay."

Given permission, both cat and dog immediately launched themselves at their bowls and began to gobble down their meals. The way they went at it you'd think they hadn't eaten for days.

Shaking her head, Stephanie turned to walk back into the kitchen. But her smile faded with each step as she recalled what Dani had said. Thorne could fix the internet out here? And Harper had mentioned the trouble he'd been having with getting someone out to take care of it?

The fact of the matter was that he *had* managed to arrange for someone to come look at it. A service guy had been out just last week to take care of the problem, and he'd fixed it too as far as she could tell. At least, he'd got it going again after the last time it had dropped out for hours. It was a little slow now, and flickered on occasion, but it hadn't completely dropped out again since then, which was a relief. Between the research she did and emails to and from her editor, agent, and readers, Stephanie depended heavily on the internet. Having it drop out on her repeatedly like it had been doing had been a terrible pain in the arse. The point was, though, that it had been fixed, so why would Harper say otherwise?

Although, Stephanie thought, while talking to Elvi a couple days ago, she had mentioned the bit about the internet being slow and flickering. She wouldn't be surprised if the lovely lady had immediately gone all mama bear and got ahold of Harper about it. Maybe he'd been trying to arrange for a serviceman to come out again, but was having trouble getting an appointment this time.

"That must be it," Stephanie muttered to herself as she quickly closed her laptop and cleaned up the small mess she'd made at the island while preparing dinner for Felix and Trixie. She considered making herself something to eat too and went to open the refrigerator door, but she wasn't really hungry and nothing inside looked all that appealing. Besides, Stephanie doubted she'd have the time to fix herself anything. Felix and Trixie were superfast eaters and usually wanted to go out for their before-bedtime walk the moment they'd finished their meal.

As if having heard her thoughts and agreeing with them, Trixie gave one solid woof, drawing her gaze to where both dog and cat had finished their meals. Felix was now idly licking his paw while Trixie stood staring at her expectantly.

"Right. Time for a walk," Stephanie said wryly, closing the fridge door and walking toward them.

Sunrise was only half an hour or so away when she stepped outside, but the sky was a lot brighter than it had been the last time she'd come out. It was still a dark blue-gray overhead, but streaks of brilliant red, then orange, and finally bright yellow colored the sky closer to the horizon. It was stunning and silent. At least the voices that usually filled her head were. Instead, now all she could hear were the birds stirring from their night's rest. Their many and varied chirps and tweets had never sounded so beautiful.

Smiling to herself, Stephanie took the three shallow steps off the porch and started across the yard, automatically heading for the path that ran along the right-hand side of the small lake that took up the center of the property between the two houses. Or perhaps it was really just a large pond. She never knew what to call it. It was actually an old gravel quarry that had filled with water decades ago. That being the case, it was an almost perfect rectangle, with the longer sides running from the front of the property where Drina and Harper's house was to the back of the property where her house was.

Whatever it should be called, she knew it took up twenty acres of the forty-acre property, and that fish had been added to it at some point over the years. Perch, sunfish, blue gill and largemouth bass now thrived in it, along with a few snapping turtles. Harper had removed the old wooden dock that had been rotting out when he'd bought the property, and replaced it with a modular floating dock that would last forever. It now had a pontoon boat docked at it, along with a Jet Ski, a paddleboat, and two paddle bikes. He'd also shipped in truckloads of sand to cover what had been gravel shores on either end.

For all intents and purposes, it was now a small lake rather than a pond, at least Stephanie thought so. To her, ponds were much smaller with lily pads in them, and there were a few of those on either end of the property too, but she didn't consider the larger body of water a pond. In her opinion, ponds didn't get waves on them, and the lake did when the winds were high. Not large ones, the water wasn't deep enough for that, but it got waves nonetheless.

"Felix! Don't wander off too far," Stephanie called when she noted that while Trixie was sticking close to her side for their walk, the cat was rushing up the long tree-lined lane toward the front of the property where Drina and Harper's house was.

"Damned cat," she muttered to herself, picking up her pace when the tabby continued forward without even slowing or glancing around to acknowledge her words. Looking down at Trixie, she gave her a pat for staying by her side and said, "He's probably hoping to catch some poor sleepy bird before it's quite awake and alert enough to escape him. That cat's a killer."

If Trixie understood her words, she didn't seem unduly concerned by the knowledge that Felix was a bird killer. Eyes bright and tongue lolling she simply stared up at her, apparently happy just to be at her side, walking the property.

Shaking her head, Stephanie glanced up the lane again, her gaze sliding over the trees that lined the fourteen-foot-wide path that stretched out more than a thousand feet before her. Large maples and majestic old oaks formed a bower overhead, and shaded the grass she was traversing, as well as the various flowers that grew close to the tree trunks as if they'd been planted there at one time, but had grown wild since. Her gaze slid over deep red irises, yellow-edged red tulips, and large patches of little white flowers that she thought were called snow-in-summer or something.

It was a truly lovely walk, and one she took several times a day, marveling at the artistry of nature with each pass. But this morning in particular, the sights and sounds around her made Stephanie's heart feel oddly full. Or perhaps that was the absence of the voices in her head, she acknowledged. For once she could truly appreciate the beauty and serenity of where she lived and recognize how lucky she was.

She reveled in that feeling for a moment, until movement ahead caught her eye just as Felix darted off to the left toward the lake.

"Damned cat. He definitely has the scent of a bird," Stephanie told Trixie, and broke into a run in the hopes of catching up in time to prevent the carnage that would no doubt occur.

Moving at the incredible speed that having the nanos allowed, she covered the distance quickly, arriving at the end of the lane where the grass gave way to tar and chip, and reached out in two directions. One of the solid paths continued forward and then split around a center aisle of grass and trees to make two lanes on either side of the natural median that ran up to two gates to the road. The second, however, turned sharply left and slanted downhill, stopping where the sand started on the right side, and continuing on into the lake on the left, making a ramp into the water. It was where Harper put the boat in. The path to the right was the one Felix had traveled.

Stephanie glanced toward Drina and Harper's house as she started to take the turn, but there wasn't much to see. The trees and bushes in the yard blocked most of her view of it, but there didn't appear to be lights on inside. Perhaps Thorne had gone right to bed on arriving, she thought, and knew the drive down here from Toronto would have taken probably three hours. He could have been tired and—

Her thoughts died abruptly as her gaze slid away from the house now on her right side and moved to the area in front of her. Already halfway down the ramp to the water, Stephanie stopped running and simply stared. Oh yeah, Felix had found a bird, all right. A big one. Or maybe an angel. Damn, the man in whose lap Felix was standing was gorgeous. Like breathtaking. Stunning. Beautiful, Stephanie thought, and just stood there gaping at him until Trixie caught up and rubbed against her on the way past. The poor dog had obviously run full out to try to keep up with her and was now overheated, because she didn't even slow, but charged down the rest of the ramp and straight into the water to cool off.

"Oh dear," Stephanie breathed, managing not to wince as the dog frolicked briefly in the water. If they'd been heading to bed after this walk, she'd have been upset knowing she'd have a wet dog leaping into bed with her the minute Trixie thought she was asleep. Fortunately, she had to stay up to let in the grocery delivery guy, so all she had to worry about was wet and sandy floors and possibly a wet and sandy couch if Trixie managed to get on it before she could stop her.

Sighing, she continued down the ramp, careful now not to look directly at the man on the dock who she assumed was Thorne. Stephanie was assuming that because, while his hair was a pure white she'd never seen before, she didn't see any evidence of wings. At least, she didn't until she reached and crossed the short span of beach before the dock and stepped onto it.

Thorne was sitting on the corner storage box that sat halfway up the dock. It was attached on one side to the portable watercraft port where the Jet Ski was docked, and on a second side to the main dock itself while the third side hung over the water, attached to nothing. He was facing the direction she'd come from, leaving her a side view as she started up the dock, which was why she hadn't seen his wings at first. Now she did. They were folded and pressed tight to his back at the top, and then hung down the side of the storage box, stopping just inches above the water. At first, they appeared simply brown, but as Stephanie continued up the dock and got closer, she could see that they were actually a mix of various browns from a lighter version of milk chocolate to a dark chocolate. They too were beautiful, and she admired them briefly before raising her gaze to his face and hair.

The man had an art-worthy face. Michelangelo would have wanted to sculpt a statue of him, Da Vinci would have painted his portrait, and Stephanie wished she had the skill to do both. Failing that, snapping his picture and making it her screensaver so that she could simply stare at him every day was appealing too. Or would have been if she was some psycho stalker chick, which she wasn't, Stephanie reminded herself when one of her hands slid into her pocket to clasp her cell phone.

Sighing inwardly as she released the phone, Stephanie let her gaze trail over his face, taking in his strong chin, full lips, straight nose, and the most incredible golden eyes she'd ever seen, before sliding up to his pure white hair. Which wasn't hair, she realized now that she was closer. The man's head was covered with small white feathers lying flat to his scalp. Like a bald eagle, she thought, and had a sudden desire to run her fingers over it to see if it was as soft as it looked.

Startled by the thought, Stephanie stopped about six

feet from the man, forced her gaze back to his face, and said, "You must be Thorne."

He nodded in response, but his expression was unreadable. Thorne wasn't smiling, but he wasn't frowning at her either. He was just watching her almost warily, as if leery of her reaction to him, and Stephanie supposed that was fair. The guy was one of a kind, and had to worry how others would react. Well, she supposed he wasn't really one of a kind. From what she knew there had been a handful of people on Dressler's island with wings. But he was certainly the first half-man/half-bald-eagle she'd encountered. That being the case, Stephanie wasn't sure what approach to take here. Should she be polite and act like he was perfectly normal? Or would he find that fake? Maybe she should be authentic and ask the questions she suddenly had about his wings and the feathers on his head. Or would that offend him?

For the first time in thirteen years, Stephanie had no idea what someone was feeling or thinking, and suddenly missed the ability to hear people's thoughts that she'd earlier been weeping with joy over losing.

"Ironic," she muttered, and then glanced to the heavens and added, "You have a weird sense of humor."

"What?" Thorne asked.

Stephanie lowered her gaze and focused on him again. The man was now staring at her with curiosity. Probably wondering if she was a crazy lady talking to herself like that, she supposed, and wondered if it would help or make matters worse if she admitted she'd been addressing God. Probably worse, she decided.

Not sure how she should be acting, Stephanie did what she always did and simply acted like herself. Taking another step up the dock, she announced, "I'm Stephanie McGill, Dr. Dani McGill's sister. I live in the house at the back."

She gestured toward the back of the lake as she spoke, and then glanced down at Trixie when the now soaked boxer came prancing up onto the dock next to her. Petting the top of her head, the only part of the beast that didn't appear to be wet, she added, "This soggy stink-bottom is my soul sister and best buddy, Trixie."

"Soggy stink-bottom?" Thorne questioned, his lips twitching with amusement.

"Soggy because she jumps in the lake every chance she gets, and stink-bottom because she has the stinkiest farts *ever*," Stephanie explained, considering him with interest. His voice was deep and strong, the kind she considered sexy. But he also had an accent, one that was hard to pin down. There were some British inflections in there, but some Spanish as well. But then she knew that Dressler and his wife had been Brits, while the maid who had helped raise him was native to Venezuela, so the Spanish accent could be her influence, Stephanie thought.

Her gaze shifted to the gray tabby who had climbed halfway up Thorne's chest to alternately rub his face on Thorne's wings where they rested against his shoulders, and lick them. Amusement quirking her lips, she finished the introductions with, "And the cat presently molesting you is Felix."

Thorne lowered his gaze to the tabby and gave it a stroke down its back that had Felix writhing with pleasure. "He's very affectionate."

Stephanie snorted at the claim. "The only time he shows affection is when he wants food, and what he's doing with all that rubbing his face on you is marking you with his scent," she informed him. Tilting her head, she eyed her cat consideringly as he continued to lick and rub himself almost obsessively anywhere he could reach Thorne's feathers, first the tops of his wings, then the feathers on the side of his head. "I'm thinking he sees you as his next meal."

"What?" Thorne asked with amused disbelief.

Stephanie shrugged. "Fortunately for you, he just had a can of salmon. Otherwise, he might be doing more than licking those wings of yours."

Thorne shook his head as if the very idea was ridiculous, and then stood and set Felix on the box where he'd been sitting before turning to face her. She wasn't sure what he was doing, until he held a hand out down low and clucked his tongue. Trixie reacted like the traitorous ho she was, and immediately rushed forward to first sniff and then lick Thorne's fingers.

Stephanie winced when the dog then pressed her wet body up against Thorne's legs. It was an invitation for him to pet her, and one he accepted, apparently not at all upset that she might be ruining his very expensive-looking, very tight brown leather pants. Very, very tight, Stephanie thought, her gaze traveling over his narrow hips and long lean legs before coasting up to his chest and arms in the matching leather vest he wore.

Damn, Stephanie thought, the guy had wide shoulders that could give Dwayne Johnson a run for his money, yet the arms themselves, while nicely muscled, weren't as bulky as The Rock's were. Most of the muscle seemed to be in his upper chest and shoulders. Probably to power those wings, she thought.

Realizing she was gawking and that Thorne had

noticed, Stephanie grimaced and shrugged. "Sorry. But it's not every day a gal meets a superhot guy with wings."

"Superhot?" he echoed, sounding surprised.

Stephanie snorted at his reaction. "Oh, please. You must know you're absolutely gorgeous," she said, and when he simply stared at her wide-eyed, she muttered, "Okay, so you didn't know. Well . . . now you do," she said simply, and then patted her leg, drawing Trixie back to her side.

Bending down, she gave the dog an affectionate pet as she said, "Dani ordered groceries for you. They should arrive sometime between ten and noon. I'll open the gate for the delivery guy and he'll leave yours at your door before driving out to give me mine. You might want to avoid the windows until he leaves."

Straightening, she eyed him briefly before adding, "Dani also said Drina warned her that there wasn't much in the house to eat until the delivery. Are you hungry?"

Thorne was silent for a moment, his expression considering, and then he said, "I could eat."

"Well, let's go see if I have anything you'd be interested in then," she suggested, and turned to head off the dock, saying, "Come on, Wiggle Butt, let's go home."

Three

For one moment Thorne thought Stephanie was calling him Wiggle Butt, but then his gaze dropped to the dog as she hurried to keep up with her mistress and he noticed that Trixie did wiggle her butt as she chased after her. It was her happily wagging tail that caused the wiggle, and it made a wide, amused smile curve his lips.

Shaking his head, Thorne glanced at the cat, who was now standing on his hind legs on the storage box, and pawing at his left wing to get his attention.

"You don't see me as a meal, do you, boy?" he asked. Not expecting an answer, he then scooped up the gray tabby and strode after Stephanie McGill.

The woman was walking fast, Thorne noted as he followed her onto a long tree-lined path. He immediately wondered if that was because she was uncomfortable around him and trying to get some space. He wouldn't have been surprised if she was. He supposed he must seem odd to her.

Although she had said he was superhot, Thorne recalled, and found himself smiling at the memory. No one had ever told him he was superhot before. His mother and Maria had told him he was handsome, but they were family. Well, technically, Maria was his mother's maid, but in reality she had become a member of the family over the years, and as such, she, like his mother, was biased. Of course, there were females on the island he'd grown up on, other victims of his father's experiments who had obviously found him attractive, and he'd even encountered an immortal female or six the last half dozen years who had shown that they thought him attractive. But in his—perhaps somewhat limited—experience, females didn't generally just announce they thought men were good-looking or hot, let alone superhot.

Thorne had been so startled by the compliment that he hadn't returned the favor and said he thought she was very attractive . . . but he did. The woman was a long cool drink of superhot in his eyes. She had a lovely face, beautiful golden blond hair caught up in a ponytail on the back of her head, and a slim, coltish figure even in the open-bottomed joggers and the loose gray jersey with blue shoulders and long sleeves. She was also barefoot, he'd noticed, and for some reason Thorne found that sexy as hell.

Weird, he thought, and then grunted in surprise when a sharp pain in the top of his wing drew him from his thoughts. Thorne turned his head sharply to see the cat chomping down on it. Scowling, he shifted his hold to the cat's upper body and tried to pull him away, but the animal just bit down harder on the wing edge.

"I told you he saw you as his next meal."

Thorne glanced around to see that Stephanie, apparently hearing his grunt of pain and looking back, had seen the problem and was hurrying toward him. She was using the incredible speed immortals had and was stopped in front of him almost before he'd recognized she was coming back. He had to make a concerted effort not to start or take a step back in surprise, and then he simply stood there while she forced Felix to release his bite.

Once the cat had removed his teeth from the wing, Stephanie took Felix from Thorne's arms and stepped back to offer him an apologetic grimace. "He's a bird killer."

"And sees me as fair game despite my weighing ten times more than him?" he asked wryly.

"I didn't say he was a smart bird killer," she pointed out with amusement.

"Hmm," Thorne murmured, smiling faintly as they started along the path again, this time together. They walked in silence for a moment, Thorne's gaze sliding over the long, shaded lane through the trees, before he commented, "It's beautiful here. Quiet too compared to the city."

"Yes."

The word was almost a sigh and he glanced at her with curiosity to see her gazing at their surroundings with appreciation, as if she had never noticed them before. It made him ask, "Have you lived here long?"

"About a year," she admitted. "Harper bought the property a couple years ago. It only had their house on it then, and it was a dump. They had to do extensive renovations and landscaping. It took a good six months to fix it up. They pretty much had to gut the place and start over."

Eyebrows rising, Thorne glanced back toward the house he was staying in, but it was already completely hidden from view by the trees and bushes everywhere on the property. In fact, all he could see from where they were walking was trees, bushes, flowers, and the occasional glimpse through the greenery of the neighboring field on their left, or brief peeks of the lake on their right. He could also see the large warehouse-like building at the end of the path by the driveways. A large white monstrosity that was big enough to hold eight or ten cars from what he could see. Harper had called it the shop when he'd given him the keys to the house he and his wife, Drina, owned. He'd said it was where the lawn mowers and other things were kept and where he would find the fishing gear if he felt like fishing while here.

"Once they'd finished renovating the house," Stephanie continued, "they brought me out to test it."

"Test it?" Thorne asked with confusion, turning to glance at her.

Stephanie hesitated, but then asked, "How much do you know about immortals?"

Thorne considered the question briefly, and then said, "I was told that immortals are descendants of Atlanteans. That Atlantis truly did exist, was somewhat isolated from the rest of the world, and—as some sources suggest—was much more advanced than everyone else at that time. That they bioengineered nanos to treat illness and wounds without the need for medicine or surgeries. But that these nanos had the unexpected side effect of acting like a fountain of youth to their hosts, keeping them young and healthy indefinitely. Unfortunately, the nanos use blood for much of their repairs, as well as to power and regenerate themselves—more blood than a human body can produce. This problem was handled with blood transfusions in Atlantis, but when it fell, the Atlanteans who carried nanos were the only ones to survive, and found themselves joining a world that was much less developed. There were no more transfusions or even any real science yet in the rest of the world, and the nanos forced a sort of evolution on their hosts to survive. Immortals developed fangs to get the blood the nanos needed to support their work."

"And the other ways they evolved?" Stephanie asked.

"Your kind are faster than mortals, stronger, and can see in the dark," he listed off, and when she didn't respond and seemed to be waiting, he searched his mind for the answer she was looking for and then said, "Oh, yes, apparently you can read and control mortals without the nanos, and even immortals who are younger than you. Although I understand those abilities don't work well with myself and some of my father's other victims?"

It was a question. Just because the immortals he'd encountered so far couldn't read him didn't mean they all couldn't. If Stephanie could read or control him, he'd prefer to know and stay the hell away from her. He'd been controlled enough in his life.

"Yes. You're unreadable," she said easily.

Thorne felt himself relax a little, but asked, "And what about the control thing? Can you control me?"

She stopped walking at the question, her expression surprised, and he assumed that meant she hadn't considered whether she might be able to control him or not. Now, though, she turned to peer at him. Her expression was intense and focused on his forehead as if she were trying to see through into his brain.

Thorne waited, but after several moments, she blinked her eyes once and shook her head as she relaxed.

"Nope. You're safe. No controllability there," she assured him almost cheerfully, and started walking again.

Thorne fell into step with her, but pointed out, "You still haven't told me what Harper brought you out here to test out."

"Ah, well . . ." She paused, hesitancy claiming her face briefly, but finally she sighed and said, "Well, I seem to be a little sensitive to hearing thoughts."

"You mean reading minds?" he asked dryly.

Stephanie shook her head. "It's not really a case of reading them. At least not for me," she qualified. "Mostly it's like someone has turned a radio on and I can't *not* hear. Only, usually it's like everyone in the house, as well as all the neighboring houses, has turned on radios at full blast and they're all blaring at me with this constant, loud, overwhelming madness of clashing sounds and thoughts."

Thorne's eyes had grown wider as she'd spoken. She was describing something that sounded to him to be absolutely horrible, but doing it in a cheerful voice.

"It's maddening," she admitted, still sounding chipper.

"And all immortals experience this?" Thorne asked with a frown, thinking that this explained why many of the immortals he'd met were grim and usually taciturn with little to say. At least, the males he'd met often were. The women were usually the opposite, but even some of them were salty in his experience. But he could understand why they would be if their minds were constantly bombarded with other people's thoughts.

"No. From what I understand most immortals can block it out, or it isn't as loud for them, or they only need to block those in close proximity. Unfortunately, I appear to be extremely sensitive or something and pick up everyone within more than a mile radius, and can't block them out."

Thorne's eyebrows pulled together and shifted down at this news. It didn't sound very pleasant. The thoughts of everyone within a mile radius blaring in your head like a bunch of overloud radios and not being able to block it? In the city that could be thousands of people's thoughts pouring into your head like competing radios playing through a window. He didn't think he could bear that. He didn't know how she did, and began to worry that the cheerful way she talked about it might be a sign of mental instability, which would be a damned shame. The woman was beautiful, and seemed smart. It would be sad if her sensitivity, or inability to block these voices, drove her mad.

Pushing that thought away for now, he reasoned slowly, "So, the test was to see if being out here with acres of farmland between you and your neighbors would help with that?"

"Exactly," she said with a nod. "Harper had their house insulated with soundproofing and a lot of other things in an effort to block those thoughts for me, then had me come out and live there for a couple weeks on my own to see if it helped."

"And did it?" Thorne asked with curiosity.

"Not really," she admitted, and then confided, "The

soundproofing and stuff used to work when I was younger, but became less helpful as I grew up. I seemed to be able to hear more and from farther away with each passing year," she confessed with the first sign of unhappiness since they'd started talking about it. "But being out in the country did help. With the houses separated by fields, there are fewer people in the vicinity for me to have to deal with, and that was helpful," she assured him.

Thorne nodded, not surprised to hear that. "So, on learning this, Harper and Drina then built a second house for you?"

"Oh, hell, no!" Stephanie said firmly, giving him a scowl for the suggestion. "Like I'd let them do that."

One eyebrow raised, Thorne asked, "So the second house was always here?"

"No." She shook her head. "When I told them it was great, perfect, and I couldn't hear a thing in the house, they—"

"Wait, wait," Thorne interrupted. "You just told me it doesn't work."

"It doesn't," she assured him. "I lied."

Thorne frowned at the admission.

"Scowl at me all you like, but I lied for their sakes," she said, appearing unconcerned by his opinion. "They were all worrying themselves sick about me, afraid I'd go mad and blah, blah, blah." She shrugged. "And it *was* better out here. With so few people's thoughts in my head, I could actually have a thought or two of my own, and the headaches were much reduced."

"I see," Thorne murmured, and he did see. He had family who worried about him too. It was why he was here in Canada rather than at home on his island. So that his mother and Maria would stop worrying about him.

"Anyway, as I was saying, I told them it was awesome and everything was great out here, and they immediately offered me the house and land as a birthday gift."

Thorne's eyebrows rose again at the crazy generous offer.

"But I have more pride than that," Stephanie said solemnly. "Everyone has been worrying and working for years to try to make things easier for me. Dani and Decker, Elvi and Victor, Harper and Drina, and everyone else have spent tons of money trying to help. They even try 'not to think' when I'm around to help keep me from being overwhelmed." She chuckled softly after saying that and told him, "I know this because I heard them thinking, 'Do not think anything. Clear your mind so you don't burden her with more thoughts.'"

Stephanie shook her head. "So, I refused the offer of the house. Told them I'd rather they keep it so they can visit when they wish, and I'd buy the back end of the property from him and build my own house facing the lake," she told him, and then grimaced. "Of course Harper fought it. He wanted to do this for me. But I pointed out that I didn't want to feel like a charity case, and also they could come visit often, but sleep in their own house where, between their insulation and mine, their thoughts wouldn't disturb me.

"In the end, that was the only reason he gave in," she admitted. "And he still intervened a bit. I got to pay for everything, but he oversaw the construction to ensure they were quick about it and did everything right. Which I did appreciate, since thanks to him they built my house faster than they renovated his. I was able to move out here a little over a year ago. And here we are."

Thorne glanced around with surprise to see that while she'd been speaking, they'd made it to the end of the tree-lined path, crossed the yard to the side of a second house that was a mirror to the one he was staying in, and were stepping onto a covered porch where the main entrance waited.

Curious, he glanced around at the landscaping, noting the line of hedges at the front of the patio, the four shallow stairs down to a large area covered in stone tiles, an open-sided gazebo with a ceiling fan and lights that gave shelter from the sun to the long table and six chairs under it. There was a pond about ten feet to the right of the gazebo, out in front of the corner of the house, with tall grass and flowers surrounding it, and a wide path between it and the house that led to a grassy area in front of the house that extended a good hundred feet before dropping off at the beach. There was also an enclosed gazebo some thirty feet in front of and to the left of the open structure. It was about eighteen feet by twelve feet in dimension, with screened windows making up the top six feet of the building, and only the lower part solid. It sat at a slight angle, overlooking the lake and the path they'd just come from.

Thorne stared around with a sort of wonder. Everything here was like a mirror image of the house he was staying in. Even the plants, bushes, flowers, and tall grasses were similar. They weren't exactly the same—the color of the flowers here were reds and pinks and purples rather than the yellows that predominated the other house, and the tall grasses were of differing varieties than used there—

but otherwise, it could have been a reflection of the yard of the house he was staying in.

"Coming?"

Thorne glanced around to see that Stephanie had already entered the house and was peering out at him through the open door.

"Sorry. I was just looking around," he explained, starting forward again. "It looks very like the yard of the house I'm staying in."

"Yeah." Stephanie grinned as she closed the door behind him and locked it. Then she headed through the entry and across an open space in front of the kitchen. "I loved what Harper and Drina had done at their house and pretty much mirrored it here, just using different colors."

Thorne murmured something of an agreement as he glanced around. Like the outside, the inside was a reflected image of the house he was staying in. Once out of the entry, there was a long, large kitchen on his right, and a dining area on his left with a clear glass railing around it, the only separation between it and a large room that sat three feet below the dining area but had to be thirty or forty feet wide and nearly as deep with a high cathedral ceiling and a front wall that looked out over the lake. That wall was made up completely of glass, giving an amazing view of the surrounding land and the lake. He couldn't see the house on the other side of the lake, though, he noticed. There were two small islands on this side of the lake, or perhaps islets would be a better word since they were so small. Neither was more than twenty feet across, and both were covered with trees and bushes that blocked any view of the other house. He couldn't even see the dock from here. But then the same had been true from the other side of the lake. He'd been told there were two houses on the lake, but hadn't been able to see this one from the house he was staying in, or even when he'd walked out onto the dock. It had made him wonder, but now he understood. The two little islands blocked both houses from each other.

"Did Harper have the islands made?" he asked with interest.

"No." Stephanie stopped and turned to look out at the view of the lake. She then bent to set Felix on the hardwood floor as she explained, "They were there when he bought the place. I guess that's where the dragline equipment was stationed when it was still a quarry. But their position is why I had the house built on this corner, the islands with all their trees act as a privacy fence between the two houses. Perfect, huh?"

"Actually, yes, it is rather perfect," he admitted with a faint smile, and then turned to look at the kitchen at the back of the house. Like the house he was in, it had sliding doors on the far end, overlooking a deck. But where the cupboards in the house he was in were a pale wood, these ones were a glossy, pure white on the upper cupboards, and a stunningly bright blue on the bottom as well as on the cupboards that made up the long island that took up the center of the kitchen. He'd never seen a kitchen quite this big.

"Don't feel bad if you don't like my kitchen. The blue usually shocks people. My brother-in-law, Decker, claimed it would blind him to have to look at it all the time."

Thorne glanced to Stephanie with surprise and shook

his head. "I don't find it blinding at all. It's perfect. It goes well with the white and brightens the kitchen. I imagine even on the gloomiest day, or at night, this kitchen is cheerful and bright."

"It is," she agreed, beaming at him, and then she glanced around the kitchen and commented, "Which is ironic, since the color is Evening Blue, which you'd think would be darker rather than this almost electric blue."

Thorne didn't respond to that, but peered over the kitchen again and commented, "It's big. The kitchen, I mean."

"Yeah." She smiled crookedly. "Well, the kitchen is the heart of the home. Big hearts are good."

Thorne nodded. The tiny kitchen of the small house on the island was where he, his mother, and Maria had spent most of their time while he was growing up and even after he'd become a man. He suspected it was that way for most people. Obviously, it was for Stephanie.

"Well, let's see what I have to feed you," Stephanie said, walking into the kitchen. Opening the refrigerator door, she peered in and then began poking through the contents and asked, "What time of day is this for you?"

Thorne glanced at the watch on his wrist. "It's nearly six thirty."

Stephanie laughed softly and glanced his way. "Sorry. I meant, are you normally a night person? Is this like a snack before bed, or are you an early bird and this is breakfast or maybe lunch since you must have been up for four or more hours now to drive here from Toronto?"

"Oh. Usually this would be morning, but I rested yesterday afternoon and early evening so that I could drive down on the motorcycle last night."

"I suppose driving during the day would have caused a stir," Stephanie commented, her gaze sliding over him briefly before she turned to the refrigerator again. "But bacon and eggs are good at any time of day. Do you prefer omelets, eggs over easy, or scrambled eg—" She stopped abruptly, her eyes going wide, and turned an alarmed gaze his way. "I'm sorry. Do you eat eggs? I mean . . ."

"I am not a chicken, Stephanie. I eat eggs," Thorne said with amusement, guessing her dilemma, and watched the blush that rose up her neck to cover her face as her dismay gave way to chagrin.

"Sorry," she muttered, and turned quickly back to the fridge to retrieve a carton of eggs and a package of bacon.

Feeling bad for her, he said, "There's no reason to be embarrassed. You aren't the first person to worry that offering eggs might offend me."

Stephanie sighed and shrugged her shoulders as she walked around the island to the large range that took up three feet in the center of one side. She set the items she'd collected on the counter next to the range, and then opened the drawer directly under the range to retrieve a frying pan before saying, "I've never met anyone like you before. Which shouldn't surprise you, but I guarantee it means I'll probably trip up and accidentally insult you a time or two. My apologies in advance."

Thorne found himself smiling at the wry confession. She was incredibly honest. First telling him he was hot, and now admitting that she'd probably slip up and make errors that might offend him. Most people he met either tried to act like there was nothing at all different about him, or kept their distance because of his differences.

She seemed to be taking it in stride, though, and he liked her honesty.

Something wet nudging his hand drew his gaze down to see her boxer beside him, pressing her muzzle into his hand. Recognizing it as a bid for attention, he took a moment to pet the friendly creature, and then glanced around, wondering where the cat had gone. When he spotted him on one of the chairs that were as high as bar stools that lined the end of the counter between the kitchen and dining room, his gaze narrowed. The cat looked like it was about to launch itself at him. Not eager to have the little fiend bite his wing again, Thorne straightened and walked into the kitchen proper to stand across the island from Stephanie.

"What can I do to help?" he asked as she continued to gather items—a spatula, a butter dish, salt and pepper, two plates . . .

"You can make us both a coffee and start on the toast if you like," she suggested easily as she moved around the island to gather forks, spoons, and knives from a silverware drawer next to the sink that sat in the center of the end counter. She then glanced at him to ask, "Do you drink coffee? If not, there's a little orange juice left in the fridge and more coming later."

"I enjoy coffee," Thorne assured her, and looked around until he spotted the single-cup coffee machine on the end of the counter near the opening into the kitchen.

"Coffee cups are in the cupboard above it. The coffee pods are in the top drawer under it, and there's a small bucket in the second drawer down to throw the used pods in when you need to switch them out," Stephanie said as he moved to the machine.

Nodding, Thorne retrieved two cups from the upper cupboard and then opened the top drawer under the machine. His eyes widened when he saw the slots dividing the different flavors of coffee. There were Tim Hortons original blend pods lined up and separated neatly from various flavored coffees all with their own divided sections: vanilla hazelnut, pumpkin cappuccino, German chocolate cake—all lined up nicely next to hot chocolate and even tea pods. The woman was very organized.

Thorne decided he liked it as he selected one and asked, "What kind of coffee do you want?"

"Vanilla hazelnut," Stephanie responded, sounding distracted, and then added, "Medium strength with one sugar and two splashes of mocha creamer, please. The mocha creamer and normal cream are on the right-hand door of the fridge."

Thorne smiled as he set up the cup and pod and pushed the necessary button. He then moved to fetch the creamer from the refrigerator, which stood two cupboard lengths away to his right, cutting the long stretch of upper and lower cupboards in half. Returning to the coffee machine a moment later, he glanced around, noticing that the cupboards past the refrigerator on this side of the kitchen stopped at a set of glass French doors in the side wall at the far end of the kitchen, which had to be thirty-five feet long. The borders on the doors were the same blue as the lower cupboards, with frosted glass filling the center.

"My office."

Thorne glanced around with confusion to see that Stephanie had sliced open the package of bacon and was now laying out the strips in the frying pan.

Stephanie didn't even glance up when she explained, "The French doors are to my office."

"Oh." He nodded, despite the fact that she wasn't looking at him, and then noticed the solid, single white door at the end of the cupboards on the other side and asked, "What about the single door?"

"The laundry closet," she explained, glancing along the cupboards behind her toward the door in question. "The washer and dryer are in there the same as at Drina and Harper's house."

"I didn't really explore much," Thorne explained. "I dropped my gear inside the door to the garage, took a quick look into the kitchen and front room, then walked outside to watch the sun rise."

Stephanie smiled crookedly. "I like watching the sun rise before I go to bed. But I sleep through the morning and get up sometime around noon."

"That's what? Four or five hours of sleep?" Thorne asked with surprise.

"I'm not a big sleeper," Stephanie said with a shrug as she finished laying out the bacon and grabbed a bowl to begin cracking eggs on the rim and releasing the contents into the bowl. Glancing up then, she pointed out, "You never said what you prefer: scrambled, over easy, or would you prefer an omelet?"

"Scrambled," Thorne decided, not wanting to be a bother and thinking that would probably be easiest for her to make.

Stephanie moved around to the fridge to retrieve a carton of milk, stopped to grab a fork on the way back, and set to work on the eggs. Thorne watched her add milk, salt and pepper, and then attack it with the fork before he turned to the coffee machine as it finished spitting out the first cup of coffee. It was only after he'd set the second cup to start and shifted his attention to adding the sugar and mocha creamer to the first cup that he noticed how domestic and comfortable this all seemed. It reminded him of home, where he, Maria, and his mother often worked together to prepare meals.

"Taste it and see if it's okay or you need more creamer," he suggested, carrying the first coffee over and setting it down beside Stephanie.

"Perfect," Stephanie assured him after stopping her stirring to take a sip. "Thank you."

"My pleasure," Thorne responded as he returned to the coffee machine to fix his own coffee. Aside from the small container holding spoons next to the coffee machine, there was a clear glass bowl full of sugar. A rubber lid covered it. Organized, Thorne thought again, but asked, "Do you have ants here?"

"Yes," Stephanie said dryly. "I don't know how they get in, but they do and they drive me crazy getting into anything and everything they can. Hence the lid on the sugar bowl," she added.

Thorne nodded, lifted his cup to taste it, and smiled. Good. He then lowered the cup and glanced around in search of the toaster.

"The toaster is on the other side of the refrigerator. The bread is in the drawer under it," Stephanie murmured.

Thorne glanced at her sharply, and then moved along the counter to find the white four-slice toaster sitting on the white-and-gray marble countertop just past the refrigerator as promised. A white porcelain butter dish stood next to it and the bread was in the drawer underneath as she'd said.

Taking out the bread, he began to pull out slices and deposit them in the slots on the toaster, asking, "You're sure you can't read my mind?"

Stephanie chuckled at the question. "Positive. I just saw you looking around and guessed that was what you were looking for."

When Thorne glanced at her a little dubiously, she arched an eyebrow. "I wouldn't bother lying about that."

"You admitted to lying to your loved ones about the insulation in the house blocking people's thoughts," he pointed out.

Stephanie shrugged, and then said bluntly, "Because I love them. I don't love you or care what you think."

Thorne nodded solemnly, not at all offended. What she said made perfect sense. They'd just met. She wouldn't lie to save his feelings or prevent him from worrying. She probably wouldn't have cared if her being able to read his mind might have made him uncomfortable. Besides, none of the other immortals he'd met had been able to read him. Not even the very old and apparently most powerful immortal, Lucian Argeneau.

"Your sister told me you're a writer," he said, pushing down the lever to start the bread toasting. Thorne then leaned against the counter, his arms crossed over his chest as he watched Stephanie cooking the bacon.

She glanced up from the pan, her expression slightly wary. "Did she?"

"Yes. Fiction, she said."

A smile tugged at her lips at that, and Stephanie shook her head. "She calls it that because she's uncomfortable admitting I write horror."

Thorne blinked in surprise. "Really? You write horror?"

She hesitated, her head tilting a little one way and then

the other in a gesture that he suspected meant so-so, and then admitted, "Actually, a lot of what I write is nonfiction, but gets published as horror fiction."

Thorne's eyes narrowed. "How does that work?"

She took a moment to turn over the strips of bacon in the pan, and then said, "The first book I wrote started as a . . . well, sort of as a journal, I guess. A recounting of what happened to Dani and me when we were attacked and turned. It was at the suggestion of Marguerite's son-in-law, Greg . . ." Stephanie paused and glanced at him with a frown. "Have you met Marguerite?"

"I was staying with her in Toronto before I came here," Thorne admitted.

"Oh." She nodded. "Okay, well, as you may or may not know, Greg Hewitt is married to her daughter, Lissianna. They're life mates, and he's a psychologist, or psychiatrist or whatever. Anyway, Dani and Elvi ganged up on me and made me see him a couple of times after we were first turned. They thought it would help."

"Did it?" Thorne asked with curiosity.

"I guess. Maybe. A little," Stephanie said uncertainly, and then shook her head. "Actually, probably not much, but that wasn't his fault. I was dealing with a lot. Everyone's thoughts were in my head, swamping me, making it impossible to concentrate on my own thoughts or feelings. I was also afraid of letting him know anything about my being able to hear so much, so I wasn't very honest and forthcoming, which is probably important in counseling," she admitted, and then sighed and said, "Anyway, he thought it might be cathartic for me to write down what happened and how I felt about the attack and losing my family and everything. So, I did. And it actually did kind of help, I think. At least it made me feel better, so after that, every time they sent me out to chase down their rogues, or had me sift through horrible memories of victims, I wrote that down too."

The toaster behind him popped and Stephanie paused to remove the first batch of crispy bacon from the pan before adding fresh strips of raw meat, while he buttered the toast and dropped more bread in the machine. Thorne then turned and watched silently as she finished up, his mind going over what she'd said. There was a lot to unpack there and it was raising questions in him.

Before he could sort out what he wanted to ask first, she'd finished laying in the fresh strips of bacon and continued. "Like I said, when I first started, it was supposed to be just a personal journal. But then about eight years ago, when I was twenty, I was cleaning out my room and came across the journals. I never read them after I wrote them, or even while writing them," Stephanie explained.

"But that day you did," he said solemnly, and she smiled.

"Yeah. Though I'm still not sure why," she admitted wryly, and shrugged. "Whatever. I started with the first one I'd written, the one about Dani and me . . . and it was actually really well-written if I do say so myself." Stephanie smiled crookedly and glanced up to tell him, "I had actually written them in the third person, like a story. Greg would probably say that it was some sort of attempt to distance myself from what had happened, and it probably was, but it made writing them easier. It also made reading them, years later, much easier. It was like reading something that had happened to someone else, and despite knowing how that first story ended, I couldn't stop."

Her gaze shifted back to the bacon she was cooking. "And then I got this crazy idea . . . Marguerite's eldest son, Lucern, is an author. He actually documents how his family members find and claim their life mates, but it gets published as paranormal romance. The family view them as historical documents, but the rest of the world sees them as bodice rippers or something," she said with a chuckle.

"And you thought why not publish your journals, which are actually historical accounts, as horrors," he guessed.

"Yeah." Stephanie grinned at him. "I thought it was crazy. I mean, when I was still just your average, know-nothing, mortal teenager, I used to dream of being a writer when I grew up. I never really thought it would happen. But those journals were sitting there and it wasn't like I had a lot of career options thanks to my not being able to get a postsecondary education. So, I thought, what the hell? Why not give it a go?"

Stephanie shook her head slightly, as if still marveling at the course her life had taken. "So, I typed them all up, editing as I went. Once I was done, though, I wasn't sure what to do with them. I didn't have an agent, and from some research online learned that getting an agent was next to impossible, but that getting published without one was equally nearly impossible. So, I decided I'd go the self-pubbed, online route."

"Couldn't you have just controlled an agent to make them work with you?" he pointed out, and was pleased when Stephanie glanced up at him with disgust.

"Of course I could have. I could have controlled an editor or publisher and made them publish me too, but that would have been cheating," she said a little stiffly.

"I mean . . . what should I have done after that? Stood in bookstores and controlled people to make them buy my books too?" She snorted at the idea, and shook her head. "I wanted to earn my way. If I was going to just control my way through life I might as well have controlled my way into Jeff Bezos's office and made him give me a couple million or billion dollars. Or maybe made him marry me and take everything when he cocked up his toes."

Stephanie clucked with distaste. "Why even live if you aren't going to actually do stuff for yourself, but just coast through making others do the heavy lifting for you?" She shook her head. "Not for me."

Thorne smiled at her outrage, pleased by that as well. It seemed to him from the news he read that a lot of people would prefer to coast through life, living off of others, rather than work and earn their way. He was glad she didn't.

"Anyway," Stephanie said as she shifted her attention to turning the bacon sizzling in the frying pan, "I self-published online and, much to my amazement, that first book did pretty well. It wasn't huge or anything, but it gained a small following, and those readers were kind of rabid. They spread the word—talking about it, writing reviews, pushing it to other readers, and so on. My second book did even better, and the next better still.

"I mean, I wasn't Stephen King successful, but money was coming in and my fan base was almost doubling with each book," she told him. "After the fourth book, the word had spread so far that a couple of publishers emailed, saying they were interested in publishing me in paper and asking for the name of my agent."

"Which you didn't have," Thorne said as the toaster

popped behind him again and he turned to the duty of buttering once more.

"No," she agreed with amusement. "But I got one pretty quick with those emails in hand. Fortunately, a good one. She got me a pretty amazing deal and—" when she paused briefly, he glanced over his shoulder to see her peering around the kitchen "—five years and five three-book contracts later I was able to build this house."

"Fifteen books in five years?" he asked with surprise as he finished buttering the toast.

"They were all already written from events that took place between when I was fourteen and twenty or so. They just had to be edited and typed up from journals to Word documents," she explained.

"What will you do when you run out of journals?" Thorne asked with curiosity as he finished with the toast and turned to peer at her.

Stephanie snorted at the suggestion. "Like that would happen. Lucian drags me out regularly to help with one rogue or another. All I have to do is write up what happened when I get back home. And I'm pretty fast at typing."

"Lucian Argeneau," Thorne murmured, recognizing the name of the head of the North American Immortal Council.

"Yes." She glanced to him and smiled wryly. "I gather you met him in Venezuela when he was looking for your father's island?"

"I did," he admitted, keeping his face expressionless.

Apparently, not expressionless enough, he realized when Stephanie chuckled and said, "Yeah. He's a hard-ass on the outside. But that's just a cover." Amusement fading, she told him solemnly, "He's really a very good man under all that cold steel he shows everyone. He's just the guy burdened with keeping everyone safe, and believe me, it weighs heavy on him." She turned the bacon again, and added, "I'm sure he acted all arrogant and grim when you first met, and didn't thank you for leading him and the others to the island to rescue everyone. But I know he was grateful as hell for it and will never forget what you did for us when you risked flying to the mainland to find him."

Stephanie raised her head, and added, "And it's the same for me. I had family in those cells on the island. If you hadn't helped, they might still be there. So, thank you, Thorne."

"It was nothing," he said gruffly, uncomfortable with the gratitude. Especially since what he'd done had really been self-serving.

"It wasn't nothing," Stephanie said firmly. "If someone had seen you on the mainland . . ." She shook her head, not bothering to say what would have happened. But she didn't have to. He knew. He'd have been shot out of the air and, if he'd survived, would have ended up in some government facility somewhere, spending the rest of his days being poked and prodded and tested like a lab rat. But it had been a risk he'd been willing to take to free himself, his mother, and Maria from his father's tyranny.

"Can you pass me the toast?"

Thorne blinked his thoughts away to see that Stephanie had transferred the last of the bacon to the paper-towel-laced plate she'd put the first batch on, and was now opening the French doors of the upper of a pair of double ovens to place it inside. Turning, he picked up the toast and walked over to slide the plate into the oven next to the bacon, then stepped back to watch with fascination as she closed the double doors.

"I didn't know they had ovens with French doors," he admitted as she began to tap on the digital screen at the top, setting the oven to keep the contents warm.

"Yeah, they haven't been around that long, but I was so happy when I saw them in the appliance store," she said enthusiastically. "My arms aren't long enough for an upper oven with a drop-down door. I had to put stuff in from the side and was forever burning myself on the side wall," she explained. "With this oven I never burn myself. Well, not so far anyway," she added, and then murmured, "Knock on wood," and did just that, knocking twice on the wooden surface of the cupboard next to the ovens.

Thorne smiled at the superstitious action, and then noticed that her coffee cup was empty and snatched it up. As he carried it to the coffee machine, he commented, "I didn't realize you weren't born immortal. I just assumed that since you and your sister are both immortal that there was a whole family of immortal McGills out there, like the Argeneaus."

"No. Just me and Dani," Stephanie said quietly as she gave the scrambled eggs one more stir before pouring them into the frying pan. She grabbed a spatula and began to push the quickly gelling eggs around in the pan before adding, "We were on the way home from a family weekend up north in cottage country. Dani had come from work and drove up by herself. At the end of the weekend, I asked to join her for the ride home to avoid being cramped in the family van with the rest of my siblings. We were attacked by rogues when we stopped for snacks for the ride."

Thorne considered that as he made both himself and Stephanie a fresh coffee. He wanted to ask more about that, wanted to know what had happened, but considering it had been published as a horror, he decided now wasn't the time. So, instead, he commented, "And now you're a rogue hunter as well as a horror writer?"

"Part-time," she admitted. "For a while I was afraid that being a hunter was the only career that would be open to me. Fortunately, this writing gig turned out pretty well, so I only help on the harder cases now."

"Why would you think hunting rogues would be the only career open to you?" he asked, glancing around at her with surprise.

"Well, with my sensitivity to hearing other people's thoughts, it wasn't like I could go anywhere as populated as a university or college," Stephanie pointed out dryly. "I couldn't even work as a waitress with all the voices in my head. I'd go mad, or just shrivel up into a ball of agony and probably set myself on fire or something. The headaches were killer."

Thorne felt his eyebrows draw together at that news as he finished making their coffees, and said, "I thought the nanos would prevent things like headaches and such?"

"I guess they do for immortals. I mean, I've never heard of them having headaches unless they get a head wound and then it's just the nanos healing them. But nothing works the same with me," she muttered with disgust.

Thorne was frowning over that when she announced,

"The eggs are done. Would you rather eat at the dining room table or the island?"

He glanced toward the dining room table and the view beyond. It was beautiful, but there was a large vase of flowers on the table that would have to be moved, and all the food would have to be carried to it. The seats at the counter would be easier, so he said, "In here is fine."

"Good choice," Stephanie assured him.

Thorne smiled faintly and started to carry the coffees to the counter that ran between the kitchen and dining room. The back half was open underneath the counter-top, and several chairs sat there, facing the kitchen itself. He had assumed that was where she expected to eat, so was surprised when she said, "Over here."

Thorne glanced around to see that she was carrying a bowl full of scrambled eggs to the far end of the island by the sliding doors. It was only then he noticed that there were two chairs there—one on the end, and one at the side. He followed her with the coffees.

"You can have the end. Better view," Stephanie said as she set down the eggs, and headed back toward the oven.

Thorne put down the coffees, and then glanced around to see that she hadn't returned to the oven after all, but had stopped at the drawers just past the chairs to retrieve a couple of place mats. When she collected the silver-ware and plates next, Thorne moved around her and used a folded dish towel that was lying on the cupboard to retrieve the bacon from the oven. While Stephanie set the table, he brought over the bacon and returned for the toast, but when he swung back it was to see that she had sort of frozen in the act of setting down a fork, a stricken expression on her face.

"What is it?" he asked with concern, returning quickly to the end of the island.

"I didn't think—Can you sit?" she asked uncertainly. "I mean, your wings . . ."

Thorne relaxed, a faint smile curving his lips, and then he set down the toast and turned his back to her so that she could see his wings. He'd let them lay flat down his back before this, but now shifted them to the sides.

"Oh, wow," Stephanie breathed, and he glanced over his shoulder to see her coming around to stand behind him.

Thorne turned his face forward and simply waited as she got a closer look.

Four

"So, your shirt and vest are Velcroed together under the—where your wings are attached to your upper back."

Thorne blinked, surprised by Stephanie's comment about his clothes rather than the fact that he could move his wings as he had.

"So, you have to reach back and do them up like a woman puts on a bra?" she asked.

"Yes, I suppose," Thorne admitted wryly as he felt her fingers drift over the back of the cloth covering his lower back. He'd never thought of it that way.

"Oh, they fasten around the neck too," she said suddenly, and Thorne stiffened a little as her fingers brushed the side of his neck just above the leather. The brief contact sent an unexpected shiver of pleasure through him that had his feathers ruffling a bit before he caught the instinctive reaction and reversed it.

"Sorry," Stephanie murmured, and he could actually feel her heat move away from him as she stepped back.

"It's fine. You just startled me," Thorne muttered, turning to see her heading back around to the side of the island. Her expression was oddly troubled, though, he noted.

"We should probably eat before the food gets cold," Stephanie said as she sat down.

Thorne stared at her silently. It seemed to him that she was avoiding looking at him now, and he wasn't sure what that meant. Had the brief ruffling of his feathers offended her somehow? Or had it simply pointed out to her how different he was? That he was, ultimately, a freak.

Irritated with such unproductive thoughts—the kind he'd believed he'd overcome years ago—Thorne gave his head a shake and shifted his wings to sit down in the end seat, then let his wings relax to hang down on either side of the counter-height chair.

The meal was somewhat awkward after that. At least it was for Thorne. Stephanie was silent, her head down, and it left him feeling uncomfortable and unwelcome. It was the complete opposite of the atmosphere earlier while they'd worked together and talked, and he regretted losing that.

"I'm sorry."

Thorne glanced up from his plate with surprise at those softly spoken words.

Stephanie grimaced and said, "I didn't mean to ruffle your feathers. I shouldn't have touched you without permission."

His eyes widened incredulously at the solemn apology.

He'd thought she was disgusted by him, but she seemed to be suggesting she'd felt bad for . . . touching him? Without permission? He almost assured her that the apology was unnecessary and she could touch him anytime, anywhere, and any way she'd like, but caught the words at the last moment as he realized how they would sound.

Not that he didn't mean it. Thorne would be happy for her to touch him again . . . anywhere and as often as she'd like. He liked this woman. A lot. He enjoyed talking to her, and listening to her . . . and he was attracted to her as well. His skin still tingled where she'd touched the side of his neck. He'd like to see if her touch had the same effect in other places, but suspected it was probably too soon to make such admissions. Thorne wasn't sure. He hadn't exactly been raised in polite society where he could learn social customs and mores.

Hell, he'd spent the majority of his life with just his elderly mother and Maria for company. It was only the last six years or so that he'd spent time with others his own age, and that had been the other hybrids, results of his father's experiments who had spent their lives trapped on the island as well and had no better clue about social niceties than him.

Of course, there had been female immortals on the island these last years. Hunters who had been staying on the island to try to help those who looked normal enough to join society, as well as to guard against Dressler returning to the island. Most of them had been mated, though. And he suspected the experience he'd had with the five who weren't mated wasn't typical of human relations.

So, basically, Thorne didn't have a clue how males

and females got along normally. For instance, was it appropriate for him to touch her? Even just to clasp her hand, or touch her arm? And what about kissing? Thorne wondered as he watched her lips move. How long would it be before he might kiss her? Was there a standard time length between meeting and when kissing might be appropriate? And should he ask for permission first? Because he really had a terrible, mounting urge to cover her mouth with his and—

"Earth to Thorne!"

He blinked as those words got through his thoughts. Stephanie had spoken them in a half amused and half exasperated voice that suggested she'd said them more than once, or at least had been trying to get his attention for some time.

"I'm sorry. Yes?" he said, forcing his gaze away from her luscious mouth to her beautiful eyes.

"Did you want some eggs?" She gestured toward the bowl she was holding out.

"Oh. Yes. Thank you," Thorne murmured, taking the bowl from her and grimacing as he said apologetically, "I'm sorry. I was thinking."

"About what?" Stephanie asked with interest as she took several pieces of bacon before passing the plate to him.

Thorne quickly searched his mind for a more acceptable answer than "about kissing you" as he set the eggs aside and accepted the bacon. But by the time he'd taken several rations and set the plate down the only thing he'd come up with was, "You mentioned you had family members in the cells on the island. I know Decker was there, and that he's your sister's husband?"

A crooked smile curved Stephanie's lips. "Yeah. I was

upset about that. Legally he might only be my brother-in-law, but really he's become like a true brother. The older PITA brother every girl needs."

"Pita?" Thorne asked uncertainly.

"An acronym for Pain In The Arse," Stephanie explained with a grin, and when Thorne raised his eyebrows, she shrugged. "All big brothers are PITAs at times, and Decker's no exception. I think it's the job of big brothers around the world."

"Ah." Thorne nodded.

"But Uncle Vic was in there too," she added.

"Uncle Vic?" he asked with confusion. "I thought you and your sister were the only McGills who had been turned and—"

"Yeah. Sorry." She rolled her eyes at herself. "After I was rescued from Leo—he was the creep rogue who turned both my sister and me," she stopped to explain. "Anyway, after I was rescued and finished turning, I was sent to Port Henry to live with Elvi and Victor Argeneau. Victor is Lucian's brother. Well, one of them. They have a lot of brothers and sisters. I think," she added with a small frown. "I mean, I know of seven or eight brothers and two sisters, but I suspect there are more who just haven't made their way to Canada yet."

Thorne nodded encouragingly.

"So, Victor is one of Lucian's younger brothers, and he and his wife, Elvi, took me in and became surrogate parents to me. I pretty much lived with them until I moved here. Well, half the time at least," she added. "The other half of the time was split between Drina and Harper, and Beau and Tiny."

"Drina and Harper Stoyan who own the other house?"

he said, not really asking, but just verifying that he was right.

"Yes," Stephanie said before popping some scrambled egg into her mouth.

"And who are Beau and Tiny?" Thorne asked with interest. "I think you mentioned this Beau before. She's a hunter?" This time it was a true question.

Stephanie finished chewing the food in her mouth, swallowed, and said, "Yeah. Beau and Tiny escorted me to Port Henry. It's how they met and found out they were life mates," she added with a grin. "Beau and Tiny kind of adopted me as a . . . a little sister I guess is the best description. They both, along with Beau's partner, Eshe, tend to be teamed up with me when I'm dragged out on hunts too." Her expression turned solemn before she added, "Beau and Eshe were also in the cells with Uncle Vic and Decker."

"Beau and Eshe," Thorne murmured, mentally running through the immortals he'd met after the hunters had swarmed the island and battled his father's men.

"Beau's pale as death with fuchsia-tipped black hair, and Eshe has gorgeous dark skin and short hair with the tips dyed so that it looks like it's on fire."

"Ah." Thorne nodded as an image of the two women instantly came to mind. "They stayed at the house and helped Maria's granddaughter, Sarita, through the turn."

Stephanie smiled. "Yeah. They liked her. Said she'd make a good hunter."

When Thorne raised his eyebrows, she laughed and added, "That's a high compliment from those two."

"Ah," he said with understanding, and then tilted his

head and asked with curiosity, "Did Dani and Decker live at Victor and Elvi's too?"

"No." Her smile faded, some of the light went out of her eyes, and she seemed to close up a bit. Before Thorne could ask further questions, Stephanie suddenly straightened, her smile returned—though it looked somewhat forced—and she said, "You do know I've been doing all the talking, right?"

Thorne's eyes widened at the accusation in her tone.

"You just keep asking questions, and I just keep answering," she pointed out, and then announced, "Now it's your turn."

"My turn?" Thorne asked, a sliver of alarm sliding through his body and making his feathers ruffle before he could catch the natural reaction and stop it.

"Oh, wow."

Thorne glanced to Stephanie warily as he forced his body to relax. "What?"

"I'm guessing that ruffling thing is because you're alarmed that you're now going to be on the hot seat?"

Thorne frowned and glanced down at his chair, but didn't see any wires or anything else suggesting it could be heated.

"It's an expression," Stephanie said with amusement. "It means I'll be asking you some possibly uncomfortable or embarrassing questions now, and you're stuck in the hot seat figuring out how to answer them."

"Oh," he muttered, relaxing back in his seat and eyeing her warily.

"So? Was the ruffling an alarm response?"

"Perhaps," he said quietly.

She opened her mouth to speak, hesitated, and then her

eyes widened with dismay and she asked, "Was it alarm too when I touched your neck?"

"No," Thorne assured her solemnly, not wanting her not to touch him out of worry that she was upsetting him.

She tilted her head. "Startled?"

Knowing she was asking if that had been why he'd ruffled up when she'd touched him, he nodded. Though that wasn't fully the truth. He *had* been startled by the tingle of pleasure that had shot through him, but not the touch itself.

"Okay, so it's like an emotional boner," she said with a grin. "Telling when you're upset or startled."

Thorne's eyes widened incredulously.

Stephanie laughed at his expression and shook her head. "Relax. I'm just teasing. You looked really worried about what I might ask and I didn't mean to stress you out so was hoping to lighten the moment."

Thorne forced himself to relax, or tried to. The woman was a bit unpredictable, coming out with somewhat shocking comments every once in a while. At least, shocking to him, but then what the hell did he know? He'd spent most of his life isolated on an island with two elderly ladies for company.

"What's it like to fly?"

The question brought his focus back to Stephanie and he considered the question, but after a moment admitted, "I'm not sure how to answer that."

Stephanie raised her eyebrows. "Don't you fly? Wait," she added quickly, "I know you fly. You flew to the mainland to warn Lucian and the others," she reminded him, as if he could forget that.

"Yes. But . . ." He paused, trying to figure out how to

explain his problem to her, and then asked, "How would you answer if a person with no legs asked what it was like to walk?"

Stephanie sat back, her expression thoughtful for a moment, and then grimaced. "I see what you mean," she admitted, but then smiled faintly and added, "But I think you actually just answered the question with your question."

"I did?" he asked with surprise.

She nodded. "To a person without legs, walking would be . . . a freedom they've never enjoyed. I imagine it's the same for having wings and flying."

Thorne's eyebrows rose. Stephanie was right, of course.

"Okay, so I'll ask you an easier question," she announced, and then leaned her elbows on the island top, propped her chin on the heels of her hands, and asked, "How did you learn to fly?"

Thorne grimaced at the memory that question brought to mind. "You've heard the expression sink or swim?"

"Yes. Of course."

"Well, it was that kind of deal," he told her grimly. "Willis, one of Dressler's men, threw me off the cliff in front of our cottage. It was fly or die."

Her eyes widened in horror. "Really?"

Thorne nodded.

"On purpose?" she asked.

"Yes. Apparently, Dressler wanted to know if I could fly, so he sent Willis down with instructions on what to do. He came into the cottage in the middle of the afternoon, grabbed me up, dragged me to the cliff with my mother and Maria following, screaming hysterically and trying to pull me away from him. They couldn't manage that, however, and once at the cliff's edge, he apologized, said it was on my father's orders, and tossed me out into the air," Thorne told her. "I was four and a half years old."

"Oh my God, that bastard," Stephanie breathed the words. "I can't believe he—But you flew?" she asked with concern. "Of course you did, you're here and still alive."

Thorne shrugged. "Mostly I think I just kind of glided more than actually flew that time." Smiling wryly, he added, "Although I do more gliding than flapping of wings anyway as a rule once I get into the air."

Stephanie didn't even seem to hear that; she was shaking her head slowly, horror on her face, and asked, "What if you hadn't been able to fly? What if you'd just dropped like a stone? You could have died. I mean, I thought he was just a mad scientist, but he's a fricking psychopath."

He didn't argue with her. Dressler *was* a psychopath, and he'd hurt a lot of people. It was why Thorne wouldn't acknowledge having any relationship to the man who was technically his father. Maybe. He wasn't one hundred percent positive the man's DNA was anywhere inside him. The bastard had added so many different varieties of animal DNA to the fertilized egg that eventually became him that it might have eradicated all traces of Dressler's. At least, that's what Thorne told himself. He hated having any connection to the man, let alone being a result of his seed. He certainly didn't consider him a father.

"Wow," Stephanie muttered, and stood up to begin gathering her plate and silverware. "There are way too many mean, crazy bastards in this world."

Thorne grunted something of an agreement as he too stood and started to gather the items from their meal.

"And that crazy asshole managed to get himself turned and is still out there, but now a crazy immortal asshole,"

Stephanie pointed out with disgust as she stomped to the sink.

"Perhaps," Thorne agreed as he followed her with the items he'd gathered. "Maybe we got lucky and he didn't survive the turn, but died after fleeing Venezuela." He noted the way Stephanie stiffened at those words and suspected she had some knowledge that the man still lived. Not wanting to hear that, Thorne quickly added, "Even if he is alive, though, I doubt he's happy."

"What?" she asked with surprise, glancing around from rinsing her plate. "Why?"

"From what I know of him, he was an arrogant ass who enjoyed money and all the accolades of his position as a respected professor," Thorne said solemnly. "Now he's on the run, there are no more accolades, and since my mother closed out their accounts and moved her money to where he can't reach it, no more money."

"Until he takes control of some poor unsuspecting mortal and takes their money," she said dryly.

Thorne was frowning over that possibility when the dog suddenly let out a woof.

Stephanie glanced around to where the boxer was standing by the door, and sighed. "Really, Trixie?" she asked, as if expecting an answer, and then grimaced and said, "Although come to think of it, I don't recall you going potty while we were on our walk."

The boxer barked again as if in response, and Stephanie gave an exasperated huff. "Oh, very well, just let me put the dishes in the dishwasher and we'll go outside."

Shaking himself out of his surprised state, Thorne set himself to the task of helping her quickly clean up the kitchen.

Five

"It's hot," Stephanie commented as they stepped out onto the porch and a wall of humid heat met them.

"Hmm," Thorne murmured, pulling the door closed just in time to prevent the cat from following them out. "Is it not usually this hot?"

"Not in May," she said, following the boxer down the four short steps to the stone patio and then crossing to the table and chairs under the open awning on the left of the path. "Although I suppose that's not true. The weather will probably bounce around for the next couple weeks. Really hot, and then milder, or even chilly. We've been known to even have brief, mild snowfalls in May other years, so . . ." She shrugged as she settled in one of the chairs around the table. "You never know what you'll get this time of year. But give it another month and the weather will be consistent and crazy hot," she told him, and then frowned and asked, "Will you be here in a month, do you think?"

Thorne stopped and leaned his shoulder against one of the wooden beams that held up the metal roof of the awning, his gaze following Trixie as she sniffed her way around the small enclosed yard between the stone patio and the sandy path down to the beach. "Good question. I originally thought I'd only be here a week, maybe two. But apparently things are more complicated than expected."

"Things?" she asked gently.

Thorne hesitated and scowled out toward the lake for a moment, before saying dismissively, "Just some stuff."

Stephanie was silent. She was a little disappointed that he hadn't admitted that he was here to have his wings removed, but supposed it was too much to expect that he'd trust her enough to blab such personal and private information at this point. She wished he would, though, because she really wanted to know why he wanted to be rid of his wings.

Her gaze slid down his body, following the curve of the wings pressed tight to his back. To her they were beautiful. Stunning, even. And she thought it must be amazing to be able to fly. Stephanie couldn't even imagine the freedom involved in that ability. At how the world must look to him as he soared over the land, the sun on his back and the wind in his face. Why would he give that up?

"What's that?"

Stephanie tore herself from her admiration of Thorne's wings to glance at him in question.

"I heard a buzzing sound from inside the house," he explained.

Eyebrows flying up, Stephanie stood and hurried for the door, opening it just as a second buzz sounded. Recognizing it as the gate buzzer, she glanced at the clock on the wall as she hurried across the entry and around the kitchen counter, headed for the monitor at the far end of the island.

It was eight thirty. She was surprised that it was that late already. It had just been six thirty when they'd headed back to her house to start breakfast, and it didn't feel like two hours had passed since then. Reaching the monitor next to the far end of the island, she checked the images of the front gates, her eyes widening when she saw the delivery truck at gate one.

"What is that buzz?" Thorne asked, coming around the island now as well, his expression perplexed.

"The front gate. The groceries are here," Stephanie explained as she pressed the button to open gate one for the driver.

"Already?" Thorne asked with surprise, and she turned in time to see him check his watch.

"Yeah. Dani said the delivery wouldn't be until sometime between ten and noon. Looks like they're early, though," she muttered, her gaze shifting between him and the screen where she could see the gates opening and the delivery truck easing slowly forward.

Stephanie sensed rather than saw when Thorne moved closer to watch the delivery truck pick up speed once it was through the gates, and roll quickly to the walkway to the porch of Drina and Harper's house. They watched silently as the driver, a man in his late twenties, hopped out, walked around to retrieve a box from the passenger seat, and carried it out of camera view, only to pop up on another camera view a moment later as he crossed the covered porch of Drina and Harper's house to set the box down by the door.

"You have cameras of the other house too?" Thorne asked with surprise as the deliveryman walked off-screen of that camera only to pop up on the driveway shot again and get back in his truck.

"Just the outside," she assured him. "And the monitors over there show the outside shots of my place too."

"Hmm," Thorne murmured as they watched the truck start to move again, headed for the tree-lined path to the back of the property.

Stephanie watched until the truck moved out of shot, and then glanced around briefly before suggesting, "Maybe you should wait in my office."

Thorne looked toward the still open entry door and frowned. "Trixie's still outside. She was doing her business when I came in, so I—"

"I'll get her," Stephanie assured him, and headed for the entry. "But Cory usually insists on carrying my groceries in for me, so . . ."

"Right. The office," Thorne said quietly, heading that way.

She heard an odd note in his voice, and glanced over her shoulder, but he was turned away, opening the doors to the office and slipping through. She couldn't see his expression, but supposed she didn't really need to see it to know he was upset at the need to hide.

Stephanie couldn't really blame him. She couldn't imagine what it must be like to be so different you had to hide yourself all the time like he had to. She did understand the being different part, but at least she didn't have to hide herself from the rest of the world for fear of the consequences of being seen. Although she did hide away to avoid people's thoughts. Still, she could go out in public if necessary, painful as it might be, but Thorne couldn't. Dani had said he wanted his wings removed so that he could have a chance at a normal life and this certainly highlighted that need. He couldn't even risk being seen by the delivery guy.

Reaching the door, she leaned out and called for Trixie, then petted the dog when she rushed to her side. "Good girl. Inside."

The boxer rushed past her into the house, and Stephanie closed and locked the door, then frowned as she noted the muddy paw prints on the floor. "What did you—? Oh, damn, Trixie! You went in the pond!" she accused, and then cursed and turned to open the closet door to retrieve one of the towels she kept stored there for just this purpose.

"Get over here," she growled, closing the door and glancing around for the dog. Her eyes widened incredulously when she saw that Trixie was ignoring her and instead was pawing at the closed double doors to her office.

"Trixie," she exclaimed with disbelief at the usually obedient dog, and rushed into the kitchen after her. Stephanie had just got to the dog's side and was reaching for her with the towel when one of the French doors opened. Thorne took in the situation at a glance, snatched the towel from her, opened the door wider for Trixie to enter, and assured her, "I'll dry her down. You worry about the groceries."

Stephanie stared briefly at the door after he closed it between them, and then shook her head and rushed back to the closet to fetch a second towel. She was crawling across the floor on her hands and knees, wiping up the muddy paw prints as she went, when a knock sounded at the door. Shifting back to sit on her haunches, Stephanie glanced around and gave a half smile, half grimace to the man peering through the glass door. She instinctively raised a hand to wave him in, and then realized he was carrying two boxes and couldn't open the door.

Muttering under her breath about where her brain was this morning, she scrambled to her feet and hurried over to open it for him.

"Sorry," Stephanie said as she stepped back, pulling the door with her to let him in. She was itching to take the boxes from him, but after a year of weekly deliveries she knew better than to try. Cory was only in his mid- to late twenties, but he was a country boy, raised on a farm by a mother who trained him to be polite and helpful. He never let her carry the boxes.

"Trixie make a mess?" Cory asked with amusement as he strode in, heading for the kitchen as usual.

"Yeah. She went in the pond again," Stephanie said with disgust as she closed the door. Hanging the dirty towel over the nearest of the chairs lined up along the kitchen counter, she followed him to the island where he set the boxes directly across from the refrigerator.

"Where's Trixie now?" Cory asked, glancing around for the dog as he shifted the upper box off to sit next to the lower one on the island countertop. "She's usually here sitting pretty for her treat."

He'd barely finished speaking when a woof sounded from the office. Stephanie wasn't surprised. Trixie loved Cory, or perhaps it was more honest to say that Trixie loved the treats he always brought for the spoiled boxer. Trixie also recognized the word *treat*.

"I closed her up in my office so she wouldn't drag mud

through the house," Stephanie said as she began removing bread and the dry and canned goods from the box and putting them away. Stephanie always did this while he was here. She could hardly open the refrigerator to put away the cold stuff. He'd see the neat stacks of blood in her fridge and that would raise all sorts of questions. Wanting to forestall any suggestion that she fetch the dog out, she added, "No treats for her today. She's been a bad girl playing in the pond and dragging mud inside. Besides, now that the groceries are here, we'll be heading to bed. The last thing I want is to have to get up in an hour or two to let her out again."

"Yeah," Cory said sympathetically as he watched her unpack her groceries. "I figured you'd been up all night as usual and wouldn't want to wait any longer than necessary for your groceries. That's why I brought them out first thing when the boss mentioned an order was called in on a rush for the front house, and he'd said he couldn't do it any earlier than noon, but would deliver both at the same time."

"Thank you, Cory. I appreciate it," Stephanie said sincerely. The man was easygoing and cheerful, and usually she didn't mind their brief chats when he delivered, but she found herself anxious for him to leave today. She didn't like the fact that Thorne was stuck in her office so long as this man was here. She was also a little uncomfortable that Thorne was presently in her office. Not that Stephanie worried that he would snoop or get into anything he shouldn't; she was just suddenly aware that while she kept the rest of the house clean, her office was always a mess. It was where she spent most of her time when working. In fact, she barely left it, except to let Trixie out for a potty break, or to make

Trixie, Felix, and herself a meal. She even ate at her desk. Which meant that there was probably a used plate in there, a dirty coffee cup or two, an empty water glass or three, a back scratcher, moisturizing cream, an open pack of beef jerky, Post-it notes stuck to every surface, several pens lying around, half without their caps on because she sucked that way and was forever setting her pen down, and then when she was unable to spot it right away the next time she wanted to make a note would grab another rather than sift through the stuff on her desk.

There would also be a midsized pile of mail she'd received but left to open until she met her deadline, stacks of printed chapters as Stephanie liked to edit from paper rather than from the computer because she was quite sure she caught more errors in her writing that way. There was probably also a fine layer of crumbs and dust on her keyboard, desk, and everything else. The dog blanket she kept on her couch for Trixie and Felix to sit on while she worked would be dirty and no doubt disheveled, and she was quite sure that her sandals, and at least two pairs of slippers, were lying about on her floor from previous potty trips with Trixie. She tended to grab shoes from the closet on the way out, and then forget to kick them off until she got back to her desk. She'd then forget they were there until she got to the door and would have to grab another pair from the coat closet for the next trip out.

Yeah, her office was a pigsty at the moment, Stephanie acknowledged, and Thorne couldn't possibly fail to notice that being stuck in there as he presently was.

"How are the edits going? Will you get them done on time?"

Stephanie dragged her gaze from the closed office doors and stared at Cory blankly.

"Last week you mentioned some edits had arrived the day before I came out and you were rushing to get them done," he reminded her with amusement. "Will you have them done on time?"

"Oh, yes." Stephanie forced a smile as she nodded. "Yes, they're nearly done now. I expect to finish tomorrow. Well." She frowned slightly, and then added, "Later today for the rest of the world, I guess, but tomorrow for me since I haven't been to bed yet."

"Yeah, this is still Friday for you, huh?" Cory said with amusement as he began to mosey his way out of the kitchen.

Stephanie murmured in agreement as she followed, and then added, "One of the hazards of keeping the weird hours I do. My hours and days are always all screwed up."

Cory chuckled as he reached the door and then opened it, saying, "Well, I'll look forward to reading the book when it comes out. See you next week."

"Yes. Next week," Stephanie murmured, and started to close the door behind him, but paused when he suddenly stopped to glance back.

"Oh, by the way, will there be two deliveries again next week? Or just the one?"

"Probably two," Stephanie admitted. "But the usual time will be fine from now on."

"Okay," Cory said, and started across the porch, headed for his truck.

This time Stephanie waited until he was in his vehicle and starting the engine before closing and locking the door.

"He sounded friendly."

Stephanie glanced around just as Trixie reached her and nudged her hand for a pet. Accommodating the request, she scratched behind the boxer's ear and offered Thorne a wry smile as he came around the kitchen counter. "It's the country. They're all friendly out here."

Thorne's eyebrows rose slightly. "Is that a law?"

Stephanie chuckled at the teasing question, but merely said, "Seems like. At least, everyone I've met seems to abide by it."

"Good to know," Thorne said as he crossed toward where she still stood by the door. Pausing in front of her then, he said solemnly, "I too should go and let you get your sleep. You apparently have work to do when you get up."

"It's no biggie," Stephanie murmured with an awkward shrug as she stepped out of his way. "A couple hours' work at most and I should be done."

Thorne merely nodded and reached for the door handle, then paused with surprise when it didn't move.

"It's locked," Stephanie said, flushing slightly and reaching around him to unlock the door. When she noted the surprised expression on his face, she grimaced, and muttered, "Habit," by way of an explanation, and avoided his gaze as she stepped back again. Uncomfortable in the brief silence that followed, she added, "You'd better get back and get your groceries put away. Dani probably included butter and milk and stuff in your order. It shouldn't be left out in the heat long or will spoil. Let me know if there's something you want that she didn't think to order and I'll take care of it for you."

"Thank you. I'm sure what she ordered will be sufficient," Thorne said quietly as he pulled the door open and stepped out onto the porch. "Thank you, though . . . and thank you for the lovely meal and company."

"My pleasure," Stephanie said quietly.

"And let me know when you're done your work. I'll come out and take a look at your internet setup, then."

"Oh. Okay. Thanks," Stephanie said, and grabbed Trixie's collar to stop the dog when she tried to follow him out of the house. They both watched silently as he crossed her porch to the walkway, but when Trixie whined and pulled, making it obvious she wanted to follow Thorne, Stephanie closed the door and watched him through the glass panel as she murmured, "Yeah. I know. I like him too."

Trixie didn't respond.

"He's a nice guy. Easy to talk to. Good sense of humor . . . and woo baby, he sure is pretty too, huh? Did you see that face on him?" she asked, glancing down to Trixie to see the dog now sitting, and staring up at her with eyes wide and tongue hanging out. Stephanie grinned. "That's exactly how I felt."

She turned back to the view out of the door as Thorne reached the walkway and started down it toward the driveway, before adding, "And his chest and shoulders too! I mean, seriously? They're enough to make a gal want to tackle him to the ground and climb all over him. A shame his wings hide his butt, though. Although they're pretty magnificent. But I'd be interested in seeing if his tush is as gorgeous as the rest of him."

The words had barely left her mouth when Thorne suddenly stopped walking. His body half turned while his head continued a bit farther so that his wide, amazed eyes could find hers through the glass window.

Stephanie smiled and gave him a little wave even as

she asked Trixie out of the corner of her mouth, "You don't think he heard me, do you? Nah, he couldn't have heard me. He doesn't have the hopped-up hearing of an immortal."

One of Thorne's eyebrows rose at the comment, and despite the door being closed, thanks to her own advanced hearing, she heard him say, "No, I have the hopped-up hearing of a bat, which Dressler also included in my DNA."

"Oh!" Stephanie was quite sure she turned as red as a cherry at that point. "Sorry. I was just . . ." She waved vaguely, unable to come up with any possible excuse to dig herself out of the embarrassment she'd dug herself into. She considered claiming she was just trying out lines for a story, but doubted he'd believe it, so just offered an apologetic shrug and chagrined smile.

Much to her relief, Thorne didn't continue her humiliation, but simply turned and started to walk again.

"Damn, Trixie, that was embarrassing, huh?" Stephanie whispered with mortification as she watched Thorne stride away. After three steps, though, the wings hanging down his back suddenly parted, half lifting away to the sides to reveal his butt in the tight, faded blue jeans he was wearing. They remained up and out of the way for several minutes as he walked, giving her an unimpeded view of his derriere, which was nicely curved and full, and as impressive as his chest. All she could do was grin like an idiot. Obviously, the man wasn't offended by what he'd heard. And he was showing her his derriere. Did that mean he was interested? The possibility caused a giddy sensation to roll over her as she watched him walk out of sight.

Shaking her head at her own foolishness, Stephanie

smiled down at Trixie as she turned away from the door. "That man is a hottie. Beautiful face, amazing chest, awesome tush, and freaking wings. The man has it all . . . and he did show me his tush so I'm thinking he might be interested in . . ."

Stephanie paused, unsure what she was interested in when it came to Thorne. She definitely found him attractive, and liked him, and she couldn't read his mind. Well, she hadn't tried to read his mind, but she normally didn't have to try. As a rule, thoughts just came at her. On the other hand, no one's thoughts were coming at her right now, and she'd heard a lot of the hybrids from Dressler's island couldn't be read, so not hearing his thoughts might not mean anything. But she hadn't been able to get into his mind to control him either.

"And when I touched him . . ." Stephanie murmured, recalling the moment when she'd brushed her fingers over the skin near the small feathers along the nape of his neck. She'd felt a tingle of something along her own neck, a tremor of pleasure and excitement that made her shiver again now in response to the memory.

Shared pleasure? The possibility had her attention. Shared pleasure was a common sign of having met a life mate. As was not being able to read or control someone. Although the fact that he was a hybrid made that symptom iffy for her. Not to mention the fact that her reading abilities appeared to be on the fritz at the moment.

The thought made her stop and close her eyes as she tried to open her mind to the voices she usually heard inside her head. The constant barrage of ideas, hopes, fears, anger, memories, and dreams of anyone within what she would guess was more than a mile radius that normally bombarded her mind.

"Nothing," Stephanie muttered, opening her eyes after a minute when the only thoughts in her head were her own. It had been a relief earlier, and really still was . . . mostly. But now a sliver of concern was sliding in to join the relief and enjoyment of her suddenly peaceful mind. Like a snake slithering into a garden, worry was writhing its way into her thoughts. What was happening? Why didn't she hear anyone? Was something wrong?

"Maybe it's a brain tumor," she muttered, but knew that couldn't be the case. The nanos wouldn't allow something like that to happen.

Glancing to Trixie, she asked, "Do you think I should mention it to Dani? She's a doctor. She might know something. Or at least she'd know who to ask about it."

When the boxer just stared back, Stephanie grimaced and said, "You're right, of course. She'd just freak out and then worry herself sick until she found out what had happened. If she was able to figure it out," she added on a grumble.

Dani, Drina, Victor, Elvi, and even Lucian, among others, had all been trying for years to understand why her ability to hear the thoughts of others was so amplified, all without results. Which had left them just worrying themselves silly over her. It had just gotten worse when she'd started picking up on little hints of what the future held for certain people. They'd started watching her with anxious eyes, practically tiptoeing around her like they thought she might crack and explode at any minute. They'd also done anything and everything they thought, hoped, or believed might minimize the effects on her. They were all terrified she would turn into a no-fanger, the vicious crazy version of the fangless immortal or Edentate, which was what she was. At least she hoped she was still an Edentate and not a no-fanger. After all, crazy people didn't usually know they were crazy. On the other hand, she hadn't run amok and started slaughtering people yet, so hopefully . . .

While the others had tried to hide their worries from her, it had been impossible. Stephanie had been able to hear their concerns, and the hopes and plans and efforts they'd made to try to help her. She'd wanted to reassure them that all was well and she would be fine, but hadn't been able to make herself do it. She hadn't thought it would be fair, because when the voices in her head had been at their worst, it had been maddening and she too had feared losing her mind. She had often been left just covering her head, curling up into a ball on the floor, and crying herself to sleep, which had given her the only respite she could find . . . At least until the voices woke her up again.

No, she decided now, telling any of the people who cared for her about the sudden silence in her head would be a bad idea. At least for the moment. She didn't need everyone worrying even more about her. Who was to say this would be any different?

A whine from Trixie drew her attention to the dog just as she raised a paw to brush it down her leg. The boxer then took several steps across the dining area toward the living room and stopped and looked back at her expectantly and released one loud woof.

"Right. Bedtime," Stephanie said, recognizing the message the dog was giving her. She started moving again, but then stopped as her gaze slid to the kitchen and the groceries waiting on the island. Turning her feet in that direction, she told the boxer, "I just have to put the cold stuff away first so it doesn't spoil."

Much to her relief, Trixie didn't bark again in protest; she simply followed her into the kitchen and flopped on the floor beside her when Stephanie stopped at the boxes and began taking out items. She was quick about the task, and was equally quick about brushing her teeth and washing her face before leading Trixie into the bedroom to go to bed.

Six

Thorne put the last of the groceries away, and then walked out into the dining area to take in the view from the large room on the lake side of the house. His gaze automatically tracked to where the islands hid the house at the back of the property. A smile curved his mouth as his mind turned to Stephanie and her words when she'd thought he couldn't hear her.

She thought he was a nice guy, and easy to talk to, and she found him attractive. Stephanie had been more specific than that, talking about his body and face and wanting to see his ass. She even liked his wings, he recalled.

Thorne reached back with one hand and ran it over the edge of one wing. His wings were a part of him. He'd had them his whole life and when young had thought it was perfectly normal. It was only as he grew up and saw the way his father's men treated him that he'd realized he was a freak.

The newcomers to the island—the immortals and even a few mortals who had come to help them after the raid—had been kinder and more polite. Even so, they'd still looked on him and the other hybrids with an amazement that emphasized their oddness. And more than one had reacted with a shock and pity that was quickly hidden, but still seen for all that.

But not Stephanie, Thorne thought. She'd come rocketing around the trees in search of her cat, only to come to an abrupt halt when she saw them on the dock. Her eyes had immediately widened. However, those wide eyes had been trained not on his wings, but on the cat as she took in the way Felix was rubbing up against him. She'd then relaxed and approached with obvious amusement and the information that the cat wasn't showing affection, but marking him as his next meal.

The memory made him smile. Stephanie hadn't seemed to pay his wings much attention other than a curious glance or two. And, more importantly, the first thing she'd said, when she didn't think he could hear her, wasn't about his wings but his face, and that was more telling than anything. Thorne was pretty sure she didn't see him as a freak, but just an attractive man. Well, an attractive man with wings, he supposed. But a man just the same. He liked that. He liked *her*, and wondered what he should do about that . . . if anything.

Thorne frowned at the last thought. He was in Canada to have his wings cut off. He'd hoped it would be a simple operation, like amputating a leg. But it turned out it wasn't so simple. Dani was afraid the operation could kill him. Did he have a right to start up something, and perhaps get emotionally involved with Stephanie, when he might soon die? Would she even be interested in a relationship with him?

"Slow your roll, buddy," Thorne murmured to himself on a sigh. He was getting way ahead of himself here and knew it. They'd just met, for Christ's sake. And frankly, he wasn't sure of his situation . . . or hers for that matter. He had no idea what she wanted, or even what he wanted at this point. But she was a beautiful woman who had already made one hell of an impression on him. Thorne suspected he could become very serious about her very quickly.

The problem then became him. Having a relationship with her might set them up for a world of hurt if he died on the operating table, or hell, even if he didn't. Either way, he wouldn't be around long. Once he was able, Thorne was returning to Venezuela. He owed it to his mother and Maria. After all their sacrifices and the way they'd risked themselves to protect and take care of him all these decades, he could do no less than look after the two of them in their dotage.

Meanwhile, Stephanie was obviously happy and settled here on her little piece of paradise in Canada. He doubted she would want to move to the island he'd grown up on. Besides, once he was rid of his wings, his mother and Maria wanted to move to the mainland. He suspected that Stephanie, with her sensitivity to people's thoughts, would not survive there. Not with her sanity intact anyway.

But again, he was getting ahead of himself. They'd just met, and while Thorne found her incredibly attractive and knew the feeling was reciprocated, that didn't necessarily mean anything was going to come of it. Maybe he was worrying about things that wouldn't be an issue and should just relax and enjoy her company for now. A little light courting shouldn't be an issue.

Except that Thorne wasn't sure he knew how to do that. For all his years on this earth, he'd led a very sheltered life. Hell, he'd spent all but the last six years alone with his mother and Maria. Circumstances forcing him to remain a virgin until the hunters had raided the island and chased his father off of it, freeing them all. Of course, he'd definitely made up for that since then. In fact, according to his mother and Maria, he'd been acting like a rutting bull these last six years.

If Thorne was honest with himself, they were right. Once free of the threat of his father, he'd had affair after affair with not just a good number of the female hybrids on the island, but with several of the immortals and even a few of the mortals who had come to help them sort out their lives. And rutting bull was a perfect description. There had been little in the way of care and concern, or even conversation, in his encounters with other hybrids. Looking back, it seemed to him that they'd all been trying to erase the memories of their lives to that point by indulging their carnal sides.

It had been a little different with the immortals and mortals he'd got involved with, but not by much. With them it had been more of a brief fling. In truth, he suspected the women had approached him out of curiosity as much as attraction.

Stephanie, however . . . she was different. She truly found him attractive, and his interest in her was more than sexual. Not that he didn't want to bed her. He did. Just recalling the sensation he'd experienced when she'd touched him lightly made a shiver run through his body again. But he also wanted to know everything about her,

her past, her present, her future hopes and dreams. Her opinions, her likes, and so on.

Thorne just wasn't sure he had the social skills to carry that off. Sit him in a room with a couple of old ladies, and he'd be good. But talk to a beautiful young woman like Stephanie and draw her into conversations? Yeah, no. His confidence there was pretty much nonexistent.

Although he'd done well enough that morning, Thorne pointed out to himself. In truth, cooking and eating with her had felt familiar and comfortable, like being at home with his mother and Maria.

"Odd," he muttered, his gaze scanning the lake and islands again as he wished that he could see her house. Had she gone to sleep? Or was she working on her edits before bed? Thorne wondered. The thought recalled him to the fact that a lot of her journals had been published as fiction.

Turning abruptly, he headed for the double doors at the far end of the kitchen. They had led into Stephanie's office in her house, and it was the same here as well, he saw with satisfaction when he opened the doors to the room. While her office was painted a sky blue with a white couch, white blinds, and built-in white bookshelves across the back wall behind an obviously custom-built desk painted the same blue as her lower kitchen cupboards, this office was painted tan, had a dark brown leather couch, beige blinds, and dark wood bookshelves and desk.

He liked Stephanie's better. It was brighter and much more cheerful, Thorne decided as he crossed to the shelves and began to scan the books on them.

Dani hadn't just told him that her sister was an author, she'd also mentioned that Stephanie's writing name was

Anna Stephens. Essentially different versions of her first and middle name, Stephanie Anne, reversed.

There was a whole row of Anna Stephens's novels on one shelf. Thorne pulled out the first one and turned it to read the blurb on the back.

> Young Stella MacGregor had an idyllic life. A close, loving family, good friends, excellent grades, and her first part-time job was the dream job she'd been hoping to get since she was twelve. Life was good . . . until the family's yearly vacation in cottage country. At first it was great, lots of fun, laughter, and bonding with her siblings and cousins. It was on the ride home that things went wrong. An innocent stop for goodies for the return drive ended in Stella and her older sister being kidnapped by a pack of brutal, knife-wielding psychos who would teach her that life wasn't all laughter and love. They'd teach her that having good things meant having something to lose, that madness was only one small decision away, and that evil can wear a handsome face. They'd teach her the true meaning of horror.

Thorne slowly let out his breath, and turned the book over to peer at the cover. It was a young blonde girl in dark woods with blood on her face, neck, and soaking into the neckline of her T-shirt. He stared at it briefly, and then slowly set the book back on the shelf. He wanted to read it, and would eventually. But he'd rather hear the tale from her own lips first. If he got the chance.

That thought made him frown. Thorne had no idea how much free time he'd have in the future. He wasn't here on vacation, and doubted it would be more than a day or two before Dr. Dani arrived with a truckload of specialists and consultants in tow. After that, his time would no doubt be taken up with whatever tests and questions they'd bombard him with.

Thorne grimaced at the thought. It wasn't something he was looking forward to, but understood it had to be done.

Sighing, he turned and strode into the kitchen to start opening and closing cupboard doors to see what there was available to cook with. He had a hankering for scones. It was what his mother had always made for him when he was feeling down or stressed. Thinking of the tests and operation to come was causing a craving for the tasty goodies. He'd bake up a couple of batches of them and gorge himself, then maybe take some out to Stephanie as a thank-you for the meal she'd fed him that morning.

"Yeah, yeah. I'm coming," Stephanie muttered when Trixie's demanding bark woke her from a dead sleep. Tossing aside the warm sheet and blanket she'd been cocooned in, she pretty much rolled out of bed and then stumbled around it to unlock and open the bedroom door. The moment she did, Trixie rushed past her with another excited woof and hurried out into the hall.

Stifling a yawn, Stephanie followed the animal's wildly wagging tail down the hall and out into the living room where her gaze automatically sought out the clock on the wall. Her mouth immediately snapped closed, cutting off her yawn, and she scowled at the eager beast she was following. "Jeez, Trixie. It's just past 11 A.M., not even noon. We only slept maybe three and a half hours. Couldn't you have waited at least another thirty minutes?"

Trixie merely barked again for answer as she rushed across the open living room and dining area, headed for the door, her butt wiggling with every step.

"Yeah, right, why would you care? You drop and nap whenever you want throughout the day," Stephanie growled with irritation as she reached the door where Trixie now sat, waiting.

Glowering at the eager creature, she unlocked and opened the door for her before spotting the covered basket on the concrete pad on the other side. Her eyes widened with alarm at once as she imagined Trixie trampling the basket on the way out. However, the boxer neatly sidestepped it and didn't even stop to give it a sniff before rushing off toward the driveway.

"I guess you really had to go," Stephanie said wryly, some of her irritation with the dog fading at this proof that there was a reason for her being up.

Shrugging inwardly, she bent to pick up the basket, her nose twitching at the scents wafting from it. Stephanie didn't recognize the aroma except that it was some kind of baked good, but she groaned out loud when she pulled back the dish towel laid over the basket and saw the goodies it had covered.

"Scones," she moaned, lowering her head to inhale deeply. God, they smelled good.

"Sorry. I didn't mean to wake you."

Stephanie stiffened at that deep baritone voice, and jerked her head up to stare blankly at Thorne. The man was standing at the end of the walkway, calmly petting an adoring Trixie as he eyed Stephanie and she now understood that Trixie's sudden urge to get outside hadn't had a thing to do with needing to relieve herself. She'd heard, smelled, or just sensed in that way dogs had that Thorne was out here and had wanted to see him.

"I thought it would be safe enough to leave them on the porch and go. I didn't consider that Trixie would raise a ruckus at my creeping around outside."

"You weren't creeping around. You were bringing me baked goodness from Berry Pickers," Stephanie said at once, and then frowned and asked, "How did you get these from Berry Pickers? I would have thought . . ." She let her voice trail off rather than say that his wings would have made that impossible.

"I'm not sure what Berry Pickers is, but I didn't get those anywhere. Your sister ordered raspberries in the groceries, and Drina had chocolate, flour, and so on in the cupboards, so I made them myself," Thorne assured her, not seeming offended at the question.

Stephanie stared at him blankly, and then looked down at the scones. They were huge golden triangles with bits of chocolate and raspberries throughout. They looked perfect. And he'd baked them? Those two points didn't seem to want to gel in her mind. They just didn't seem to go together. Thorne could bake.

Well, *maybe* he could bake, she thought, and plucked one out of the basket, raised it to her mouth, took a bite, and then closed her eyes and moaned as she chewed.

"Oh my God! So good," she proclaimed once she'd swallowed the bite of food. Opening her eyes, Stephanie cast a disbelieving gaze his way. "You baked these? Yourself? Like you can *cook*?"

"Yessss?" Thorne said, drawing out the word uncertainly, as if unsure why that would be an issue.

"You can cook and you brought me goodies. Oh-my-Gawd-I-think-I-love-you," Stephanie squealed, and then took another bite of the scone and turned away. As she headed into the house with the basket in hand, she mumbled, "Need coffee. Come," around the flaky deliciousness in her mouth and left him to follow as she headed for the coffee machine.

Thorne stared blankly at the door Stephanie had left open, her words ringing in his ears. *Oh-my-Gawd-I-think-I-love-you.* Well, that was . . . Damn, he thought.

Thorne knew she wasn't being serious, but the words had drilled their way inside his head, and then shot south toward his chest, lodging there like heartburn. The idea of being loved by a woman like her was causing an ache that he wasn't sure he liked.

Giving his head a shake, he glanced down at Trixie. "Do you think she's awake enough to realize that she's only wearing a very tiny, white T-shirt that doesn't cover her black panties, which have Badass Bitch written on them?"

Apparently not as impressed with the skimpy outfit as Thorne had been, Trixie leaned into his side and yawned. Yeah, the sight of Stephanie in those teeny black panties and the tight T-shirt that stopped just below her obviously braless breasts had left Thorne dry-mouthed. He'd barely managed to croak out his apology for waking her, and now felt like it had been the lamest thing he could have said. He definitely wasn't a sweet talker, Thorne acknowledged, but told the boxer, "I'll take your completely uninterested yawn as a no."

When that got no reaction from the dog, he asked, "How upset do you think she'll be when she realizes?"

A sudden yelp of dismay from inside drew his gaze to the open door. When the sound was followed by the slap of running feet that grew more distant with each step, Thorne smiled wryly. "I think that answers that."

Shaking his head, he gave Trixie one last pat, and then started forward, tugging off his computer backpack as he went. "Come on, girl. We'll make your mother some coffee to help her get over her embarrassment when she comes back from dressing. If nothing else, she can hide her face behind the cup."

He led Trixie inside, and headed into the kitchen. He set his backpack on the island where they'd had breakfast, and then walked to the coffeemaker at the opposite end of the kitchen.

Thorne made Stephanie's first. Vanilla hazelnut with one sugar and two splashes of mocha creamer, he remembered, and went to the fridge to collect the creamer once he'd got the Keurig set up and started. As it had been that morning, the creamer was on the bottom shelf on the right-hand door. Thorne snatched it up and started to close the door, but then paused when he caught a glimpse of something deep red on the left-hand side of the refrigerator. Pulling the left door open, he stared with curiosity at the bagged blood stacked neatly on the top shelf.

There were quite a few bags, more than two dozen, perhaps as many as three dozen. It made him wonder how many she had to consume a day. Magda, one of the immortals he'd had a brief fling with on the island, had told him that how much blood an immortal needed daily often varied. Some older immortals could even go days without needing to consume any, while the youngest or newly turned usually needed as much as a dozen bags a day.

The sound of Stephanie's voice caught his attention and had him turning his head slightly to listen, but Thorne couldn't understand what she was saying. Thinking she was probably talking to Trixie, something he'd witnessed her doing before, he closed the refrigerator door and turned to carry the creamer back to the coffee machine.

He had just finished fixing Stephanie's coffee and started his own when movement out of the corner of his eye drew his attention to Trixie. The boxer was lying on a dog bed next to the dining room table, chewing on a bone. Yet Stephanie's voice could still be heard from somewhere on the other side of the house, a low murmur of sound that was making him extremely curious.

After the briefest hesitation, he picked up Stephanie's coffee and followed the sound of her voice through the living room, into a hall, and then to a closed door of a room on the left. Pausing there, he listened, now able to hear what she was saying.

"Right, Felix? I mean, usually I'm out here alone and could romp around naked outside without anyone seeing," she muttered, sounding agitated. Thorne found it rather endearing that she talked to her pets, and wondered if all pet owners did it. He'd never had a pet himself, though he'd always wanted one. He imagined Trixie and Felix went a long way toward easing the loneliness Stephanie must feel with circumstances forcing her to avoid others. Much like him, really, he thought. While their circumstances were different, Thorne understood the loneliness of an almost solitary existence.

"You don't think he thought I knew he was there and

deliberately dressed like this for him or something, do you?"

Thorne's eyebrows rose at the words. He hadn't thought that for a minute. Especially not with her bedhead and bleary, bloodshot eyes. It had been obvious she'd just woken up and stumbled out. Hence his apology for waking her.

"Not that I wouldn't have if I'd known he was out there," Stephanie said now. "I mean, the guy is superhot and jumpable, and I would have dressed for him had I known he'd be on my stoop. But I surely would have picked out something sexy rather than this ridiculous getup."

Thorne's eyebrows crawled even farther up his forehead. Superhot and jumpable? His heart did a little hop in his chest even as his cock did the same in his pants. Damn! The feeling was mutual. But he couldn't think of a single thing that could be sexier than her skimpy panties and the cropped T-shirt that had hugged her small breasts so lovingly.

"Ah, well," Stephanie continued. "I need to just take a deep breath and chill. I'm not even sure if he's interested in me. I mean, he was sweet moving his wings to show me his bottom earlier, but . . . what did that even mean? Was that because he's interested? Or just to . . . well, I don't know," she admitted, sounding frustrated, and then muttered, "I need to read a book on human mating habits or something. I am so far outside the loop on that stuff it's pathetic. I'm probably the only twenty-seven-year-old virgin on the planet."

Thorne stiffened at these words, more than a little surprised by them. He hadn't considered that a woman as beautiful and vibrant as Stephanie might be inexperienced in that area. But now that he'd heard the words, he realized he should have expected it. She lived out in the middle of farm country and avoided people to prevent having her mind overwhelmed with their thoughts, so she hadn't been bar hopping or whatever else normal people did to meet members of the opposite sex.

Aside from that, from the little she'd told him, it sounded like she had been pretty protected and sheltered by this Elvi and Victor and the others who had taken her under their wing after being turned, and she'd said that had happened at fourteen. It was possible she hadn't even been kissed before her life was turned upside down, and certainly wouldn't have been since. Probably. There was no way to know for sure.

"I haven't even been properly kissed, Felix. How humiliating is that?"

Okay, Thorne thought as he turned and headed back toward the kitchen with Stephanie's coffee, there *was* a way to know and now he did. He definitely needed to take a step back and stick to friendship with her. He was not going to deflower the woman and then fly out of her life whether it be by dying or literally flying on a plane back to Venezuela. Besides, if she was a virgin, living out here in the middle of nowhere as she was, she probably wasn't on birth control. What if he got her pregnant? Dear God, what would that even look like? Would she have a bird boy or girl with fangs? Or could she even? She was immortal, surely the nanos would—

Well, frankly, he didn't know what the nanos would do. Would they eradicate the nonhuman DNA and replace it with human? Could the nanos replace DNA? He didn't think they'd probably allow the nonhuman DNA to remain, so he supposed they'd just destroy it, aborting the fetus.

Oddly enough, that thought bothered him. For a minute, while he'd considered the worry of getting her pregnant, a small quiet part inside of him had seemed to unfurl. It was one that was enamored of the idea of having a child with Stephanie—a beautiful little girl like her, or a sturdy little boy like him. But he was pretty sure that wasn't possible, so stomped on that unfurling part of himself viciously as he turned into the kitchen and headed for the island.

Seven

Stephanie pulled her hair back into a ponytail, fastened it with a scrunchie, and then turned to peer at herself in the mirror over her dresser. Her nose immediately wrinkled with displeasure. She'd decided to dress down in an effort to ensure Thorne didn't think she'd tried to seduce him with her outfit, or lack thereof, when she'd stepped outside this morning.

But she may have gone a little overboard, Stephanie acknowledged to herself as her gaze slid over the sweatshirt and joggers she was wearing. They were both at least three times too big for her. They were Decker's, left behind at Christmas. He and Dani had spent a week here for the holiday. They'd bedded down at Drina and Harper's house during the stay in an effort to give her a break from having to hear their thoughts at least while sleeping, but they'd spent most of the rest of that week with her—decorating the tree, baking, playing board games, and putting together jigsaw puzzles when weather kept them indoors, or cross-country skiing, snowmobiling, and just walking around the property on nicer days.

The snowmobiling was why Decker's joggers were still here. He'd decided to take a little jaunt across the lake at one point. Only the lake wasn't fully frozen. Stephanie would have told him as much if she'd had the chance, but Decker had found that out the hard way.

Stephanie had brought her snowmobile to a halt at the edge of the lake and shouted a warning to him. He hadn't heard it over the engine of his own snowmobile. Dani had stopped beside her and was just asking why she wasn't continuing when Decker's machine had crashed through the thin ice.

While Dani had shrieked with horror and dismay and rushed toward the water on foot, Stephanie had just grimaced and waited for Decker to walk out of the water. They were immortal, after all, but she didn't blame Dani for forgetting that and freaking out in the moment.

They had been on her end of the lake when it had happened, so she'd taken Decker back to her place while Dani had gone back to Drina and Harper's place to fetch him dry clothes to wear. The clothes he'd taken his dunking in had still been in the dryer when the couple had returned to the other house to sleep, and they'd left the next day without them.

Stephanie had kept them neatly folded on her dresser for months intending to give them to him the next time they visited. But seeing them today, she'd put them on. Now she was rethinking that. While she'd chosen them as the least sexy thing she had available, they went beyond unsexy and just looked ridiculous.

Grimacing, Stephanie quickly tugged off Decker's clothes, tossed them in the laundry hamper next to her dresser, and then grabbed what she'd normally wear, a pair of white shorts and one of her roomier T-shirts, plain, no saying at all, just a white one. She donned those quickly, didn't even check herself out in the mirror afterward, but simply snatched up the basket of scones and headed determinedly out of her room, afraid that if she stopped to look at herself she'd change her mind and decide this outfit wasn't good enough either. Or find some other way to delay going out to the kitchen and facing Thorne after his *seeing her in her underwear*. Honestly, sometimes she couldn't believe her luck. Or lack of it.

Pushing these useless and defeatist thoughts aside, Stephanie strode out to the kitchen, vaguely aware that Felix was following her. She wasn't sure what she'd expected to find once she reached the kitchen, but it wasn't Thorne seated at the island, tapping away furiously at the keyboard of a laptop open in front of him.

"Good morning," Stephanie said lightly as she carried the basket of scones over to set on the island. "Whatcha doing?"

"Checking your internet speed," he answered, and then glanced up and smiled easily before offering, "Good morning."

Stephanie smiled crookedly and turned to head toward the coffee machine.

"I made you a coffee. It's here."

Stephanie swung back in surprise, her gaze following his nod toward the cup of coffee on the place mat on the side of the island.

"Vanilla hazelnut, one sugar, two splashes of mocha creamer," Thorne said when she stared blankly at the cup.

He didn't mention it, but Stephanie could see that he'd also got out two small plates and butter. The man had taken care of everything. Damn! Baking, coffee making, table setting . . . Thorne was a domestic diva . . . or a domestic dude or whatever it would be for a guy.

She joined him at the island, grabbed a scone, took a sip of coffee, and glanced at the laptop Thorne was using. Stephanie watched him work as she took a bite of the tasty pastry. His expression was very intense and serious, a small frown starting to pull at his lips.

"Speed not good?" she asked after several moments of silence punctuated only by the rat-a-tat-tat of his typing. Stephanie suspected he must have the keyboard on typewriter sound, because that's what it sounded like. Hers didn't do that.

"Yes, and no," Thorne answered with a more obvious frown. "There's a serious lag at times. I just can't figure out why."

"Hmm," Stephanie murmured, glancing over her shoulder and through the open doors of her office toward her own computer. The lag as he called it was what had been driving her crazy since the tech guy had repaired her internet after it had dropped altogether. The difference in speed before and after the crash had been noticeable to her. It was only slower by seconds, but the fact that she was aware of the difference made it irritating. Stephanie was not a patient girl.

"I'm going to take a look at your router and wiring," he announced, standing up. "Harper said it was in the basement?"

"Yeah, but don't you want a scone first?" she asked, pushing the plate toward him.

"I had at least a dozen of them before I came to drop

these off to you. This batch is all yours," he told her with a faint smile.

"Really? All of them?" she asked, eyeing the scones and silently beginning to count them.

"Every last one," Thorne assured her with an amusement that suggested her greedy delight was obvious. "I'll be right back."

"Hmm," Stephanie murmured before taking another bite of her scone. He could go wherever he liked so long as he left the scones here.

"Oh, uh . . ."

Stephanie swallowed her mouthful of scone and glanced around in question. "What?"

"Where's the door to the basement?" Thorne asked with a little chagrin.

"Around the corner there," she said, gesturing toward the entry. "Take a left just past the front counter; you'll pass the garage door and then the basement door is straight ahead," she directed. "The router and everything are in a cabinet on the center wall downstairs. It's—Oh, hang on. I'll show you," she finished, grabbing her coffee and taking it and her scone to follow him.

"You don't have to," Thorne protested at once. "Stay and enjoy your coffee and scone."

Stephanie shrugged the suggestion away. "It's easier just to show you where it is. And I can drink my coffee down there as easily as up here. Then I can answer any questions you have without you shouting them up the stairs, or having to come back up to ask them."

She didn't give Thorne a chance to argue, but moved past him and around the corner to the short hall with the garage door on the right and the basement door straight ahead.

"This is your router," Thorne murmured once she'd shown him to the shelf holding all the internet and security stuff. Picking up the box with three antennae coming out of it, he looked it over, then set it down, and glanced at the other machines and wires. "The rest of this is your security system?"

"Yeah. At least, I think so. I'm not very tech-minded. I just call someone in when I have problems."

Thorne nodded, his attention on the router again as he examined it. He then looked over the other stuff briefly before shaking his head. "I don't see anything here that would account for the lag."

Stephanie grimaced. It wasn't really what she'd hoped to hear.

"I think I'll take a look outside."

Stephanie glanced at him with surprise. "Outside?"

"Where the cable comes into the house. It could have been damaged, chewed on by animals, or bent or something." He shrugged. "Not sure if that could do it, but I may as well look while I'm here."

"Okay." She stepped back, and looked up, eyeing the wire running between the joists overhead. They followed them across to the outer wall, and Stephanie grimaced as she glanced along the wall and guessed where they were. "It looks like they come out under the deck off the kitchen. That could be fun."

"Fun as in not?" Thorne suggested dryly, eyeing where the lines went out of the house as well.

"Pretty much," she agreed with amusement. "At least, I wouldn't find crawling around under the deck fun. Fortunately, it's more than two feet off the ground so you should be able to get under there even with your wings. Although they'll probably be covered in cobwebs and dead bugs when you get out. You might need to hose them down afterward."

Thorne grimaced at the possibility, but then shrugged as if it was to be expected and followed her to the stairs.

"So, I'm guessing you're self-taught when it comes to all this computer stuff," Stephanie commented as she watched Thorne lay down the first strip of cardboard half under the deck and half outside of it and then kneel on it to push the stack of the long rectangular pieces of cardboard ahead of him under the deck.

"Good guess," Thorne said, smiling faintly at her where she sat with an umbrella in one hand to protect her from the sun, and a flashlight in the other, ready to light the way for him . . . from outside of the deck.

She had insisted on helping, and this was the only way he'd let her. Thorne didn't want her under the deck with him, claiming it would be too claustrophobic with the two of them there. Stephanie didn't know about that, but since she hated spiders, earwigs, ants, mice, and absolutely every other creepy-crawly and critter she worried might be under the deck, she was happier to help from outside of the deck anyway.

Stephanie was presently sitting on her own strip of cardboard. They'd got all of them from her recycle bin. They had once made up the packaging for a bookshelf she'd ordered for the living room. She had a lot of books.

"Ready?" she asked now, flipping on the flashlight in preparation of shining it into the opening to help guide him as he maneuvered himself and his cardboard strips under the deck. Once he reached the wall, he had his own little flashlight to usc to chcck the cable. Her presence was just to make his journey a little easier.

"Ready," Thorne agreed as he set out his next strip of cardboard in front of the one he was on, and then began to worm his way under the deck.

"I bet you were a little whiz at computers as a boy," Stephanie said as she leaned forward and angled the flashlight to get as much of the light around his body as she could to illuminate the way in front of him. "You were probably a gamer too since you were stuck on your father's island your whole life. It must have been your only connection to the rest of the world."

"Bad guess," Thorne grunted as he paused to slide the stack of cardboard ahead of him again. "We weren't allowed computers while my father ruled the island. We've only had them the last six years since your people raided it and freed everyone."

"Really?" she asked with surprise.

"Really," he assured her. "He wouldn't let us have anything that might allow us to communicate with the outside world. No phones, computers, radios, iPads, Kindles. Nothing."

Stephanie grunted at this news, trying to imagine what that must have been like. She'd known about, and had access to, computers since she was a kid. She couldn't imagine growing up without them. "What about television?"

"No television when I was young. But we got one about twenty years ago, and a VCR to watch movies," he told her.

Stephanie's eyebrows rose at the not having television when he was young bit, followed by the getting one twenty years ago. The man didn't look any more than twenty-five or thirty years old. So, twenty years ago he would have been around five or ten. That was still young.

"There was no cable or anything on the island," Thorne pointed out. "So, VCR and a television to watch movies on was the only way to go."

"What did you do to pass the time before getting the VCR and television?"

"Read." The answer was succinct if somewhat muffled from under the deck.

"Read?" Stephanie echoed with confusion. "What did you read if you didn't have computers and presumably Kindles to read on?"

"Books," he said with an amusement that suggested that was the obvious answer.

"Right," Stephanie murmured wryly, thinking of the shelves of books in her house. Although most of them were her own in English as well as every other language they were published in. She'd never read even the English ones once she'd finished editing them and they were published. Instead, she read several other authors of horror, as well as sci-fi and suspense, always on a Kindle. Different strokes for different folks, she supposed.

"We had tons and tons of books," Thorne went on as he maneuvered deeper under the deck. "My mother demanded them and insisted Dressler buy them on a regular basis. She even signed up to several of those book-a-month clubs, and we kept reading even after we got the television. The movies were more of a 'once a week' thing while books were every day."

Stephanie nodded and then asked, "So, were you homeschooled?"

When she saw him stop moving forward under the deck and glance back toward her, she explained, "I'm presuming there wasn't a school on the island, but you're well-spoken and obviously smart. Homeschooling would seem to be the answer."

"Yes. I was homeschooled. My mother oversaw it, but Maria helped at times too."

"What about after the raid on the island? Did you take online courses on computing or something?"

"No. That's self-taught," he answered.

"Seriously?" Stephanie asked with amazement.

"Yes." Thorne quirked an eyebrow in question. "Why so surprised?"

"Because computers are basically incomprehensible to me," she admitted with a grimace he couldn't see. "It's like Greek. But much more useful than Greek would be to me since I'm a writer. There's nothing more frustrating than losing the story you're working on and not knowing how to reclaim it."

"Ah," Thorne murmured. "Well, I find computers easy to understand. Unlike people, they work on pure logic."

Stephanie shifted the flashlight a bit to help better light Thorne's way, and asked archly, "Is that a suggestion that you don't find me very logical, Mr. Dressler?"

"Not at all," he assured her. "And my last name is Salter."

"Salter?" she echoed with confusion. "I thought Dressler was your—"

"My mother reverted to her maiden name after the dust settled six years ago," he interrupted to explain. "And I took it as well. We're both Salters now."

"Ahh," Stephanie murmured with understanding. "I'm sorry. I didn't know."

She could almost hear the shrug in his voice when Thorne said, "How could you?"

Stephanie merely nodded to herself. She had no trouble understanding why he and his mother had reverted to her maiden name. She herself wouldn't want any connection to a man who had performed horrible experiments on her either.

Dressler was completely conscienceless. A monster, Stephanie thought, and shuddered a little at the memory of her encounter with the man. She could still feel the horror she'd experienced when he'd decided to take her with him and "get her on his table." Thank God Tiny and Decker had arrived when they had or she knew she'd even now be living in a cage somewhere, suffering horrible and painful experiments at the hands of that bastard.

She'd heard some of the things he'd done to the immortals he'd kept captive on the island—cutting limbs off, cutting them in half, drowning them, setting them on fire. He apparently hadn't felt the least compunction about torturing those people either. As far as he was concerned, it was just science.

A surprised grunt from Thorne had her leaning down to peer under the deck. The beam of her flashlight was on his wings as he lay in the dirt, but he had reached the wall where the cable went in and had the little flashlight she'd given him out and shining on some kind of box.

"What is it?" she asked.

"I'm not sure. It's . . ."

She saw him open the box, and her eyebrows rose when he began to mutter under his breath.

"I need wire cutters," he said suddenly.

Stephanie glanced at the paraphernalia Thorne had

laid out near her in front of the deck. He hadn't been able to drag it all under with him, so had left some things behind for her to pass to him if needed. Setting aside the umbrella for a minute, she picked up the wire cutters and bent forward to get a good look at where she needed to aim. She then tossed them toward his left side. Afraid of hitting him, she didn't put enough power behind the throw and they landed next to his upper legs rather than his shoulder as she'd hoped. Fortunately, he was still able to reach them with a little stretching.

"Thanks."

"Do you need anything else?" Stephanie asked, trying to see what he was doing.

"No. I've got it."

Nodding, Stephanie sat back and glanced around, then slapped a mosquito who had dared to land on her and try to take blood. There were a lot of them buzzing about in the bushes around her. She hated mosquitos too. The vampires of the insect world. Stephanie grimaced to herself at the thought and then glanced back under the deck when she heard movement. Thorne was backing out from under the deck, dragging his cardboard and other items with him. She kept the flashlight on until his feet appeared at the opening, and then turned it off, snatched up her umbrella, and stood to get back out of the way.

"Did you find the problem?" Stephanie asked with curiosity as he pulled out everything from under the deck and closed the door the men had put in the skirting around the base. Her gaze was on the small black box he'd brought out with him. It hadn't gone in with him.

"Yeah. I'm pretty sure I did," Thorne said grimly, and then glanced around with narrowed eyes before saying.

"Let's get all of this put away and then I'll check the internet and see if it's working all right now."

Stephanie cast a quick look around, wondering what he had expected to see or was looking for, and then helped him gather up the cardboard and tools. She left the black box to him, but eyed it with curiosity as they walked back around the house.

They went in through the garage door, dumped the cardboard back in the recycle box, put her tools away, and then headed into the house with the black box. Trixie greeted them as if they'd been gone for days rather than the twenty minutes to half hour they'd been out front. Thorne left her to pet and calm the animal and went directly to his laptop to start tapping away on the keyboard again.

"Soda, water, or coffee?" Stephanie asked as she fetched Trixie a treat.

"Coffee, please," Thorne responded almost absently, his attention on his computer.

Stephanie made them both coffees, her gaze sliding toward the box with curiosity when Thorne opened it and pulled out one of the items inside to examine briefly before continuing to type on his computer. A moment later he did the same with what looked to her to be a small router or something. By the time she'd finished and was carrying the coffees over to the island, he was closing the box, his expression even grimmer than it had been since he'd come out from under the deck.

"Okay. Lay it on me," Stephanie said as she set the coffees down and claimed her seat. "What was in the box and why was it under the deck?"

"The box is—Well, there's a coupler and a hub and—"

Pausing when he noted her expression, he frowned and asked uncertainly, "What?"

"Nothing," she said at once, and then grinned and added, "I just find it supersweet that you're mentioning these things as if you expect me to know what they are, or what they do."

"Ah." Thorne smiled wryly and shook his head, but then sighed and said, "Basically, someone was spying on you."

"What?" she gasped with amazement, and Thorne nodded.

"They'd spliced into your line and were capturing everything you sent out and everything you received and transmitting it to a third party," he said solemnly. "That was the cause of the lag."

Stephanie stared at him blankly for a minute, and then shook her head and asked uncertainly, "By sent out and received, you mean my emails?"

"Your emails, and anything you looked up online," he said.

Stephanie stared at him for another moment as that information circled in her head and then blurted, "Well, that makes no sense. I mean, how would they even get under the deck to do that with the security I have? And why would they bother? I don't—Oh!" she interrupted herself suddenly, and grimaced. "Of course. They must be after Harper's business info. He's developing some kind of new—Why are you shaking your head?"

"Because this wouldn't give them Harper and Drina's information," he explained. "Only yours."

"What? But that's crazy! I don't do anything anyone else would want to know. I email Elvi, Beau, Drina, and Dani once a week. I video chat with them too, but that's it. Just boring stuff like, how are you? What's happening? Crap like that. Otherwise, all I do is research things once in a while for my books and email my editor and—Okay. Why do you look like you're saying bingo in your head?"

"Because I am," Thorne admitted with a wry smile. "It's probably someone after your books."

"Yeah, no, I don't think so," she said at once. "I mean, I have some rabid fans, but not crazy Annie Wilkes types who would do something like that."

"Stephen King's *Misery*," Thorne said at once, obviously recognizing the character she was referencing. *Misery* was a book about a psycho fan—Annie Wilkes— who kidnapped and did horrible things to a writer.

Stephanie smiled faintly at the fact that he'd read the book too, but said, "Yeah, well, I don't have those kinds of fans. Like I said, rabid ones, not crazy."

Thorne tilted his head with interest. "What's the difference?"

"Rabid fans order the book ahead, or know the day it will be out and get it that day. They talk it up to everyone they know and suggest they read it, they join fan groups that talk about the series, and they write lovely fan letters telling me how my stories helped them realize that even living nightmares end and life will get better afterward. Stuff like that," she explained. "While crazy fans are just crazy. I haven't received a single letter or email I would say was from a crazy fan."

"Maybe crazy fans don't write to the authors they're fixated on," he said reasonably, and then pointed out, "Since I'm guessing you rarely if ever leave this place, and don't do anything else that would attract a stalker, the only draw has to be your writing."

Stephanie considered that unhappily and then reluctantly nodded. "Fair enough, but how would a fan know where I live? It's not like my address is out there on the Net. I do everything writing related through a PO box in town."

Thorne's eyebrows crawled up his forehead, his expression disbelieving. "If you're referring to the four or five buildings on the corner that I passed a few minutes before reaching here this morning, it's a damned small town, Stephanie. It wouldn't be hard to stake out your PO box or—Hell! Just ask questions at the corner store or coffee shop I drove past," he said dryly, and then added, "That Cory guy who delivered your groceries knows who you are and is obviously a fan. I'm sure he brags to all his friends that he delivers to you. He might even have told some of them where your house is."

Stephanie scowled at him for the suggestion. She definitely didn't want it to be one of her readers who'd got ahold of her address because Cory was flapping his gums, but beyond that she really didn't want it to be one of her readers at all. She loved her readers. They wrote her such lovely, encouraging letters. Sometimes they even sent her little gifts—little notebooks to write in, and handmade items that she cherished. Unfortunately, other than her writing, she couldn't think of any other reason someone might bug her internet, or hack it or whatever.

Unable to argue the point, Stephanie changed the subject instead and muttered, "Well, it couldn't have been on there long, or I'm sure the tech guy would have noticed it when he fixed the internet."

Thorne stiffened and speared her with his eyes. "The tech guy? Someone was out to fix the internet already?" he asked sharply, and when she nodded, said, "Harper told me he couldn't get anyone out here. That he was told it would be weeks before anyone could come fix the problem."

"Yeah, he told me that back when I first lost service too," Stephanie admitted with a shrug. "But he must have harassed them after he said that, because the service guy showed up the next day, and got the internet up and running. Although I did notice it was slow afterward, and I complained about that to Elvi just the other day. She probably put a bug in Harper's ear about it, and he meant he was having trouble getting someone out *again* when it was basically up and running but just slow. So—You're shaking your head again."

"When he gave me the keys to the house before I left Toronto, Harper told me the internet was down. He said he couldn't get anyone out to take care of it, but would call again today," Thorne told her solemnly. "As far as he knows, no serviceman has come out."

"Well . . ." Stephanie frowned.

"I was more than a little surprised when I got to their house and found the service was fine. I thought it must just be yours that was out. That's why I brought my laptop with me when I brought the scones out, to check it. I was going to do it from your porch because I thought you would be sleeping or working, but then you came out and I was able to do it from here."

"And it was up and running," Stephanie murmured.

Thorne nodded. "It was a little slow, though, compared to Harper and Drina's, so I thought I'd see if I couldn't fix that for you."

"Thank you," she said quietly, and then added, "But obviously my internet people had an opening come up, after all. They did come out and get the internet back up, and they probably just didn't bother to tell Harper because they figured I would."

"Or maybe this service guy wasn't really working for your internet provider, but is the one who set up the hack on your system," he countered.

Stephanie shook her head at once. "No. How would some random weirdo know I was having internet problems and would be expecting a service guy?"

"Maybe he cut the line at the road so that you'd call for service, and then showed up when he felt a safe amount of time had passed and you'd be expecting a techie to come out. Then he set up his hack, and repaired the line afterward," Thorne said slowly, as if reasoning it out as he spoke.

"Well, that was stupid, then," Stephanie said, and pointed out, "Once the real service guy showed up, he'd have found the gear."

Thorne nodded, but then said, "Unless the guy phoned in claiming to be Harper and canceled the service call."

She was scowling over that possibility when he asked, "Did this guy go under the deck like me?"

Stephanie grimaced and admitted, "I'm not sure. I mean, I assume he did but I was cooking Felix's tuna balls and Trixie's dog food. I wasn't watching him. But," she added, "when he buzzed at the gate, he said it was an easy fix and outdoor, so he wouldn't have to put me out any. He'd pretty much be in and gone. And he was. He was done and heading back down the driveway in no more than the twenty minutes or so that it took you to climb under the deck, remove the couplers and whatever, and crawl out." Sighing, she reluctantly admitted, "I suppose he could have been the one to put in the hacking stuff."

Stephanie paused briefly, and then grimaced and told him, "It was after 8 P.M. when he showed up. I thought it was kind of late for a service call, but he said I was the last stop of the day and they'd all been working overtime the last few weeks because they're so busy. At the time, I was just so glad to be getting the internet back up . . ." She shrugged helplessly, feeling foolish now, but added, "And knowing how much trouble Harper said he had getting someone to come out, it didn't seem beyond reason that they'd work overtime to catch up." Shaking her head, she sighed. "I guess that was stupid of me. I should have called the office and verified he worked for them."

"Why would you? His excuse sounded perfectly reasonable. I would have believed it," Thorne assured her, and she appreciated the attempt to make her feel better, but merely nodded, her thoughts turning to the fact that someone had apparently hacked her internet. The idea seemed surreal to her. Just unbelievable and crazy.

"Are you all right?" Thorne asked.

Stephanie nodded a little distractedly, still trying to accept that someone had gone to all that trouble to read her emails.

"Are you sure you're all right?" he asked with concern.

"Hmm?" She glanced at him in question, surprised at the depth of the concern on his expression. "Sure. Why wouldn't I be?"

Thorne hesitated, and then said carefully, "Well, I'd

expect you to be a little more upset about this. Someone was spying on you," he pointed out.

"Yeah. Weird, huh?" Stephanie muttered, and then gave a short laugh. "I mean, it's kind of hard to believe . . . and I guess I'd be more upset if there was the possibility that something personal and private might have been read, but my emails since that tech guy got my internet going again just haven't been that interesting. In fact, reading them must have been boring as hell for him."

When Thorne merely arched an eyebrow, she told him, "This week Elvi emailed me several recipes, Beau emailed to whine about not getting enough time alone with Tiny due to work, and Drina emailed about the plans she and Harper were making to visit a friend in England next month," she listed off, and then shrugged. "I thanked Elvi for the recipes, commiserated with Beau, and told Drina I wanted to visit with her and Harper before they go to England. That's it. Hardly earth-shattering stuff."

"What about business emails?" Thorne asked.

"There were none," she answered with a wry smile. "I mean, I got a fan letter or twenty, but my editor hasn't written since sending me the edits the day before my internet went out, before the techie came and could have put the hacker stuff on."

"And you haven't finished them to send back yet," Thorne realized.

"No," she agreed. "So basically the poor schmuck who hacked me paid out a bunch of money for all the gear he hooked up, and got nothing for it." Stephanie shook her head. "In truth, I find it hard to believe he even did it, and just feel sorry for the idiot," she said wryly, and then added, "But, of course, I'll be more careful in future about who I let in. I guess I'll have to check with my internet provider before buzzing anyone through the gate, and maybe keep an eye on them and read their minds too to be sure they aren't up to no good."

Stephanie frowned even as she said it, annoyed to have to go to such lengths because some idiot had thought he might get a free copy of one of her books before it was published. At least, she assumed that had been the plan. She couldn't think of any other reason someone might hack her like that.

"That's probably a good idea," Thorne said, closing his computer. "But for now, we found the hack, your line is clean, and there's no more lag on your internet speed."

"Yes." Stephanie sighed the word and then managed a smile, and said, "Thank you for that. I never would have checked the wires, or—" She grimaced and shrugged. "The hacking thing would have been there forever."

"My pleasure," Thorne said easily as he put his computer in his backpack. "I'm just glad I was able to do something. Harper and Drina refused to let me pay rent to stay in their beautiful house, so it'll make me feel better if I can at least help out while I'm here. Which reminds me . . ." he said as he zipped up the backpack. "If you have anything you need done while I'm here, let me know and I'll do what I can."

"You mean like gardening, baking, or me-owing the lawn?" she finished, eyes wide as she realized what had nearly slipped out. Dear God, her brain just went south around this man. Stephanie couldn't believe she'd said that. While she was a gal who usually said what she thought, offering herself up in a "Coffee, tea, or me?" way was just one step beyond her comfort level.

"Me-owing?" Thorne echoed with obvious amusement.

"Mowing," she said, feeling her face flush with embarrassment.

"Ah, of course, and I'd be happy to do any of those if you like," he assured her as he stood up and slung his backpack over one shoulder and wing. "But I should probably head out and let you get to your edits. I heard you tell your delivery guy that you hoped to get them done today and I've taken up enough of your time."

Stephanie wanted to protest his leaving. She liked spending time with him. But she'd already embarrassed herself enough for one day, and she did have to finish those edits, so she nodded and stood to walk him to the door.

"Thanks again," she murmured as he reached for the door, and then when he tried to open it and nothing happened, she said, "Oh, sorry. It's locked." Reaching past him, Stephanie flicked the thumb turn to unlock it and then stepped quickly back, her arm tingling where it had brushed his as she'd reached around him, but said, "Habit," to ensure he didn't think she'd been trying to lock him in with her like some sex-starved virgin. The truth was Stephanie locked every door she could, every chance she got, and had done so ever since the attack where she was turned. She didn't want to admit that to him though.

"A good habit," Thorne said simply as he now opened the door. "Good luck with your edits."

Stephanie mumbled a thanks, and then closed the door and locked it behind him as he crossed the porch to the walkway. This time, she didn't stay to watch him leave. She was a little disgruntled at the moment, and turned away to head into the kitchen, rubbing her still tingling arm as she went.

They'd only spent time together twice so far, but he'd seemed a little different to her this time. Distant, she thought. He'd definitely kept a physical distance from her, and then when her arm had brushed his as she'd unlocked the door for him, he'd stiffened and his feathers had ruffled again. He'd also pulled away. It was possible that he'd experienced the same tingling she had and that had startled him, but considering he'd also seemed somehow emotionally distant to her this visit, she didn't think that was the case.

Stephanie wasn't sure what had changed between that morning and this afternoon to make him withdraw, but he'd been easygoing and much warmer that morning, chatting easily, joking, teasing, and even showing her his bottom. She'd liked that Thorne better. The Thorne from this afternoon might as well have been wearing a big billboard reading Not Interested. Keep Your Tush-looking Eyes to Yourself.

"So, probably not a possible life mate," she muttered to herself, thinking that surely if they were possible life mates he wouldn't have been able to instill this sudden emotional distance between them. The thought was a depressing one and Stephanie sighed as she headed into her office to work.

Eight

Thorne wasn't sure where he was when he first woke up. It took a moment for the cobwebs of sleep to clear from his mind so that he could recognize the living room of Drina and Harper's house. He'd sat down to read and fallen asleep. Not surprising, he supposed. He'd got up at 1 A.M. that morning to get ready for the drive down here, and while he'd laid down beforehand, he'd had trouble getting to sleep and had probably only managed a couple hours of shut-eye.

"Coffee," Thorne muttered, returning the recliner to its upright position and getting up. His gaze moved to the wall of windows as he headed into the kitchen, noting that he'd slept so long that the sun had gone down. Not long ago, he guessed by the fact that the sky was gray rather than full dark, but it had set just the same.

Wondering if Stephanie had finished her edits and what she was doing, he set up a cup and pod in the machine and pushed the button, then walked over to the refrigerator to grab the cream. His gaze automatically moved to the security monitor as he went and he froze when he spotted movement on one of the eight camera images. Forgetting about the cream, he walked over to the monitor and narrowed his gaze on the camera view of the front entrance to the property and the man presently climbing over the fence beside the entry gate.

Thorne didn't recognize him, but then he didn't know anyone around here. However, it wasn't the guy he'd watched deliver his groceries that morning on Stephanie's monitor, and it wasn't any of the immortals he'd met since arriving in Canada. He watched until the man made his way up the driveway, past this house and obviously headed for Stephanie's, and then Thorne turned and hurried for the door.

Stephanie finished the email to her editor, attached the file with corrections, hit Send, and sat back in her desk chair with a little sigh. That was done.

She ran her foot over Trixie where the dog lay under her L-shaped desk. "Mommy's finished work, baby. Do you want to go for a walk?"

Stephanie wasn't surprised when the boxer immediately scrambled to her feet and moved around her chair to get out from under the desk. Trixie was a good girl, and let her work when she needed, but she must be bored, Stephanie thought as she pushed her wheeled desk chair back and stood up. "Okay, we'll go for a walk and then I'll feed you."

Her words made Trixie stop and turn to bark at her

and Stephanie grinned. "What's that? You'd rather eat first?"

When the dog opened her mouth, let her tongue hang out, and wagged her tail energetically, Stephanie chuckled. "I'll take that as a yes you'd rather eat first, shall I?"

Trixie barked again. Whether it was in agreement or not, Stephanie couldn't say, but moved out into the kitchen to grab the dog's food as well as Felix's. She was just setting the food on the counter and wondering where the cat was when something soft rubbed against her lower leg. Usually Felix also sat in the office with her while she was working, but today he'd taken up position by the door to look at the world outside instead. Probably watching for Thorne, Stephanie had guessed. Both animals seemed as enthralled with the man as she was, though for different reasons.

Stephanie had just put Trixie's food in the microwave to warm up when the dog started barking wildly. It was the danger bark, not the hurry-with-my-food-already-woman bark, and Stephanie turned sharply to see what had her attention.

Seeing that Trixie was standing at the sliding doors to the deck off the kitchen, Stephanie walked quickly to her side to look out. Her eyes widened incredulously when she saw Thorne in the bushes beyond her deck, wrestling with a man. The pair of them seemed evenly matched when it came to strength, and were grappling for the upper hand in the tussle.

Stephanie started to unlock the sliding doors and then gasped in shock when she saw the flash of fangs before the stranger suddenly went for Thorne's throat. Unlocking and dragging the door open, she bellowed in fury and charged across the deck. Stephanie vaulted over the railing, aiming her feet at the man attacking Thorne. She hit him hard, her heels slamming into his shoulder. She heard the crunch of bone breaking, and the man staggered back away from Thorne as she landed between them.

She started toward Thorne's attacker, but when he scrambled back to his feet and immediately made a run for it, she let him go to hurry to Thorne instead. Stephanie had seen the blood spray from his neck when she'd knocked the immortal away and was more concerned about Thorne than his attacker at that moment. She could hunt that bastard down later, if necessary. Right now she wanted to be sure Thorne hadn't taken a fatal wound.

"Let me see," she said, rushing to his side and kneeling next to where he'd fallen when he and the other man had broken apart.

"I'm fine," Thorne growled, his hand pressed tight to his throat and remaining there when she tried to pull it away.

Her eyes widened at his strength. She was immortal, and while she didn't have fangs, she did have all the other abilities, including superstrength, yet he was able to keep her from pulling her hand away. Frowning over that, she asked, "Who was that guy?"

"Your hacker," Thorne said, sounding angry. "I saw him climb over the fence and followed to see what he was up to and he came straight here. When I saw him pull another one of those black boxes out of his jacket and kneel to open the hatch in the deck skirting, I confronted him."

Stephanie's mouth tightened at this news. She'd

thought this whole hacking business resolved with Thorne's finding the box. It seemed not, she thought, but was more concerned about Thorne at the moment and said, "You need to let me see your wound, Thorne."

When he snapped his mouth closed and shook his head, she didn't argue with him. Instead, Stephanie simply picked him up.

"I can walk," Thorne snapped, beginning to struggle in her arms.

Ignoring him, Stephanie leapt up and forward, easily clearing the raised railing. She landed on the deck with a thud that sent a jolt through both of them. It stopped Thorne's struggles long enough for her to carry him inside and set him on his feet next to the island.

"Sit," Stephanie ordered as she hurried from the room. She went to the bathroom to fetch a washcloth and towels. She didn't bother looking for antiseptic, bandages, or anything of that nature for the simple reason that she didn't have things like that. Stephanie didn't need them. The nanos fixed up everything for her pretty quick without the necessity of first aid. She didn't even have rubbing alcohol, for heaven's sake, or real alcohol, which might have done in a pinch, because she had no need for rubbing alcohol and drinking liquor would have very little effect on her so she didn't bother with it.

Cursing under her breath at the lack of first aid equipment, Stephanie headed back to the kitchen with the washcloth and towels.

Thorne was sitting at the end of the island when she returned, hand still pressed to the wound. Ignoring him, she set the towels and washcloth down next to him, then grabbed two bowls, ran warm water into one, grabbed a spoon and sharp knife, and then got the ginger root out of the fridge before retrieving honey and a small bottle of lavender essential oil from the cupboard.

"What are you doing?" Thorne asked with bewilderment as he eyed the honey and ginger.

"I don't have any antibiotic or antiseptic here, so I'll have to make you one."

His eyes immediately narrowed as he watched her pour some of the liquid honey into the bowl and start working on the ginger. "You are not putting honey and ginger on me. And oh my God! What is that? It stinks," he complained when she opened the lavender essential oil.

Stephanie smiled faintly at the complaint. She'd bought the lavender essential oil to use in her diffuser because it was supposed to be soothing, but just like Thorne, she hadn't cared for the scent at all. Which was lucky for him, because it meant she still had almost a full bottle of it. Stephanie had read somewhere that lavender had antiseptic qualities, so intended to dab it on his wound, or maybe pour it over it. But she wasn't sure if she should use it full strength or water it down with something.

Stephanie pondered the issue as she peeled and ground up the ginger.

"You're wasting your time," Thorne growled, sounding annoyed. "You are not putting that stuff on me."

"I don't have any anti—"

"I don't need antiseptic, I'll heal just fine without it," he assured her. "And if you think you're going to slather me with that gunk, you and I are going to tussle."

"You say that like it's a bad thing," she muttered, and then realized what had come out of her mouth, and closed her eyes briefly. When she opened them again, she pushed the ginger and honey away with exasperation, and picked up the washcloth and water instead. "Fine. Then at least let me wash the blood away and get a look at the wound to see if I should call Dani and have her come sew you up."

When she dipped the washcloth in the water and began to wring it out, Thorne scowled and said, "I don't need Dani to sew me—"

His words ended on a startled curse when she used immortal speed to rush around the island and tug his hand away from the wound before he'd even realized she was moving.

Considering that she hadn't been able to shift his hand at all outside, Stephanie knew it was only catching him by surprise that had allowed her to this time. But she was the one who was surprised when she got a look at the wound. The size and shape told her that the bastard had tried to rip his throat out. Fortunately, he'd failed. But the wound appeared deep.

Stephanie suffered some confusion as she peered at it. While there was some blood on his neck and covering his vest, there wasn't as much as she would have expected, and the wound appeared to have already stopped bleeding. That was odd. Mortals didn't stop bleeding that quickly, especially after taking a wound like this. The crimson liquid should be pouring down his throat.

Leaning closer, and unconsciously inhaling the coppery scent, Stephanie wished she could lift the flap of torn skin to see how deep it really was. She was afraid it would cause him pain and start the injury bleeding again, though, and didn't want to do that.

With her thoughts taken up by such concerns, Stephanie was caught completely by surprise by her own actions when she suddenly licked his throat. She didn't consciously decide to do it. She hadn't even noticed that she'd leaned closer to his neck. It was as if her tongue, or body, had a mind of its own. Worse yet, it wasn't some dainty little lick with the tip of her tongue that she gave him either. It was a full on dragging of her tongue from the base of his throat, up to the wound . . . and the effect was electric. The taste was good, which told her that she'd gone too long without taking blood. But it was the sensations that roared through her body in response to the greedy caress that had her pulling back.

Stephanie meant to apologize and get the hell away from him, but while she was able to pull her face back from his neck, she couldn't seem to make her body move away from Thorne. She didn't want to. She wanted to crawl into his lap and lick him again . . . everywhere, and Stephanie was struggling with that urge when she shifted her gaze to Thorne and saw the smoldering look on his face. Before she could quite work out what that meant, he caught her by the arms, drew her between his knees. and kissed her.

Oh yeah, he was definitely her life mate. That was the last coherent thought Stephanie had before she was completely overwhelmed by the sensations his kiss stirred in her. And as she'd guessed, she'd never been properly kissed before. The lame, sloppy mashing of mouths followed by nibbling at her lips that Stephanie had experienced at the few school dances she'd attended before she had been turned were nothing like what she was experiencing now. This was passion and need. This was Thorne trying to suck her soul out of her body even as she did the same to him.

Stephanie had no idea what she was doing or if she was doing it right. She was all sensation and hunger, her mouth moving of its own accord, her body doing the same. Clutching at his shoulders, she moved up between his legs as far as she could go so that she could press her upper body more firmly against his. She then moaned into his mouth as her breasts rubbed against his chest through their clothes and her nipples woke up from their lifelong slumber with an excitement that shot straight down between her legs.

Thorne must have felt it too, because his moan followed hard on hers and then she felt him tugging at her T-shirt before he gave up and simply ripped it open. The tearing sound just added to her excitement, but it seemed to startle Thorne and he broke their kiss to pull back slightly and shake his head as if trying to clear it before muttering, "I'm sorry. I shouldn't—"

"Don't stop," Stephanie gasped, taking his hands in hers and covering her now bare breasts with them even as she pressed her mouth to his again. It was all she had to do. Even as his hands closed over her small breasts, his tongue was thrusting past her lips.

Stephanie kissed him eagerly back, and then cried out into his mouth as he began to knead her breasts, his rough palms scraping over her nipples. The friction immediately had the sensitive buds hardening with excitement.

In the end, Stephanie didn't crawl into Thorne's lap; he lifted her onto it so that she straddled him. He then broke their kiss and ducked his head to claim one excited nipple. Drawing it into his hot, wet mouth, he lashed it with his tongue and then sucked, before nipping and then lashing it again as his hands moved down to clasp her hips and urge her more firmly against the hardness in his pants.

Besieged by the duo of sensations roaring through her body in growing, overwhelming waves, Stephanie lost her mind a little. Clutching at his shoulders, she braced her feet on the footrests on either side of the chair and shifted herself against him, riding the hardness that was giving her so much pleasure. She'd only managed to do that twice when Thorne released her nipple on a growl and caught her under the ass, pressing her tight to his chest and hips as he erupted out of the chair.

"Bedroom," Thorne got out between clenched teeth as he carried her from the kitchen. "Your first time isn't going to be on the kitchen island."

Some of Stephanie's excitement shifted aside at those words and she asked with alarm, "You can tell it's my first time?"

"Hell, no. You're the least virginal virgin I've ever met. I overheard you tell Felix," he explained. She didn't get the chance to consider that. They'd reached the bedroom by then and he stopped long enough to kick the door closed behind them, shutting Trixie and Felix out, and then threw her on the bed.

Stephanie hadn't even finished one bounce when he was on top of her, his body pressing her down into the mattress as his mouth covered hers again. She kissed him back at once, moaning as he ground himself against her. She then reached around his back, found the Velcro of his vest under his wings and ripped it open. Stephanie followed that up by undoing the Velcro at his neck and then tugged the vest out of the way when he lifted his chest a bit for her to do it.

They both moaned when he relaxed against her again, the hairs on his chest teasing her hard nipples. He kissed her again then, his tongue thrusting into her mouth as his hips ground against hers. Stephanie instinctively spread her legs so that his hardness rested against the apex of her thighs, and they both groaned at the friction when he ground against her again.

"God!" Thorne gasped as he tore his mouth from hers and raised his upper body slightly to grind against her more firmly.

Stephanie cried out at the sensations shooting through her, and then opened her eyes with surprise when his hands were suddenly on her breasts again when they should have been holding his upper body off of her. She blinked in surprise when she saw that he was holding himself up with his partially open wings, leaving his hands free to caress her as his hips continued to rub against her where they were nestled between her thighs.

Eyes wide, she shifted her gaze to his face and their eyes met and held as he caressed and kneaded her breasts.

"Oh, Thorne! Oh, please," she pleaded when he then rolled and gently pinched her nipples, ratcheting up the sensations he was causing to an almost unbearable level. He lowered himself slightly in response, just far enough that he could bend his head to kiss her, and then one of his hands left a breast to glide down her stomach to the waist of her shorts. Even as she felt them open, his hand was sliding inside and down between her legs.

Stephanie cried out into his mouth and jerked under him at the caress, her body trying to writhe with the pleasure suffusing it despite being pinned down by his. Thorne immediately gave up caressing her other breast to allow that hand to move down to the top of her shorts, to begin shoving them over her hips even as his other hand continued to caress her. But then he gave up the caresses altogether, broke their kiss, and rose up on his knees between hers.

A surprised gasp slipped from her lips when Thorne caught her by both ankles and raised them in front of his chest. He smiled at her startled expression, and then gently, almost reverently, kissed first one ankle and the other before grabbing the waist of her shorts and dragging them up her legs and off, taking her panties with them.

Stephanie heard her clothing hit the floor as her legs dropped back to the bed, but her attention was on the fact that she was now splayed out before him completely nude and with her legs wide open because he was between them. Thorne had noticed this as well, and decided to take a moment to enjoy the view. There wasn't a damned thing she could do about it short of telling him to stop and get on with it. Stephanie was actually about to do that when he suddenly reached down and ran his fingers lightly over the damp, excited flesh between her legs.

They both gasped and jerked at the caress, and then Thorne shook his head with bewilderment. "Dear God, I've never experienced anything like this. I want to make your first time good for you, but just touching you gives me pleasure. I'm afraid I'm going to—"

His words ended on a startled gasp as Stephanie sat up and kissed him. She wasn't so innocent that she didn't know about premature ejaculation and understand that it was what he was worrying about. But there was no such thing as premature ejaculation for an immortal and their mate. If he orgasmed, she would too right along with him. However, Stephanie had no desire to stop what they were doing to explain that to him, so she kissed him aggressively for a moment and then reached between them to touch his erection through the heavy fabric of his leather pants.

The sharp pleasure that shot through her at the tentative touch told her that it was the right move. It also guided her on what to do next and she began to rub him more firmly through the material as he took over their kiss and forced her back to the bed with his body.

Already experiencing his pleasure with him, when Thorne reached down and slid his fingers between her thighs to caress her as well, Stephanie reached her tipping point. Crying out into his mouth, she arched up against him. She was vaguely aware of her hand tightening around his erection, and felt her body react as another overwhelming wave of pleasure rode through her, and then her poor mind couldn't take any more and dragged her down into darkness. Thorne's own roar of release was the last thing she heard.

Stephanie woke up hungry, though not for food. Grimacing at the cramps attacking her stomach, she squeezed her eyes tightly closed for a moment rather than open them, hoping the cramps would go away. But, of course, they wouldn't. At least, not until she fed.

Sighing, she gave up and opened her eyes, then froze as she saw that what was covering her wasn't her usual weighted blanket but a very large brown wing. It was only partially open, just enough to curve around her, and it was surprisingly warm, and very soft. It was also lighter than she would have expected.

Stephanie stared at the wing briefly, taking in the beautiful and varying shades of chocolate in the feathers, and then she turned her head to peer at Thorne. The man was lying on his stomach next to her, eyes closed. His face was relaxed in sleep, and he was breathing deeply.

He was out for the count, Stephanie thought, and wasn't surprised. It was a well-known fact that life mates suffered postcoital faints, or loss of consciousness as the male of their kind preferred to call it. Not that there'd been any actual coitus, Stephanie acknowledged wryly. They hadn't made it that far. She was still a twenty-seven-year-old virgin.

Sighing at the thought, Stephanie shifted her gaze back to the wing covering her, and wondered if Thorne would wake up if she moved it. Probably, she decided, and didn't want him to. She needed to feed and didn't want Thorne to see that. Stephanie hated drinking blood. Always had. Unlike immortals with fangs, she couldn't just slap a bag to her teeth and let them empty it without the need to taste the liquid they were taking in. Without fangs, she and Dani both had to drink their blood. She hated that. It was disgusting. Not because of the taste so much. When Stephanie was really hungry—and she usually was before she could force herself to feed—it actually didn't taste too bad. If she was desperately hungry—like ready to run down the next mortal she encountered and start gnawing on them—it even tasted good. But that didn't make it any less disgusting and stomach-turning for her to have to do. Stephanie just couldn't get past the fact that she was drinking *blood*. The last thing she wanted was to have to do it in front of Thorne and see her own disgust mirrored on his face.

That being the case, Stephanie held her breath and, rather than move his wing, started to slide sideways on the bed to slip out from under it. She hadn't got more than an inch when the end of the wing suddenly curled farther down around her and rolled her toward Thorne. Her own eyes wide with surprise, she saw that his were now open, and a sleepy smile graced his face.

"Good morning," he murmured, and then grinned wryly and added, "Or I suppose I should say good evening since it's after midnight."

"Is it?" Stephanie asked with surprise, and instinctively glanced over her shoulder to try to see the bedside clock. When she couldn't see it because of her angle and his wing, she said, "Alexa . . . what time is it?"

When her clock responded, "The time is 12:22 A.M.," she looked back to Thorne to see him peering past her with curiosity.

"You have a talking clock?" he asked with interest.

"I have Alexa," she corrected. "She tells me the time, plays music, turns lights on and off . . ." Stephanie shrugged.

Thorne's face relaxed into a smile. "Yes. I've heard of Alexa for controlling lights and such. I didn't know the system would tell you the time."

"She does lots of things. I can find out the temperature outside, what the weather is supposed to be for the day or week, get recipes . . ." She hesitated, and then admitted, "That's all I really use her for, but I know there's other stuff she'll do."

"Hmm." Thorne's gaze shifted back to her. Noting

the expression on her face, he raised his eyebrows in question.

"I didn't know you could do that with your wings," she explained, her gaze moving with curiosity over the feathered appendage cocooning her. "I didn't know they could curl around . . ." She paused to frown, and then said, "Well, I mean, I've seen birds do that in cartoons, but I never thought it was real."

"You thought all they could do was flap," Thorne suggested, and when she nodded, he shook his head and glanced along his own wing. "No. They're basically extra arms, but with less functional hands."

"Really?" Stephanie asked with surprise, and Thorne glanced back to her and nodded.

"Pretty much," he assured her. "They have the same bones from the shoulder to the wrist. It's just the hands that differ. The hands on my wings have only three phalanges compared to my hand having five."

"Phalanges? Fingers?" she asked uncertainly.

"Yes." Thorne smiled. "My wings have a very short thumb and two longer fingers basically, compared to the thumb and four fingers on my hands."

"Oh." Stephanie eyed his wing as she considered that. She would have liked to feel it up to find the bones he was talking about, but thought that might be rude. It also might lead back to more coitus or noncoitus and passing out again, and while she wouldn't mind that at all, aside from a pressing need for blood, she was the mother of two fur babies and as such had responsibilities that should be seen to first. Turning reluctantly away from his fascinating wing, Stephanie met his gaze and said solemnly, "I need to get up and feed Trixie and Felix."

"Already done," Thorne assured her.

"What?" she asked with surprise, and when he nodded, she asked, "When?"

"About twenty minutes ago. I took them outside afterward too. My coming back to bed is probably what woke you. You were shivering, sleeping on the covers. I didn't want to disturb you, so I put my wing over you to warm you, but that probably woke you up in the end," he admitted with a slight frown.

It was an expression Stephanie was now wearing as well. "You . . . you didn't faint after we . . . ?"

"Oh yeah. Like a Victorian miss," he assured her with wry amusement, and then arched an eyebrow. "Care to discuss why that happened?"

Stephanie opened her mouth, closed it again, and then shook her head. She wasn't ready to explain to him about life mates and that their experiencing the shared pleasure, and passing out afterward, meant that he was hers. It was too soon. She didn't want the man running screaming into the night.

Thorne looked disappointed by her nonanswer, and then sighed and started to lift his wing away from her and shift as if to get up as he said, "I should probably get up and—"

His words died and he stopped moving when she placed her hand on his chest. It had been instinct for Stephanie, a response to his withdrawing. It was highly effective at preventing that. She felt the tingle and shiver that went through him both under her hand and as it rushed through her own body, and then his wing was curling around her again and drawing her closer even as his hand slid around her head and angled it to where he wanted. When his lips lowered to hers, she opened to him at once.

Thorne kissed her with a hunger that she responded to immediately. It sent a rush of warm sensation through her body, making her stretch and arch against him, which just caused more uproar in them both. Moaning into his mouth, she reached for him then, running her hands over his arms and shoulders, and then down and around to grasp and squeeze his behind.

Her eyes opened in surprise when she felt the bare flesh there under her fingers. He'd still been wearing his leather pants during their first go-round. They hadn't made it to removing them, but he must have taken them off before getting back in bed after feeding Trixie and Felix. They were gone now and she moaned into his mouth as her grasp on his behind had him grinding against her, his very evident erection rubbing over her pelvis.

The action made Thorne growl into her mouth, and then he broke their kiss on a gasp and suddenly turned her onto her back in the bed. He came over her then, but while his lower body pressed against hers, he held his upper body up with his wings, leaving several inches between their chests.

"We have to slow down," he panted, even as his hands began to move over her body, sliding up her sides and over her stomach before gliding up to cover her breasts. They both groaned when he closed his hands over her small buds and began to knead. Still, Thorne repeated, "We have to slow down. I want to make this good for you."

"Yes," Stephanie agreed, but opened her legs so that she cradled his hips, then braced her feet and raised her hips up to rub against him, making them both groan.

"Stephanie," he protested on a moan.

"Yes. Please, Thorne. Yes," she panted, repeating the action and almost sobbing with need as his erection slid against the nub of her excitement.

"God, you're so hot and wet," he growled, shifting his hips into the motion now as well, and gliding across her again. But Stephanie wanted more, needed more, and the only more she could think of was—

"Oh God!" Thorne gasped, and froze when she shifted her hips and he slid partway into her rather than just rub against her. Eyes wide, he met her gaze, concern and need fighting on his expression. "Did you—? Are you—?"

Breathing heavily, Stephanie licked her lips. She hadn't been sure what to expect. Of course, she'd heard there could be pain the first time, but had briefly forgotten that while chasing her orgasm. However, while it felt odd to have him inside of her, and she could feel her body stretching to take him all in, there wasn't any actual pain. In truth, all she was feeling was pleasure, which she suspected was coming from Thorne himself. Holding on to that pleasure, Stephanie thrust herself up again, determined to get the pain, if there was any, over with. But he slid home easily and without causing her any discomfort. Again, all she was feeling was his pleasure and a vague sense of fullness.

Stephanie had hoped Thorne would take over then and start to move, but instead he remained stiff as a board over her. He was watching her with a strained expression as concern and desire fought on his face. Realizing that he was remaining still in an effort not to hurt her, and to let her set the speed, Stephanie lowered herself slightly and then raised herself again, and then

did it again and then again as wave after wave of slowly
mounting pleasure coursed over her. But it was better
when Thorne finally gave up his considerate stillness,
grasped her hips, and took over. He began to pound
into her then with a vigor and a passion that pushed
them both over the edge to pleasure before darkness
closed in.

Nine

"No. Not on the bed."

Stephanie opened sleepy eyes at those hissed words to see Thorne standing on the other side of the bed, a tray of delicious-smelling goodies in hand. He was scowling firmly at something on the floor, and Stephanie raised herself up on her elbows to peer over the side of the bed. Trixie was there, frozen in the crouching position she usually took before jumping up on something. The boxer was meeting Thorne's gaze and not moving, but not relaxing her pose either. Stephanie realized Trixie was trying to decide if she should listen to Thorne or not, and solved the dog's dilemma by saying, "In your basket, Trixie. No bed."

The boxer immediately relaxed her pose with a little huff of either disappointment or disgust, and then turned to pad over to the dog bed in the corner. Once she'd laid down on the ergonomic dog mattress, Stephanie turned her gaze to Thorne.

Smiling wryly, he raised the tray slightly and said, "I come bearing breakfast in bed."

Stephanie immediately shifted to a sitting position and arranged her pillows behind her so she could lean back in comfort. Beaming at Thorne, she then patted her lap, ready for the tray.

Much to her amazement, however, he just shook his head and set the tray on her dresser before walking around the bed to her side, saying, "You need to feed first."

Stephanie's smile turned into a scowl when he stopped at the bedside table and picked up one of four glasses of red fluid waiting there. Her shocked mind pointed out that he'd actually opened and poured four bags into large glasses, and lined them up on the table for her, and that there was even a straw in the one he was holding. It was so sweet . . . and so unwelcome.

"I don't want all your effort to go to waste and breakfast to get cold," she said with a forced smile. "I can drink the blood later."

"Judging by the fact that you licked the blood off of my throat after I was injured, and that that was hours ago, I'd say you can't wait," Thorne countered solemnly.

Stephanie had rather hoped he either hadn't noticed at the time, or had forgotten about that after everything they'd done. Apparently not, though, and that realization had her flushing with embarrassment and guilt. "I—"

"I know you dislike feeding," he interrupted sympathetically. "Dani said it's because you have to actually drink it, but—"

"Dani told you?" she asked with dismay.

"Not deliberately," he said quickly. "We were in the office at Marguerite and Julius's home. Dani was explaining that she wanted to bring in different specialists to consult on me when Decker came in with blood. He pointed out that she'd neglected to feed that morning, and insisted she do it now. He then apologized to me for the interruption, but explained that Dani and you both disliked feeding and put it off as long as possible as a rule, which was dangerous. Your sister got annoyed and said the two of you only disliked it because you had to actually drink it. That maybe if you could feed like other immortals, you wouldn't be so resistant to it."

Stephanie relaxed a little as he finished. Dani hadn't been telling tales. At least not specifically about her. Noting his determined expression, she sighed with resignation and took the glass from him. Stephanie then stared down into the dark red liquid, trying to work her way up to drinking it.

Even after thirteen years, feeding for Stephanie was something of an ordeal. She tried to look at it like taking medicine, but this medicine looked like blood, smelled like blood, and—sadly—tasted like blood. Stephanie had a real problem drinking blood. It was purely psychological and she knew it. In her mind, only monsters like Dracula and Leonius Livius drank blood. Stephanie didn't want to be a monster.

Unfortunately, that ingrained belief that drinking blood made you a monster was contrary to the reality that if she didn't feed, her hunger could build to a point that it made her do things that would make her that monster.

Frankly, it was all one huge pain in the ass. Drinking blood, hearing everyone's thoughts, all of it, and she still cursed Leonius Livius daily for visiting this hell on her.

Except, of course, that she was no longer hearing everyone's thoughts, Stephanie recalled. Which should be a good thing, but really just had her worried. It was nice not to be constantly bombarded with other people's thinking, but it was worrisome that it had stopped so abruptly.

"I'll make a deal with you," Thorne said suddenly, drawing her attention back to the situation at hand. "You drink and I'll answer any questions you have about me to help distract you."

Stephanie almost explained that she was just thinking, and she'd drink the blood without his offer, but when she glanced up to say that, her gaze landed on his neck and she bit back the words. He'd obviously showered. His hair was still a little damp, and the dried blood that had been on his throat last time she'd seen it was gone. But what really changed her mind was that she could see that the wound itself seemed to be well into healing. It wasn't mending as quickly as it would on an immortal, but it was definitely healing faster than it would with a mortal.

Curious about that, she nodded, and said, "Okay. Why is your neck healing so fast? And why did the bleeding stop so quickly when it happened?"

Thorne's expression made it clear he wasn't pleased with the question, but he stuck to the deal and said, "That would be the cockroach in me."

Stephanie blinked. "I'm sorry. What?"

Thorne grimaced and then sighed with resignation and walked around the bed to climb in beside her on his hands and knees. He took a moment to arrange his pillow so it was tucked under his chest and then dropped to rest on it, and cushioned his chin on his arms so that he could watch her as he spoke. "Once upon a time there was a complete and utter prick named Dressler."

Feeling her lips twitch at the singsong storyteller voice he was using, not to mention his cheerful description of his father, Stephanie ducked her head to her straw and began drinking to hide her response as he continued.

"This cruel and uncaring bastard was utterly devoid of any kind of empathy or conscience, and in the normal course of events, surely would have landed in jail for murder or some such thing. However, Dressler had two things going for him—he was handsome, and he was beyond clever. He was also obsessed with the idea of creating the perfect human," Thorne added dryly. "To this end, he made it his business to become very good at identifying DNA sequences responsible for certain traits or behaviors in people, and then isolating and extracting them. He wanted to create a superior race of genetically modified humans using the DNA for what he considered the best traits. To him that was strength, intelligence, speed, etc. . . . You get the idea."

Stephanie nodded and continued to suck at her straw as she waited for him to go on.

"But then one day he went to the movies and saw *Spider-Man*, and he started to consider the possibility of using animal DNA combined with human to make this superior race. This way he could have real spidermen and even bird people and several other more interesting results."

Stephanie had stopped sucking on her straw and lifted her head to blink at him with surprise at the mention of the movie *Spider-Man*. "Really?"

"No." Thorne grinned at her, and then shrugged and admitted, "I wanted to be sure you were paying attention."

"I'm paying attention . . . Despite the fact that this seems to be a long and meandering way to explain your body's handling of an injury, I'm listening," she assured him, her tone acerbic. "Now tell me what really made him turn his interest to animal DNA."

"The truth is, I don't know. It wasn't in any of his notes and he never told anyone. At least, not anyone who admitted it. All we know is that while he started out working with human DNA, he quickly switched to adding animal DNA to the mix," he said with a shrug.

"Oh. Okay, go on," Stephanie murmured, and then began to suck on her straw again.

"Anyway, unfortunately for Dressler, while it isn't illegal to genetically modify embryos, it *is* illegal to implant them. Actually, I'm not sure if it was even illegal to implant them back then. Dressler was a bit ahead of the game when it came to splicing DNA and things like that. I believe it wasn't really a thing until the 1970s, and this was back in the late fifties, early sixties. There might not have been laws against it yet.

"However," Thorne continued heavily, "he was foolish enough to lecture on the possibilities of this process and his ideas were not well received by his peers. He was considered a Dr. Frankenstein of his time, and shunned by one and all. He was even drummed out of the very prestigious university where he was a junior professor. Unable to secure another position in England, Dressler moved farther afield and eventually was hired as a professor of genetics at a university in Venezuela."

"So that's how he ended up in Venezuela," Stephanie murmured. She'd wondered about that back when the whole island situation had been going on.

Thorne nodded. "The government was also corrupt

and he probably figured he could get away with more there."

"Probably," Stephanie agreed.

"Anyway," Thorne went on, "a year later, while on a visit back home in England, he encountered the beautiful and gracious heiress Elizabeth Salter."

Stephanie smiled around her straw at his description of his mother and the affection clear in his voice.

"Knowing how much power and protection her money would offer him, Dressler set out to capture Elizabeth's hand in marriage," Thorne went on. "Young and naive, Elizabeth was easily swept up in the romance and adventure he offered. She ran away with him to marry and live in Venezuela and her fate was sealed.

"Dressler, you see, had realized that the only way to carry on with his genetic experiments was to do so in secret. So, with Elizabeth's money, he bought two islands off the coast of Venezuela—a small one with a lovely little house on it where they could live while his compound and their permanent home was built on the larger one.

"Everything seemed fine at first to Elizabeth, except that her husband always seemed to be away working." Pausing, Thorne glanced at her and pointed out, "He could hardly carry on the caring, loving husband routine full-time."

When Stephanie nodded in understanding, he continued. "So, Elizabeth was missing her husband and became depressed because of that, or so she thought. But her dear husband was actually drugging her every night at dinner to make her sleep so that he could give her hormone shots without her knowledge."

"Hormone shots?" Stephanie asked with surprise.

"They were to stimulate her ovaries to produce more eggs," he explained. "No doubt they were affecting her mood as well, of course, but since she didn't know about them . . ." He shrugged.

"She assumed she was just missing her husband," Stephanie finished for him, and asked, "How did he harvest the eggs?"

"He drugged her," Thorne said simply. "Dropped a couple pills in her after-dinner drink, and then extracted the eggs. Then he started the hormones again for more eggs. He did this to her over and over again during their first year of marriage."

"Dear God," Stephanie breathed.

Thorne nodded grimly. "Anyway, the reason for all of these eggs was so he could create me. Well, not me specifically, but he wanted to create a hybrid with the different animal DNA that he had decided would make up a superior being." Thorne paused briefly, his expression grim, and then told her, "He apparently had several failures. I was told that the lab in the basement of that little house on the island they first lived on was full of jars of mutated fetuses that hadn't been viable."

"He grew them in jars?" Stephanie asked with disbelief.

"No," Thorne said with a faint smile, and shook his head. "He fertilized the eggs and did his little DNA splicing deal to them, and then implanted them in my mother in batches of six embryos. He did this six times before it was a success . . . well, a success by his standards."

"Six times?" Stephanie asked with horror. "You mean your mother was pregnant six times?"

Thorne's mouth tightened. "And miscarried five, sometimes more than one fetus. All between three to four months. Father performed autopsies on them to see what went wrong, then pickled them in jars, and stored them on shelves in his basement lab like trophies. He would then adjust and recombine the DNA he was using for the next batch in the hopes of a more successful outcome."

"Bastard," Stephanie muttered, shuddering with disgust at the heartlessness of the man, but said, "Your poor mother must have been devastated."

"Mother didn't really remember," Thorne said almost wearily. "He apparently kept her drugged for most of that first year or two during the egg harvesting and the pregnancies that didn't carry to term."

"Wouldn't continually drugging her be bad for the babies?" Stephanie asked with a frown. "I mean, that could be the reason she lost so many."

"It may have contributed to it," he agreed solemnly. "Although from what I've been told, those fetuses were deformed and probably not viable on their own."

"You haven't seen them?" she asked with curiosity.

Thorne shook his head. "I was given the option before they were destroyed, but chose not to. I'd seen enough of the devastation he'd caused on the island. I didn't need to see more to know the man was a monster."

Stephanie nodded in understanding. She'd heard what Dressler had done on the island, but these fetuses were from his wife's eggs and his sperm. They were his *children*, and he'd experimented on them like . . . And poor Elizabeth, she thought. Thorne's mother had been mistreated horribly. Stephanie couldn't imagine how devastating it must have been for her once he was no longer keeping her drugged and she understood what he'd done.

"When did he stop drugging your mother? He did stop before the raid, didn't he?"

"Oh, yes, decades before," he assured her. "He stopped the drugs when she reached her fifth month of pregnancy with me and there were no signs of problems." He fell silent for a minute, and then said, "She gave birth to me in their bedroom on the island with only Maria to help her."

"The housekeeper?" Stephanie asked, trying to recall what Mirabeau and Eshe had told her about the two women.

"She started out as a housekeeper, but after my birth she became much more than that. She was a friend and companion to my mother, and a nanny and *tía* to me."

"*Tía* means aunt?" Stephanie asked, sure she'd read that somewhere.

"Yes."

Stephanie nodded and then asked, "Why did Maria have to help her? Where was your—Dressler?" she finished, just catching herself before she said *father.*

"Mother had locked him out of the room."

Stephanie's eyebrows rose at this news. But then she thought about it and decided that Thorne's mother had probably sorted out that something was wrong once he'd stopped drugging her. She had to have some memories of all the miscarriages. Aside from that, the time loss she'd suffered when he drugged her must have made her suspicious.

"So, that's the story of how I came to be," Thorne said, hopping off the bed and walking around to take the now empty glass from her. Removing the straw, he placed it in a fresh glass, and then handed it to her.

"Thank you for sharing that with me," Stephanie said solemnly as she took the glass. "But you still haven't explained why there was so little blood from that man trying to rip out your throat, and why your wound appears to be healing so quickly."

"Right." Thorne grimaced, but walked back around the bed, climbed in next to her again, and said, "The answer to that is in what I am."

"A really hot and sexy guy?" she asked lightly, hoping to jolly him out of the grimness that had suddenly dropped around him like a dark cloak.

Her words actually made his lips twitch, but then his expression became more serious and he said, "As I said, Dressler wanted what he considered the best traits for his new race of beings."

"Like wings?" she suggested, her gaze sliding to where the wings were neatly tucked away and pressed tight to his back.

"Yes. Apparently, he thought they would come in handy. I'm not sure how. It didn't say in his notes. Maybe he was thinking it would save money on airfare," he said sarcastically.

Stephanie chuckled at his words as she sucked blood up the straw.

"Eagles also have keen eyesight," Thorne commented. "He included the genetic makeup for that as well."

"And bat hearing," she said, recalling Thorne's comment when he'd heard her through her door.

"Yes. The human hearing range is between 20 and 20,000 hertz, but bats can hear frequencies up to

200,000 hertz. Obviously, he thought that would come in handy in this superior race."

Stephanie's eyes widened. She'd definitely not be saying anything she didn't want him to hear when he was around.

"But he also wanted strength to be a trait," Thorne said now.

"Oh! I know this one," Stephanie said excitedly.

Thorne raised his eyebrows. "Okay. What do you know?"

"He used dung beetle DNA for strength," she guessed, and explained, "I read they're the strongest animal in the world."

Thorne was grinning, but shook his head, and assured her, "Not the dung beetle. While you're right, and they are the strongest creature relative to their size, he decided to stick with animals rather than insects for that trait and went with the gorilla."

"Oh," Stephanie murmured.

Thorne raised his eyebrows. "You sound disappointed."

"Well, I kind of am," Stephanie admitted with a shrug as she set the now empty second glass on the side table and picked up the third. She transferred the straw to the new glass, and then turned back to admit, "I had a whole slew of poop jokes come to mind when I thought it might be dung beetle. Now they're just useless."

That startled a laugh from Thorne and he peered at her with disbelief. "Seriously? You'd make fun of my genetics?"

"Well, sure," she said as if that should be obvious. "I mean, if you had dung beetle DNA in you, how could anyone resist using that against you?"

Thorne gaped at her with disbelief for a moment as

she began to suck back her blood, and then said, "You're a heartless hussy, Ms. McGill."

Eyes widening, she let the straw pop out of her mouth and squealed, "Oooooh! I always wanted to be a hussy. And I can be . . . now that I'm not a twenty-seven-year-old virgin anymore. Thank you for that by the way."

"My pleasure," Thorne said wryly, and then, his expression becoming more serious, he asked, "Speaking of which, are you okay?"

"Oh yeah. It didn't even hurt," Stephanie assured him, and then added, "Dani said it was agony for her the first time, so I was expecting the worst, but it didn't hurt at all. Must be that life mate mojo," she said thoughtfully.

"Life mate mojo? Care to explain that to me?" he asked mildly.

Stephanie snorted at the suggestion. "No. Especially not when you still haven't explained your incredible healing abilities."

When he groaned, she commented, "You said something about the cockroach in you. Is that the answer? Is your ability to heal really because of cockroach DNA?"

"No," Thorne assured her, and then grimaced and added, "I don't know, but the consensus is no."

"The consensus?" she asked.

Thorne nodded. "Dani got ahold of as many of Dressler's notes on his experiments as she could in preparation for the operation we're hoping can be performed. But some of his notes were destroyed either by him or during the raid. Unfortunately, some of the ones about me were among the destroyed pages. What remained mentioned the eagle, the bat, the gorilla, and the axolotl. They think the axolotl is partially responsible for my healing abilities because they can regenerate their limbs and other body parts. But it doesn't explain the lack of bleeding even on serious injuries when I have them."

"The axolotl?" Stephanie said with confusion. "What is that?"

"It's sometimes called the Mexican Walking Fish, but it's really a salamander," he explained.

"And it can regenerate its limbs?"

Thorne nodded. "And some organs, I think. But like I said, that doesn't explain the lack of bleeding, so Rachel—she's a doctor friend of Dani's . . ." he explained.

"Yes. I know her. She's married to Marguerite's son, Etienne," Stephanie murmured.

"Right. Well, she suggested maybe Dressler included cockroach DNA, because they have hemolymphs that stop bleeding," he told her. "But Dani said that couldn't be, because cockroaches have an open circulatory system and I don't. So, she thinks dolphin DNA is more likely."

"Dolphin?" Stephanie asked with interest.

"Yes. Dolphins apparently heal quickly from shark bites with little evidence they're suffering pain from the wound. They're also resistant to infection, have some sort of protection against hemorrhaging, and she mentioned something about their wounds healing back to looking near normal or something." He shrugged. "Anyway, she thinks dolphin DNA was used."

Stephanie stared at him thoughtfully, recalling the moment when his attacker had basically ripped his throat open. Thorne hadn't screamed out in agony, or even appeared pained by the action. Dani might be on to something, she thought.

"So, there you have it," Thorne said now. "All we know about my genetics. I'm a freak. Only part human. The rest of me is a mix of several animals. In fact, I'm probably more animal than man."

His tone of voice made her eyes narrow slightly. Thorne sounded almost ashamed and somewhat depressed as he made that admission. She recognized those feelings and the self-loathing she suspected he felt for being what he was. It was exactly how she felt about being an Edentate and possible future no-fanger. For a moment, Stephanie didn't know what to say. She didn't see him as an animal or flawed. He was all man to her despite his wings, but she suspected saying that would have little effect. He wouldn't believe her, or he'd think she was just being kind. So, instead she said, "Alexa . . . play 'Closer' by Nine Inch Nails, please."

Thorne looked confused for a moment until the song started to play. Stilling, he listened to the words.

Stephanie watched the flicker of emotion cross his face and then the chorus started and he blinked, his eyes shooting to her. A smile tugging at his lips, he took her half-empty third glass and leaned over her to set it on the bedside table. His arm brushed her body as he did, setting it tingling.

"You're a naughty girl, Stephanie McGill," he rumbled as he then used his wings to lift himself and shift over her.

"I always wanted to be naughty," she whispered as his body came down on hers. As he began to kiss her, the song played on, certain lyrics burning themselves into her soul. "My whole existence is flawed . . . Isolation . . . you make me perfect . . . you are the reason I stay alive."

Stephanie suspected Thorne might be that for her. A reason to stay alive. She'd had very few of those these last nearly thirteen years. But she thought that could be different for her with Thorne here. It already was.

Ten

Thorne was placing the bacon and toast in the oven to keep warm when he heard the bathroom door close. Stephanie was up. Smiling faintly, he turned the burner down under the empty frying pan and walked over to start a cup of coffee going for her. He then went to retrieve the mocha creamer from the refrigerator, paused when his gaze landed on the bagged blood, and after a brief hesitation grabbed two bags of that as well.

Stephanie had only had two and a half glasses of blood that morning, each of the large glasses holding a pint. She probably needed more than that, so he quickly grabbed two glasses and the scissors he'd used to open the bacon package earlier. He then snipped the end off of one bag, let the contents pour into the glass, then did the same with the second.

The coffee was done spitting into the cup by the time

he'd finished with that and thrown out the empty bags, so he quickly fixed it with the one sugar and two splashes of creamer she liked before returning to his hot pan and the eggs he'd already broken. He was just beating them with a fork when Stephanie arrived in the kitchen. She was wearing a robe, and her hair was damp from what must have been a superquick shower.

"Good morning," she greeted, offering him a shy smile as she entered, and then chuckled wryly as she glanced to the window and saw the darkness outside. "Or good evening, I guess."

"Good evening," Thorne said with a smile, and then nodded toward the counter behind her where he'd lined up her coffee and the two glasses of blood. "There's coffee there for you, and blood too since you didn't finish it."

Her smile faded a little, but she sighed with resignation and picked up one of the glasses of blood first. She didn't use the straw he'd set out and that Dani had claimed she and Stephanie tended to use to drink it. Instead, Stephanie plugged her nose and gulped down the blood like she was chugging beer.

Stilling, Thorne watched her guzzle one glass of blood after the other. But when she then moved to the sink to rinse the glasses, he gave himself a shake, bestowed one last thrashing on the eggs, and poured them into the hot pan.

"You're making breakfast again. What happened to the one that you brought into the bedroom earlier?"

Thorne glanced toward Stephanie as she moved back to the counter to claim and drink from her coffee cup. "It was omelets, and they were hardening and turning color by the time I woke up so I decided it would be better to start again. But don't worry, I used the stuff from my own groceries both times."

Stephanie lowered her coffee cup and lifted surprised eyes to him. "You mean you went back to Harper and Drina's and brought back your own groceries?" she asked with disbelief, and when he nodded, she shook her head. "You didn't have to do that. You're welcome to anything here."

Thorne just shrugged. "Why can you and Dani not use your fangs to feed? Why do you have to drink the blood? Is it a genetic anomaly like Victor Argeneau and his son have?"

"You know about Uncle Victor and Vincent?" she asked with surprise.

"He was on the island," he reminded her. "They had to bring in blood donors for him to bite once he was free. They said bagged blood is no good to him. That he and his son both have to feed directly from a vein to get the nutrients they need."

"Yes," Stephanie murmured.

Thorne glanced up from the eggs he was stirring around the pan, and seeing that she was drinking her coffee and looking lost in thought, he prompted, "So is it something like that for you and Dani? A genetic anomaly? I mean, I know you can drink bagged blood, but why do you have to have it from a glass rather than drawing it up through your fangs?"

"Yes. It's a genetic anomaly kind of thing," Stephanie answered vaguely, and when Thorne glanced to her again in question, she set her coffee down and walked around the island to stand behind him.

"You look particularly scrumptious this morning, Mr. Salter," she murmured, sliding her arms around him from behind.

"Are you trying to avoid answering my question?" Thorne asked, stiffening as his body immediately responded to her nearness and touch. Desire was rushing up through him like a warm wave of need, and he was sure she was doing this deliberately to distract him . . . But it felt so damned good.

"Of course not," Stephanie whispered by his ear before nipping at it, sending a sharp shiver of pleasure through him. "But I can think of better things to do with my mouth than talking."

Thorne sucked in a sharp breath as one of her hands slid from his waist, down to cup his groin through the jeans he'd changed into when he'd gone to fetch the food. Not just his cock, but his whole body stiffened under the caress when she squeezed him through the heavy cloth.

"Stephanie," he growled in warning, his breath already reduced to shallow pants. "I'm cooking here."

"So am I," she assured him throatily. "You make me so hot."

Thorne groaned and leaned his head back as she pressed more firmly on the growing erection pushing against his jeans.

"I've never given a blow job before, Thorne," she confessed a little breathlessly as she continued to squeeze and caress him through his jeans. Then her other hand moved down to unsnap the button at his waist, and undo his zipper before she added, "I think I'd like to give you one."

"Oh God," Thorne moaned as her hand slid into his

pants and closed around his erection, then drew it out into the open air.

"You should probably turn off the range," Stephanie gasped, excitement clear in her voice as she stroked him.

Cursing, Thorne did better than that. Not only did he turn off the stove, but he then knocked Stephanie's hand away from his cock and turned to scoop her up and set her on the island. He heard the egg bowl and some other paraphernalia hit the floor as he slid her onto the countertop, and didn't care. All he could think of was claiming her, taking her there on the island, feeling her hot, wet heat encompassing his hard cock and her body warm and trembling as he gave her pleasure.

Stepping between her legs, he tugged her robe open, and was immediately on her like a ravening animal, his hands and mouth trying to explore every nook and cranny at once as she fell back to lie on the cold countertop. She was hot and so responsive, her body writhing beneath his caresses, and her moans bringing on his own as just giving her pleasure caused the same white-hot excitement he knew she was feeling to course through him.

Thorne almost came without ever entering her, but caught himself at the last moment and straightened to thrust into her so that he could feel her body pulse and squeeze him as they both found their pleasure.

Stephanie woke up slowly, a satisfied smile curving her lips as she stretched in the bed. She felt marvelous, sated . . . Damn, sex is awesome, she thought, and opened her eyes.

Sunlight was creeping around the vertical blinds

covering the sliding doors in her bedroom. She smiled at the sight and then glanced to the side, her smile not shrinking one bit when she saw that she was alone in the bed. While Thorne had been there the first two times she'd woken after they were intimate, he hadn't been there the last three. Instead, he'd been in the kitchen. Two of those times she'd found him making breakfast that they'd yet to eat. That was three breakfasts they'd let go to waste so far, she thought; the omelet he'd brought into the bedroom, the bacon and eggs she'd found him making the first time she'd gone out to the kitchen, and French toast the second time she'd found him there.

The third time she'd found Thorne in the kitchen, he hadn't bothered to start breakfast. He'd had coffee waiting, though, that she hadn't finished before they were rolling around on the floor, ripping each other's clothes off.

Stephanie felt kind of bad about that. She really loved sex with Thorne, but she had other needs to, and would have liked to have had some of the omelet, or the bacon and eggs. She definitely would have liked to try the French toast, but Thorne kept asking questions she didn't want to answer, and the only way Stephanie could think to waylay uncomfortable conversations was through sex. It was certainly effective. It took very little effort to lure Thorne into forsaking his questions and having sex. Which was a good thing because inexperienced as she was, Stephanie had no idea how to be subtle about it. Hell, the last time around, he'd asked his question and she'd simply stood up, removed her robe, and then planted herself in his lap.

Her smile faded a little as she recalled the flicker of disappointment and even a hint of anger that had crossed

Thorne's face before he'd given in and kissed her then. It made Stephanie think she wasn't fooling him at all, and he knew what she was doing every time she jumped him like that. But she didn't know what else to do. She couldn't explain what she was to him. How did you tell your life mate that you were a monster? It would have been bad enough if she were an immortal. Accepting that was expecting a lot of someone, but an Edentate, and possible future no-fanger?

"God in heaven," Stephanie breathed, closing her eyes. She couldn't accept what she'd become. How could she expect him to?

Of course, Stephanie knew she'd have to tell him eventually if she wanted them to be life mates, but . . . Well, he might be a possible life mate to her, and yes, the sex was hot and amazing, and yes, she liked him. Hell, even Trixie and Felix liked him. But—

"It's so scary," she whispered, opening her eyes.

What if she asked him to be her life mate and he said no? Or what if he said yes, and then realized later that he couldn't bear living with a blood-drinking might-someday-become-a-no-fanger gal? Or even worse, what if he said yes and then died having this operation he was here for?

What if she let herself love him and he didn't love her back?

What if he broke her heart? Stephanie didn't think she could bear that.

Stephanie had suffered and endured a lot since that fateful day she and Dani had been snatched from the grocery store parking lot in cottage country. But she didn't know if she could handle falling in love with Thorne and then losing him or watching him turn away from her in disgust. Either eventuality might be what pushed her over the edge into madness.

The clack of doggy nails on hardwood followed by a whine announced Trixie's arrival seconds before the boxer leapt up on the bed and proceeded to lick her face energetically.

"Oh! No! Trixie, stop!" Stephanie protested on a laugh, her dark thoughts disappearing at once under the boxer's loving. She tried to push the big dog off, only to have Trixie scoot right back to her, so she said, "I'm getting up. I'm getting up."

Trixie stopped licking her then and leapt off the bed with a bark, then walked around to her side of the bed and barked again.

Shaking her head, Stephanie pushed off the sheet and weighted blanket and slid her feet to the floor. "Fine. I'm coming. Thank you for stopping Mommy from becoming a pathetic, maudlin lump. Now let me get dressed and we'll go out and see Thorne," she said, urging the dog out of the way so that she could get to the closet.

The last time Stephanie saw her robe, it was lying in a crumpled mass on the kitchen floor where she'd dropped it. Which was also where she and Thorne had ended up finishing what she'd started, and where they'd passed out. He had apparently carried her to bed when he woke up, just as he had done all three times she'd seduced him in the kitchen. The other two times he'd brought her robe back with her, though, and laid it across the end of the bed. This time, he hadn't. She'd have to dress.

"Probably a good thing, because I need food," Stephanie muttered to herself as she opened the closet door and considered what she should wear. "I guess I'll have to think of another way to avoid answering questions this time. At least until I've had something to eat."

She considered her clothing options briefly, and then thinking she should probably take Trixie for a walk before the dog got destructive out of boredom, Stephanie asked Alexa what the weather was like outside thinking that would help her decide what to wear. Her eyes widened incredulously when she heard the answer, fifty-eight degrees Fahrenheit and overcast.

They'd gone from hot to cold. But then it was May, she reminded herself with a shake of her head. The weather always bounced around in May.

Giving up any idea of a dress or shorts, Stephanie grabbed a pair of jeans and a T-shirt, then walked around to her dresser for underwear and a bra before heading out of her room and straight into the bathroom.

Ten minutes and a quick shower and brush of her hair and teeth later, Stephanie made her way out to the kitchen with a smile that faded to confusion when she found it empty.

"Where's Thorne?" she asked the room at large as she glanced around. She then looked down into the Muskoka room at the front of the house. When Stephanie didn't see him there, she crossed the kitchen to her office and peered in there, but it was empty too.

Turning, she found Trixie standing at the mouth of the kitchen, eyeing her expectantly and tail wagging. As soon as the boxer saw her looking, she walked to the door.

"Sorry. Do you have to go outside?" Stephanie asked, following the dog, but in the back of her mind she was thinking maybe Trixie was leading her to Thorne, and she followed her to the door and out after opening it. But Trixie merely headed onto the lawn, and began sniffing around for a place to relieve herself.

Sighing her disappointment, Stephanie rubbed her arms against the morning's chill and glanced around as she waited, but her mind was on Thorne and why he wasn't there. She'd got so used to his being there when she woke up that his absence was . . . well, she was disappointed, depressed, afraid. Did this mean he'd lost interest?

Stephanie recalled the disappointment and anger that had flashed on his face the last time she'd seduced him rather than answer his questions, and bit her lip. Was he angry at her?

He'd told her all about himself, even the different DNA used to make him, but she hadn't really told him much in return.

That thought made Stephanie frown as she realized that basically he'd given her a medical rundown of his genetics. He hadn't really told her about himself. Not *really*. For instance, she had no idea why he would want his wings cut off. He hadn't even admitted to her that that was the reason he was here in Canada. He'd merely mentioned "the operation we're hoping can be performed." Who was the *we*?

But that was only one of the things she didn't know about him. She also didn't have any idea what his life was like on that island now that it was Dressler-free. Or if he wanted to live there forever, or would consider moving somewhere else, like Canada, maybe.

In fact, while Thorne knew she was a writer, Stephanie didn't even know what he did for a living. If he worked. His mother apparently had lots of money. Did he live off of that? Or had he found some way to fill his days and make an income?

The more Stephanie thought about it, the more she decided he had no right to be mad at her for avoiding his questions. He wasn't exactly overwhelming her with information either.

On the other hand, Stephanie thought unhappily, if she hoped to have a relationship with him and claim him as her life mate they'd need to really talk. She'd need to tell him everything. Including what she was.

Part of the problem with that, though, was that Stephanie wasn't sure what she was anymore. For years she'd been terrified that she was halfway between an Edentate and a no-fanger and likely to slip into full no-fanger at any moment. The constant barrage of voices in her head had been that bad. But now those voices had gone silent. Did that mean that her mind had fought off the no-fanger like a mortal body would fight off a virus? Or was this like the calm before a storm, and when that storm hit, she'd go full-on no-fanger?

Stephanie needed to know that before she could even consider a relationship with Thorne. As her disappointment at his absence this morning proved, she already liked him too much, and was starting to care for and even depend on him. Stephanie didn't think it would be fair to drag him into her life if she was about to become a sick monster like Leonius Livius.

But how was she supposed to figure that out? Stephanie considered that as she watched Trixie search for the perfect potty spot, and the only thing she could come up with was that she had to go be around mortals. She had to see if she would hear their voices when she was actually in their presence. Maybe the sudden silence was just her mind finally learning how to block the voices. Maybe it had just taken her longer than it took most people.

"Yeah, sure. Nearly thirteen years of almost crazy and you're suddenly good," Stephanie muttered derisively, but then sighed and pushed the negative thoughts out. She had to do something. She couldn't just live in this state of semistress forever, waiting to see what would happen next. It was time to be proactive.

Trixie's nudging her hand drew her gaze down to the dog and she managed a smile. "All done? Let's go inside, then. It's cold out here and Mommy has to grab a coat and go into town."

Thorne watched Stephanie lead Trixie back inside her house, and then straightened from the monitor he'd been glued to since returning to Drina and Harper's house.

He'd woken up this morning, after their last sex session, feeling . . . well, frankly he wasn't sure how he'd felt. Dirty? Used? Basically, just bad. It was obvious that Stephanie wasn't willing to share anything of herself with him except her body. Every time he'd asked a question of her, she'd evaded, avoided, or just plain distracted him with sex. The damned woman hadn't even been subtle about it the last time. He'd asked what a life mate was and she'd just stripped off her robe, jumped in his lap, and rubbed on him all naked and warm and sweet-smelling.

Thorne felt himself go hard just at the memory, which pissed him off. He loved sex with Stephanie. It was amazing, incredible, addictive even . . . and he couldn't stand it for all those same reasons. Because though he'd asked her what a life mate was, Thorne already knew the answer.

While Thorne's relationships with the immortal women on the island had been mostly about sex, he had done some talking with them. Moira, one of the women he'd spent time with, had been a widow who had actually found her life mate, enjoyed two hundred years with him, and then had lost him in a house fire four hundred years ago. Even after all those centuries she had wept when Thorne had done something that had reminded her of her mate. He'd immediately apologized for offending her, though he hadn't known how he might have. At which point she'd assured him that he hadn't offended her, that he'd simply reminded her of her deceased life mate in that moment. She'd then explained what life mates were to immortals, and the signs that an immortal had met one.

She'd mentioned a renewed interest in different passions, such as eating and sex for older immortals who had lost their interest in such things. Which, of course, did not include Stephanie. She was too young to have lost those interests. Moira, though, had also said life mates couldn't read or control each other. That was a little trickier since most immortals couldn't read or control him anyway, and he didn't have the ability to read or control others. But it was the last two symptoms she'd told him about that did mean something to him. Moira had said that life mates shared dreams, and shared pleasure during sex, and she'd said that sharing that pleasure was so overwhelming that they had a tendency to faint on orgasm.

Thorne hadn't shared any dreams with Stephanie that

he knew of, but he'd definitely experienced the shared pleasure. Every time he'd touched or caressed her, he'd felt excitement and pleasure shoot through his own body as if he was the one being caressed. And he'd definitely fainted at the end of each sexual experience. As he'd said to Stephanie, like a Victorian virgin. He knew that meant he was a possible life mate to her. But when he'd asked her about life mates, she hadn't admitted he was hers. Instead, she'd avoided talking about it.

Just as she avoided talking about why she had to drink blood rather than take it in through her fangs as other immortals did. That one he didn't already know the answer to. He'd been curious when Dani had mentioned that her and her sister's reluctance to feed was because they had to actually drink it. But he hadn't felt it was his business to ask her about it. With Stephanie, though, he'd asked, and it was she who apparently felt it was none of his business, because she hadn't been willing to tell him.

And that told Thorne all he needed to know. Stephanie was happy enough to screw him silly for as long as he was here, but she wasn't interested in claiming him as a life mate.

In his heart of hearts, Thorne feared that was because of what he was. That despite what she said, and that she seemed to accept him, she really saw him as less than human because of his DNA. And he couldn't even blame her for it.

If it didn't hurt so much, he'd laugh at the irony. Here he'd been the one worried that she might get too attached and get hurt when he left. But he was the one hurting, because he'd fallen for her hard and fast. He'd even started to consider how to prolong their relationship. Thinking perhaps he could convince his mother and Maria to live in Canada. Or maybe he could convince Stephanie to make the island their home base. If she was as immune to the thoughts of hybrids as everyone else, living there should be a good place for her. There were only a handful of immortals on the island now, still helping, still keeping an eye out for Dressler's possible return. But he could send them away if necessary.

Thorne had had all sorts of crazy thoughts on how to make a relationship with Stephanie work. It was all he'd thought about every time he'd woken up before her. He'd spent the time waiting for her to wake up, cooking and considering how they could work things to be together. He'd even considered not risking the operation he'd come here for . . . Until he'd realized she wasn't interested in extending their relationship to a lifetime. Then all he'd wanted was to get away from her and lick his wounds. In fact, he'd wanted to leave the moment he'd woken up in her bed that last time. Thorne had known that if Stephanie woke up before he got away, he was weak enough that all she'd have to do was smile or touch him and he'd be lost to another round of passion.

So, he'd got up, got dressed, and started out of the house. But then he'd recalled the bastard who had hacked into her system once already, and then had climbed the fence yesterday and tried again, attacking him when Thorne confronted him. He'd been worried about the fact that he couldn't lock the door behind him on the way out. What if the bastard returned while he was gone and she was sleeping? If he knew that hacking wasn't going to work anymore, he might move on to something else. Kidnapping and hurting Stephanie, for instance.

That possibility had kept him from leaving. At least

until he'd heard Stephanie talking to Trixie. Knowing then that she was up, Thorne had slipped from the house and come back here to watch the monitor. He'd been relieved when he'd seen Stephanie let Trixie out. At least he'd known she would be able to lock the door when she went back in and could defend herself if the creep who had climbed the fence yesterday returned.

Had it really only been yesterday evening? Thorne asked himself with a frown. It felt like days, or even weeks, had passed since he'd been injured and first made love to Stephanie. A lifetime.

Movement on the camera caught his eye and he stiffened and focused on it, half expecting to see the creep climbing the fence again. He was not expecting to see the garage door of Stephanie's house opening and her red SUV pulling out.

What the hell was she thinking? Thorne wondered with alarm. She shouldn't be going anywhere. Not when some crazy stalker immortal was out there.

Cursing, he straightened and headed for the door.

Eleven

Stephanie nearly had a heart attack when a big flying beast suddenly dropped out of the sky and landed in the driveway in front of her car. Slamming on the brakes, she stared wide-eyed for a moment, her mind slow to recognize that the huge winged animal she was looking at was Thorne. It was the wings. They were freaking huge! Stretching a good ten or twelve feet to either side of him. She'd never seen them open before. He always kept them tightly bunched up on his back. She'd had no idea they were so large.

Once she realized it was him, Stephanie dropped back in the driver's seat and simply stared. He was positively stunning. Majestic. The most beautiful man she'd ever seen, and he was speaking to her. Stephanie realized that when she stopped ogling his pretty wings and his muscular body in the tight jeans and T-shirt he was wearing, and shifted her gaze to his face where his lips were moving.

Leaning forward, she turned off the SUV's radio and then pushed the button to lower her window and leaned her head out to ask, "Were you saying something? I couldn't hear you over the radio."

Exasperation crossing his face, Thorne drew his wings in and she watched with fascination as they shrank away behind his back to rest neatly there.

"Awesome," she breathed with wonder, and honestly had no idea where all that wing went. How did it lay so flat to his back like that?

"Stephanie."

"Hmm?" She forced her avid gaze from his shoulders where she could just see a hint of the tops of his wings. Only a hairbreadth on the top of each shoulder, really. So little showed that they were noticeable only because they were dark brown while his T-shirt—no doubt another item of clothing missing most of its back and Velcroed on—was white. Focusing on his face, and ignoring the way his fists were propped on his hips like some father from the fifties, Stephanie asked, "Were you saying something?"

"I asked you where you thought you were going," Thorne informed her in a growl.

Stephanie raised her eyebrows at his tone, but said, "To the grocery store."

Thorne's scowl faded at once, replaced with concern. "Did they forget something in your delivery? What do you need, sweetheart? If I have it, it's yours."

Feeling her heart get all mushy at those words, Stephanie smiled at him, but said, "No, they didn't forget anything. I might pick up a few things while I'm there, but mostly I just want to go read . . . Cory, the delivery guy," she finished after a hesitation. She could hardly tell him that she just wanted to read anyone and every- one she encountered to see if she still could. But reading Cory was a good idea anyway. That way she could find out if he'd given out her address to anyone. Maybe. The man with the black box had been immortal. He might not have asked Cory questions at all. He could have just read his mind.

"Read the delivery guy?" Thorne asked. His eyebrows drew down together and he shook his head. "No."

"Excuse you?" Stephanie said with amazement. "Did you just tell me no?"

"It's not worth the risk," he said firmly. "You have a stalker out there somewhere, and he's proven he has no problem with violence. Now that he knows you have protection here, and he can't get in to hack your system again, he might pull an Annie Wilkes and kidnap you or something."

"He's not going to kidnap me in the middle of the grocery store," Stephanie said with exasperation, and then assured him, "I'll drive straight there and straight back."

"No. I can't let you do that," Thorne said determinedly, crossing his arms over his chest and glaring at her.

"You're not the boss of me," Stephanie snapped with outraged disbelief. "You don't get to tell me where I can or can't go."

"Maybe not, but I can stand here and refuse to move so you can't go anywhere," he countered, and then added with solemn apology in his voice, "It's for your own good. You know it's not safe to go out alone. If you had someone else with you, fine. But not alone."

Stephanie glowered at him resentfully, mostly because now that he'd mentioned the creep who had tried to hack her and had attacked him, she was recognizing that going out alone might be a bit risky. And she should have thought of that. But much as she hated to admit it, in her upset over her inability to hear anyone anymore and what it meant, she'd completely forgotten about her stalker guy.

That was what infatuation, sex, and disappointment over being abandoned by said "infatuate" and sexual partner did for you, Stephanie thought grimly. It stole your good sense.

On the other hand, she really needed to sort out why there was suddenly this silence in her head, Stephanie decided. And then what he'd said made her straighten in the driver's seat and she said abruptly, "Fine. I won't go alone. Come with me."

"Me?" he asked with amazement.

"Do you see anyone else around here who can go with me?" she asked dryly.

Thorne scowled and then raised his arms and his wings. "You know I can't do that. I can't ride in cars. I can't sit on my wings. And even if I could, I can't go out where anyone might see my wings."

Stephanie considered the problem briefly, wondering if telling everyone they encountered that it was a Halloween costume might work. She decided that was doubtful, especially since it was May. And then she smiled as another idea came to mind.

"Fine," she said, turning off the engine and gathering her purse. Getting out, Stephanie closed and locked the SUV doors and walked past him, headed for Drina and Harper's house. "Come with me."

When she didn't hear him follow her right away, Stephanie glanced over her shoulder and barked, "Seriously, come on. Or I'll just run to town on foot. If I use immortal speed, it should only take five minutes or so to get there."

He followed her then, but cursed as he did it and didn't look happy at the doing.

"What are you up to?" Thorne growled with suspicion as he followed her across the living room of Harper and Drina's house a moment later and toward the hall to the bedrooms. "Seducing me again won't get me to let you leave. I'm trying to keep you safe."

"I'm not *up to* anything," Stephanie assured him, and then added grimly, "And I certainly wouldn't try to seduce you. I wouldn't want to wake up alone again wondering what I did that was so wrong that you'd leave without a goodbye or even a note scribbled on the memo pad on the corner of the island."

Thorne felt himself wince at her words, but then scowled and gave her some truth as he followed her into the hall. "Well, honestly I didn't think you'd care. The fact that you weren't willing to tell me anything about yourself suggested you weren't interested in a relationship, just a fling, and flings don't leave notes when they leave in the morning."

Much to his amazement, she gave a short laugh at that and said, "Oh, because you shared so much about yourself?"

"I told you everything about me," he said, outraged that she would suggest otherwise. It seemed to him he was the only one who had done any real talking at all. All she'd done was ask questions.

"You told me everything about your *genetics*," Stephanie snapped, pausing to open the door to the master bedroom. "I'm great if I need to know your medical background for anything, but I know absolutely nothing about you the man."

"That's not true," Thorne said at once, but frowned and slowed down even as he said it as he started to run through their conversations in his head.

"Oh?" Stephanie asked as she headed into the bedroom. "Aside from your genetic makeup, I know that you live on an island in Venezuela with your mother and your *tía* Maria. That you were homeschooled by them. That you like to read, and that you watch movies once a week," she listed off as she crossed to the door to the walk-in closet.

Disappearing inside, she added, "But I knew everything but the reading part before I'd ever even met you. And what I don't know is what you do for a career, or if you even have one. If you have a pet or friends on that island. What kind of movies you enjoy . . ." Pausing, she came to the door of the walk-in closet and tossed what looked like a cream-colored sweatshirt at him.

"Put that on," Stephanie ordered before disappearing back into the closet. "I know you've read *Misery*, but is that because you enjoy horrors? Or just because it was one of the books sent by the book of the month club? And you haven't even told me that you're here to have your wings amputated, let alone why you would want to do something so ridiculous. But, oh yes, I'm the one not communicating," she said heavily before appearing in the doorway again, this time carrying a long leather coat similar to the one she was wearing. Both of them were the same color, which matched his wings, Thorne noted with interest, and then his gaze shifted to her face and he saw that Stephanie was compressing her lips with irritation as she realized that he was standing there just holding the sweatshirt. "You haven't put the hoodie on."

"It has a back," he said stiffly.

"I had noticed," she said dryly. "Put it on, please."

Thorne scowled at her, but shifted the cloth around to stick his arms through the sleeves and then yanked it on over his head. He didn't pull it down over his wings, though.

Clucking with irritation, Stephanie laid the leather coat on the foot of the bed and walked over to him to begin tugging the large shirt down his back over his wings. "There's something else I didn't know. That you can't dress yourself."

"I can dress myself," he growled, taking over pulling down the sweatshirt with a hood. "But this shirt covers my wings. I don't wear clothing that restricts my wings. It's uncomfortable."

"So are bras, but we women have to wear them every day, so suck it up, buttercup," Stephanie growled right back as she walked over to collect the leather coat.

Thorne was still gaping at her when she returned with the long leather coat. Ignoring that, she held it out.

"Put it on."

"Why?" he asked from between clenched teeth.

"Because you're going to town with me and this will hide your wings," she said quietly, all of the heat seeming to have slid out of her after her rant of moments ago.

Thorne hesitated, but recalling her saying she'd run to town on foot if necessary, and not wanting her out there on her own with a stalker around, he gave in and tugged on the long leather coat, but didn't do it up, and said, "This isn't going to work."

"Isn't it?" she asked quietly, looking him over. Shifting her gaze to his head, she said, "You need to pull the hood on."

Sighing, Thorne yanked the hoodie out from under the coat's collar now laying heavily against his wings, and pulled it over his head. The moment he did, Stephanie nodded, a small smile tugging at her lips.

"Take a look," she suggested, waving toward the walk-in closet.

Eyebrows rising, Thorne walked around her to the door to the walk-in closet. He was surprised to see a full-length mirror on the wall opposite the door, but even more surprised to see his reflection. With the hoodie covering the small white feathers on his head, and the long coat covering his wings—

"I look normal," he said with awe.

"Yet still sexy as hell," Stephanie said almost resentfully, and then sighed. "Come on. We can take your motorcycle."

Thorne watched her go and then turned to look at himself again in the mirror. Like Pinocchio, he'd always wanted to be a real boy while growing up. Now he looked like one and didn't have to wear a motorcycle helmet to do it.

"Thorne?"

"Coming," he said, and turned away from the seemingly human-looking male staring back at him to follow Stephanie out to the garage.

It took some maneuvering to get them both on the motorcycle. In fact, at first Thorne didn't think they could do it. To ride together, he had to set his wings so that they rested on either side of Stephanie's outer legs behind him, but the coat, a leather duster, was not split up the center in the back, so caught on her and bunched up there. It left the ends of his wings exposed on either side of her legs . . . until Stephanie undid her own long leather duster, and shifted it to rest over the ends of his wings.

Thorne had worried that the material of her coat would shift or be blown off his wings during the ride, but she'd assured him that wouldn't happen, and they'd set off.

Thorne had a motorbike on the island. It had belonged to one of Dressler's men, and was left behind after the raid. He'd appropriated it and had used it to boot around the island when he was in a hurry, or just jaunted around on it for fun. And, of course, he'd ridden down here from Toronto on a motorcycle Marguerite and Julius had arranged for him to use. But he'd never had a passenger on a motorcycle before. He liked it, at least with Stephanie, but it was sweet torture, having her arms around his waist and her upper body pressed to his back. For some reason it made him think of what she'd said, and he again pondered her accusation that he hadn't told her much about himself.

Now that he was considering it, Thorne realized it was true. He hadn't told her about his interests, or . . . well, anything other than his genetic makeup. Which was rather shocking when he thought of it. He'd spent his whole life wishing to be seen as more than Dressler's experiment, and yet that was most of what he'd told her about himself.

In truth, by that scale, he did know more about Stephanie than she knew about him. Thorne not only knew where she lived, but had been there. He knew she was a writer. That she had a dog and a cat that she spoiled rotten. He knew she had friends that she considered family, like Drina and Harper, Beau, and a whole host of others she'd mentioned. He knew she was lonely but very independent.

He also knew that she could get demanding and even snarky when the situation called for it, Thorne thought as he recalled her snapping at him that bras were uncomfortable too but women wore them every day, so suck it up . . . buttercup? He still couldn't believe she'd said that. But then he supposed he'd deserved it. He'd been acting like a petulant child, complaining that he didn't like wearing things that restricted his wings.

Although that was true, Thorne thought now. He had always hated covering his wings. It was why his mother and Maria had begun making him clothes that didn't cover them and had to be Velcroed around him. It wasn't just a matter of preference, though. He had a deep-seated aversion to it, and suspected it was an ingrained kind of thing. A bird unable to use its wings was as good as dead when survival meant being able to take flight at an instant's notice. But it wasn't the first time he'd had his wings covered like this, and wouldn't be the last. It was also good practice for him. It would allow him to see what life might be like without his wings.

The ride to the grocery store didn't take long. It was finding somewhere to park that was an ordeal. Stephanie refused several spots he suggested, including one directly in front of the grocery store. She had him circle the small block that made up the tiny town three times before settling on a spot at the back of a parking lot behind the town's only bank. It was down the street from the grocery store and there were at least three other spots on the street itself that were closer. Thorne didn't understand why she insisted on parking so far away and in such an isolated spot until she got off the motorcycle first and his tail feathers were briefly on view.

He didn't comment, but quickly dismounted himself and made sure his coat had dropped to cover his wings again before they set out up the street. They walked in silence, Thorne's gaze sliding over everything and everyone they passed, drinking it all in. When Stephanie turned into the grocery store, he followed her in and then froze, his senses overwhelmed with all the new sights and sounds.

While he'd seen grocery stores in movies, Thorne had never actually been in one before. It was different than seeing them on a television screen. This one, with no more than six or eight short aisles, seemed a lot smaller than the ones in movies where there appeared to be dozens of very long aisles. Here there were also people, sounds, and a certain ambience that you didn't feel watching movies. There were also smells, he noticed, and closed his eyes as he separated the different aromas assaulting him. Thorne could smell fruit, spices, and . . . dead meat.

"Thorne? Are you coming?"

Opening his eyes, he glanced around to see Stephanie looking back at him with curiosity from halfway up this first aisle.

Nodding, he moved forward, his gaze sliding over the fruits and vegetables stacked up on either side of him as he passed.

"So, how do we find Cory?" Thorne asked once he'd reached Stephanie's side.

"It's a small store," she said with a shrug. "We can just wander around until we spot him."

Thorne nodded, his gaze moving to the blueberries beside her. Thinking that he had a recipe for blueberry and lemon scones that Stephanie might like, he suggested, "Maybe I should get a cart. In case there's something we want to buy."

"How would we get groceries back to the house on the motorcycle?" Stephanie asked, looking dubious at the prospect.

"Right," Thorne murmured, but thought they should be able to manage one lemon and a container of blueberries. He had the rest of the ingredients for his scones back at the house. Nodding to himself, he picked up one of the little green cartons of blueberries, and then hurried back toward the front of the store to collect a lemon as well.

When he then turned back toward Stephanie, she had continued walking, shaking her head as she went. But he knew she wouldn't be shaking her head when she tasted his scones.

Thorne had nearly caught up to Stephanie again when the fruits and vegetables gave way to dairy for the back half of this first aisle and his gaze landed on the eggs. Thanks to making three breakfasts that had never been eaten, Thorne had gone through nearly the entire carton of eggs Dani had ordered delivered to him the day he arrived.

Just yesterday, Thorne realized with a little shake of the head.

He decided he really should replace the eggs, or he'd be without for the better part of a week until the next delivery. Stopping, Thorne picked up a carton and set it in the crook of his arm and then looked around for Stephanie. She was no longer in the aisle. Hurrying to the end, he turned the corner and then glanced down the next aisle, relaxing when he saw her about halfway down, talking to a female employee.

Assuming Stephanie was probably asking where Cory was, Thorne walked up beside her just as the store employee said, "It's in aisle four on the top shelf. I can show y—"

Her words cut off abruptly when Stephanie reached out and touched her arm. At first, Thorne thought the girl was just startled, but then he noted that her expression was now blank, and when he looked at Stephanie he saw the concentration on her face and knew that she was reading and controlling the girl.

Thorne had barely realized that when Stephanie apparently released the young woman and she turned and walked away.

He heard Stephanie let out a slow breath as she watched the girl go, and turned to look at her, surprised to see confusion and worry on her expression. Concerned, he asked, "Did she know something about our hacker?"

Stephanie glanced at him sharply, obviously surprised to find him at her side. But then shook her head and continued down the aisle, her expression unreadable.

Thorne followed slowly, his gaze considering. It remained that way over the next twenty minutes as he picked up things here and there and watched her stop, touch, read, and control every other person she passed in the store. Not just employees, she was reading shoppers too. Her expression just grew more unsettled and confused with each person she did that to, and it seemed obvious she wasn't finding whatever she was looking for . . . Which Thorne was quite sure was not Cory the delivery guy. Stephanie was searching for something. He just didn't know what.

"Thank you."

Stephanie glanced up with surprise at Thorne when he said that as he held the door for her to exit the grocery store. Smiling wryly, she pointed out, "I'm the one who's supposed to say that when you hold the door. Not you. And thank *you*."

"You're welcome. But I meant for bringing me here," Thorne said quietly as he let the door close behind them and they started down the street back toward the bank.

Stephanie eyed the *four* bags of groceries he'd purchased and shook her head. "You won't be thanking me when you're trying to sort out how to fit the groceries on the motorcycle."

"I'll manage," he assured her, and then hesitated before admitting, "I didn't mean for taking me to the grocery store to shop. I meant—I've never been in a grocery store before," he blurted, and then added wryly, "Actually, I've never been anywhere. And I've never even been able to walk around in a town before like this. It's been . . . nice."

Stephanie stopped walking and stared at Thorne blankly as his words registered. He'd never been in a grocery store. He'd never walked the streets of a town. He'd never been *anywhere*. She knew she should have realized that would be the case, and Stephanie supposed in some part of her mind she had, but she hadn't really thought about it, or what it meant, and hearing him say the words was just heartbreaking.

Swallowing, she glanced back to the tiny grocery store they'd just left, and then around the street. Her town didn't have a grocery store, just a post office, coffee shop, and corner store as he'd pointed out the other day. But this town, with a bank, a corner store, a small hardware store, a liquor store, a furniture store, two small mom-and-pop restaurants, and its tiny grocery store all crowded on both sides of one short street, was only about ten minutes away from her home and at least more populated. Which is why she'd come here rather than the smaller village she lived in.

But even this town seemed a pathetic place to take Thorne for his first and possibly only outing among other people. Because it might be his only outing if the operation he wanted wasn't viable. Of course, if it was, and Dani could remove his wings, he could go wherever he liked. But if not, he'd return to his island in Venezuela and live like a hermit, never seeing anyone who wasn't already a part of his life, and never visiting grocery stores, or walking small town streets, or . . .

"Come with me." Grabbing his arm, Stephanie urged him to the curb, glanced quickly both ways, then ushered him across the street and into one of the storefronts.

Twelve

"What are we doing here?" Thorne asked quietly when Stephanie stopped just inside the door she'd dragged him through to allow her eyes to adjust to the dimmer interior.

"This is a diner," Stephanie explained, eyeing the available tables. Spotting a booth along the wall, she caught his arm and tugged him behind her as she crossed the small, cramped space. Stephanie let go of Thorne so that she could slide in one side, expecting him to move around and slide in the other. She was halfway across the seat before she realized he was just standing there.

Stephanie was about to ask what the problem was when it clicked for her. He couldn't sit on his wings. Cursing, she quickly slid back out and looked around again. There was an empty table in the center with actual chairs around it, but that wouldn't do either. He couldn't rest his wings on either side of the chair without risking the open coat separating and showing his wings. She was just about to panic, thinking this had been a mistake, when Thorne took her arm and began to urge her toward the back of the restaurant.

They were nearly to the sitting counter at the back before she noticed the two bar stools that were empty. They were the old-fashioned kind that were covered with red faux leather and spun on their metal base. Letting out a breath of relief, Stephanie took a seat once they reached the stools and watched Thorne negotiate the seat himself. She was concerned he'd have an issue, but instead of sitting down from in front as she had done, he stopped behind the stool and swung one leg around it, sat, and drew his other leg around.

"Impressive," Stephanie said with a faint smile.

"I'm not just a pretty face," he told her.

That surprised a laugh out of her, and then she turned as a waitress approached on the other side of the counter. She was petite and seventy years old at least, but she still held a hint of the beauty she must have been when younger. Her name tag read Lauren.

"Hello, folks. Can I interest you in the breakfast special? Or should I fetch you menus?" Lauren asked, smiling at them cheerfully.

"What's the breakfast special?" Stephanie asked.

"Toast, two pancakes, hash browns, two eggs any way you like 'em, and a choice of bacon, sausage, or ham," she listed off quickly, and then grinned. "And coffee, of course. Or tea if you prefer."

"I'll have the special," Stephanie decided.

"So will I," Thorne agreed.

"Okay, bacon, sausage, or ham?" she asked Stephanie.

"Sausage, eggs over easy, and coffee," Stephanie answered, listing all her preferences.

Nodding, the waitress turned to Thorne. "And you, handsome?"

Thorne smiled faintly. "Sausage, eggs sunny-side-up, and coffee, please, Lauren."

"Ah, good looks, that accent, and manners too," Lauren said with a shake of the head and then told Stephanie, "He's a keeper," before hurrying off.

Stephanie watched the woman go and then turned to Thorne to see him grinning at her.

"I'm a keeper," he announced with a grin.

"Yes, you are," Stephanie said solemnly.

Thorne blinked at her serious tone, and then glanced to Lauren as she returned with two steaming cups of coffee.

"Your breakfasts will be out in ten minutes," Lauren announced as she set down the cups, and then gesturing to the napkin holder with ketchup, sugar, and a bowl of creamers around it, she added, "The cream and sugar are here. But let me know if you need more, or prefer sweetener."

"No. Sugar's good, thank you," Stephanie murmured since the woman was looking at her as she spoke. Stephanie supposed she encountered more women than men requesting sweetener.

"Good. Give me a wave if you need anything," Lauren said before beetling off again.

Smiling faintly, Stephanie grabbed a couple creams and a sugar and started to fix her coffee even as Thorne did the same.

She was taking her first sip of what was actually very

good coffee when he suddenly announced, "I'm a free-lance editor for a large publishing house in Britain."

Stephanie turned to him with surprise. "You're an editor?"

Thorne nodded. "But I've only been doing it since the raid. Before that . . ." He shook his head. "Well, basically there weren't any jobs on the island unless I wanted to work for Dressler, and that was out of the question."

"Oh yeah, definitely," Stephanie agreed grimly.

"But one of the first things Mother did once Dressler was gone was contact her old friends. She immediately got in touch with Margaret, her dearest friend from before her marriage, and gave her a basic rundown of what had happened, and why all contact had been cut." Stopping, he smiled crookedly, and said, "Well, she gave her a somewhat edited version that left out genetic experiments, hybrids with wings, immortals, etc."

"Ah." Stephanie nodded, not surprised to hear this. The Enforcers would have insisted on it. The last thing they would have wanted was attention on the island, the hybrids, and, by extension, the immortals since they had been victims there too.

"Anyway, it turned out Margaret had inherited and still ran a publishing house in Britain." He paused briefly, and then admitted, "Well, really, she holds the title, but her daughter actually runs it now. Anyway, after several emails, Margaret arranged for me to try out as a freelance editor. They emailed me a manuscript along with guidelines of what to do. I edited and sent it back, and they liked my work. Now they send me all the books I can edit." He smiled wryly. "Considering my love for books, I thought it would be a dream job."

"Isn't it?" Stephanie asked, her eyebrows rising slightly.

"Actually, it kind of ruins the enjoyment of the book when you're having to stop and make corrections and such all the time," he admitted. "But maybe that's me."

"Hmm," Stephanie murmured, but supposed that could be an issue. He no longer got to just read for enjoyment.

"So, I've started doing some programming on the side, and may eventually switch to that full-time so I can go back to reading for enjoyment. Or maybe I'll just do both," he said with a shrug.

"That sounds—Oh." Stephanie paused to smile at Lauren as she appeared on the other side of the counter to top up their coffees. "Thank you, Lauren."

"My pleasure." The older lady beamed at them both, and hurried off.

Stephanie and Thorne both took a minute to doctor their coffees and take a sip, and then Thorne set his cup down and announced, "I always wanted a dog growing up, but that wasn't possible. Nothing got on the island without Dressler's approval, and the only animals he allowed on the island were ones he wanted to harvest DNA from."

"Oh," Stephanie said, a little confused at the abrupt topic change.

"I did make friends with a couple of birds," he said now with a faint smile. "I wouldn't call them pets, because they were free. I would never have put them in a cage, but I used to take them orange slices and they came around every day to see me, and sometimes flew with me."

Despite her confusion at the topic change, the comment made Stephanie smile as she imagined Thorne with his huge wings flying around an island with a couple of tiny birds for company and feeding them orange slices.

"In truth," Thorne continued, "besides my mother and Maria, they were my only friends until the raid. The other hybrids, the ones who weren't kept in cages and were allowed to move around the island, they . . ." He sighed and shook his head. "They knew Dressler was my father and wanted nothing to do with me. Most suspected I was a spy for him. Others just hated me because he was my sperm donor."

"I'm sorry," Stephanie said solemnly, thinking it was unfair. He had been as much of a victim as the others.

Thorne shrugged. "Most of them have loosened up since the raid. I suspect the immortals told them I was not a spy, did not interact with Dressler, and was as much a victim as them. Whatever the case, I've made a few friends since the raid. Only one of them I'd consider a close friend though. Santiago."

"Santiago?" Stephanie queried.

Thorne nodded as he took another sip of coffee, and then said, "Dressler used his sperm and the egg of one of his victims and similar animal DNA to my own to make Santiago."

"So, he's a half brother," Stephanie reasoned, and then frowned and said, "Wait. One of his victims? An immortal?"

"No. Dressler didn't just kidnap immortals. He kidnapped mortal men and women too for their DNA, and was doing that long before he discovered immortals and changed his focus. Santiago's mother was one of them. She was a student at the university. One of his, we think. He lured her out with some extra credit project. She never left. He kept her locked up and drugged, harvesting eggs and impregnating her like he did my mother. She killed herself shortly after Santiago was born."

"Oh God," Stephanie breathed.

She was still contemplating that when he announced, "And I like action movies with a little suspense thrown in. Although I've enjoyed the Marvel movies, and *Guardians of the Galaxy* might be my favorite movie of all so far."

It was then Stephanie realized he was going through the list of things she'd used as examples when she'd been proving her point that he hadn't told her anything about himself either. In fact, he'd gone right through the list. Pets? Career? Friends? Movies? Check. Check. Check. Check. Dear God, that meant it was her turn, she realized.

"Stephanie?" Thorne said with concern when she remained silent.

"*Guardians of the Galaxy* is my favorite too," she blurted.

"Oh, that was a fine movie," Lauren announced, drawing their attention to her arrival. "My Ronnie and I really enjoyed it."

Seeing the numerous plates their waitress was carrying and balancing up her arm, Stephanie quickly shifted her coffee cup out of the way so the woman could set them down. A plate of toast, a plate with pancakes, and a plate with her sausage, hash browns, and eggs immediately slid in front of Stephanie. Her gaze moved over the mouthwatering food, and then she turned to see Lauren setting Thorne's last plate down.

"Now you two enjoy," Lauren ordered before sailing away.

"Did you see? She had all six plates," Thorne said with admiration.

"I know, amazing, right?" Stephanie said with wonder.

They smiled at each other, and then both turned to start eating, but Stephanie was distracted as she considered that now that he'd answered her questions about him, he'd expect her to answer his. She just had to work out which ones she was willing to address, or what she should say.

Thorne had asked about life mates, she recalled. But that was . . . Man! How did you tell someone that they were your life mate? Most of the immortals she knew had botched that talk badly. Besides, should she even tell him when she still wasn't sure what was going on with her? She hadn't learned much at the grocery store. Well, she had and she hadn't. Stephanie had learned that she could still read and control people, but she actually had to read them as opposed to just being flooded with their thoughts like it used to be, and she also had to be touching them to do it. Which was miles away from the skill level she used to have in that area. If she could call it that. Stephanie hadn't had any control of it before. Not over hearing, or not hearing, she'd just been bombarded by it all.

She supposed she could just explain life mates to him without saying that he was hers. Of course, he'd probably work that out, but—

"You mentioned I hadn't told you that I'm here to have my wings amputated. Or why," Thorne said suddenly.

Eager to avoid having to talk herself, Stephanie turned to him at once, her eyebrows raised in question.

"I want to have the operation for my mother and Maria," he told her solemnly, and before she could respond, he said, "They spent my entire life before the raid protecting and fighting for me. Dressler wanted to experiment on me, you see, to find out which DNA had taken, and what I could do and so on."

Stephanie winced at the thought of the experiments he would have done to find out those things. She couldn't even imagine how Thorne would have suffered.

"But my mother still had control of the money. She had to sign off on every withdrawal he made. There was nothing Dressler could do to change that. It was in her father's will," he explained. "So, my mother agreed to give him any funds he wanted if he left me alone. She also threatened to cut him off and kill herself if he didn't."

Stephanie's head went back as if from a blow at those words, her eyes widening, and Thorne nodded.

"She would have done it too," he said solemnly. "And he knew it."

"But wouldn't he then inherit the money himself?" she asked with confusion.

Thorne shook his head. "If mother dies, everything goes to her cousin. Her title, the castle, money, everything."

Stephanie blinked. "Castle?"

"My mother is a duchess," he explained with a faint smile.

"Oh," she breathed, her eyes wide, and then frowned. "Wait. Why would everything go to some cousin if she dies? Shouldn't it go to you?"

"There is no me in the human world," Thorne said quietly. "My birth was never registered. Legally, I don't exist."

"I see." Stephanie sighed the words, a bit disgruntled at this news. Dressler had stolen so much from him.

"And Maria lost everything the day I was born," he continued. "Helping my mother give birth, and seeing me . . ." Thorne shook his head. "Dressler couldn't let her leave the island and tell anyone what she'd seen. He made her write to her husband that she was leaving him and their son and staying with my mother on the island."

"Damn, he's an evil piece of shit," Stephanie growled, and then sighed and said, "So she stayed with your mother in that little house on the island and helped raise and protect you?"

Thorne nodded. "Maria was also the message carrier after my mother was wheelchair-bound. She—"

"How did that happen?" Stephanie interrupted.

Thorne grimaced. "After Dressler sent his man down to throw me off the cliff, they were afraid of what he'd do next. He'd broken the agreement not to experiment on me," he pointed out. "Mother punished him by refusing to sign any more money orders for him as she'd said she'd do. But when he threatened to take me to his labs if she didn't, she had to give in to keep me safe with her. But both Mother and Maria were afraid of what he might do next, so they started planning an escape. They were going to try to get to one of the boats and slip away in the night." Thorne paused and frowned before admitting, "They would never tell me the specifics of what happened, but Mother was injured somehow in the attempt and paralyzed from the waist down. She was wheelchair-bound from then on, and after that, Maria was the one who had to go to Dressler and fight to get me clothes, schoolbooks, etc."

Thorne stopped to take a sip of coffee, and then sighed. "Those two women are the only reason I'm alive and whole. And now that we're free of Dressler, they want to move to mainland Venezuela and for me to go with them. Which I obviously can't do with wings."

"Which is why you want the operation," she said softly.

"I don't really want it at all," he confessed on a weary sigh. "I mean, part of me does. I would be normal, could live wherever I want, and so on. But the other part . . ." Thorne hesitated, and then tried to explain. "My wings are a part of me. I love the freedom of flying, I love coasting on the air currents, looking down on the world below."

He smiled at the thought, and seemed to be lost in the memory of flying, but then his smile faded and he said solemnly, "But my mother and Maria both lost a chance at any kind of a life themselves and spent almost every minute of the first fifty-two years of my life before the raid, fighting for and caring for me. I owe them both a life," he said unhappily. "I can't give them back what they lost to protect me, but I can at least make their last years happy and comfortable. So, for my mother and Maria, I will cut off my wings, and probably pluck my head to look human. I feel like it's the least I can do to pay them back for all they did for me."

"Twenty-two," Stephanie said absently as she pondered the position Thorne was in. He didn't want to have his wings removed at all. He was only doing it for his mother and Maria, because he felt he owed them for all they'd done for him. Surely, his mother and Maria knew this? How could they let him do it? The only thing she could think was that they didn't know he didn't really want to remove his wings. That was the only thing that made sense. Two women who had sacrificed so much for him weren't likely to then turn around and demand he cut off body parts so they could spend their few remaining years in the city. It just didn't fit.

"What?" Thorne asked with confusion, pulling her back to the conversation. When she peered at him blankly, he said, "Twenty-two what?"

"Oh." She smiled faintly. "You said they looked after and protected you for fifty-two years before the raid, which was six years ago. That would make you fifty-eight," she pointed out with amusement. "Which obviously you're not. So, you must have meant twenty-two. Or thirty-two is possible, I suppose, although you look damned good for thirty-eight, if that's the case."

Thorne was silent for a minute, and then said gently, "Stephanie, my mother is eighty years old. She was twenty-two when she had me. I'm fifty-eight years old."

"What?" she gasped with disbelief, and then shook her head. "No way!"

He nodded solemnly. "I promise you I am."

Stephanie shook her head again in denial. "But you don't look more than twenty-five. Thirty tops."

"Yeah," he said slowly, and then grimaced. "That would be the *Turritopsis dohrnii* DNA."

"The who?" she asked blankly.

"The *Turritopsis dohrnii* DNA," he repeated, and then added, "It's also called the immortal jellyfish."

"Right. The immortal jellyfish," Stephanie muttered, and took a deep breath, then expelled it again before saying, "Okay. Explain."

"The immortal jellyfish has a rare cellular mechanism called transdifferentiation," he began, but halted when Stephanie shook her head.

"Dumb it down, please," she said. "I have no idea what transdifferentiation is."

"Right. Sorry," he muttered, and then simply said, "Think Benjamin Button."

Her eyes widened with horror at once and she gasped, "You're going to revert back to a baby with diapers and everything?"

"No," Thorne said with quick alarm, and then frowned. "At least, I haven't so far." Sighing, he shook his head, and said, "The jellyfish I mentioned can go all the way back to a polyp and then they . . ."

"Start over again?" she suggested when he hesitated.

"Close enough," Thorne muttered.

"But you won't," Stephanie said worriedly. "You won't go back to a polyp, or the human version of one?"

Thorne shook his head. "No. But three times now—when I was thirty-five, forty-five, and fifty-five—I have kind of . . . reverted?" he suggested, not sounding certain he was using the right phrasing, or at least something she would understand.

"Okay," Stephanie said slowly, and then asked, "Reverted to what?"

"A younger version of me."

She thought about that and then asked. "How?"

"A fever and kind of a coma-like state, or stasis," Thorne answered, and then explained, "Shortly after my thirty-fifth birthday, I came down with a fever. The second day of the fever, I didn't show up downstairs at the usual time, and Maria came up to check on me. She said she couldn't wake me no matter what she did and

I was burning up. Mother couldn't get upstairs in her wheelchair, so it was up to Maria to take care of me, and she did everything she could think of to try to bring down my fever, but nothing worked. And then suddenly, it just stopped. My temperature returned to normal, and a day later I woke up."

Smiling faintly, he said, "Maria thought it was a miracle. She spent most of that first day giving thanks to God for saving me . . . when she wasn't helping me drink water, eat, and get to the bathroom for a bath. I was pretty weak at first," Thorne told her. "But I was desperate to clean up and couldn't wait to regain my strength for a bath." Grimacing, he explained, "I was covered with this slimy ooze when I woke up, like my body was pushing gross stuff out through my pores."

Stephanie stiffened and sat up on her stool. "That's what happens during a turn."

Thorne nodded. "Yeah. I saw it with Sarita when she turned, and it looked like the same gross substance was oozing out of her pores that comes out of me when I have the fevers."

"Huh," Stephanie murmured, wondering if the scientists in Atlantis had studied this immortal jellyfish while producing their nanos. Although the gross ooze bit only really happened during the turn for immortals. Thorne said this had happened to him three times. Pushing these thoughts away, she asked, "So when you woke up, you looked younger?"

"Not much," Thorne said with a faint smile. "I mean, I was only thirty-five the first time it happened. I had maybe the beginnings of crow's-feet at my eyes, a couple sunspots on my hands, and my feathers were getting a little thinner on my head and a little dull-looking. But when I woke up from the fever, the crow's-feet and sun-spots were gone, and my feathers were thick and shiny again. I looked ten years younger too. I also had more energy, felt a little stronger." He shrugged. "I aged normally from there and then, shortly after my forty-fifth birthday it happened again: fever, coma, oozing skin, and then waking up looking and feeling a decade younger. Not so much younger that others would notice, but I noticed. And I wasn't as weak when I came out of the coma that time, and even less so this last, so my body must be adjusting to the process."

"And the last time was . . . what? Three years ago?" she asked.

Thorne nodded.

"So, you transdifferentiate or revert or whatever every ten years to a twenty-five-year-old and then age another ten years to looking about thirty-five once more, only to have these fevers and revert back to being twenty-five again? At least physically."

"Yes," he said. "Dani thinks that the mix of DNA keeps me from reverting all the way back to a polyp, or I guess a zygote, fetus, or baby in human terms."

Stephanie simply stared at him for a minute, and then laughed. "You are such a freak."

Seeing the way Thorne stiffened and that he hadn't taken it the way she'd meant it, Stephanie added, "But then so am I, so I guess we were made for each other."

Thorne relaxed a little, but not fully, and shook his head. "You aren't a freak. You were born a perfectly normal and beautiful human baby and were given nanos that make you immortal with a need for extra blood because the nanos use blood to keep you healthy and young. And you're one of many immortals out there. Not a freak."

"I'll argue the point with you later," she assured him. "But right now, I have an idea that might save your wings."

Rather than looking happy, Thorne looked wary. "What kind of idea?"

"What if I found your mother and Maria immortal life mates?" she suggested.

"What?" He looked shocked.

"Stay with me here," Stephanie said soothingly. "They sacrificed a lot to keep you safe and raise you as healthy and well as they could."

"Yes, they did," Thorne said firmly, but still looked wary, as if expecting her to try some underhanded way to convince him not to amputate his wings.

"Right. They did. I completely agree with that," she assured him, and then asked, "But do you really think living a couple years in Caracas or Maracaibo can make up for that? I mean, as humans they don't have a lot of years left in them, Thorne. They could die a year or even a month after you have your wings amputated and move them."

"I'm aware of that," he said grimly.

"And Venezuela is a communist country, isn't it? I know it has the highest murder rate in the world, and that kidnapping there is like a national pastime."

"Which is why I cannot let them move to the mainland by themselves," Thorne pointed out unhappily.

"Uh-huh." Stephanie nodded her head, and then asked, "But what if they were both immortal?"

"What?" Thorne sat up as if she'd zapped his butt with live wires.

"I'm pretty good at recognizing life mates for immortals, Thorne. At least I used to be," she added with a frown, and then shrugged. "Maybe I could find them both mates, and if I can't, I'm sure Marguerite would help too. Then they could have a whole life, and a partner who cares for each of them. That would do more to make up for their lifetime of sacrifice than a couple of months or years in a dangerous city, don't you think?" Stephanie asked, and then realized she'd never answered his question about what a life mate was. He couldn't know what she was suggesting. "I'm sorry. You asked earlier what a life mate is and I never answered. It's—"

"I know what a life mate is, Stephanie," he interrupted gently.

Shaking her head with confusion, she said, "But you asked me—"

"I wanted to talk about it, and about the fact that I know I am yours," Thorne said solemnly, and then grimaced. "But when you avoided the question and then started doing the distract-me-with-sex thing any time that topic or your feeding differences came up, I decided you weren't interested in having me as a life mate and I was just a playmate for you. A fling. It's why I left this morning. I'm falling for you, Stephanie, and it's not just that the sex is crazy hot and addictive. It's you as a person. You just get me. We fit together. We've both had to live isolated from others. We have the same taste in food, the same sense of humor. I like just sitting and talking to you even. I want to be a part of your life, and not just for a week or so. For a lifetime."

Stephanie swallowed, her stomach turning over at his words. She wanted that too, but wasn't sure if she could have it. If she was going no-fanger—

"I want much more than to be your plaything, Stephanie. So, if that's all that's on offer, please let me know. I'll pack up and head back to Toronto until the operation, and save myself some heartache."

Her eyes widened with dismay at the thought of his leaving. Stephanie had never meant to make him feel like he was just a plaything or a fling to her. Thorne was already so much more than that. But would he still want to be her life mate if he knew that she wasn't an immortal? That she was an Edentate who might go no-fanger?

There was only one way to find out, Stephanie supposed, and said, "No, Thorne. You aren't just a plaything. I really care for you too, and it would make me very happy to have you as a life mate. But—"

The ding of her phone had her stopping and glancing down with a frown as she reached into the pocket of her duster to retrieve it. Seeing the message on the screen, she muttered, "What the—?" She opened her phone, then tapped the security camera app.

"What is it?" Thorne asked, leaning in to look at her phone with her.

"I got a notification that gate one just opened at the house," Stephanie muttered, waiting impatiently for the security app to open. God in heaven, it was slow. It always was. Her best guess was that it was the downloading and streaming all the cameras that caused the delay. But that was just—

"Oh my God," she gasped when the cameras popped up already streaming and she saw all the vehicles in the driveway in front of Drina and Harper's house.

"Is that Dani?" Thorne asked, moving his head up right next to hers to get a better look at the tiny screen.

Stephanie tapped the tiny image that had the view of

all the cars presently littering the driveway, her mouth compressing as it filled the screen and she saw that the woman who had just got out of the first car was indeed her sister, Dani.

Thorne breathed out beside her, his voice resigned when he said, "I guess she's brought her specialists down and will want to examine me and stuff now."

"Those aren't specialists," Stephanie growled as she examined the men in the second car through the front windshield, even as the doors opened on either side of the SUV to allow them out.

"Hmm?" Thorne had started to straighten away from her, but paused at her words and leaned back to look again as three men got out of the car behind the one Dani and Decker had apparently ridden in. "Is that Bricker getting out of the back? And I'm pretty sure the one who just got out of the front passenger seat is Lucian."

"And Anders getting out of the driver's side," Stephanie finished for him, her gaze already moving on to the people exiting the third vehicle. "And Drina and Harper. I wonder where little Jenny is?"

"Drina and Harper's daughter?" Thorne asked, moving in closer to peer at the image on her phone. "I don't see her in the car."

"They must have left her with Elvi," Stephanie murmured, and then fell silent as they watched Harper leave Drina to talk to Dani while he hurried up to their house.

"I don't recognize the man with them, but the two women getting out of the second to last car are Eshe and Mirabeau," Thorne commented, leaning closer to the screen to get a better look at the trio who had got out of the SUV behind Drina and Harper's, and the couple now stepping out of the car behind that.

"The man with Eshe and Mirabeau is Tiny, Beau's life mate," Stephanie told him, and then added, "And the couple getting out of the last SUV are Nicholas and Jo Argeneau." Stephanie shook her head then and said fretfully, "There must be trouble they need my help with."

"Yes. Probably," Thorne murmured, sounding concerned. "They wouldn't send this many people out about a stalker."

Stephanie stiffened, her head jerking around to spear him with sharp eyes. "Why would they send anyone about the stalker? They don't know about him."

"Sure they do. I called Harper this morning to clarify whether or not he had arranged for the service guy who came out."

"But you didn't tell him about the hacker guy, right?" Stephanie demanded.

Her sharp tone made Thorne straighten and look at her with surprise.

"You didn't tell him about the black box," Stephanie pressed. "And his jumping the fence and coming back?"

Her voice was trembling with anxiety and fury, and Thorne seemed mystified by it as he said, "Yes. I did."

Stephanie groaned and closed her eyes.

"Someone should know. In case anything happens," Thorne pointed out. "And someone needs to look into the guy. What if he comes back when I'm not here and attacks you?"

"Right," she breathed out with defeat, and then shrugged. "Fine. You told him. And then he no doubt told Drina, who immediately called Dani, Elvi, and Beau, while he conference-called Lucian and Victor, and they all worried themselves sick until they had a powwow to decide how to handle this latest issue." She shook her head wearily. "Nothing new here, folks, just another thing to worry about when it comes to 'Little Stephanie.'"

Thorne frowned, as much at her exhausted tone and the defeated slump to her shoulders as at her words. "Another thing to worry about?"

"Oh yeah, that's all they do is worry about me," Stephanie told him almost resentfully as she began digging in her pocket.

"Isn't that what family is supposed to do?" he asked gently.

"Maybe," she acknowledged unhappily as she dragged her wallet out and retrieved a couple of twenties. One twenty would have covered the bill, but she tossed both on the counter, and stood up, adding, "But I doubt most people have to deal with their loved ones' fears that they'll go crazy, turn rogue, and start slaughtering mortals willy-nilly."

Thirteen

Thorne stared at the empty spot where Stephanie had been a moment ago, her words running circles inside his head. He then snatched up the grocery bags he'd set on the floor by his stool and hurried after her. He caught up to her on the sidewalk in front of the store next to the diner, and matched his stride to hers. He then eyed her with concern as he asked, "I'm guessing you would rather I hadn't told Harper about the hacker?"

"Good guess," she growled.

Thorne nodded to himself, and then admitted, "I'm just not sure why."

"Are you kidding me?" she barked with disbelief. "Did you see the army of hunters now sitting in the driveway at the house?"

"Yes, but they must think your stalker warrants this large a response. Harper probably recognized him from my description, and—"

"He didn't," Stephanie snapped.

"You don't know that," he argued.

"I do," she assured him with what sounded like an unshakable certainty.

"Well, then why would so many of them come down here?" Thorne asked with frustration.

"Because they worry about me," she snarled, stopping to whirl on him. "All of them: Dani, Decker, Elvi, Victor, Mabel, DJ, Tiny, Beau, Drina, Harper, and even Lucian. They all worry. It's what they do, and because they do, I have to ease their worries by acting like everything is fine and dandy, when most often my head is splitting with pain, the voices are driving me mad, and I just want to vent to someone. But dear God! I don't dare do that. It would make them panic. They might think I've gone no-fanger, and put me down like a dog, or at least lock me up or put me under guard until they're sure I'm not. So, it's the Happy Stephanie Hour for me twenty-four/ seven no matter how I really feel, and it's freaking exhausting," she bellowed.

Thorne glanced around nervously to be sure no one was close enough to have heard her tirade. Fortunately, they appeared to be the only ones on this end of the street at the moment, he saw with relief. Though there was a van presently parallel parking a couple of shops up on the opposite side of the street. But their darkened windows were closed, making it unlikely they'd heard anything. He hoped.

Sighing, he turned back to Stephanie in time to catch the realization on her face and the regret that followed. Thorne knew she was now sorry, not only for her carelessness in choosing to let loose here, but also for giving away so much. He also knew she'd shut down the conversation now if given half the chance, but Thorne had no intention of letting her do that.

"What is a no-fanger?" he asked before she could try to backpedal and play her "Happy Stephanie Hour" thing.

She blinked at the question and then sagged with exhaustion and shook her head with disgust. "Of course you don't know what a no-fanger is. When the immortal hunters explained who and what they were after raiding the island, and even about life mates, of course they didn't bother to include explanations about the bastard children of their group, the no-fangers and Edentates."

Running a weary hand over the top of her head and down her ponytail, Stephanie shook her head. "It doesn't matter. I'm sorry I vomited that all over you. I guess the stress of worrying about not hearing voices anymore and what it means is getting to me. Please just forget everything I said and—"

"I'm not forgetting anything," Thorne interrupted firmly, catching her arm when she turned as if to continue walking. Meeting her gaze, he said, "I'm your life mate. I want to help. Don't shut me out."

When Stephanie hesitated and glanced around, he took her arm and started her moving again, but just up the street to where he'd spotted a bench. Urging her to sit down, he joined her on it, taking a seat from the end of the backless bench, just as he'd done with the stool. Straddling it, and facing her, Thorne said, "Please explain what no-fangers are and why anyone would believe you are one."

Stephanie was stiff and silent for a minute, but then let her shoulders slump and cleared her throat before turning to face him on the bench. She considered him briefly, before asking, "Do you know what Edentata means?"

Thorne raised his eyebrows at the question. He was a well-read man, and from some of that reading he did know what Edentata meant. He simply had no idea what it could have to do with immortals. Finally, he said, "As far as I know, Edentata and Edentate are an order of mammals with few or no teeth, like anteaters and armadillos. I've never heard of them called no-fangers, though, and have no idea what that could have to do with immortals."

Stephanie paused as if debating what she should say, and then told him, "When Atlantis fell and the immortal survivors found themselves without blood transfusions available to them, not all of them developed fangs."

Thorne felt his eyebrows rise at this news. No one had mentioned this bit of information to him, but he reasoned it out. "So, there are immortals who are fangless, and they're called Edentates, no-fangers, and Edentata."

"Any immortal without fangs is called Edentata. But then they divide into Edentates and no-fangers," she explained solemnly.

"Why the distinction?" he asked at once. "What is the difference between Edentates and no-fangers?"

"Edentates are basically just immortals without fangs," she explained, and then licked her lips in a gesture that looked nervous to him before she added, "No-fangers are batshit crazy immortals without fangs who run around terrorizing mortals and immortals alike."

"So, no-fangers are rogue Edentates?" Thorne suggested, and when she nodded, asked, "Well then, why not just call them rogues like they do with immortals who attack mort—?"

"Because they're nothing like rogue immortals," Stephanie interrupted, and then stopped to frown and said, "Well, I suppose they are, really, but the difference is that while immortals might go rogue after centuries of being lonely or whatever, no-fangers are just born crazy . . . or maybe they go crazy too, but much more swiftly than rogues." She shrugged as if she wasn't sure, and continued. "With no-fangers it's not a result of loneliness and a long life, it's something to do with the nanos they got."

"There were different nanos?" Thorne asked. This was something he hadn't heard before.

Stephanie nodded. "Apparently, the first batch they tested didn't work out so well. A third of the people given them died, a third were fine, and a third went crazy violent and psychotic. So, the scientists went back and reworked the nanos and came up with the second batch that worked much better. No one died as a result of getting them, no one went crazy, and all seemed well other than the need for extra blood like with the first batch," she explained. "At the time, though, the recipients of the second batch and the sane survivors of the first batch were grouped together and simply called immortals. It wasn't until Atlantis fell and the nanos started making the recipients evolve to get the blood they needed that they realized there was a difference. While all of them developed night vision, mind reading, mind control, and extra speed and strength, only the recipients of the second batch of nanos developed fangs. The recipients of the first batch didn't."

"Interesting," Thorne murmured, wondering why the recipients of the first nanos hadn't developed fangs along with the recipients of the second batch. It must have been some kind of programming difference in the nanos. But what? What could cause insanity and a lack of fangs? He pondered that briefly, until Stephanie continued.

"Leonius Livius, the man who attacked and turned both Dani and me, was a rogue Edentata."

Thorne's head jerked up at this news, his gaze finding hers. "He was . . . ?"

"No-fanger," she said grimly when he hesitated to finish the question.

"And both you and Dani . . . ?" he asked.

"Edentates," Stephanie said solemnly, and then, mouth tightening grimly, she added, "So far."

Thorne's eyebrows rose. "It can change? You can seem fine after the turn and then later . . ." He didn't finish the sentence because he couldn't think of a way to finish it that wouldn't be insulting.

"Go crazy and start slaughtering people indiscriminately?" she suggested, and then shook her head. "I don't know. Nobody seems to know, and believe me, Lucian has contacted everyone he can think of for the answer. Pretty much everyone who knows me has tried to find out. But there aren't a lot of Edentata around whether Edentate or no-fanger. Not that the no-fangers would answer any questions," she added dryly before explaining, "Most of the Edentata were slaughtered millennia ago thanks to Leo's father, who decided he wanted to be king of the world. To do this, he kidnapped a lot of Edentate and immortal females to breed his own army of sons. He apparently started with Edentate women because the immortals were less likely to notice their sudden disappearance. He'd kill their mate, take the females, use them until they were useless to him, and then kill them off.

"When he'd wiped out the majority of the Edentate females, he turned his attention to immortal women." Smiling grimly, she told him, "That's something they did manage to learn while trying to find out more information about Edentates and no-fangers. They didn't know he'd concentrated on Edentate females first, and decimated the population that way. They had assumed the lack of them was natural selection. The women refusing to have children because the odds of them surviving and being healthy and well were so bad. Like Dani and me."

Thorne's eyebrows rose. "You both decided not to have children to avoid passing on the Edentata nanos?"

She nodded unhappily, and then said, "I'm sorry. If that changes things for you—" Stephanie stopped uncertainly when he chuckled. "What?"

"Sweetheart, with the DNA soup that I'm made up from, I don't even know if I *could* have children. Well, obviously I can't have them myself, but you know what I mean," he said with mild amusement, and then shook his head. "And if by some miracle I did get you pregnant, I'd be afraid of how they might turn out, or what exactly they would be. From the descriptions of the failed fetuses in the basement of Dressler's first house . . ." He shook his head. "The idea of what might come of it would be enough to give me nightmares."

"Oh," she breathed, relaxing a little.

Thorne considered her solemnly for a minute, and then said, "Your family are concerned that your sensitivity to people's thoughts could turn you from an Edentate to a no-fanger."

"Basically, yes. They know I can't shut out the thoughts coming at me and worry that could be what makes no-fangers . . . no-fangers. That they can't shut out all the noise and find peace and it eventually drives them mad."

"But Dani doesn't have this issue?" he asked.

"No. Thank God," she breathed.

"But now the voices have stopped? You don't hear people's thoughts anymore?"

Stephanie stiffened and glanced at him sharply. "How did you know that?"

"You mentioned it when you apologized for—as you put it—vomiting all that over me. You said you guessed the stress of worrying about not hearing voices and what it means was getting to you."

"Oh," she breathed, sagging slightly and looking away with a grimace before shrugging. "Yes. I'm not hearing the thoughts of everyone around me right now, and while it's nice, it's also worrisome since I'm not sure what it means."

"Did it just slowly fade out? Or—?"

"I'm not sure," she admitted, and looked embarrassed. "The nights are always quieter. People go to sleep and may have the occasional dreams, but their thoughts aren't running nonstop while they're sleeping. That's why I work nights and sleep during the day. To avoid as much of the mind chatter as possible," she pointed out. "But this week was even quieter than usual, even during the day. Lois and Jack, our neighbors next door on the left, are up in Ottawa visiting their daughter and her family. Ed, our neighbor across the street, takes in abandoned and neglected horses, and he and his wife, Penny, left a couple days ago for Alberta to pick up a horse that needs a new home, and then Bill on our other side is spending most of his time at the hospital. His mother had a stroke."

"So, you're saying that there have been less people around to hear," Thorne reasoned.

Stephanie nodded. "And when the numbers get really low, I can kind of block them out. I mean, they become like background noise. White noise or whatever. So, I'm not sure when exactly they stopped, but I noticed it while doing an online chat with Dani."

Thorne considered that, and then asked, "Did anything happen before the voices stopped? Did you hit your head, or . . . ?" He let his voice trail off when she began to shake her head.

"Nothing. I—" Stephanie paused and looked thoughtful for a minute. "Well, I did fall asleep editing."

Thorne raised his eyebrows. "Is that unusual?"

"Oh yeah. I never fall asleep sitting up," she said with a crooked smile. "Heck, I'm lucky to sleep in bed. But that night, I dozed off for an hour or two, and the ding of my phone woke me when Dani texted she was ready to chat. I was a little panicked then, rushing to get my laptop up and running on the island so I could get Trixie and Felix their dinner while we chatted, and then I got online, said hi to Dani, and noticed her hello back was the only voice I was hearing and it was with my ears. There was nothing but silence in my head. Well, and my own thoughts," she said with a faint smile.

"So, it could have happened while you were sleeping, or the sleeping could have been a result of it," Thorne said slowly.

"A result of it? What do you mean?" Stephanie asked with uncertainty.

"Well, you say you have trouble sleeping, but you've slept a lot since I've been here. I woke up before you every time we . . . slept," he said with a crooked smile. "Maybe the constant barrage of voices in your head is why you had trouble sleeping in the past, and you fell asleep at your desk because the voices had stopped and you were exhausted. From almost thirteen years of little sleep."

Stephanie raised her eyebrows at the suggestion. "That's possible, I suppose. But it still doesn't explain why the voices have stopped."

"But the voices haven't stopped altogether. You were reading and controlling people in the grocery store," Thorne pointed out.

Stephanie nodded, unsurprised he'd noticed her doing that. It wasn't like she'd been trying to hide it. She'd been too determined to check absolutely everyone she could to be sure she could still read people. "Yes, but I had to actually touch them to do it, and really focus, which is so totally the opposite of how it normally is. Or was, I guess," she added.

Thorne tilted his head, sure he heard regret in her voice, as if she actually missed the voices that had been such an overwhelming force in her head before. He'd read once that you could miss something you lose even if you hated it when you had it. He guessed after years of hearing so many voices in her head, the silence might be a bit overwhelming. It would be like living alone after years growing up in a big, boisterous family. At first there would be relief and joy, but he wouldn't be surprised if loneliness followed until the person adjusted to life alone.

"I wish I knew why it's stopped," Stephanie grumbled, looking somewhat vexed.

"Maybe you've just learned to block the voices," Thorne suggested hopefully.

"After nearly thirteen years?" she asked with disbelief. "And surely it would be a more gradual quieting down, or fading or something? Wouldn't it?"

Thorne shrugged. "We learn some things fast. I certainly didn't learn to fly in little hops and skips. It was one minute I'd never flown at all, and then whoosh! I was flying."

"Well, yeah, but that's because someone threw you off a cliff," Stephanie said with disgust.

He couldn't argue that point, Thorne supposed, but said, "I don't think you're going mad or no-fanger. Do you?"

When Stephanie shook her head and glanced around the street, he followed her gaze, noting that there was only one person on the road besides them and they were rushing into the grocery store, rubbing their arms against the chill as they went. It seemed the cooler weather was keeping others indoors, he thought.

"I don't feel like I'm going mad," Stephanie finally said. "But it doesn't really matter what you or I think. I'm more concerned with what Lucian and the others make of it."

That made his brow furrow with concern. "They won't know unless you tell them, will they?"

Stephanie barked out a little laugh at that. "Lucian can read me. He'll know," she assured him, and then stood up. "Come on. We might as well go back and face the music. They'll all be in a panic by now because neither of us are there."

Thorne stood slowly and followed her, his mind taken up with what she'd said as they crossed the street in front of the bank. Lucian would know she wasn't hearing the thoughts of others anymore, and if he worried it was a sign she was going no-fanger, he could put her down like a dog, or at least lock her up or put her under guard until they were sure.

The very idea of that happening both enraged and scared the hell out of Thorne. They'd just finally opened up to each other, and admitted their growing feelings, and their willingness to be life mates. They still had a whole lot to sort out—his operation, how they could be together, whether Stephanie might be able to find mates for his mother and Maria . . . A whole lot. But with his genetic makeup, Thorne had never expected to find a woman willing to be with him in a real relationship, someone willing to spend their life with him. He'd thought he'd be alone forever. But Stephanie, she was perfect, and she cared about him and did want him for a life mate. He was feeling hopeful for, really, the first time in his life, and the possibility that anyone could just take that away . . .

As they stepped up on the curb in front of the bank, Thorne caught her arm and turned her toward him.

Stephanie peered up at him in question once she faced him, and then her lips curved in a knowing smile. "You're going to ask me to carry the groceries for the ride home, aren't you?"

"What?" He followed her gaze down to the bags hanging from his wrists, and shook his head. "No. I can handle it. I just wanted to say I'm sorry I told Harper about the stalker and brought them all down on you. I didn't know."

"I know you didn't," she assured him solemnly. "And I'm sorry if I snapped at you when I first found out."

"That doesn't matter," Thorne said, shrugging it off. Stephanie had been venting. Something she apparently hadn't been able to do with anyone for quite a while. Not even her sister. Knowing that, Thorne felt honored that she'd trusted him enough to vent to him, and share her fears with him. He wanted to be worthy of that. "I won't let anyone hurt you, Stephanie. Not even Lucian. I'll be right by your side the whole time he and the others are here, and I'll keep you safe. And if anything happens, I'll get you away and we can flee to the island or somewhere else if necessary, but I promise I won't let them put you down or lock you up."

Stephanie's eyes widened with surprise at the offer. A fine sheen of tears swam across her eyes, making the beautiful silver green shine, and then she placed her hand on his cheek and rose up on her tiptoes as if to kiss him. It never happened. Instead, she suddenly stiffened, and slapped her hand to the side of her neck. He saw her fingers move over something, and then Stephanie's eyes widened and she muttered, "Oh, fuck," before sagging in his arms.

Thorne was so startled at her curse that he was almost too slow to catch her. Fortunately, he had fast reflexes and, even with the delay, managed to press her to his chest and keep her from falling to the ground.

"Stephanie?" he said with concern, shifting his hold on her so that her head lolled over his arm. It was then he saw the dart in her neck. His eyes widened at the sight, and then he felt something thud into his shoulder. Turning his head, he stared at the dart sticking into the leather of the coat, and then started to glance around, scowling when the next dart hit him in the face just below his right eye.

Cursing now himself, he shifted Stephanie to free one hand and reached up to remove the dart, then tried again to see where the missiles were coming from. He spotted the hacker who had attacked him at Stephanie's standing on the sidewalk some twenty feet away. Thorne's gaze next slid to the blond man with him and he immediately stiffened, his entire body seeming to swell with rage as he recognized him. He'd seen that face before . . . in photos and a painted portrait in the big house on the island. Thorne had made sure to have them all removed before moving his mother, himself, and Maria into the main house after the raid. They had all been of Dressler at various stages in his life. The bastard now looked like the younger version of himself from the older photos thanks to having been turned immortal.

Thorne wasn't surprised when Dressler reached out and urged the hacker to lower the dart gun he was aiming at him. The bastard knew darts didn't work on him; it was something they'd both found out when he'd had Willis shoot him while he was out flying one day back before the raid. That was one attack he hadn't mentioned to his mother. He'd been hit with the dart, pulled it out, looked at it, then dropped it in the ocean and angled around until he spotted Willis on the cliff with a gun in hand. Thorne hadn't had to ask why he'd done it. Willis didn't do anything Dressler didn't order. But Thorne hadn't wanted to upset his mother with the news that Dressler had sicced the man on him to test out something else. He hadn't wanted her worrying about what he might try next.

"Well, who do we have here?" Dressler said, bringing Thorne's focus sharply onto his nemesis. "Another interesting individual who's resistant to the darts like Ms. McGill there. They don't put her down fully, and don't affect you at all . . . or are the effects just delayed with you?" the monster asked, his gaze becoming sharp and interested. "Are you feeling woozy?"

Thorne's eyes widened as he realized Dressler, the monster who had made his life such a misery and haunted his nightmares, didn't even recognize him. His own blood.

"Can you speak?" Dressler asked sharply when he didn't respond. "Perhaps the dart is having an effect, after all."

"I can speak," Thorne growled. "And no, I don't feel woozy, just nauseous at the sight of you, frankly."

He saw something flicker on the man's face at the sound of his voice, and then Dressler's eyes narrowed on him, taking in his facial features more closely. Thorne knew the exact moment he realized who he was. Dressler's eyes widened slightly, and shock crossed his face.

"Thorne?" he said with amazement, and when Thorne didn't bother to respond, he gave a little disbelieving laugh. "I didn't recognize you, son."

"I'm not your son," Thorne growled with disgust. The man was no more his father than the bald eagle whose DNA he shared was.

Ignoring his denial, Dressler smiled and said, "You look human without your wi—Where the hell are your wings?" he interrupted himself to demand, sounding for all the world like an outraged father who caught his son without his pants on.

"I cut them off," he lied coldly.

Fury filled Dressler's face and then receded before he said coolly, "Well, that was foolish. You could have flown away if you hadn't done that."

Or if they weren't restricted by the shirt and coat he was wearing, Thorne thought grimly, shifting Stephanie and lifting her into his arms.

"Well, this turns out perfectly for me," Dressler announced. "I have both Ms. McGill, who I've wanted to get on my table since encountering her last fall, and you, who I've wanted to do tests on since you were born. I guess this is my lucky day."

"You're not going to touch her," Thorne growled, fury roaring through him at the very thought and setting his feathers ruffling under the clothes covering them.

His instincts were urging him to set Stephanie down, go after the bastard and his latest stooge, and tear them both limb from limb. But they were both immortals, strong and deadly, and with Stephanie there he couldn't take the risk. If he lost the battle, and she was captured, the pain and torture his father no doubt planned to subject her to would be his fault. So, despite the fact that he'd like nothing more than to end the bastard who gave him this life, fighting was out of the question. Which meant fleeing was the only option.

"Get the Glock out of the van, Stacy."

Thorne stiffened when Dressler whispered that order to his underling. Apparently, the man had forgotten he'd given him the hearing of a bat, or perhaps he wasn't sure what DNA had taken and what traits Thorne had besides the obvious. Which was why he wanted to test him, he realized. Whatever the case, since the darts didn't work on him, his sperm donor intended to just straight up shoot him. Thorne wasn't "down with that" as he'd heard Bricker say while he was in Toronto.

Even as the man Dressler had addressed as Stacy turned to jog toward a large white van fifty feet away, Thorne began to move. He immediately burst into a run while, at the same time, he shifted Stephanie and hefted her over his shoulder. He held her with one arm across the backs of her thighs, the grocery bags hanging from that wrist banging against her calves. Hoping he wasn't hurting her, he pressed her legs tight to his chest, and charged straight for Dressler.

As Thorne expected the man didn't stand and fight. He'd spent decades hiring muscle to do his fighting for him. He'd even had his latest flunky, Stacy, shooting the gun.

Dressler's first reaction when Thorne started bearing down on him was to react like a deer in headlights. He froze, eyes wide and horror on his face, and then he scrambled to get the hell out of the way, managing to trip himself up. When he crashed to the ground, Thorne charged past him, continuing around the bank to the parking lot.

Fourteen

Thorne spent the seconds it took to cross the parking lot behind the bank considering how the hell he was going to drive a motorcycle with an unconscious Stephanie. He briefly contemplated just keeping her over his shoulder, but it would affect the weight distribution on the motorcycle. That could be a problem when taking corners, especially if he had to take them at high speed. Besides, he needed to keep his hands on the gears, which meant he couldn't hold on to her, and she might tumble off his shoulder.

That left only one option. Reaching the motorcycle, he mounted up, caught Stephanie by the lower legs, and tugged her down to sit facing him with her legs spread and each riding over his thighs and hanging down behind him.

Thorne kept her leaning against him at first, so that she'd be out of the way while he started the engine, then eased her quickly down so that her back was between the handlebars, her shoulders over the headlight, and her head dangling over the front wheel guard. He was just debating if this was a good idea when sudden shouting drew his attention.

Glancing up, he saw that Dressler and Stacy had caught up and were pushing past a couple getting out of a car near the entry to the parking lot. Even as he looked, Stacy was raising the Glock he'd gone to fetch, aiming it in his direction.

Thorne didn't wait to see more. Stephanie had made him park facing into the parking lot to make it less likely someone would catch a flash of his wings as they dismounted. That worked well for him now. He didn't have to walk the bike back, or turn it, but could just go. Thorne nearly unseated both him and Stephanie by giving the bike too much throttle in his panic to avoid the bullets Stacy started shooting at them. Grinding his teeth, he eased up on the throttle and drove over the slight curb into the empty lot next to the parking lot rather than drive toward the exit and into a hail of bullets.

Thorne felt something hit him in his back, a solid thud like someone had punched him, and figured one of the bullets had got him, but he'd didn't suddenly have trouble breathing, or feel faint or anything, so figured it must have missed everything vital. He wasn't going to count on getting that lucky twice, so sped up as he crossed the weed-filled lot, heading for the street at the end of the main road.

Thorne was aware of the sudden silence behind him, and knew that meant Dressler and Stacy had probably stopped shooting to go for the van. They'd be on his ass in a minute if he didn't put some distance between them. His teeth grinding together, he glanced worriedly at Stephanie. He couldn't see her face, however; her head was hanging down over the headlight, so that—if she was awake—she was getting an upside-down view of the road ahead as he increased their speed to zip out of town.

Thorne was slowing for a turn when he heard squealing wheels and the rev of an engine behind him. A quick glance back as he took the corner showed a white van careening onto the road he was even now leaving.

Mouth tightening, Thorne sped up again but frowned when the bike didn't pick up as quickly as he'd hoped, or even as quickly as it had during the drive down from Toronto. He didn't know if it was the added weight, or the weight distribution of Stephanie's torso resting so far in front, but he'd lost a hell of a lot of pickup, and he worried it would allow the van to catch up.

Setting his teeth, Thorne just kept at it, trying to coax more speed out of the bike, and keep ahead of the van. Much to his relief the motorcycle did eventually speed up a bit. It was just slower to accelerate, he realized. Thorne still wasn't sure he could outrun the van, though. But he was going to do his damnedest. He'd barely had that thought when he realized they were coming up on the next turn. This was onto a much busier road, a back highway that traveled from Chatham to London.

Thorne felt sweat begin to bead under the leather duster as he watched the traffic passing ahead and realized he'd have to come to a full stop and wait for an opening to cross traffic into the northbound lane. A full stop for possibly long enough for the van to catch up to them. If that happened, Thorne had no doubt Dressler would have Stacy shoot him and then just drag him and Stephanie into the van and they'd disappear into cages somewhere to be experimented on. The possibility pushed him to do something incredibly stupid.

The turn he had to take was a left, and there was a gas station on the corner on the left side of the road. Thorne crossed the presently empty lane for oncoming traffic, and cut through the gas station rather than go right to the corner. That wasn't the stupid part. The stupid part was that he didn't stop or even slow before exiting the gas station through the highway side exit. He simply drove out onto the highway headed the wrong way into oncoming traffic.

Horns honked and vehicles swerved, though it wasn't really necessary. He wasn't actually on the road itself, but on the verge that ran alongside it, which fortunately was tar and chip and not loose gravel. Thorne ignored the honking and curses shouted his way as car after car rushed past, and stuck to the side of the highway, trying to get his speed up to equal that of the traffic moving in the same direction he was, on the opposite side of the road. He risked a glance over his shoulder after a moment, relieved to see the van stuck at the mouth of the gas station driveway. Too big to do what he was, the van was having to wait for a chance to enter traffic. Thorne hoped they had a long wait, but wasn't counting on it.

The minute he reached the speed traffic going their way was moving at, Thorne took a deep breath, picked the first opening between vehicles that he thought was large enough, and swerved across the lane of oncoming traffic. He narrowly missed getting clipped by a semi as he shot into the lane he should have been in from the start.

Thorne didn't breathe again until he'd managed to fit the motorcycle into traffic between a car and a pickup with little more room between them than he needed. He was quite sure he heard cursing from the pickup driver as he slid in front of him, but at least the guy didn't lay on the horn. Thorne had barely had that thought when the sound of several horns erupted from behind. They were accompanied by the screech of breaking tires and then the shriek of rending metal.

Glancing over his shoulder, Thorne saw that the van had decided to make its way into traffic whether there was room and time to do so or not. Two cars were now on the side of the road, one a dark blue PT Cruiser that had white paint all up its side, and the other was a little red smart car. Dressler, or Stacy, whoever was driving, had obviously sideswiped the Cruiser and forced it off the road. Presumably, the smart car had swerved to miss the tangling vehicles and ended up spinning out.

The white van was now six or seven cars behind him on the two-lane highway. With the traffic as heavy as it was, they probably wouldn't be able to move up closer without forcing more cars off the road. Unfortunately, Thorne wouldn't put that past Dressler. But even if he didn't go that far to catch up, the man obviously knew where he and Stephanie were staying, or at least where Stephanie lived. Stacy was the hacker who had attacked him when he'd confronted him by Stephanie's deck. They could just follow them there.

Thorne briefly considered veering off and heading somewhere else, but didn't think he'd be able to outrun the van with the slower acceleration issue the motorcycle had right now. He didn't want to be caught in the middle of nowhere and forced off the road. On the other hand, there were presently twelve immortals at the house who could help them.

The thought brought a grim smile to Thorne's lips. Whether it was just bad luck to run into the two men in town, or they'd followed them from the house, Dressler and Stacy couldn't know about the arrival of the others. Thorne could lead Dressler right to the men waiting at the house and finally watch his tormentor get the justice he deserved.

Grabbing and holding on to that thought, Thorne surveyed the highway ahead. Spotting the road that he had to take to return to the house, he began to slow for the turn. He risked a glance at what he could see of Stephanie then, and felt relief course through him when he saw her fingers twitching. Shifting his gaze to the bottom of her chin—all that he could see of her from the neck up with her head back as it was—he saw that she was trying to lift her head and almost reached out to help her. But he didn't want to risk it with the turn coming.

Leaving her where she was for now, Thorne concentrated on negotiating the corner and then picking up speed again. Once he had the motorcycle going as fast as it could, he took the chance to reach for the front of Stephanie's coat and yank her upright.

Thorne winced when her forehead slammed into his chin, and then glanced down briefly to see that her eyes were open and her mouth was moving. Frowning, he turned his gaze back to the road and angled his head closer to hers so that he could hear her and still see where he was going.

"Gate," was all Stephanie said, and then she sagged as if her head was just too heavy to hold up.

Thorne eased her back against the handlebar and spared a moment to be sure she'd settled all right. He then concentrated on the road ahead as the word *gate* circled through his mind. The gate at the house was electric, and painfully slow. You also had to be relatively close for the remote to work. You couldn't hit the button from halfway up the road and have the gate be open by the time you arrived at it. Dani had told him that while giving all of her various warnings and instructions to him before he'd left Toronto. She'd said you had to be no more than three or four car lengths away for it to work, and then you had to sit at the gate and wait for it to finish opening.

At least you did if you were in a car, Thorne thought suddenly. If you hit the remote three or four car lengths away, the gate would start opening, but wouldn't be wide enough apart for a car to pass through by the time it got to the gate. However, it might be open wide enough for a motorcycle to slide through.

Pinning his hopes on that, Thorne began to slow for the turn onto Stephanie's road and glanced over his shoulder again. Alarm coursed through him when he noted that the van had gained on them much more swiftly than he'd expected. It was only twenty feet back now, close enough they could have tried shooting him again, but hadn't.

Wondering over that, Thorne took the turn, and immediately tried to coax the motorcycle back up to speed as quickly as possible. Even as he did, he found himself instinctively hunching his shoulders against the expected bullets that would surely now start flying.

When that didn't happen, Thorne glanced over his shoulder again with bewilderment, wondering what the bastard was up to. The van had closed the distance between them a little more and was one car length away now . . . and still no gun appeared. The bastard knew exactly where he was going and, thanks to Stacy's stint pretending to be a serviceman, knew how slow the gate was to open. Dressler probably planned to trap him between the van and the slowly opening gate and pick him off at his leisure, Thorne realized. Oh, Dressler wouldn't kill him. Then he couldn't perform his experiments on him. He'd probably just shoot both of his legs to make it so he couldn't escape. And maybe his arms so he couldn't fight.

Hoping he was right and the gates would be open wide enough for them to slip through when they got there, Thorne reached into his pocket for the remote, only to come up empty. It was then he recalled that Stephanie had it. She'd grabbed the remote off the counter on the way out of Drina and Harper's house, and opened the gate for them when they left, then had probably pocketed it after pressing the button to close it once they were through.

Thorne would have been cursing up a storm at that realization if he'd had the time for it, but he didn't, and instead his mind immediately switched to figuring out what to do. The plan he came up with wasn't a great one, but he didn't think it was absolutely awful either. There were presently a dozen hunters at the house with incredible hearing. If he continued past the house, shouting out on the way by, surely one of them would hear. They had that supernano hearing, after all, and if even one glanced around at the shout and saw he and Stephanie being pursued by a van, surely they'd open the gate, and probably even start out after them. All Thorne had to do was keep driving and wait for the cavalry to catch up to them. Or, alternately, he'd ride around the admittedly very long, rural block a couple times, repeating the procedure until they did hear, and opened the damned gate for him.

Shoulders tensing, Thorne began to slow a bit as he approached the first driveway to Stephanie's home, and started to search for the vehicles he'd seen in the camera image. At first the trees and bushes that filled the front lawn hid them from view. He was nearly to the driveway itself before he spotted the tail end of a black SUV. Thorne immediately began to bellow like a wounded bear, which was one animal he didn't have DNA from.

Thorne thought he saw movement in the driveway as they rode past, but couldn't be sure. And then the shooting started.

He didn't know if Dressler had seen something that told him there was help at the house and so decided to bring the chase to an immediate end, or whether the fact that he wasn't stopping at the house was the reason for the sudden onslaught of bullets, but whatever the case, they weren't messing around now. Thorne felt a bullet punch into his shoulder, another hit him about midback just below his lungs, and then another hit his lower back near his spine. He never figured out if any of them were mortal wounds, or if a lung or anything else important had been hit, because it was then he caught something out of the corner of his eye and turned to see that the van was in the opposite lane and overtaking them. Dressler was driving, and Stacy was now hanging out the front passenger window, aiming his gun not at him, but the front tire of his motorcycle.

Thorne instinctively hit the brakes and tried to swerve away from the van, hoping to keep him from hitting his mark, but it was too late. Even as he swerved, the tire blew, and with the wheel turned, he lost control.

Stephanie woke up on a scream that she silenced the moment her eyes opened. It was an automatic response. The part of her brain that was always terrified that someone would realize she wasn't handling the voices in her head as well as she tried to pretend she was immediately went into protective mode, shutting down everything to make her seem as normal as possible while she tried to cope. But dear God, coping was hard this time. The voices in her head were back full tilt, and after the last few days of silence, they were unbearable. Her instinct was to pull a pillow over her head to muffle the noise, but she knew that wouldn't work. She had to—

"Breathe."

Stephanie opened eyes she hadn't realized she'd closed again and found herself staring at Lucian Argeneau.

"Breathe," he ordered firmly.

"I'm fine," she gasped, panic setting in at his witnessing her losing it briefly.

"You're not fine. You need to breathe and push the voices to the background again, little girl, or you'll lose your mind," Lucian said firmly, and then growled, "And if you lose your mind and I have to put you down, I'll be very cross with you, because I know you can do this, so breathe."

Eyes widening, Stephanie drew in a shaky breath,

exhaled quickly, and then pulled in another longer and deeper one. Some of the panic immediately receded, which helped a little.

"Now, push the voices to the back of your mind. Focus on my voice rather than the echoes in your head," Lucian commanded.

Stephanie stared at him, waiting for him to say something, and after a moment she scowled and pointed out, "Well, you'll have to speak if you want me to focus on your voice."

Lucian stiffened and actually looked alarmed as he realized she was right, then straightened and bellowed, "Dani McGill Argeneau Pimms, get in here!"

Dani must have been standing just outside the door, because it opened at once and her sister rushed in, concern on her face as she glanced from Stephanie to Lucian and back.

"Speak," Lucian ordered. When Dani peered at him uncertainly, he added, "Talk to her. Give her something to ground her, so she can push the voices back."

"Oh." Nodding, Dani managed a smile and turned to Stephanie. She opened her mouth as if to say something, and then just stood there, mouth agape.

"Oh, for God's sake," Lucian growled. "I thought you women were 'all about communication'? Leigh and the girls are constantly telling me that women are better at it than men. Wait until I pull this out as proof she's wrong the next time she's going on about it," he muttered, and then turned to Stephanie and said abruptly, "You were gone when we got here. Dani was alarmed because you never leave and Thorne shouldn't have been running around in broad daylight with *wings* for anyone to see.

I called Mortimer and had him do that thing he does where he finds phones. He found yours in some little town whose name escapes me at the moment."

Dani had closed her mouth when he began to speak, but opened it now, probably to tell him the name of the town, but he barked, "You had your chance to speak and blew it. I'm talking now."

Dani closed her mouth and bit her lip. Whether it was to keep from snapping at him, or to keep from laughing at him, Stephanie couldn't say. Personally, she would have been laughing at him. The man was beyond annoyed at simply having to talk.

Grunting, Lucian turned to scowl at her. "Anyway, I left Bricker and Anders here in case we missed you and you returned before we did. They were to call if that happened, and that's what took place. While we were poking around that little town, you two came back here on the motorcycle with a van hard on your heels and some bastard hanging out the window, shooting at you. Thorne took four bullets, you took two, but the real problem came when they shot out the front wheel of the motorcycle. Thorne lost control and crashed the bike into that big tree just outside the fence on the edge of the property. Bricker—"

"Is Thorne all right?" Stephanie asked at once, sitting up in bed as concern crashed down over her, doing more to push back the voices in her head and make her concentrate than Lucian's talking had been doing before that.

While Lucian glowered at her for interrupting, it was Dani who said, "He was badly hurt in the accident. You both were, and the bullet wounds didn't help, but I think he'll be fine."

"You think?" Stephanie asked sharply.

"He's gone into stasis," Dani told her gently. "He's feverish, and unresponsive, but I think that's just—"

"Wait," Stephanie interrupted with a frown. "By stasis, do you mean that thing he says happens? The fevers and coma because of the topsy-turvy dora jellyfish DNA he has?"

"*Turritopsis dohrnii*," Dani corrected.

"Whatever," Stephanie said impatiently. "Is that what's happening to him?"

"Yes. We believe it is." Dani nodded.

"But I thought that only happens every ten years. Thorne said—"

"It happens in the *Turritopsis dohrnii* when it's injured," Dani explained. "It—"

"He's healing," Lucian interrupted impatiently. "And I need answers to know what to do here, little girl. So, I'm going to finish telling you what we know, and then you will fill in the blanks. Understood?"

Dani and Stephanie both turned to look at him with surprise. The man rarely spoke, but apparently, now that he'd started, he wanted to finish. When he glared and repeated, "Understood?" they both nodded silently.

"Right. So, as I was saying, you two crashed into the tree. By the time Bricker and Anders got the gate open and were able to get out to you, two men were trying to untangle you both from the wreckage of the bike and drag you to the van. They had Thorne free and had left him lying on the ground nearby while they worked on freeing you." He paused briefly, as if debating whether to tell her, but then just said, "The handlebars were wrapped around you like a belt with one of them through your ribs, and the headlight was embedded in your skull."

Eyes widening with dismay, Stephanie raised one hand to her rib cage and the other to her head to feel around for the wounds that she'd suffered.

"They're healed," Lucian said with an exasperation that suggested she should have expected as much, and Stephanie supposed she should have. She wouldn't be awake with a headlight piercing her brain.

"So," he continued in a long-suffering voice, "the two men gave up and took off in their van when Bricker and Anders came out in the SUV. The men considered giving chase, but decided you two needed to take priority." His expression as he said that suggested he wasn't wholly in agreement. "So, they called us to let us know what had happened and set to work detangling you from the metal."

"By the time we got back, they had freed you, got you both inside, put you each in a bed, and started you on blood."

"But they didn't know what to do for Thorne," Dani put in now. "He'd gone into stasis."

Stephanie nodded, but asked, "How long—?"

"The crash was forty-eight hours ago," Lucian answered without letting her finish the question. "You've both been unconscious since then, and that is how long I've waited for my answers, Stephanie. I'd like them now. Who is this person who was hacking your system? Who were the men in the van and why were they shooting at you? And what in the bloody hell were you doing out and about in daylight with Thorne, for Christ's sake? If anyone had seen his wings—"

"No one saw his wings," Stephanie said soothingly. "Didn't you see the hoodie and duster he was wearing? They covered everything. He looked like a perfectly normal guy in them."

"His clothing was pretty shredded and covered with blood and other things," Dani explained. "The men didn't want to ruin the sheets in the bed, so stripped him before putting him in it. We never saw what he was wearing."

"Blood?" Stephanie asked with concern. "I thought Thorne couldn't bleed a lot? He hardly bled at all when the hacker ripped his throat open. He said it has to do with the dolphin DNA."

"The blood and other matter on him was mostly yours," Dani said gently.

"Oh," Stephanie breathed, suspecting by other matter she meant bits of brain. It had to go somewhere when the headlight tried to move in.

"Why were you in town with Thorne?" Lucian repeated.

Stephanie hesitated, and then muttered, "I needed to go to the grocery store and Thorne came with me because he didn't think it was safe for me to go alone."

Lucian stared at her so hard and so long she knew he was sorting through whatever thoughts were in her head to see if she was telling the truth. She could feel him in there. Fortunately, while the voices in her head had receded somewhat as this conversation had proceeded, they were still in there causing havoc and she was having to concentrate very hard to separate their discussion from the thoughts and feelings of others coming at her from every direction. Stephanie was hoping that would be confusing to him too, but in case it wasn't, she blurted, "Dressler."

Lucian stiffened, his gaze focusing on her face rather than her forehead. His voice was almost threatening when he asked, "Dressler what?"

"He was one of the men in the van," she said at once. "The other was the hacker, so I can only presume he works for Dressler. We were just heading back to the motorcycle with the groceries to come home when I got shot with a dart right there on Main Street. I think Thorne was shot too, but it didn't seem to affect him."

Stephanie quickly recounted their escape from town and the ride back to the house with the van chasing them. As had happened the last time Dressler had shot her with a dart gun, Stephanie hadn't lost consciousness, and had been awake and slowly regaining feeling and strength the whole time between then and the collision with the tree so was able to give a full accounting. She even recalled the crash, or at least the start of it. Things got fuzzy after the first impact. She supposed having a headlight lodged in your head would do that, but didn't bother to mention it as she finished her tale.

Fifteen

"**D**ressler," Lucian growled the name with disgust once Stephanie had finished recounting her version of events in town and the ride back.

"How did he know Thorne was here?" Dani asked Lucian with concern. "You don't think one of the hybrids on the island is still in contact with Dressler and passing him information, do you?"

"No," Stephanie said at once, drawing her sister's gaze. "Or if there is, they didn't tell him Thorne was here. Dressler was surprised to encounter him. He didn't even seem to recognize him at first, and once he did, he thought it was just good luck that he could get both of us when he'd started out after me. Apparently, he's eager to get Thorne 'on his table' too," she added dryly.

"On his table?" Dani echoed with a sickened expression, and then frowning, she asked, "And what do you mean 'too'? Why would he want you on his table?"

"Because the darts don't work on Stephanie like they should, and he, no doubt, wants to know why and how or if he can use that to avoid capture," Lucian explained abruptly.

Stephanie looked to Lucian with alarm. She hadn't realized he knew that while the dart had temporarily incapacitated her, it had failed to knock her out completely. Lucian had been badly burned in the explosion Dressler had set off in the house they had gone to raid, yet despite his blackened and charred condition, she'd been told he'd acted like he'd suffered nothing worse than a sunburn. He'd slapped a bag of blood to his fangs, waited for it to empty, then had got to his feet and started barking orders between bags of blood. That being the case, she'd hoped he hadn't noticed that she'd been conscious and already partially recovered when Decker had carried her back through the woods to the first house, while Beau had stayed unconscious for another twenty minutes or so. She was quite sure Decker hadn't said anything.

"Decker didn't have to say anything," Lucian assured her. "I miss very little."

"Well, apparently I miss a lot," Dani said impatiently, and glowered at Stephanie. "Why didn't you tell me the darts don't work on you? And neither you nor Decker mentioned that Dressler was the one who shot you. How did that little piece of info get left out?"

"We didn't want you to worry," Stephanie said soothingly.

"We? We who? Not Decker?" Dani's voice was getting higher with her upset.

"Dani," she began, intending to calm her and lie if she had to, to keep Decker's butt out of trouble. But before

Stephanie could attempt damage control, Lucian continued his abrupt questions.

"Did you get any indication from Dressler as to where
he'd planned to take you?"

"I—He shot me before I even realized he was there in
town," Stephanie said evasively, and knew by the way
one eyebrow slid up on Lucian's forehead that he hadn't
missed the evasion.

"And after?" he prodded, his eyes narrowing. "What
did you read from him after he shot you?"

When Stephanie looked away, desperately searching
for an answer he'd accept that didn't include the fact
that she could no longer read anyone without touching
them—

Wait, she thought, that couldn't be true anymore.
The voices were back in her head. She could hear the
thoughts of everyone in the house; it just took some effort to separate and identify which thoughts belonged
to whom. Bricker was hoping this case didn't drag on
much longer because he was missing his Holly. Anders was considering what he should get his Valerie for
her birthday. Jo and Nicholas were both thinking they
should volunteer for the next walk around the property
so they could get some alone time. Tiny, Mirabeau, and
Eshe were apparently playing cards with Drina and
Harper because all they were thinking about was the
hands each held, at least on the surface. Decker was outside the bedroom listening to everything and wondering
how much shit he was in with Dani over not telling her
about Dressler. Dani was fretting over the fact that both
Decker and Stephanie appeared to be keeping secrets
from her, and Lucian—

Stephanie's head shot up, her eyes wide with alarm.

She wasn't at all surprised to see that Lucian's gaze was focused on her forehead, his expression concentrated.

"You couldn't read him," he barely breathed the words he was so stunned.

"Of course she couldn't," Dani muttered irritably, still upset at not knowing about Dressler. "The man's obviously crazy, and immortals can't read the insane. Even Stephanie can't read them."

"She can," Lucian told her absently, still digging around in Stephanie's head. She could feel him there again now that she wasn't distracted with everyone's thoughts.

"What?" Dani turned on her with alarm. "You can read the insane? No immortal can read the insane."

Stephanie grimaced. "Well, they aren't missing anything."

"You couldn't read anyone before the accident," Lucian muttered now, drawing her wary gaze back to him. "And haven't been hearing people's thoughts at all for several days."

"What? Is this true?" Dani asked, her voice rising again with panic.

Stephanie opened her mouth to admit it was, but never got the chance before Lucian snapped, "Why wasn't I told?"

"You?" Dani asked, giving him a dismissive look. She then turned on Stephanie to demand, "Why didn't you tell me? I'm your doctor. You need to tell me this stuff."

Stephanie rolled her eyes at that claim. "You aren't my doctor."

"The hell I'm not. I'm the only doctor you see," Dani argued.

"I see you because you're my sister, not for medical

stuff," Stephanie said with exasperation. "I'm Edentate, Dani, I don't need a doctor any more than you do."

"Fine! But I *am* your sister, and you should tell me stuff like this. I need to know what's going on in your life. I need to know—"

"If I'm about to turn no-fanger and need to be put down?" Stephanie finished for her quietly when Dani cut herself off abruptly.

Guilt crossed Dani's face and was clear in her mind, but so were her thoughts, the same ones Stephanie had been hearing for years. The fear that she was different. That she heard too much and saw too much. That it would drive her mad, make her no-fanger, a ravening animal like Leonius, and then she'd have to watch her own sister being put down like a rabid dog.

"Stephanie," Dani began, worry and guilt struggling on her face. "I—"

"Enough! We do not have time for this," Lucian barked, and then scowled and said, "Dani, Stephanie does not tell you anything that goes on in her life, at least not the truth, and she does that because she knows you are not worrying that she *might* turn no-fanger, but *when* exactly she *will* snap and have to be put down. She knows you are forever looking for signs that she is on the verge of it, trying to prepare yourself for what will follow. It terrifies and disheartens her, and puts a great burden on her all at the same time. She feels she has to protect you and not make you worry more by telling you basically *anything*. You have failed her as a sister."

Several emotions crossed Dani's features: guilt, outrage, disappointment, anger . . . Rage won out. "You sanctimonious prick!" she snapped at Lucian. "You sit there saying I've failed her, but you can't honestly say you haven't been thinking the same things."

"I can," Lucian assured her calmly. "Stephanie is intelligent and logical and has an incredibly strong mind. Unlike the rest of you, I think she will come out at the other end of this just fine."

Stephanie's eyes widened incredulously on Lucian at those words. The man was not prone to offer compliments, but those were some pretty big ones coming from him, and for some reason they made her eyes glaze over with tears. Perhaps because he was the first person who might believe in her. She said *might* because she'd never picked up those thoughts from him in the past.

On the other hand, Stephanie realized, while he worried about her in general, she'd never picked up thoughts from him suggesting he thought she would go no-fanger. Come to think of it, Lucian rarely thought anything about her at all. At least, not in her presence, she realized, and felt her lips quirk up with a wry smile as she understood. Lucian was older than dirt. He'd seen a lot of serious shit in his very long life, and had been smart enough—not to mention disciplined enough—not to think anything he didn't want her to hear.

"She *can* beat this," Lucian told Dani firmly, drawing Stephanie's attention back to him as he added grimly, "If the rest of you don't convince her otherwise with your certainty she cannot."

"Do you really believe I can?" Stephanie asked in almost a whisper, desperately needing the reassurance.

Lucian turned, met her gaze dead-on, and held it as he said bluntly, "If I didn't believe that, I'd have put you down long ago rather than let you suffer as you have."

Stephanie drew in a slow breath and nodded once, believing him.

Lucian then glanced from her to Dani and asked, "Now, can we return to the topic at hand? Dressler?"

"Yes, of course," Stephanie said, making herself sit up a little straighter.

Lucian didn't wait for Dani to agree, but said, "We need to catch the bastard this time. I will not accept his escaping again."

Stephanie understood his frustration. They'd just missed him in New York some years back, and then again at the raid last fall, but they'd had other near misses besides that. She knew there had been several raids on nests the last six years where it turned out Dressler was the sire starting the nest, but no longer in attendance. The man had a knack for knowing when to get out and move on. Almost like he did have someone warning him. But that wouldn't be a hybrid. It would have to be someone close to the rogue hunters, or a hunter him/herself.

"Did Mortimer figure out how Dressler got his hands on the dart gun?" she asked suddenly.

"No." Lucian didn't hide his frustration. "As far as we know no one has lost a weapon, and none of our people are missing, so he couldn't have got it by killing or kidnapping one of our people and taking their weapon."

"Hmm," Stephanie murmured with a small frown. It troubled her that they couldn't sort that out. It meant they had no idea how many of the special weapons he had. Leaving that issue for now, she sighed and said, "The easiest way to catch Dressler is to just hang around and wait for him to come after Thorne and me again."

"He wouldn't try to come after them again, would he?" Dani asked Lucian with concern. "Not now that he knows there's a small army of hunters here waiting for him."

"But does he know that?" Stephanie asked. "He knows two immortals interrupted his taking us this time. Heck, if they were busy and distracted trying to untangle me from metal, they may not even have noticed where Bricker and Anders came from and could have thought they just happened along for a visit, or something. So, as long as you don't have a small armada of SUVs on display in the driveway, there's no reason he should know there are more than Bricker and Anders here, and that might not stop him if he has a nest somewhere around here with more men to help him take us."

Lucian stared at her, his face expressionless for a moment, and then he stood abruptly and strode from the room, bellowing for Anders and Bricker.

"The SUVs are in the driveway, then, I take it," Stephanie said dryly.

Dani nodded.

"Yeah. That's what I thought," Stephanie said wryly, and began to push aside the sheets and blankets covering her.

"What are you doing? Do you need to use the bathroom?" Dani asked with concern, quickly fetching a robe that had sat folded on the dresser.

"I want to see Thorne," Stephanie announced, grimacing when she discovered that while Bricker and Anders had removed her outer clothes, they'd left her bra and panties on her. Unfortunately, her bra had not escaped the blood she'd lost in the accident. It was now stiff and itchy with the dried stuff. She removed it quickly, and then reached for the robe Dani was holding, eyebrows rising when her sister hesitated to give it to her.

"You really shouldn't be up yet, Stephanie," she said finally. "You need more blood. Get back in bed and I'll—" The words died when Stephanie shook her head and took the robe.

"I want to see Thorne," she insisted, and quickly shrugged into the robe, surprised to find it was her own. Someone must have fetched it from her house, Stephanie thought, because this wasn't her place, but one of Drina and Harper's guest rooms. Not surprising, she supposed. If she and Thorne had been as badly injured as Drina had said, the men would have wanted to get them to the closest place with blood and beds.

"Which room is he in?" Stephanie asked, tying the sash of the robe as she headed for the door.

"In the room next door," Dani admitted. "But I really think it would be better if you got back in bed. Thorne is fine, and you and I need to talk. I should apologize for—"

"Nothing," Stephanie said firmly, opening the bedroom door and leading the way out. "You should apologize for nothing. You can't help how you feel. I know you care, and I know you're scared for me and have been for a long time. I've been scared too. Afraid I'd just flip my lid one day and become a female Leonius." She shuddered at the thought before straightening her shoulders and saying determinedly, "But I won't let that happen. Lucian's right. I can beat this."

Stephanie opened the door to the guest room Thorne was in and stopped dead at the sight of him. Bricker and Anders had laid him on his stomach in the bed, but left him uncovered. No doubt they'd been concerned about injuring his wing feathers or something, she thought, and let her gaze move over the folded chocolate-brown wings covering his back from shoulders to midcalf as completely as a blanket would have. The man who had seemed so big and strong and beautiful just the day before appeared almost shrunken in size now, and he was so pale and still.

Swallowing, Stephanie crossed to the bed and eased to sit down on the edge of it, her hand moving toward his upper arm, and then stopping when she noted the sheen to his skin. After a hesitation, she ran one finger lightly down the few inches of arm not covered by his wing and then turned her hand over to examine the goo on the tip of the finger. To Stephanie, it looked exactly like the substance that oozed out of the pores of mortals during a turn. She assumed it was injured cells or whatnot being forced from the body as it repaired itself.

"Stephanie, you need blood," Dani said with concern. "You've seen for yourself that he's fine. Let's go to the kitchen and feed."

"I want to stay with Thorne."

There was a brief silence and then Dani said, "Sitting here staring at him won't make him heal faster. From what I understand this stasis lasts three or four days."

"Yes. Thorne told me that," she admitted.

"Well then, there's no reason to sit here. Let's go get you some food and blood."

"Later," Stephanie said, leaning over to grab a tissue from the box on the bedside table. She wiped the ooze from her fingertip, and then crumpled the ball in her left hand as she reached out to run the fingers of her right hand lightly over the nearer wing.

Dani was silent now, at least verbally, but her thoughts were still going and Stephanie could hear the worries she was now having, so wasn't surprised when Dani said, "Steph . . . I know you can't read Thorne, and it was probably a relief to have someone around whose thoughts weren't coming at you all the time. But none of us can read him."

Stephanie turned to peer at her, one eyebrow arched. "And?"

Dani bit her lip and then said, "I just want to make sure you aren't attaching some significance to it, and maybe getting a crush on Thorne. I mean, he's a good-looking guy, and super nice, but your not being able to read or control him doesn't make him a possible life mate to you."

"Shared pleasure does, though," Stephanie pointed out solemnly, meeting her gaze.

"Yes. But you'd have to have sex with him to know if—" Dani stopped, her eyes widening at Stephanie's expression, and then gasped, "You didn't!"

"We had sex and experienced shared pleasure," she admitted. However, while her words were calm and matter-of-fact, Stephanie wasn't as insouciant as she was trying to appear and could feel her face heat up with what was probably the mother of all blushes.

Dani wasn't handling it much better. For a minute, Stephanie was afraid she might actually be having a stroke. Her face flushed, then paled, then flushed again while her mouth was moving in an almost chewing fashion with no words coming out. Finally, her voice oddly squeaky, she asked, "You had sex?"

"And experienced shared pleasure," Stephanie repeated slowly, pretty sure that was the most important part here. It had been the whole point behind her telling her.

"You lost your virginity?"

"And gained a life mate," Stephanie pointed out. "Besides, I didn't really lose it. I mean, I didn't set it down somewhere and forget where I put it. I just . . . well, I guess I gave it to him."

"You gave him your virginity," Dani sighed, her eyes glazing over with tears.

"Yeah. You're really not getting the point, sis. Thorne is my life mate."

"I know that," she assured her impatiently. "But this is . . . My baby sister is a woman now."

"I'm pretty sure I was a woman before having sex," Stephanie said dryly. "I mean, his dick isn't a magic wand." She paused, and then said, "Well, it is pretty magic, but he didn't wave it around before putting it in and suddenly turn me into a woman."

"Oh my God, you had sex!" Dani squealed excitedly.

"Yeah . . . I mean, I'm twenty-seven. It was about time, don't you think?"

"Oh, for God's sake! You are so ruining this for me!" Dani snapped. "In the old days you would have shared all the details, and we'd be squealing and giggling and munching out on junk food."

"The old days," Stephanie muttered, her gaze turning grimly to Thorne.

"Yes. The old days," Dani said solemnly. "When you used to treat me like your favorite big sister. Which you haven't done since we were turned. Now I get weekly chats where you tell me about work, and your pets. Nothing about you. Your feelings or hopes. Or even what the hell has been going on," she added a little heatedly. "Do you know how much I've worried about you? Or how guilty I've felt because I have Decker and you don't have a mate? Or how much I've worried that you'd never find a partner or relationship, that the voices in your head would someday overwhelm you and you'd never know the happiness of a loving relationship, you'd just—" Realizing what she was saying, she stopped abruptly, alarm on her face, and it was Stephanie who finished for her.

"Wander through life all alone, my mind tortured, until I gave in to the madness?" she suggested, and then shook her head. "You see, now that's why I don't tell you anything."

"I didn't mean—"

"You didn't mean to tell me, but it's what you've been thinking," Stephanie interrupted solemnly. "Dani, I can hear your thoughts. I could from the moment I was turned, and Lucian was right, you wrote me off years ago as a lost cause."

Dani stared at her with a tortured expression for a moment, and then her shoulders sagged and she said, "So I did fail you as a sister."

"No," Stephanie said on a sigh. "It's fine. You can't help your fears."

"Then why did you stop talking to me? You used to tell me everything. But ever since the attack you've shut me out and—"

"*I* shut *you* out?" Stephanie gasped with disbelief. "Are you fucking kidding me?"

"You did," Dani insisted. "And I miss the old Stephanie. I miss my sister. We need to discuss this and—"

"All right, you want to discuss this?" Stephanie interrupted coldly, fury unfurling inside her. "Fine. Yeah, you suck as a sister."

Dani's head went back slightly and she closed her eyes briefly as if she'd suffered a blow. But then she let her breath out on a sad sigh and shook her head. "I'm sorry if my fears about you going no-fanger were—"

"Your sucking as a sister doesn't have a damned thing to do with that," Stephanie snapped. "It's the way you acted after we were turned."

"The way I acted?" Dani said uncertainly. "If I did something back then that upset you, I'm sorry, but I was trying to do what was best for you."

Stephanie raised her eyebrows. "Oh. Right. So, I guess I should thank you for abandoning me after the most traumatic event of my life."

"Abandoning you?" Dani gasped with disbelief.

"Yes, abandoning me," Stephanie growled. "I was a kid, Dani. I was attacked by a psychotic bastard who turned me into—" She shook her head. "I didn't even understand at the time what I'd become. But while I was still struggling with that, you tell me we can't go home anymore, that Mom, Dad, our brothers, sisters, aunts, uncles, and cousins . . . hell, even my friends, they were all told that we'd died in an accident and were now off-limits."

She swallowed thickly at the memory of that blow when she'd been given the news, and then said, "I'd lost everyone in one fell swoop. But I thought, it's okay. At least I still have Dani." Her mouth twisted with a humorless smile when Dani winced. "Yeah, no. You were off banging Decker all over the world, dumping me on Elvi and Victor, who were—by the way—*complete fucking strangers.*"

"I'm sorry. I know it was hard, and I didn't really want to leave you, but everyone was telling me it was for the best. You'd be safe from Leonius in Port Henry, and I was supposed to help them lure Leonius in so they could capture him," she pointed out. "But I insisted they tell me everything that was going on with you, and—"

"Oh yeah?" Stephanie interrupted to ask. "So where were you when I ran away?"

When Dani stared at her blankly, Stephanie reminded her, "When Anders was going to take me back to Lucian because they were *concerned* I might not be quite right in the head because of the Edentata stuff."

She knew when Dani's breath slowly left her that she recognized what she was talking about. Stephanie nodded. "Yeah, so if they told you everything that was going on with me, why didn't you come to find me when I ran away and went home?" she asked, but didn't give her a chance to answer before saying, "I *needed* you. I was so alone and lonely, and afraid. I knew I couldn't go home, but I needed my big sister and thought—" She shook her head, refusing to admit her running away had been a cry for help, and then continued bitterly, "But who came to find me? Not you, Dani. Not my sister. Drina and Harper did. Two people I hadn't even met a week earlier." She snorted. "So yeah, forgive me for thinking you suck as a sister for abandoning me when I was fourteen years old."

"Fifteen," Dani corrected quietly.

A short humorless laugh slipped from Stephanie's lips and she said wearily, "Barely fifteen."

"Steph, I'm sorry. I—"

"Stephanie. Come."

Stephanie turned to the door at that abrupt order,

relieved at the interruption that would save her from having to hear excuses and apologies. She saw Lucian walking away down the hall and stood to follow at once, but her gaze slid over Thorne as she went. She didn't really want to leave Thorne, but when Lucian gave an order, it was best to listen. At least in these situations, with rogues around and Lucian trying to catch them. Especially this time when the rogue was a threat to both her and Thorne.

Sixteen

"Sit," Lucian ordered when Stephanie followed him into the kitchen.

She moved automatically to the far end of the island. It was where she always sat in her home.

As it was in her house, the security monitor was on the counter right next to the end of the island. Stephanie glanced at it out of habit as she sat down, and movement on the camera view of the front of the shop immediately caught her eye. Anders was backing one of the SUVs into the shop where the rest were already parked.

"I see you moved the vehicles out of the driveway," she murmured, managing a faint smile.

"It was a good idea," Lucian admitted, and the comment made the tension in her shoulders ease. The guy was a hard-ass. He'd come down on you like a ton of bricks if you messed up, but he also acknowledged when you had good ideas and such. Not with lots of fanfare or anything, just a simple acknowledgment. Oddly, it was enough from him. At least for her.

"Close your eyes."

Rather than close, Stephanie's eyes narrowed warily at that order. "Why?"

"Just close your eyes," he instructed impatiently.

Resisting the urge to stick out her tongue at him, Stephanie closed her eyes.

"Now," he said solemnly, "we need to know if our hiding the SUVs will do any good, or if Dressler has already done a drive-by and seen them. So, I want you to sift through those voices in your head for him, and find out what he's seen."

When Stephanie's eyes immediately popped open again, Lucian barked, "Shut them!"

Heaving out an exasperated sigh, Stephanie closed her eyes once more, but said, "I don't know if I can find Dressler's voice in all of the masses crowded in my mind."

"Of course you can. You did it last fall at the nest we raided. You were able to separate his voice from the others and follow it to where he was."

Nothing could have stopped her from opening her eyes then, though they were narrowed again as she met his gaze. "How do you know that? You wouldn't listen that night when I tried to tell you there was someone else there."

Lucian merely arched one eyebrow, and Stephanie sighed to herself. Of course he'd read her thoughts at the time, but hadn't deemed it important enough to follow up then. He hadn't realized it was Dressler in the house behind the woods, because she hadn't yet known. And none of them had been aware that there were bombs

in the house, so he'd thought it smarter to deal with
the many in the house before going after the one alone
somewhere behind it, which was all she'd known at the
time.

"Fine," she groused, closing her eyes.

Stephanie took a moment to gather herself, and then
opened her mind to the voices that had been hammering
at her since she'd woken up. Not that her mind was ever
really closed to them. Much as she wished she could,
Stephanie could not completely block them out, but she
could muffle them somewhat. Like closing your bedroom door when someone was playing the stereo at a
volume so high the bass vibrated through the house. It
didn't silence it, didn't even lower the volume much, but
it was just enough to keep her from being incapacitated.
Essentially, what she was doing now was opening that
bedroom door to let the babble come in unimpeded.

Stephanie bit back a moan as sound exploded inside
her head. So many voices. So much emotion. Too much,
she thought with anxiety. It wouldn't have been before
when she was used to it, but after three days of the abso-
lute bliss of silence in her mind, this cacophony of noise
was overwhelming, and Stephanie felt panic begin to
rise in her.

"Steady," Lucian said grimly. "Remember to breathe."

Stephanie's eyes flickered under her eyelids as she
realized she was holding her breath. She sucked in a
long, deep draft of air, surprised to find it did help somewhat. Not a whole lot, but enough for the panic that had
been building in her to recede a bit. So, she exhaled to
take another deep breath and the pressure and panic in
her head eased a little more.

"Good. Now look for his voice."

"Get out of my head, Lucian," Stephanie said with irritation. She hated when he read her. Where the others couldn't anymore, he still could and it was uncomfortable for her. Not just because of what he might read either. Stephanie didn't know what it was like for others, but for her, it was a physical sensation when Lucian went poking through her thoughts. In fact, the only reason she could have missed his reading her last fall to get the info he had about Dressler and the hunt was because she'd been busy struggling with her body, trying to force it by sheer will to shake off the drug and start functioning properly again. Now, she could feel it, and it was like something abrasive was being rubbed across her brain. That alone had her resenting the hell out of his being in there.

"Find Dressler," Lucian ordered, ignoring her request and staying firmly in her mind.

"I will. Just get out of my head!" she insisted, raising a hand to her scalp as if to rub away the irritation. However, she couldn't rub her brain. Her hand dropped, but her temper rose.

"Find Dressler," Lucian repeated.

"Get out!" She'd meant to snap the words, but they came out in a guttural roar. On the bright side, Stephanie suddenly couldn't feel Lucian in her mind anymore. She could hear him, though. There was a startled grunt, followed by a loud, but short, screech of his chair on the hardwood floor, as if he'd jerked back in surprise.

Stephanie opened her eyes, and saw him shaking his head as if trying to recover from a physical blow. Frowning, she asked, "Are you all right?"

Lucian just grunted, and rubbed his forehead, muttering, "Find Dressler."

"Stubborn arse," she muttered, shaking her head as she closed her eyes again.

"Arse?" Lucian growled with irritation. "You spent too much time with Magnus before moving out of Port Henry and picked up his British expressions."

"You'd prefer I call you an ass?" Stephanie asked dryly, but didn't wait for an answer, and instead concentrated on sifting through the voices in her head, searching for Dressler's. She was pretty sure she'd recognize it. Like Lucian had said, she'd heard it before. It was calm, and cold and—There!

"What is it? Did you find him?" Lucian asked at once when she gave a small grunt.

Stephanie nodded silently, concentrating on Dressler's thoughts.

"Then he's close," Bricker commented, and Stephanie gave a little start at his voice. She hadn't heard the man approach. But then she'd been listening to the voices in her head. For all she knew, everyone could be in the kitchen now. Sometimes it was hard to hear outer sounds when the inner noise was high.

"He must have taken control of one of the neighbors on either side of here to be close," Beau said, sounding angry.

"Not necessarily," Lucian said, and then asked, "Stephanie, do you have any idea how far away a person has to be before you can't hear their thoughts anymore?"

Stephanie hesitated, reluctant to admit the truth, even to herself.

"Shall I read you to get the answer?" Lucian threatened, but the very fact that he made the threat rather than just do it gave her pause. Normally he'd just dive into her head and mine the information for himself.

Well, if she was thinking of it, which he could easily ensure by asking her the question again. She'd instinctively think of the answer. His not doing so now made her wonder what had happened when she'd yelled at him to get out of her head. Had she hurt him somehow?

"Stephanie," he growled impatiently now. "It's important."

She scowled at his tone, but knowing he was right and it *was* important, she finally answered, "Five or six miles."

Someone sucked in a shocked breath. Someone else gave a low, impressed whistle. Everyone else was silent, but it was only a surface silence. Their thoughts were going a mile a minute at this news. Worry, concern, admiration, respect, and fear filled the thoughts of those around her. It was the fear that troubled her, though. It wasn't fear *for* her, it was fear *of* her . . . and the threat she could be if she went no-fanger.

Nothing new there, Stephanie reminded herself grimly, and set her mouth as she ignored and blocked out the voices of the people around her in favor of that farther voice, Dressler.

"Are you sure?" Lucian asked finally.

For a minute Stephanie thought he was asking if she was sure that the others were afraid of her, but then she realized he was asking if she was sure that her limit for hearing people's thoughts was five or six miles. Sighing, she explained, "The Winters had a seventy-fifth wedding anniversary just after I moved in last summer. They're a couple in their nineties," she told them. "They've lived in town their whole lives and know everyone in it. So, they—or maybe it was their kids or grandkids—threw a big barbecue to celebrate and invited the whole town.

It was even in the local paper. All welcome." Stephanie smiled faintly. "I think I'm probably the only one who didn't go."

"I don't understand," Beau said, and Stephanie could hear the frown in her voice. "What's that got to do with—?"

"The Winters live on the other side of town," Stephanie interrupted to explain. "Pretty much on the edge of the township. A good seven or eight miles away. And I know pretty much everyone went because they all dropped out of my head one, two, or three at a time as they headed to the party. The last person whose thoughts I could hear was the postie in town. She had a good thirty-minute inner debate about whether she should close up the post office and go or not before giving in, putting an Out to Lunch sign in the window and heading off to the barbecue. I lost her thoughts no more than a couple minutes later," she explained, and then added, "The post office is about five or six miles away from here."

"My God," Harper murmured. "We knew you were hearing people from a distance, but a five- or six-mile radius? That must be . . . I'm surprised you go outside at all."

"Harper, she's inside right now and can hear Dressler's thoughts," Drina pointed out quietly. "The insulation in the walls and triple-paned windows obviously don't work anymore."

"But she said . . ." His voice faded away to silence and Stephanie supposed it was because he'd realized she'd been lying about that for a while now. The realization caused some regret in her, and she worried that he'd be angry with her for it, when all she'd been trying to do was ease the anxiety they were all suffering over her.

"What are you picking up from Dressler?" Lucian asked, distracting Stephanie. "Can you tell where he is?"

Stephanie zeroed in on Dressler's thoughts again, and . . . well, frankly she didn't know how she did it, but she kind of tracked them back to his physical body and suddenly could see through his eyes. Stephanie didn't explain that to the people around her, however. She didn't need them fearing her even more.

"He's in a country kitchen," she muttered, looking around the room Dressler was in. He was sitting at a kitchen table, a phone to his ear, talking to someone.

"Country kitchen?" Lucian asked. "Is that the name of a restaurant, or—?"

"He's in a kitchen decorated in the country style," Stephanie explained. "Open beams, open shelves, one brick wall, weathered surfaces, lots of wood."

Lucian gave an exasperated huff. "I don't care what the decor is, Stephanie. Do you recognize the house? Do you know whose kitchen it is and where?"

Stephanie gave a disbelieving laugh at the question. "I don't usually leave the house, much less go around touring my neighbors' kitchens, Lucian. How would I know where it is?"

"Right," he muttered, but then asked, "Well, can you tell if it's near or far by—What's happening?" he interrupted himself to ask when Stephanie sucked in a sharp breath.

She didn't respond right away. She was concentrating on the conversation Dressler was having.

"Stephanie?" Lucian prodded after a moment.

"He knows you're here," she said finally. "He's talking to someone at his latest nest. Arranging for men to come. He plans to attack."

"How many men and how long until they get here?" Lucian barked at once.

"I don't know how many," Stephanie said with a frown. "All he said was bring them all."

"Christ," someone muttered. "There were thirty rogues at the last nest he started."

"Push deeper, Stephanie," Lucian ordered quietly. "This is important. I need to know when to expect them and if we should send for reinforcements."

"It's probably a good idea to call Mortimer and have him send every available man anyway," someone said, and Stephanie recognized that it was Lucian's nephew, Nicholas Argeneau.

"Call and tell him to prepare and put them on standby, but not to send them until we say so," Lucian ordered, and Stephanie heard Nicholas move away to make the call.

"Stephanie," Lucian said now, "I need you to go deeper into his mind. We need to learn whatever we can."

She nodded, and did what she thought of as a deep dive—following Dressler's thoughts not just into his body, but into his mind, or his core, or possibly even where his soul resided. Stephanie didn't know where she went when this happened, but it usually allowed her to see things she couldn't otherwise. Sometimes it even let her see future events, and that was the case this time. Feeling almost disjointed from her own body, she whipped past flashes of his life and the tortures he'd put on others in the name of science, and into . . .

"I can't move. He shot me," she whispered.

"Who shot you? Dressler?" Tiny asked at once.

"She can't hear you, Tiny," Beau said solemnly. "Look at her eyes. She's doing that thing she does where she sees something that hasn't happened yet."

Beau was wrong, Stephanie thought. She could hear them. She could also smell, feel, and talk, but while she knew her eyes had popped open, she couldn't see anything around her, just the scene playing out in her head, and she couldn't move or stop it. This vision, or whatever it was, had to end on its own before she'd be free to move.

It was almost like an absence seizure, Stephanie thought, recalling something she'd come across while doing research a while back. She knew she froze and seemed to stare blankly into space for a bit while it happened; she'd been told that. She'd also been told that her eyes glowed oddly too when it happened, but she had no control over it. Or really over what she said when it happened.

"She shot him," Stephanie said with surprise, watching the scene playing out in her head.

"Dressler?" Lucian asked.

"She shot him," she repeated.

"You already said that, Stephanie," Lucian said quietly, tension in his voice. "Can you tell us if it's Dressler who was shot, and who the she is?"

"Dressler."

"Dressler is the one getting shot?" Lucian asked for clarification. "Is it here? Does he get shot here?"

"I don't . . ." She frowned with confusion as she turned to look around the room and found her gaze on the woman to her right in the vision. "I don't know her."

The ding of a bell sounded, pulling Stephanie out of the scene she'd stumbled into, and she blinked her eyes and put out a hand to the island to steady herself as she returned to the kitchen in Harper and Drina's house.

A long sigh from Lucian told her that he understood she'd lost her connection to Dressler, but then he turned to the others crowded into the kitchen and said, "I want the fences guarded until this is over, and tell Nicholas—Oh, there you are," he interrupted himself to say as Nicholas now entered the room. "Call Mortimer back and tell him to send as many men and women as he can find. Pull them off anything they're on and get them here. Pronto," he added grimly, and then glanced to the side and muttered, "And who the hell is that? Is that Marguerite?"

Stephanie automatically turned to follow his gaze to the monitor of camera views on the side counter, her eyes finding the source of the ding that had pulled her from the scene she'd been watching. It had been the chime that rang when the gate was opened. Another SUV had arrived and parked at the end of the walkway leading to the porch. And it was indeed Marguerite getting out of the front passenger seat, even as Julius got out on the driver's side. They all watched silently as Marguerite opened the back door to allow a short, round gray-haired woman in a black knee-length dress to get out of the vehicle while Julius moved to the back of the SUV to retrieve a portable wheelchair. He opened it and rolled it around to the driver's side back door.

Stephanie saw that he'd opened the door, but then he bent into the vehicle and out of sight briefly before closing the door and coming around the vehicle, pushing the wheelchair with a woman now in it. She was older too, her hair white, her face pale, and she was wearing dark blue dress pants and a pure white blouse.

Stephanie frowned slightly as she realized that they hadn't brought the baby with them. Marguerite and Julius took their baby girl, Benedetta, with them everywhere. Her not being with them now was somewhat surprising . . . unless they knew about incoming trouble.

"What the hell are they doing here?" Lucian muttered, and stood up. He started out of the room, and then paused to spear Stephanie with one pointing finger. "Wait here. I want to know what you saw."

Stephanie nodded as she turned her gaze back to the monitor. She then stood and walked over to use the mouse on the countertop to click on the small image of the porch, enlarging it as Julius pushed the wheelchair up the walkway toward it with Marguerite and the other woman following. She immediately sucked in a startled breath when she was able to better see the two women.

"Stephanie?" Beau asked, moving up to her side. "Are you all right?"

"Who are those women with Marguerite and Julius?" she asked almost urgently.

Beau turned to peer at the screen, but after a moment shook her head. "I don't know. I've never seen them before."

"They're Thorne's mother and his *tía*. They're staying at Marguerite's and I called them earlier today. I thought they should know he'd been hurt. I guess they must have decided to come see for themselves that he was healing."

Stephanie turned at those solemn words to see Dani entering the kitchen with Decker on her heels. She almost turned back to the monitor again then, but hesitated when she noted the tracks of tears on Dani's face and that her eyes were bloodshot. She'd been crying, and Stephanie knew it was her fault. She'd hurled some pretty hurtful words at her before Lucian had called her away. Resentment and hurt she'd kept bottled up inside for all these years had just exploded out of her. It had felt good at the time, finally saying it, but now that she could see the effect it had had on Dani, Stephanie felt guilt begin to prick at her.

"They shouldn't have come," Beau said, turning back to the screen with a frown. "It's too dangerous with Dressler planning an attack."

"Dressler's planning an attack here? On this house?" Dani asked with concern.

"I better go see what Lucian needs doing," Decker said grimly, but paused long enough to rub Dani's arm and press a tender kiss to her forehead before hurrying for the door.

"Lucian will send them back to Toronto," Tiny predicted.

"He won't," Stephanie said with certainty, turning back to look at the monitor. Lucian had stopped the small group as they'd reached the ground level porch and was talking to them. He didn't look happy, but then neither did Marguerite at whatever they were discussing, and Stephanie said, "Lucian might try to send them away, but they won't go."

"How do you know?" Beau asked with curiosity.

"Because she shoots Dressler," she answered.

"Marguerite?" Tiny asked.

Stephanie shook her head, her gaze locked on the two women on-screen.

"One of the mortal women shoots Dressler?" Harper

asked, sounding surprised, and when she nodded, asked, "Which one?"

"Both of them," Stephanie answered, and then turned to cross the kitchen to Dani. Catching her arm as she passed her, she drew her around and tugged her out of the kitchen with her. Urging her toward the bedroom where she'd woken up, Stephanie said, "We need to talk."

Seventeen

"I'm sorry," Dani blurted the moment Stephanie ushered her into the bedroom and turned to push the door closed behind them.

Shaking her head, Stephanie faced her at once and said, "No. I'm sorry. I shouldn't have gone at you like that. I—"

"Yes. You should have," Dani interrupted. "I deserved it. And I really am sorry. I never looked at it from your perspective. You'd just been through hell, and needed me. I should have insisted we stay together, but they were all telling me you'd be safer in Port Henry, and I'd never been in a situation like that, so thought it best to listen to their advice. That's the truth."

"I know," Stephanie said solemnly.

"Okay. But do you know that while I'm this big, respected doctor, I haven't got a clue what I'm doing most of the time?" Dani asked unhappily. "I mean, I know what I'm doing at work. That's easy compared to real life. In real life I don't know what the hell I'm doing, and back then it was even worse. I was a mess. Who the hell would have believed vampires are real? Or that we'd become fangless vampires? Or that one day I'd be so desperate for blood I'd be licking on a poor old man's head wound?" she asked with self-disgust, and shook her head briefly before sighing and telling her, "Back then I was just as confused and frightened and lost as you must have felt, and I listened to others rather than my own instincts. I let them convince me you'd be better off away from me in Port Henry."

Reaching out, Dani took Stephanie's hands and said, "I let you down, and I'm so incredibly sorry. I love you. I'll do whatever I can to make it up to you. I just hope someday you can forgive me."

Stephanie stared at Dani silently, listening to the thoughts in her head. Every one of them lined up with her words. She wasn't hiding or exaggerating anything. Dani had been just as traumatized and messed up as her back then and, because of that, had believed the others might have a better idea of what should be done than she did.

Sighing, Stephanie simply used their clasped hands to tug Dani into an embrace.

"I love you too," she whispered, hugging her tightly and blinking rapidly as her eyes glazed over with tears. Stephanie hated crying.

"God, I'm crying," Dani muttered, sniffling. "I hate crying."

The words brought a watery laugh from Stephanie, and she pulled back so they could both wipe their eyes, admitting, "So do I."

"And I hate fighting with you," Dani added as she turned to snatch a box of tissues off the bedside table and held it between them so they could both take some.

"We don't fight," Stephanie said wryly. "This is the first one we've had in—"

"Since the family weekend up north before we were attacked," Dani finished for her when Stephanie paused.

"Yeah," she agreed solemnly.

Dani nodded. "We haven't argued since then because you've been avoiding me ever since you were sent to Port Henry."

Stephanie didn't argue because it was the truth. She hadn't wanted all her resentment to blow up on her as it had earlier. While she'd been angry and hurt, Dani had still been the only real family she'd had left, and she'd been afraid of alienating her.

"And I let you," Dani confessed. "I've been so afraid for you, and feeling so helpless to do anything about your situation, it was just easier to not deal with it. I'm sorry for that too."

A small laugh slipped from Stephanie, and she shook her head. "We've both made mistakes, Dani. I was looking to you as some wise mother figure who could fix all my woes, completely ignoring the fact that we were both in uncharted territory."

"While I felt like I should be able to fix everything, and was kicking my own ass for being a failure because I didn't know what the hell to do," Dani said. "Lucian was right about that. It's why I got so upset when he said it. I did fail you as a sister."

"Isn't that what life is about? Mom used to say life was a series of lessons, some you pass and some you fail. The important thing is to try . . . and to learn from your mistakes so that you pass the next time."

Dani let her breath out on an exasperated huff. "See, you're the one dispensing wisdom when it should be me. I so suck ass as a big sister."

Stephanie grinned. "You said ass." When Dani wrinkled her nose at her, she added, "Don't say it around Decker or he'll think you're getting my potty mouth, and won't want you to hang out with me."

"Decker loves you," Dani assured her fondly. "He's always coming home after you work with him and the other hunters, bragging on how you helped them with this, or how you did that." Expression turning solemn, she added, "He said you saved all of their lives that day when you sensed the bomb in the house."

Stephanie shook her head. "Mostly just him, Lucian, and Bricker. And whoever went through the back door. Everyone else probably would have been fine. Maybe a little charred, but alive."

"He says the ones at the windows and sliding doors could have been killed too when the fire blew out the glass," Dani insisted. "But no matter, thank you for saving Decker."

"He's family," Stephanie said with a shrug, uncomfortable with her thanks.

"He is," Dani assured her. "And he thinks of you as a little sister. He's decided he's going to redouble his efforts to find out what he can about no-fangers and how they go no-fanger. Whether it's usually immediate, or takes time. He says Marcus told him that Basha said that Leonius seemed a perfectly normal little boy to her when he was young, but she later found out it was a facade, and that when he was out of her sight, he was torturing and killing little animals and stuff like that."

"So basic serial killer behavior," Stephanie said dryly, because she knew that was a common trend with serial killers. That they'd tortured and killed animals while young, eventually graduating to humans. "Well, the good news is I've never had, and haven't suddenly developed, an urge to kill animals of any kind."

Dani smiled faintly, but then bit her lip.

"Say it," Stephanie suggested quietly. "I can hear your thoughts."

"Right. Then you already know that Decker was wondering if your temporary loss of hearing everyone's thoughts coincided with Thorne's arrival? If so, his being your life mate might have somehow helped silence it for you."

Stephanie considered it, but shook her head. "I don't think so. I noticed the lack of voices at the start of our chat, which was what? Five thirty in the morning?" When Dani nodded, she said, "Well, Thorne didn't arrive for another hour. He had to be a lot more than five or six miles away when I first noticed the silence in my head. Probably more like fifty at the time."

"Oh," Dani said with disappointment.

"Besides, Thorne and I were talking about this, and he thinks it might be possible the voices died out even hours before that."

Her eyebrows rose with surprise. "Why?"

"Because I fell asleep editing," Stephanie admitted wryly, and then shrugged. "Look, don't worry about it. Maybe it was just a blip, or maybe I'm learning to block the voices, or maybe my mind threw up some kind of shield to give me a break from everyone's thoughts.

Whatever, it's apparently stopped; I can hear them again, and I'll handle it." She smiled crookedly, and added, "But it was nice while it lasted. It made me feel almost normal . . . when I wasn't worrying it was a bad thing," she added with a wry laugh.

"Oh, baby girl," Dani sighed, hugging her again. "I'm sorry I made you feel you couldn't tell me this stuff. You can, you know. I'll try to control my panic and just listen."

"Thanks," Stephanie murmured as they separated.

"You're rubbing your stomach," Dani pointed out then with a small frown. "You need blood."

"Yeah. I guess I'd better have some." They both grimaced at the thought of it, and then Stephanie turned to lead the way to the door, but paused with her hand on the knob as a thought struck her.

"What is it?" Dani asked, and Stephanie could hear the flood of different worries immediately cramming their way into her sister's head.

"Thorne's mother is here," Stephanie said, turning wide, alarmed eyes to her sister.

"Oh. Yes." Dani glanced to the door, and pursed her lips. "I wonder if Lucian made them leave."

"He didn't," Stephanie said with certainty. The future she'd seen wouldn't happen if Lucian managed to make them leave.

"We should go say hello, then," Dani decided, gesturing for her to open the door.

"I can't meet Thorne's mother like this," Stephanie protested at once, glancing down at herself. While the robe covered her, she was very aware that the only thing under it was a pair of panties and the dried blood that streaked her upper body and part of her lower body.

Good Lord, she thought after giving herself a sniff, she smelled like a charnel house. "I need a shower. And clothes."

"It's fine," Dani assured her. "She knows you and Thorne were in an accident. She'll understand."

"Would you have wanted to meet Decker's mother for the first time in this state?" Stephanie asked pointedly.

"Right," Dani said with immediate understanding. "Okay. Let me check the hall to see if the coast is clear. If it is, you can hustle to the shower while I run back to your place and fetch you something to wear."

"Yes. Thank you. That would be good," Stephanie said with relief, stepping aside to let her slip out of the room. She bit her lip as she waited, fretting over meeting Thorne's mother . . . and without Thorne there for support. What if his mother hated her? What if she took one look at her and—

Her thoughts died and she glanced toward the door when it opened.

"The coast is clear. Elizabeth and Maria are in the house now, but they're in Thorne's room with Marguerite. And the bathroom is empty," Dani announced, and began handing her the items she'd apparently grabbed while out of the room. Two bags of blood and a glass. She hadn't forgotten Stephanie's need for blood. "You can drink these in the bathroom while you wait for the water to warm up. It should tide you over for a bit."

"Thanks," Stephanie murmured, slipping the glass into the capacious pocket of her robe so she could carry a blood bag in each hand.

"Go ahead and I'll get those clothes," Dani said, stepping backward in the hall for Stephanie to leave the bedroom. "What do you want me to grab?"

She opened her mouth to answer as she stepped out of the bedroom, but then paused, her eyes going wide with alarm. "I don't have anything to wear."

"What?" Dani asked with surprise.

"Well, nothing appropriate to meet Thorne's mother," she explained. "I mean, I'm by myself all the time, Dani. All I own are joggers, jeans, shorts, jerseys, and T-shirts. Nothing nice enough to meet—"

"Steph, honey, I'm sure shorts and a T-shirt will be fine. She isn't the queen."

"No, it's worse. She's my life mate's mom," Stephanie pointed out.

Dani smiled at her sympathetically, but said, "You better get moving before they come. They might not stay with Thorne long. He isn't awake to visit with."

"Right," she muttered, and started forward, only to freeze when Thorne's door opened ahead of them and Marguerite appeared.

"Oh, there you are, Stephanie," she said with a smile. "I was just coming to find you. I want to introduce you to Thorne's mother and *tía*. Come, dear."

"Oh God," Stephanie breathed, and Dani immediately stepped in front of her and grasped her shoulders bracingly. "It's going to be all right."

Stephanie switched her wide eyes to her sister's face and hissed, "What if she can tell I had sex with her son?"

Dani blinked several times at that question, obviously completely unprepared for it, but then she gave a slight laugh and said soothingly, "Sweetheart, she isn't immortal. She can't read your mind to know that, and she won't just be able to tell. I mean, it's not like it's written on your forehead or something."

"Right," Stephanie breathed.

"Right," her sister echoed. "Let's do this."

Dani stepped to her side then, apparently willing to accompany her to meet Thorne's mother, but neither of them moved. Marguerite was now in the hall, but so were Elizabeth Salter and Maria Reyes.

Stephanie stared wide-eyed at the woman in the wheelchair and thought she must have been a raging beauty in her youth, because despite the awful scar marring her face, she was still lovely in her eighties.

"Steph?" Dani said gently, and when that got no response, took her elbow to urge her forward, murmuring, "Lady Salter, how lovely to see you again."

Lady? Stephanie thought with dismay, and then recalled Thorne mentioning a castle and title. She briefly panicked, wondering if she should curtsy or something. Did you curtsy when meeting a duchess, or was that only the queen?

"Steph?" Dani said with concern, drawing her from her thoughts to realize that they were all staring at her.

"Oh. Sorry, I—It's a pleasure to meet you, Lady Salter, Mrs. Reyes," she said finally, offering them both a nervous smile. While both women smiled in return, Thorne's *tía* was smiling a little distractedly, her gaze on Stephanie's hands. Glancing down, Stephanie released a little squeak of alarm when she saw the blood bags Dani had given her. Mentally kicking herself for forgetting about them, she quickly whipped both hands behind her back, and muttered an embarrassed "Sorry."

"Don't be sorry, dear. You are immortal," Thorne's mother said with understanding, and then her smile widened as she said, "And it's lovely to meet you too. Did you and Thorne experience shared pleasure?"

Stephanie blinked, opened and closed her mouth, and then turned on Dani. "You said she wouldn't be able to tell we had sex!"

Dani stared back helplessly, and then opened her mouth, but before she could respond Lucian's bellow filled the house.

"Stephanie Anne McGill!"

Huffing out an exasperated breath, Stephanie shook her head. She then turned to Lady Salter, opened her mouth, but ended up just closing it without uttering a word and heading up the hall. She had absolutely no idea what she should say to the lady.

"I told you to wait here for me," Lucian reminded her sternly when she entered the kitchen.

"Yeah. Sorry, I had to talk to Dani," Stephanie muttered, moving to the end of the island and dropping into the seat she'd occupied earlier. She then asked, "Could you tell I'd had sex with Thorne when you first got here?"

"What?" he asked with confusion, and then he shook his head. "What a ridiculous question. No, of course not. It is not tattooed on your forehead, Stephanie."

"Then how did Thorne's mother know?" she muttered unhappily.

"Because I told her," Lucian said simply.

"What?" Stephanie asked with disbelief. "You told Thorne's mother he and I had sex?"

"No," he said patiently. "Lady Salter asked if it had turned out that Marguerite was right in her belief that you and Thorne were life mates, and I said that you had enjoyed shared pleasure, proving she was indeed correct."

"If you couldn't tell by looking at me, how would you

even kn—" She cut herself off there, already knowing the answer to the question. He'd read it from her mind while he was poking around in there. Closing her eyes, she said through clenched teeth, "Oh my *God*, it's bad enough that you poked around inside my head and read such private things, but did you have to go gossiping about it like an old woman?"

"I do not gossip," Lucian said with affront. "She asked a question, and I answered."

"About my sex life!" she snapped.

Lucian's expression began to look a bit irritated, and he said, "Yes, well, we have more important things to discuss than your sex life."

"Oh, really? That's funny, 'cause it seems like you didn't mind discussing it with others."

"She is Thorne's mother, so of course would want to know if he found a life mate," he pointed out with exaggerated patience.

"I get that, Lucian. But now she's going to think I'm a ho or something. I mean, he hasn't even been here three days."

"He has been here five days now," Lucian corrected. "He arrived Saturday morning, the accident was Monday and today is Wednesday."

"Oh, right, but he was only conscious for two and a half of those days," she said grimly.

"I do not see what difference that makes. You are life mates. Long courtships are not possible with life mates," Lucian pointed out, and then his lips twitching with the threat of a smile, he added, "As for her thinking you a ho, as you so charmingly put it, you were a twenty-eight-year-old virgin before Thorne, Stephanie. No one could think you a woman of ill repute."

"Twenty-seven," Stephanie growled resentfully.

"Twenty-eight," Lucian assured her. "You were fifteen when I met you after Leonius turned you. It has been thirteen years. You are twenty-eight."

"I was fifteen years and two days old when Dani and I were taken by Leonius and his sons, and it's actually only been twelve years and ten and a half months since then. My birthday isn't for another month and a half. I am twenty-seven," she assured him, and then glanced away muttering, "Leave it to you to try to mansplain my own age to me."

Lucian scowled at her and stood to leave the room, which, oddly enough, made Stephanie panic. If he left, she'd have no excuse not to talk to Thorne's mother.

"I thought you wanted me to tell you what all I'd learned while in Dressler's mind," she protested with alarm.

"I did, and I have. I read you while you were distracted, being churlish," he announced smugly.

Stephanie frowned, and stood to trail him out of the kitchen. "Well, wait! Don't go. I could maybe read him again and see if I can learn anything else."

"You're just afraid if I leave, Marguerite will insist on your suffering through talking to Thorne's mother," Lucian said knowingly.

"I am," she admitted.

"Hmm." He paused at the door and turned to eye her, as if considering helping her out, but then shook his head. "I have to talk to the hunters and make plans. Besides, suffering is good for the soul."

"Then I must have the shiniest soul around," she muttered under her breath as he opened the door.

"No doubt," Lucian agreed as he closed the door,

and she scowled over the fact that he'd heard her. She hadn't meant him to, but she spent so much time alone that talking to herself was a habit. "A bad one I need to break while the house is full of people."

"What do you need to break, dear?"

Stephanie turned to see Marguerite pushing Elizabeth Salter's wheelchair into the kitchen with Maria at her side.

"Oh, damn," she breathed, knowing her soul was about to get shinier.

Eighteen

"Do you like dogs?"

Stephanie glanced up from the playing cards she was holding to peer at Thorne's mother quizzically. The question had come completely out of left field for her. But it wasn't the first time a query unrelated to what was going on had come from Lady Elizabeth. Although that first one about whether she and Thorne had experienced shared pleasure had definitely topped the list as most shocking. There had been many other questions over the twenty-four hours since their first encounter that had left her speechless, though.

Stephanie smiled faintly to herself. She was usually the one leaving others in that state, and while it was often something to do with her abilities, there had been occasions when something she'd said had left everyone gaping in shock. Knowing Thorne's mother was British, though, and having always heard Brits were rather conservative and proper, she hadn't expected it from her. Apparently, that reserved Brit thing had skipped Lady Salter. That, or her years alone on the tiny island in Venezuela with just Maria and Thorne for company had taken the conservative right out of her. The woman hadn't shrunk from discussing any topic with her. From when the wedding would be, to if she thought they'd adopt immortal, mortal, or even hybrid children since they couldn't have any of their own.

When Stephanie had protested that she and Thorne had only known each other a handful of days, and hadn't even discussed marriage yet, she'd waved that away as unimportant and assured her that he would, and she thought they should marry soon. She was old and didn't have a lot of years left in her, Lady Elizabeth had pointed out. She wanted to see her son married and settled before she died.

"Stephanie loves dogs," Marguerite announced when Stephanie was slow to respond. "She actually has a boxer, Trixie. The men have been taking turns feeding and walking her for you," Marguerite added when alarm immediately entered Stephanie's face at the mention of her beloved dog.

Stephanie relaxed a little, her worry eased, but not her guilt. She hadn't even thought of Trixie. She was a bad mother.

"Good, good," Elizabeth said, distracting her from her thoughts, and Stephanie turned to find the woman beaming at her as if she'd done something particularly clever. "Thorne always wanted a dog. You're going to make him so happy."

Stephanie couldn't help but smile back. The woman had proclaimed that she would make Thorne happy at least two dozen times now, and not always after asking and getting the answer to one of her many questions. Sometimes, she just blurted it out and reached out to squeeze her arm or hand happily. It was kind of sweet. In fact, so far Thorne's mother seemed like the epitome of sweet . . . despite her introductory question. She was an elderly woman who just wanted to see her son happy before she died.

Stephanie wanted to do her one better. She wanted to make Thorne happy, but she also wanted to give his mother a chance to live happily, to make up for the hell her life had been these last fifty-eight years. She wanted to do the same for Maria as well. Both women were lovely and kind, and cared about Thorne more than their own lives. So, she hadn't been at all surprised to read from their minds that they hadn't wanted Thorne to cut off his wings. They didn't even desire to spend their last years on mainland Venezuela. That had all been a ruse to get Thorne to Canada to meet her . . . because Marguerite had gone to the island, met Thorne, and thought he might be a life mate to Stephanie. For some reason, Marguerite had said as much to his mother before broaching him on the subject, and both Lady Elizabeth and Maria had insisted Marguerite not tell him. Worried that he might suffer unbearable disappointment if he got his hopes up and Marguerite was wrong, they'd determined that they had to approach this more sneakily. They'd then come up with the plan to arrange a meeting, and if things worked out . . . Grand! If not, he need never know, and wouldn't be disappointed or hurt. Both women were very pleased that it had worked out so well. But neither seemed to be considering that they had yet to tell Thorne what they'd done.

"Stephanie, dear," Marguerite said now, drawing her from her thoughts. "You're pale, and rubbing your stomach. Perhaps you should go feed."

Stephanie froze, her hand still on her stomach and her anxious gaze going to Thorne's mother, but Elizabeth just smiled and said, "I daresay Sarita's looking a little pale as well. Maybe she should go with you."

Stephanie blinked in surprise and glanced to the fifth player at the table, Maria's granddaughter, Sarita Argeneau, who was the life mate of, and married to, Domitian Argeneau. The couple lived in Venezuela where Domitian ran a handful of restaurants and Sarita worked assisting the hybrids who could pass as fully human. She was helping them decide where they wanted to live, getting them set up, and guiding them as they navigated society, among other things.

When the couple had heard that the two elderly ladies planned to visit Canada with Thorne, they'd decided to accompany them and take the opportunity to visit Domitian's sister, Drina. They'd apparently been out clothes shopping when the news had reached them that Thorne had been hurt and Maria and Elizabeth were on their way to him. They'd quickly followed, arriving at the house an hour after Marguerite and the others.

Sarita now gave Stephanie an understanding smile and nod. "Actually, I could do with a bag or two if you don't mind my joining you?"

"Of course." Stephanie managed a smile and stood up. She was relieved that Lady Elizabeth hadn't been upset or put off by the whole "feeding" thing, but now she had to feed in front of Sarita. Stephanie didn't like to feed to begin with, but drinking blood in front of other people just made it worse in her mind.

"You don't have to worry about Grandmother and Aunt Liz being upset about you needing blood," Sarita said as they crossed the living room to the kitchen a moment later. "Domitian and I broke them in for you. They've seen us feed loads of times. It doesn't bother them now."

"It might not bother them to see you slap a bag to your fangs, but I actually have to drink it like juice," Stephanie said with a grimace.

"But from what I hear, you don't drink it like juice, though," Sarita said wryly.

That made Stephanie glance to her with surprise. "What?"

"Marguerite says you hate drinking it, and juice is good. So, you probably drink it more like anyone else would drink cod liver oil, or snake wine."

"Snake wine?" Stephanie asked with disbelief as they reached the refrigerator and she opened it to pull out four bags of blood.

"It's a real thing," Sarita assured her, wrinkling her nose. "They make it in Asia, rice wine with snakes in it. The snake is supposed to die and be pickled, but I heard there have been a few cases where the snakes weren't dead and people were attacked by them when they opened the bottle."

"Ewww." Stephanie gave a shudder as she pulled a glass down from the cupboard, cut open one of the bags, and started to pour it in. "That has to be an old wives' tale."

"No. Really," Sarita said as she picked up one of the two bags Stephanie had handed her, and then grinning, she added, "I read it on the internet, so it must be real."

"Oh, well then, you're right, it must be real," Stephanie

agreed with amusement as she threw the now empty bag away, and picked up her glass.

"Of course," Sarita agreed with a grin. Raising her bag, she tapped it against Stephanie's glass and said, *"Salud,"* then slapped it to her fangs.

Stephanie watched enviously for a minute, and then plugged her nose and quickly downed her glass of blood.

"Does plugging your nose help?" Sarita asked with curiosity as she watched Stephanie snip the corner off her second bag and pour it into the glass.

"Not really," she admitted wryly, "but it makes me feel better."

"Have you ever thought of maybe spicing it up or something? To make it more palatable?" Sarita asked.

"What? You mean like putting cinnamon in it?" Stephanie asked uncertainly.

"Yes. Or maybe Tabasco if you like hot stuff. I mean, you already don't like the flavor, so it can't make it any worse and might improve it," Sarita pointed out, and then said, "Oooh, or add Tabasco, Worcestershire sauce, salt and pepper, and a celery stick and it'll be a real Bloody Mary. They serve those at the Night Club in Toronto. We went the other night, and while I didn't have any, other immortals seemed to really enjoy them."

"Really?" Stephanie asked. She'd heard of the Night Club, a club for immortals where "blood drinks" were served. But she'd never been there. Too many people. Their thoughts in her head would be overwhelming. Besides, other immortals were uncomfortable around her knowing she could hear their thoughts. While older immortals could read those younger than them if they chose, everyone knew to recite nursery rhymes if they wished to block themselves from being read. Stephanie could not be blocked. Reciting all the nursery rhymes ever written wouldn't do it. She'd hear those and their other thoughts as well. It made immortals who weren't part of her family and friend group avoid her.

Stephanie peered down at the glass of thick liquid she held, and then moved to the refrigerator to see if Drina and Harper had Worcestershire sauce. They did, and there was also celery. She then checked the cupboard for Tabasco, and found that as well.

"How much do I put in?" she asked Sarita as she lined up the ingredients.

"Hang on." Sarita pulled out her cell phone and presumably looked up the recipe for a normal Bloody Mary. Stephanie doubted they'd have the blood version anywhere. "One dash Tabasco, two dashes Worcestershire sauce. One stalk celery, and salt and pepper to taste," she read off, and then glanced to her and added, "I'm guessing you want to pass on the vodka?"

"Yeah," Stephanie agreed wryly as she began dashing in the ingredients.

"I'm thinking you might want to double up the Worcestershire and Tabasco," Sarita commented as she watched. "I mean, they only use three-quarters of a cup of tomato vegetable cocktail juice in a normal drink, and you've got more blood than that."

Nodding, Stephanie doubled up her dashes, and then went a little crazy with salt and pepper. She stuck the celery stalk in, used it to stir the liquid, and then raised the glass and said, "Here goes nothing."

"My fingers are crossed for you," Sarita told her with a smile.

"Thanks," Stephanie murmured, and then took a tentative sip. Her eyes widened slightly as the thick liquid slid over her tongue.

"What? How is it?" Sarita asked with curiosity.

"It's . . . not bad," she decided after another sip. "Not like a chocolate milk shake or something, but it's definitely drinkable." She didn't mention that doctoring it up like this also made it seem more like an actual drink and less like blood, which helped too.

"Yay!" Sarita said on a laugh.

Stephanie smiled, and then said, "Thank you. Hopefully this will make taking my blood easier."

"My pleasure," Sarita assured her, and then suggested, "You should maybe call G.G. at the Night Club and get the proper recipe and the recipes for the other drinks they make there. You might find something else you like better."

"I will," Stephanie decided, and then fell silent and concentrated on her drink as Sarita slapped her second bag on her fangs to let them take in her own drink.

"So," Sarita said a few moments later as Stephanie rinsed her glass and she threw out the empty bags. "Thorne."

Stephanie glanced at her sideways, one eyebrow rising. "Yes?"

"His wings," Sarita said. "Aren't they the most amazing things you've ever seen?"

"Oh yeah," Stephanie said, turning back to cleaning her glass. "Amazing. Majestic. Fricking huge!"

Sarita laughed and nodded. "Yeah. The first time I saw them was inside the cottage on the island. It's small, so he could only open them partway, so that each was about six feet in length. I thought that was their full size, so when I saw him unfurl them for real outside for the first time and realized he had a more than twenty-foot wingspan, I nearly peed myself. And—oh my God!— when he flapped them and took to the air . . ." She shook her head, and then catching Stephanie's expression asked, "You have seen him fly, right?"

"Not yet," Stephanie admitted regretfully. "I mean, he swooped out of the sky and dropped to the ground in front of my car, but I didn't actually see him fly, just the dropping to the ground. Mind you, that was impressive enough. I can only imagine what it must be like to see him fly."

"I'm sure he'll show you once he's up and around again. But you'll probably have to wait until you can both go to the island for him to take you up with him," Sarita said with a small frown. "It would be kind of risky to fly here."

"Take me up with him? How would that go? Would I kneel on his back or something?" Stephanie asked uncertainly, because she didn't see how that could work.

"No, silly, he'd carry you," Sarita said with a laugh.

"Oh." Her eyes widened slightly, and she asked, "Have you flown with him?"

"No. Oh God, no. Domitian would have fits," Sarita said with a grin, and then added, "Although one of Dressler's hybrids, one of them who worked for him, did snatch me off the ground and fly me for a distance when he caught me." She wrinkled her nose at the memory. "That wasn't exactly a pleasure flight, though. I'm sure it's much more amazing and awesome when you aren't afraid for your life, and struggling."

"No doubt," Stephanie agreed dryly as she turned off the water. She quickly dried her hands and they headed back to Thorne's bedroom and the game of gin rummy. When they finished the game after two more hands, Lady Elizabeth immediately suggested another round, but Sarita shook her head and stood up.

"I'm going to find Domitian and see if he needs some blood brought out. He's probably ready for some now."

"Oh dear, I should check on Julius and see if he needs some too," Marguerite said, getting up as well. As she walked to the door with Sarita, she suggested, "Maybe we should just take out a bunch and hand it out. The men and women Lucian has standing guard can't leave their posts, but might need some too."

"Good idea," Sarita announced as the pair left the room.

"Well," Elizabeth said, glancing from Stephanie to Maria. "We could play three-person rummy or just chat. Which would you two prefer?"

"I'm fine with either—" Stephanie began and then stopped midsentence as a ringing silence filled her head.

"Are you all right, dear?" Elizabeth asked, reaching out to touch her arm.

Stephanie hesitated, her head lifting instinctively and turning first this way and that as if it was like adjusting an antenna and she'd be able to hear the voices if she moved her head to just the right position.

"Stephanie?" Lady Elizabeth said a little more firmly. "What's wrong? Are you all right?"

"I . . . Yes," she said finally, exhaling a slow breath. Stephanie then managed a crooked smile and explained, "My head just suddenly went silent. The voices have stopped again."

"Oh." Rather than look as concerned as Stephanie felt,

Lady Elizabeth beamed at her. "Well, that's good, then. Maybe it will keep happening off and on for a while before stopping altogether."

"Like periods during perimenopause," Maria said with a nod. "They come, they go, they stay away a while, they come back, and then poof, they stop."

"Yes, exactly," Lady Elizabeth agreed with a smile, and turned back to Stephanie to say, "Maybe this is the come and go and eventually they'll stop altogether for you."

Stephanie had been gaping since Sarita's grandmother had brought up perimenopause and periods. Not that there was anything wrong with such a discussion. Her own mother and sisters had talked freely about periods and such, but Thorne's mother was a lady. Like a real one, a duchess and everything. And British to boot. She just wasn't living up to the image Stephanie had in her head of the British and nobility.

"Wouldn't that be nice?" Lady Elizabeth asked.

Stephanie merely smiled a bit weakly. Much as she disliked how overwhelming the voices in her head could be at times, she'd developed ways to cope with it over the years. Besides, moving out here to the country had really made a difference, and she did like being able to assist Lucian and the hunters on the tougher cases. Stephanie felt a certain sense of satisfaction knowing she was helping to make a difference. While she didn't think she'd miss the voices constantly pounding at her head, she would miss being useful in that way.

Crazy, Stephanie thought with a small shake of the head. She'd hated this sensitivity she had to other people's thoughts for as long as she'd had it. There were just some things people thought that you did not want to know about. But now that she might be losing them, she found a reason to want them? That was just crazy.

Of course, she might not be losing them at all, Stephanie reminded herself. Really, they had no idea what was happening.

A grunt from Maria distracted her, and Stephanie glanced with curiosity toward the woman now standing next to Thorne, the back of her hand pressed to his forehead.

"Has his fever broken, Maria?" Lady Elizabeth asked.

"*Sí.* He will wake soon," Sarita's grandmother said.

"How soon?" Stephanie asked eagerly, getting up to join the older lady by the bed. "He said he didn't wake up until the next day when this happened before."

"The first time," Maria agreed. "The second time, he woke up sooner, and this last time it was only a couple of hours after his fever broke that he woke up. I think his body adjusts more to the process each time."

"Oh," Stephanie breathed, her gaze moving over Thorne's face. There was more color in his cheeks now, and he looked like he was sleeping and not dead as he had for the last couple of days. He'd been as pale and still as a corpse before this, and while she'd known he was just in stasis it had been worrying to her. Perhaps after witnessing it another dozen times she'd take it in stride.

That thought had her pausing. Another dozen times? She was thinking long term. Which she supposed she should. He'd agreed to be her life mate. But she hadn't really considered what that would mean. A life together. It's why she'd been so alarmed and embarrassed by his mother's questions about the wedding and adopting children and so on. She was still getting used to the idea that she might get to keep him in her life. Stephanie hadn't yet had the chance to consider exactly what that might look like, though, and she didn't want to until she was sure that the way her ability to hear voices flickered in and out wasn't a sign she was about to go no-fanger.

"Well, now that his fever has broken, I think I might go lie down for a nap," Lady Elizabeth said suddenly. "Between worrying about Thorne, and the excitement of finding out for certain that he was a life mate for you, I didn't sleep very well last night."

"I will see you to your room," Maria said, turning from the bed and then pausing.

Stephanie was vaguely aware that the woman had stopped, but didn't think anything of it until Maria hissed her name and nudged her arm. She glanced around in question, and then stilled when she noted Maria's wide-eyed expression and followed it to the man standing in the doorway with a shotgun in his hands.

"Jack?" she said uncertainly, moving around Maria toward her elderly neighbor. "What are you doing here? How did you—?"

The rest of that question would have been "get past the men," but the words died on her lips when she saw Bricker behind the older man. He'd obviously escorted him to the room.

"I'm sure glad to see you're all right, girl," Jack said, stepping into the room toward her, his gaze sliding suspiciously over the two elderly ladies, and then to Thorne in the bed.

Fortunately, while the men had left him uncovered when they'd first put him in the bed, Maria had pulled the sheet and blanket up over Thorne to his neck when she'd arrived, and his wings were no longer on display. The back of his head was still showing, though, but with the curtains closed and the lights dimmed as they were, from the distance of the doorway, the feathers just looked like white hair. She hoped.

"All right?" Stephanie asked warily, her gaze shooting to Bricker. The expression the hunter was giving her made her think he was probably sending her silent thoughts to tell her what was up. But she couldn't hear them. He didn't know that, though.

"Yeah. Lois and I were halfway to Alberta when we got the news that the horse we were going to pick up had died. Well, we turned right around to come home, of course. We got back and were unpacking when I heard gunshots. I rushed around the truck to see some yahoos in a van chasing you and, I guess it must have been this feller," he said, gesturing toward Thorne, "on a motorcycle." He peered at Thorne briefly, and then shifted his gaze back to her, and said, "Well, I rushed to the house to grab my shotgun and tell Lois to call 911, but heard the crash while I was still in the house. By the time I got back out, the yahoos were gone and this fella—" he gestured over his shoulder with a thumb at Bricker "—and another one were there. They said everything was fine and so I went home." Jack frowned even as he admitted that, as if unsure why he'd been so easily sent away.

Of course Stephanie knew why. Bricker, or Anders, had controlled him to send him home.

"Anyway," Jack went on. "When I saw all the men showing up today, and the guns they were packing, I knew you must be expecting more trouble, so I thought

I'd best come over and see if I couldn't help out. I'm no stranger to trouble, and a mighty fine shot with this old girl," he said, nodding to the shotgun he held. "If you need me, I'm here."

Stephanie smiled faintly, touched at the offer. While she avoided most people even out here, Jack and Lois were one of the few exceptions she'd made. They were what her mother would have called "good people," and they'd been good neighbors. Harper had got to know them early on when he'd started renovating this house, and had liked and trusted them so much he'd given them the code to the gate so Jack could cut down a couple of trees that weren't faring well from the wood lot at the back behind where Stephanie's house now sat. He'd wanted them for wood for his fireplace, and had appreciated Harper letting him have it. In return, Jack had used the code to let in contractors on occasion when Harper was late arriving to meet them. Now the couple kept an eye out for trouble, and Jack occasionally walked the mail up from the road just to check on her, because he knew she was a woman on her own.

As for his comment about being no stranger to trouble, Stephanie knew that was true from some of the thoughts she'd gotten from him and his wife over the year that she'd lived here. When he was younger, Jack had run with a rather notorious biker gang. But he'd given up that life and settled down to farming when he'd married Lois. That had been part of the agreement to her marrying him. She wasn't willing to be the widow of a biker. If he wanted her for a wife, he'd have to give up that life. Jack had, and from the thoughts Stephanie had read from his mind, he hadn't regretted it for a moment.

"Thank you, Jack, that's a really kind offer, but—" Her voice died as she glanced past him to Bricker and saw his expression.

When she raised her eyebrows in question, Bricker frowned as if annoyed she wasn't getting whatever message he was trying to send, and said, "Lucian thinks we could use the extra help." Bricker's expression said otherwise, but he continued. "He sent Anders over to collect Jack's wife and bring her back here where they'll be safer if Dressler causes trouble. He doesn't want them caught in the crossfire."

Stephanie understood then. They would take care of Jack and Lois. But they probably wouldn't be keeping them here. They'd erase this whole incident from their minds and send them on a vacation somewhere to keep them out of the line of fire until this situation had been resolved.

She nodded at Bricker in understanding.

"Are those feathers on the boy's head?" Jack asked suddenly, and Stephanie glanced at him sharply to see that he had shifted to the side a bit to get a better look past her at Thorne.

"Crap," Bricker muttered, and immediately took control of Jack.

Stephanie knew he had, because the man's face went blank and his body slack . . . including his hands, which opened to let the shotgun fall. Stephanie was barely able to catch it before it hit the floor. Scowling at Bricker, she set the shotgun on the dresser. "A little warning next time, Bricker. If that gun had hit the floor, it could have gone off and hurt Thorne's mother or Maria."

"I thought you'd hear my thoughts. Why didn't you?"

he added with a frown. Something in her expression must have given her away, because his eyebrows rose suddenly. "You can't hear thoughts again?"

When Stephanie grimaced and shook her head, he said, "Damn, I better go tell Lucian. He wanted you to check in on Dressler and see if he's close enough for you to hear him again. He wants to know if his men have arrived and how soon we need to worry about an attack."

"Wait!" Stephanie barked when Bricker turned to leave the room. When he swung back, she gestured to Jack. "Were you just going to leave him here?"

"Oh." He hesitated, and then sighed. "No. I'll take him with me. Anders should be back with his wife by now, and Lucian plans to wipe their memories of this trouble and send them on an all-expense-paid trip to Toronto or something."

"New Brunswick," Stephanie said at once, and when Bricker peered at her blankly, she said, "Their daughter is married to a dentist out there. They'd probably like to visit them and spend some time with their grandkids. Tell him to check their minds to see if they'd like to go to New Brunswick. I'll pay for the flight and hotel so they don't have to trouble their daughter last minute like this."

"It's your dime," Bricker said with a shrug and led Jack away.

"That was kind," Lady Elizabeth said with approval.

"Oh, well, they're nice people and good neighbors," Stephanie murmured self-consciously as she turned back into the room. "They keep an eye on things here when I'm away helping Lucian with cases, and even when I'm home, they look out for me. The least I can do is send them to visit their daughter and grandkids," she said with a shrug, and then smiled at Elizabeth and reminded her, "Weren't you going to take a nap?"

"I'll wait a little bit, I think," Elizabeth said after a hesitation, and then explained, "I suspect Lucian will be calling you out for a chat the minute Bricker talks to him. I wouldn't want Thorne to wake up on his own."

Stephanie nodded and had just settled back in her seat when she heard Lucian bellowing her name like a wounded bear. Sighing, she shared a wry smile with Thorne's mother and stood up, only to pause when Lucian appeared in the doorway.

Nineteen

"Nothing at all?"

Stephanie grimaced apologetically as Lucian asked that for the third time, but shook her head and told him again, "I can't hear anyone's thoughts. Not even Maria's or Lady Elizabeth's."

"Damn." His gaze shifted to where Thorne still lay asleep in bed, and then over Lady Elizabeth and Maria, before returning to her. Raising his eyebrows he said, "So, we won't have any warning of when the attack is coming."

"No. I'm sorry," Stephanie said solemnly. She hadn't been at all surprised when Lucian had come to find her right away after Bricker had passed on the news that she'd lost the voices again. She was very surprised, though, at just how much guilt she was experiencing over it. Stephanie felt like she was letting him down big-time.

Lucian waved away her apology. "You said you could read people when the voices were gone last time? The people in the grocery store?"

"Yes. If I was touching them, I could both read and control them."

Lucian nodded and held out his hand. "Read me."

She stared at his hand like it was a viper, and then shifted her gaze to his face, her expression wary. "Why?"

"I want to know if you can 'deep dive' as you call it even when the voices are missing."

Stephanie was shaking her head before he'd finished talking. "I'm not going to 'deep dive' in your head, Lucian."

"Just do it," he ordered. "I need to know if you'll still be useful to me after this business is over. I want to know if you can get the answers you used to get when you still heard the voices in your head. So—" he wiggled his fingers "—take my hand and try to do your deep dive on me . . . or are you afraid of what you'll find there and too cowardly to try?"

Stephanie scowled, her shoulders stiffening and rising. The bastard was manipulating her with the coward talk, and she knew it. But it still worked, damn him. Mouth setting, she met his gaze and reached out to grasp his hand.

Sound immediately exploded inside her head like someone had turned on a radio full blast inside her skull. But just one. Lucian's mind was a hive of worries and concerns. From his worry for his wife and daughters, his other family members, and the Enforcers who worked under him, to immortals in general, and even the mortals he tried to keep safe from the rogue members of their kind. His life was a long string of worries and issues he had to take care of to keep everything from exploding around him.

"Go deep," Lucian ordered when she hesitated there on the periphery of his mind.

Stephanie bit her lip briefly, and then took a breath and followed his thoughts into that deep place everyone had. But this was nothing like the other times she'd deep dived. Dressler, for instance, was only in his eighties, a mere fetus next to this man. His memories had rushed by so quickly she'd only gotten an impression of his evil, and his complete lack of compassion or empathy for the victims of the heartless deeds he'd performed in the name of science.

Lucian, though . . . he was ancient . . . and the things he'd seen and suffered . . . Her mind exploded with pain of every kind, emotional, physical, a tortured soul, a shredded conscience. A good man who had done bad things for the greater good and lived with them every day. She saw his brother's face as he begged him to kill him. She saw his first life mate and their children die a fiery death in the fall of Atlantis, and felt his soul shrink with the grief of their loss. She saw . . . too much. It was too much. It was—

Stephanie pulled away with a cry of pain, tears streaming from her eyes as she stood gasping and gaping at him with amazement that he'd survived so much.

Lucian merely nodded solemnly. "You can still do your deep dive."

Stephanie just stared at him as he turned and walked out of the room.

"Are you all right, dear?"

Stephanie heard the words, but they didn't really pierce the agony writhing through her brain until Lady Elizabeth took her hand and gave it a squeeze.

Blinking, she glanced down at the woman in her wheel-chair, a little surprised that Thorne's mother was there. Or maybe surprised that she herself was standing there in the guest room of Harper and Drina's house. Her mind was slow to leave behind the life that had flashed before and around her as she'd done her deep dive. It wasn't a life she would wish on anyone.

"Steph?"

Blinking, she turned to the door to see Bricker entering, several weapons in his arms.

"Here, take the dart guns," he instructed, holding up his arms. "There's one for each of you ladies. Lucian wants you to keep them on you at all times until this is over."

"Oh dear, I'm afraid it won't be much use to me," Lady Elizabeth said as Stephanie relieved Bricker of the guns. "I was never a very good shot."

"Well, you probably won't need it," Bricker said sooth-ingly. "But if he gets in here, and gets close enough, I doubt you'll miss. Just keep it hidden down the side of your wheelchair, just in case."

Lady Elizabeth took the gun when Stephanie offered it to her, then slid it between her leg and the wheelchair before covering it with the skirt of the pretty blue dress she was wearing today. Nodding, Stephanie slid one of the remaining guns she held down the back of her shorts and then offered the last gun to Maria, who took it and peered at her black dress uncertainly. She did not have pockets or a back to slide it into. In the end, she retrieved her bag from the top of the dresser and slid it in there with her knitting and whatnot.

Stephanie almost told her to keep it on her, but then changed her mind. She had a gun handy, and so did Elizabeth; they should be fine.

"I'm going to put this just here under the sheet," Bricker announced, drawing her attention to the bed where he was pulling up the sheet and blanket covering Thorne's prone body to lay a machete at his side on the mattress. "It's a last-resort weapon. Just don't forget to remove it if Thorne wakes up and starts moving. It's freshly sharpened. He might cut himself by accident."

Stephanie nodded solemnly as she watched him let the sheet and blanket drop back down to cover the weapon.

"I guess that's everything," Bricker said, straightening. "Any questions before I go, ladies?"

When they each simply shook their heads, he said, "Lucian would rather you stay in the house for the foreseeable future, and if you could stay together that would be good too. Since extra hunters have started to arrive, there will be someone standing guard in the house from now on. At the moment that's me, and I'll be in the kitchen watching the cameras if you need me. Good?"

"Good," Stephanie assured him.

Nodding, he left the room and started up the hall, headed for the kitchen.

"How worried should we be?" Lady Elizabeth asked solemnly, and when Stephanie turned to her in question, she pointed out, "We've been restricted to the house and they have a guard inside with us now."

Stephanie shrugged mildly. "Lucian is just being cautious. He knows Dressler plans to attack, but doesn't know when, so is preparing for any eventuality." Forcing a smile, she added, "Lucian has been in loads of situations like this, or worse. He knows what he's doing. I wouldn't worry too much. Besides, I have it on good authority that you'll come out of this all right."

"Good authority?" Elizabeth looked perplexed for a moment and then her eyes widened. "Did you have one of your visions of the future?"

Stephanie stilled, her own eyes widening. "You know about my visions?"

"Of course, dear. You wrote about it in your book about the immortal boy and his mortal mother, among others."

"You read that?" she asked, her voice rising with her alarm.

"Dear girl, once Marguerite mentioned she thought my Thorne might be a life mate for you, and that you were a writer who wrote your actual history despite being published as fiction . . . Well, I just had to order all your books and read every one," Elizabeth assured her.

"Holy hell, and sweet jumping Jesus," Stephanie breathed.

"Now that is the one complaint I would have with your books, dear. They're very well written, and fast paced. The excitement pretty much jumps off the page at you, but you do have a tendency to cuss like a sailor," Lady Elizabeth pointed out.

"I do," Stephanie agreed weakly, trying to think of what else she might have put in the books that could have offended the woman who was essentially—in immortal terms at least—a mother-in-law whether she and Thorne married or not. Dear God, did she really want to find the woman a life mate and extend her life immeasurably?

After all, mothers-in-law were notoriously hideous to deal with. She'd heard stories where even when they started out seemingly nice they later turned into a wicked-witch-of-the-west-wannabe. Did she want to risk that?

Stephanie gave herself a mental slap for that thought. Lady Elizabeth was lovely, and sweet, and didn't deserve her even considering the thought she'd just had.

"It's probably hanging around with all those hunters that's given you a propensity to curse so much," Lady Elizabeth said thoughtfully.

"Probably," Stephanie agreed as she sidled toward the door. It was always best to blame the men in situations like this, she thought, and then said, "Did you hear Bricker shout? I think I heard him call me."

"No, I didn't, but then my hearing isn't what it used to be," Lady Elizabeth said, and then glanced to Maria. "Did you hear anything?"

Stephanie just caught the flicker of amusement and sympathy on the older woman's face before she schooled it into a solemn expression for Lady Elizabeth's sake. "I think maybe I heard something."

"I better go check," Stephanie said, and ducked out of the room before either woman could comment.

"Oh my God, Bricker, Thorne's mother has read my books," Stephanie complained as she entered the kitchen a moment later.

"So have I."

The words were uttered, not by Bricker, who she could now see was unconscious on the kitchen floor with a dart in his back, but by the man standing over him.

"Dressler," she said blankly. Though Stephanie wasn't sure why she was so surprised. She'd known for some time that everything would come to a head here. She'd recognized the guest room where Thorne was resting as the room where the future scene of her being shot and Lady Elizabeth and Maria shooting Dressler had taken place. She just hadn't thought it would happen so soon, and with absolutely no warning when the place was crawling with hunters.

"How did you get in here without the Enforcers stopping you?" she asked, once her initial shock had passed.

"They're busy," Dressler explained, and gestured toward the security monitor beside him.

Bricker must have been watching the monitor when he'd been shot, Stephanie supposed as she moved cautiously along the opposite side of the long island until she was almost even with Dressler and could see the camera views on the monitor on the counter.

Stephanie swallowed as she saw the chaos taking place outside. There were two buses pulled up to the gates, one at each of them, and while there were several dozen men already inside the fence, others were even now effortlessly leaping the gate while still more were yet coming off the buses. Decker and several other hunters had left their posts to rush to the point of the breach. They were doing a pretty good job of picking them off, but there were so many . . . and they were taking some hits of their own, she realized as she saw Anders fall, hit by a dart, and then Nicholas.

"Most of the men jumping the fence are just cannon fodder," Dressler announced. "A distraction to draw the hunters to that area so that we could slip over the fence at the other end of the property and approach the house to fetch you and Thorne out. The men remaining on the bus are the more skilled shooters."

Stephanie's gaze slid to the buses to look them over again. The first time she'd looked, she'd only really noticed the men still piling off of it. Now she noted the men not disembarking, but positioned at the windows, dart guns aimed at the hunters.

"I really only hoped they could keep the hunters busy long enough for us to get in and out. But at this rate, I might just be able to set up shop here and get all of you on my table," Dressler commented as Stephanie saw Harper go down and Drina run to his side, only to collapse across his back when she too took a dart.

Hands fisting, Stephanie stared at Drina and Harper for a moment and then Lucian's bellow sounded. She could hear it all the way inside the house. It was enraged and commanding, and had immediate effect. The hunters suddenly drew back, many grabbing a fallen comrade as they went and dragging them as they ran for the cover of the SUVs now rolling into view.

Stephanie squinted at the small image, recognizing Marguerite driving one, Dani another, and . . . Good God! Was that Elvi and Mabel in two others? And there were Victor, DJ, Magnus, Teddy, and Katricia on the ground with the other hunters, hunkering down behind the SUVs and shooting around them at the men swarming across the yard. She didn't see Magnus's wife, Allie, though. She must have stayed behind in Port Henry to watch the children, Stephanie supposed, and wondered when the rest of them had arrived. She knew Lucian had put out a call for more aid down here to prepare for Dressler's attack, but—

Well, she thought suddenly, Port Henry was only forty-five minutes away in bad traffic, and these were the people who had loved, taken care of, and protected her since she was fourteen. She supposed she shouldn't be surprised that they'd answered Lucian's call for aid when she was in trouble.

"Damn," Dressler said with disappointment as the hunters now out of range of the guns of the men on the bus began steadily picking off the men swarming over the fence. Then he shrugged fatalistically. "Ah well, as I said, I only expected them to be cannon fodder and a distraction. Now I guess we should collect Thorne and get out of here before they mow down all the men and are no longer distracted."

Turning to her, he smiled pleasantly and then gestured to her left. "Stephanie, meet Stacy. He's my right-hand man."

She turned sharply, but wasn't fast enough. The big goon who had attacked Thorne when he caught him trying to reinstall his hacking equipment, and who had been with Dressler in town the other day, was there, catching her arms and pulling them behind her back. Stephanie considered trying out a couple of the moves the other hunters had taught her over the years while working with them. One or two might have got her out of Stacy's hold, but in the end, she decided not to waste the energy. Dressler was taking her where he needed to be anyway, so she let Stacy frog-march her out of the kitchen.

Thorne woke up feeling dried out and nasty. That was the only way to describe it. He felt parched and brittle, and had a bad taste in his mouth, but didn't even have enough moisture left in his body to work up some saliva to hopefully wash away the worst of the bad taste.

"Oh, Thorne! You're awake."

Lying on his stomach, with his head turned to the side, he couldn't see the speaker until his mother wheeled her chair up the side of the bed and into his line of vision.

"Mother? What are you doing here?" he asked, his voice rough and croaky.

"Well, we heard about the accident and came at once, of course. You were in stasis when we got here, and we've been waiting for you to wake up," she explained, and then when he began to shift, intending to get up, she warned, "Don't move around too much, dear. Bricker put a machete under the sheet next to your hand there, and you might cut yourself on it. He said it was freshly sharpened."

"A what? Why the hell would he put a machete in my bed?" he asked with disbelief.

"He said it was a last-resort weapon. In case my gun, and Maria's and Stephanie's, aren't enough," she explained, and then frowned and clucked her tongue. "Stephanie will be so upset she wasn't here when you woke up. She's been at your side almost from the minute she recovered and woke up, but Bricker needed her," she added, glancing vexedly toward the door. She then sighed and turned back to smile at him. "I really like her, dear. I think the two of you will make a lovely couple."

Thorne's eyes widened, and then he felt his face flush and knew he was blushing like a schoolboy. Dear God, how did his mother know about him and Stephanie? And in case her gun, and Maria's and Stephanie's, weren't enough for what? What the hell had been happening while he was sleeping?

"Wait," he said suddenly. "What did Stephanie recover from? Was she hurt? I don't . . ." His voice trailed off as his memory slowly returned. The motorcycle, the chase, the van and Stacy hanging out of the van's passenger window shooting at him. He remembered taking several bullets and then the bastard hit the bike's front tire and—

"We crashed," he muttered.

"Yes," his mother said with relief, and explained, "For a minute there I was afraid you'd sustained some brain damage. Though I gather it was Stephanie who ended up with the headlight being driven into her brain and she seems perfectly fine, so—"

"Stephanie had the headlight driven into her brain?" he gasped with horror.

"Mmm." His mother nodded solemnly. "But she healed up nicely and seems perfectly fine, so all is good there. Now we just have to deal with Dressler, and then we can decide where to live."

Thorne merely grunted, unsurprised at the way his mother referred to the man she had married and who was technically his father. In all the years of his life she had never given Dressler the courtesy of calling him her husband or his father. Because, quite simply, he was neither. He had never been a father to Thorne in any way, and he had stopped being a husband when she'd discovered all that the man had been doing to her, the drugging, and harvesting eggs to mutate the babies they would have had. She loved Thorne as a son, but considered herself his only parent . . . and so did he.

"I was thinking we should live in Canada in the

summer and the island in the winter," his mother said now. "But then we learned that you were able to go to town wearing a duster and hoodie when it got cool, so now we're thinking perhaps it should be Canada in the fall, winter and spring, and the island in the summer," she told him, and then said excitedly, "Harper says we can build another house on one of the two unused corners of the lake if we like so Maria and I can live close by without being on top of you and Stephanie. Wouldn't that be nice?"

"Uhhhh," Thorne choked out, his mind whirling.

"And Maria and I think a nice early summer wedding is best," she announced.

"Early summer?" he repeated weakly. He and Stephanie hadn't even discussed marriage. Would she be willing? He knew she was afraid of going no-fanger and didn't want to saddle him with that issue if it was happening to her. He doubted she'd agree to marriage until she knew what was happening with this absence-of-thoughts business.

"Yes. Early summer. Actually, early June would be good, although technically I suppose it isn't really summer until June 20 or something, but it's close enough."

"Of this year?" he asked with disbelief. "Mother, I don't think—"

"Maria and I don't have a lot of time left, son. We can't shilly-shally and I do want to be alive for your wedding. I can't wait to see you all handsome in a tux."

Thorne stared at her helplessly, guilt seeping into his bones. He didn't want to disappoint her, but it wasn't wholly up to him. Stephanie—

"Oh!" she said suddenly, and turned to look at someone next to her that Thorne couldn't see. "Maria, we'll have to start work on a tux for Thorne right away. Perhaps we can buy him a nice Armani or Boss tuxedo and cut the back out to replace with Velcro."

"Yes, yes," Maria said at once, sounding as excited as his mother. "I will get Sarita to help me on the computer to order one for him and we will fix it in time for a June wedding."

"There, you see!" his mother said brightly, turning back to him. "Everything will be fine. You'll marry Stephanie, and we'll all live happily here for part of the year, and on the island the rest of the year. You, Stephanie, Maria, me, and the grandchildren. Life will be grand."

Thorne closed his eyes on a sigh, wondering how he would convince Stephanie to marry him without finding out about—His eyes popped open. *"Grandchildren?"*

"Yes, of course. You and Stephanie should adopt at least two. A boy and a girl would be nice. Maria and I can't wait to spoil our little grandbabies." She sighed a little sadly and added, "Of course, we won't live long enough to see them grow up and marry and such, but we'll get to enjoy them for however long God sees fit to let us live." Face turning grim, she added, "So, you shouldn't dally about adopting like you have about finding a mate, because we don't have that many years left as it is."

Thorne groaned and closed his eyes, guilt lapping at him again.

"Oh, Stephanie, dear. You're—"

The abrupt end to his mother's words and the sudden shift in energy in the room told Thorne there was a problem. He was about to open his eyes when his mother laid her hand on his arm on top of the blankets and snapped,

"You! Here to shoot my son in the back again, Ramsey? It should be easy since he's unconscious."

Thorne remained still, getting the message that his mother wanted him to pretend to still be in stasis. He supposed the idea had merit when his fingers twitched under the sheet and pressed up against the machete his mother had mentioned. It was literally right next to his hand. Was the handle close to his fingers? Or was it resting with the blade end nearest his hand? Either way, with that and the element of surprise, he might get the upper hand if he had enough strength.

That was the problem, Thorne wasn't certain of how strong he was just now. The first time he'd woken up from stasis, he'd needed help to get to the bathroom to shower away the sludge coating his skin. The second time, he'd managed it alone, but using the wall to brace himself. The third time, he'd been pleased to make it there with only a few stops to rest. Thorne had no idea what shape he would be in this time when he tried to rise. On top of that, if Dressler wasn't alone—

"Or is your henchman there going to shoot him for you?" his mother asked now, unknowingly, or perhaps knowingly, telling him that Dressler wasn't alone. Her voice cold, she growled with disgust, "You always did make others do your dirty work."

"And you always had a sharp tongue, wife," Thorne heard Dressler snap. His voice turning mocking, he then added, "You used to be vain too, but your little accident on the island fixed that up."

His mother didn't respond, but her nails dug into his arm, and Thorne knew the bastard had hurt her with that shot. She tried not to let him see how the large scar on her face bothered her, but he knew it did.

"I could always turn you, Elizabeth," Dressler said suddenly. "You'd have your youth and beauty again. We could make another go of it."

"I'd rather sleep with snakes," his mother responded grimly. "Besides, I'm not the foolish young girl I was when you romanced me into marriage the first time, Ramsey. I know your only interest in me is my money." Voice becoming sickeningly sweet, she asked, "Finding it tough out there without my inheritance to finance your schemes?"

"There are plenty of other women out there with money, Elizabeth," Dressler growled.

"But can you control them and make them marry you or just give you their money?" Stephanie asked, and Thorne stilled at the sound of her voice. It was the first time she'd spoken since entering the room, and he tried to tell from her voice if she'd been hurt, or mistreated by Dressler or his man. But it was hard to tell. She sounded okay, but he suspected Stephanie wasn't the type to show weakness.

"I mean, you can't take the time to romance anyone with the Enforcers on your trail," Stephanie pointed out. "So, controlling and making a rich mortal give you their money is your only option. But you haven't had anyone to train you to read and control mortals, have you?"

"Shut up," Dressler growled, and Thorne heard a strange pfft of sound that he didn't recognize. It was followed by gasps by the women in the room and then a thud that sounded like something hitting the floor. Thorne didn't know what was happening, but it couldn't be good. Hoping everyone was sufficiently distracted, he felt around with his left hand, grimacing at the fact that the weapon had been put there when he was right-handed. He'd make do, though, Thorne thought grimly as he grasped the handle of the machete.

"You bastard," his mother snapped, and he heard another of those strange pfft sounds.

But this time, no gasps followed. Instead, his father laughed and said, "You missed me, but then you always were a terrible shot, Elizabeth. Even your father used to say so when we were dating."

"I wasn't aiming for you, Ramsey." His mother's voice sounded smug.

"Goddammit," Dressler suddenly snarled with frustration.

That's when Thorne decided to move. Fingers tightening around the machete, he pushed up off the mattress to his hands and knees and then staggered to his feet, and whirled to take in the room at a glance. Stephanie was on the floor just inside the door, but Dressler's man, Stacy, was also down, lying with his head and chest on top of the backs of her legs. Meanwhile, Dressler knelt beside them, his back to the room as he checked Stacy.

From all of this, Thorne deduced that Dressler had shot Stephanie with the dart gun he was holding, while his mother had apparently shot Stacy. A nice distraction that had captured Dressler's attention allowing Thorne to get up unnoticed.

"Now how the hell am I to get Stephanie and Thorne out?" Dressler growled with fury, glowering from his mother to the unconscious man. "Stacy was to carry Thorne."

Thorne was about to gain the bastard's attention by announcing that he didn't need carrying, when Dressler suddenly straightened and started toward his mother in her wheelchair.

Thorne immediately raised the machete, only to freeze with it upraised when an explosion filled the room. Blinking in amazement, he stared at the large hole that had suddenly appeared in Dressler's chest, and then glanced sharply to Maria, who stood by the dresser holding a shotgun of all things.

"I could not get the dart gun out of my bag," Maria said with a shrug. "This was faster."

"You bitter old bitch!" Dressler suddenly roared, the wound not seeming to bother him much at all. Three things happened then: Dressler started toward Maria, murder in his eyes, and Thorne saw his mother raise her dart gun and shoot the bastard in the back even as he himself staggered forward, swinging the machete.

Twenty

"I'm sorry."

Thorne stared blankly down at where Stephanie's head was nestled against his chest. He was a bit confused to find her there when he'd gone to sleep alone. It took him a moment to sort out that this was a shared dream where her mind had joined his in sleep. While her sudden presence was a surprise, so were her words.

"What are you sorry for?" he asked with confusion.

"That you didn't get to confront your father and were the one who had to kill him."

Thorne stiffened at the words, a frown now tugging at his mouth. Shifting slightly, he caught her under the chin and raised her head slightly. Once her gaze met his, he said solemnly, "Stephanie, Dressler was not my father."

"I know he may not have acted like one, but technically he—"

"Technically I have some of his DNA in me," he interrupted her quietly. "But I also have the DNA of a bald eagle, a dolphin, a bat, and countless other animals. So, are they all my father too?"

"Oh," she said with surprise. "No. Of course not."

"Right," he said, and then assured her, "And neither is Dressler. I'd never even met the man before our encounter in town. He had no hand in raising me, and with all the DNA he spliced into me I like to think there wasn't much of his that ended up in the mix."

"I can understand that," she murmured quietly, her expression sympathetic.

Thorne nodded, but then added, "The man was nothing more than a jailer to me, as well as the man who abused and misused my mother horribly. Frankly, though I should probably be ashamed to admit it, cutting off his head was all the closure I needed. It was like putting down a rabid dog. He can't hurt my mother, Maria, or anyone else ever again. That is closure for me."

Stephanie nodded in understanding, and then a mischievous smile suddenly curved her lips and she rose up to straddle his hips.

"I like you on your back," she announced as she slid her body over his quickly waking erection where it rested under her. "Can you lay on your wings in real life too?"

"With care," he said a little breathlessly, his hands moving to her hips as she rode over his body again. God, that felt good. He closed his eyes briefly to enjoy the sensations she was stirring, and then opened them again and shifted his hands to claim her breasts to knead and squeeze them eagerly.

Stephanie moaned under the caress, her head going

back as she arched into his touch, and then she gasped, "I think I love dream sex."

Thorne chuckled and suddenly rolled them so that he was over her, though he used his wings to hold his weight off of her on the bed. Then he lowered his head to run a tongue over one excited nipple, as he released it and promised, "I'm going to lick every inch of your body."

"Please do," Stephanie groaned, her fingers gliding into the soft feathers on his head. "Then I'll do the same in return."

Thorne growled at the promise and closed his mouth over the nipple he'd just lashed, his mind filling with all the things he wanted to do to her here in their dreams where they weren't a slave to life mate passion.

Thorne woke up still smiling from the dream he'd had. It had been nice. And he was apparently a master of understatement, Thorne admitted to himself, because the dream had been more than nice. They'd talked, they'd laughed, and they'd made love—the slow sexy kind, not the ridiculously fast and furious sort that they only seemed capable of in reality at the moment.

Stephanie had assured him that should ease up in a year or two, but until then they would only be able to go slow and tender when sleeping in separate beds and having shared dreams. He'd immediately suggested they have separate bedrooms for a while then, which had made her laugh. He liked making Stephanie laugh. She relaxed, and smiled, her eyes sparkling.

Sighing happily, he lifted himself slightly off his

stomach so that he could turn his head to look toward the other side of the bed where he wished Stephanie was . . . and where he was sure she would be right now if his mother and Maria weren't here. The four of them and Dani and Decker had retreated to Stephanie's house once everything was over and the cleanup was done in Drina and Harper's house and at the front of the estate.

Thorne grimaced at the memory of that. After taking off Dressler's head, he'd dropped the machete, scooped up Stephanie, and staggered, naked, out of the room with Maria chasing after him trying to wrap a sheet around his waist, and his mother trailing in her wheelchair asking if Stephanie was okay. If he was okay.

Thorne's moment of chivalry had almost ended with him dropping Stephanie on her head. His strength had not been up to the task of carrying anyone at that moment. He'd barely been strong enough to make his own way, so it had been a relief when Dani had rushed into the house, spotted them entering the living room, and hurried forward to take Stephanie from him as she began to slip from his grasp. It was somewhat humiliating that a woman could carry her when he couldn't, Thorne supposed, but a relief just the same. He'd rather suffer a little humiliation than dump Stephanie on her head.

It was from Dani they'd learned that the battle outside was over. It was also when he'd learned that Dressler had brought two busloads of rogues he'd turned, and sicced them on them like wild dogs. Most of the battle had been the exchange of darts, but apparently there had been a little hand to hand, or machete and bat to machete, and whatever the hunters had to hand.

Fortunately, none of the rogues were trained fighters,

and the hunters had handled them easily with little in the way of injury on their side. Though a rogue or two had lost their head. That just made Thorne glad the bastard, Dressler, was dead.

Dani had told them that several hunters had taken darts before Lucian had reached the front of the property from where he'd been at the back, spotted the shooters on the bus, and sent the women out in SUVs to offer cover to the hunters as he ordered them to retreat. But by the time she'd come inside most were already recovering from the effects of the drug the dart tips were coated with, and the rest would as well, including the rogues the hunters had taken out with those same darts. Which had been a problem. The sheer number of them had been an issue. They'd all had to be transported to Toronto and the jail cells there. Although there had been some question as to whether they'd be able to squeeze all of them into the few cells they had for rogues at the Enforcer house.

Still recovering from the stasis, Thorne hadn't been allowed to help either with cleaning up inside, or collecting the rogues. Instead, they'd sent him into the bathroom to shower away the film of grunge coating him from his stasis. Meanwhile, a recovered Bricker had shot Stacy again with a dart gun to keep him under, and then had removed him as well as Dressler's body, so that Maria and Stephanie could clean up the mess in the bedroom.

Not that there was much to clean up. Dressler hadn't bled much; the nanos hadn't allowed it. They'd held on to all the blood they could as programmed, so that if someone had put his head back on his body, the nanos then could use that blood to repair and reanimate him.

Thorne didn't think anyone was likely to put the man's head back on his body. At least he hoped not.

After his shower, Thorne had found himself ushered into the kitchen and presented with a ton of food and several drink options as Stephanie, his mother, and Maria fussed over him. They'd told him more of what had happened over the days while he'd slept as the small army of hunters that Lucian had called in had seen to the last of the removal of Dressler's rogues. Watching it from the monitor in the kitchen, Thorne had marveled at how many men Dressler had managed to turn and draw into his ranks, and found the fact that he'd considered them nothing more than cannon fodder beyond horrible. The man had had no conscience at all.

It had been quite late when the last of the rogues and hunters had left. In the end, only Drina, Harper, Dani, Decker, Lucian, Bricker, and Anders had remained. While Dani and Decker had accompanied Stephanie to her house with him, his mother, Maria, Lucian, and the others had slept at Drina and Harper's house. He had no idea why, but suspected it had something to do with Stephanie's losing and regaining her sensitivity to the thoughts of the people around her and her fear that it was a sign she was going no-fanger.

That thought was enough to get Thorne up and out of bed. He intended on being at Stephanie's side until Lucian left. He'd promised he wouldn't let anything happen to her and intended to keep that promise.

Thorne quickly redonned the clothes Maria had given him after his shower the day before. They were his only option at the moment since the rest of his clothes were still at Drina and Harper's place. He then headed for the kitchen where he could hear the soft murmur of voices. Entering he found that the others had joined them from Drina's house. The kitchen was full with his mother, Maria, Dani, Decker, Drina, Harper, Bricker, and Anders all there, but no Stephanie and Lucian.

"Where is she?" he asked at once with alarm, his gaze sliding over the people moving about making coffee and tea, or just feeding on bags of blood.

"Stephanie and Lucian just left," Dani told him, knowing at once who he was asking after. "Lucian decided to go buy breakfast from the restaurant in Glencoe for everyone and wanted her to go with him."

"Glencoe?" Thorne asked with a frown.

"A town about twenty minutes from here. It's a little bigger than the one you two visited the other day. They have more restaurants," Dani explained.

Thorne nodded slowly, but asked, "Why did he take Stephanie and not someone else?"

He saw uncertainty and worry flicker across Dani's face, but in the end she sighed and shook her head. "I don't know. But I do know he doesn't think Stephanie is going no-fanger," she assured him. "Otherwise, I wouldn't have let him take her alone." She hesitated then, before admitting, "On the other hand, I do think he's up to something. I'm just not sure what."

"Hmm." Thorne muttered, and accepted the coffee she handed him, concern his overriding emotion until his mother spoke up.

"Come sit down, Thorne. We should really discuss what you and Stephanie would like at your wedding. We don't have a lot of time to plan."

Eyes widening with horror, Thorne glanced to Dani

for help, but she grinned and said, "Yes, Thorne. We should discuss the wedding. Stephanie mentioned when I got up that your mother proposed to her for you before we came out."

"What?" he gasped, his horrified gaze shifting to his mother.

"Oh, don't be silly," his mother said unconcerned. "I just told her I knew you would, and gave her the family ring so you wouldn't have to. You know the one."

Thorne did know the one. It was a family heirloom, passed down from generation to generation. His grandfather, however, had refused to give it to his mother when she'd asked for it to marry Ramsey Dressler, something she'd been upset about when she'd first decided to elope with the man. However, she'd told Thorne just before they'd left for Canada that she was glad she hadn't got to use it as an engagement ring to Dressler. That it would have tarnished it, and she wanted him to use it for his own future bride.

At the time, he'd thought his mother was talking about a possible future bride he might meet once they'd moved to the mainland after the amputation of his wings. Now he knew better. One of the things Stephanie had told him in their shared dream was that his mother had known they were life mates before they'd even met, and that the entire trip and operation were all just a scam to get them together.

Good Lord, he realized now. His mother had basically proposed to Stephanie for him. She'd even given her the damned ring. Shaking his head, he carried his coffee to the island and sat down to wait for Stephanie . . . who was now apparently his fiancée whether she was ready for it or not. God, he hoped she didn't hate him for that.

"Now that you're engaged to Thorne—"

"I'm not engaged to Thorne," Stephanie gasped, tearing her gaze from the ring she'd been staring at to scowl at Lucian.

"You're life mates. You have the ring. You're engaged," Lucian said as if it was as simple as all that.

"His mother gave me the ring," Stephanie muttered, turning her gaze back to the pretty ring Thorne's mother had slipped onto her left-hand ring finger. It was quite lovely, a bloodred ruby with sparkly little diamonds all around it. She liked it.

"She also proposed for him," Lucian said, and she was sure she caught a hint of laughter in his voice.

Sighing, she slumped back in her seat. "Is that why you insisted I accompany you to get breakfast instead of Bricker? So, you could make fun of me?"

"I'm not making fun of you," he said at once, and then added, "I am laughing at you, though. Inside."

Stephanie turned a scowl on him, but it wasn't a very successful one. Her lips kept trying to turn up with amusement, and laughter was bubbling up in her chest. The situation was so ridiculous. Only she could be proposed to by the man's mother rather than the man himself. Good Lord, at this rate, she'd be married without knowing—

"I can't marry Thorne," she announced abruptly. "I need to figure out why my ability to hear people's thoughts keeps going in and out as it does. I know you don't think I'm going no-fanger, but I won't risk marrying Thorne and dragging him into my problems until I know one way or the other for certain."

"Hmm." Lucian nodded solemnly, his gaze on the road ahead. "I thought as much."

Stephanie glanced at him with curiosity, but rather than ask what that meant, she said, "Usually you make Bricker or Anders or anyone you're with drive rather than do it yourself. How come I'm not driving right now? Is it because I'm a woman? Are you sexist when it comes to drivers, Lucian?"

"Not at all," he assured her, glancing down at the instrument panel for some reason. He'd done that a lot since they'd left the house, Stephanie thought. Was he checking the speedometer or was it something else on the digital display that kept catching his attention?

"What—?" Stephanie began, and then cried out in shock as sound exploded in her head. Voices, voices, voices. Weeping, laughing, screaming, chatting. Voices of all kinds pouring into her head like water over a break wall.

"The voices are back," Lucian said, and while she could hardly hear him over the noise filling her mind, Stephanie thought he sounded oddly satisfied. She didn't even have the capacity to wonder over that at the moment, though, with the assault she was under.

"Remember to breathe, Stephanie," Lucian said calmly. "Deep breaths. Let the noise flow over you and breathe."

Stephanie sucked in a deep breath, held it for a second, and then let it out, only to draw another. As had happened before, the deep breaths helped and the panic inside of her slowly began to recede.

"Good. Your pulse rate is slowing. You're calming down," Lucian said after a minute. "Now push the voices back. Let them flow over you and push them to the back of your mind so you can think more clearly and listen to me without their interfering."

Stephanie followed his instructions as she had the last time this had happened and tried to focus on his voice as he began to tell her his plans for Dressler's rogues. He'd already called the other members of the Council, and arranged for them to meet at the Enforcer house that night to judge the rogues and determine their future, or lack thereof. From a cursory reading of their minds as they'd loaded up the men, he suspected they'd almost all have to be put down, bar a handful who were more recent turns, had been turned unwillingly, and hadn't yet hurt anyone. Who had—even in the midst of the battle that had taken place—aimed away from the hunters, and happily given themselves up rather than hurt anyone.

Stephanie was finding concentrating on his words made bearing the voices inside her head easier, so was sorry when he suddenly announced, "We're here. I'll go in and get the food. You wait here."

Stephanie nodded, and tried not to grimace. It was easier for her to bear the voices when he was talking. Without him, she had nothing to distract her and had to relearn the ability to close the door between the voices and the rest of her mind to tone it down to a bearable level. She concentrated on that while Lucian was gone, and had just managed to metaphorically shut the bedroom door in her mind when he returned and opened the door on her side of the vehicle.

"You're doing well," he complimented after setting bags and bags and bags of food on the floor of the SUV around her feet. Presumably just to annoy her, although she supposed he hadn't put them in the back for fear they might fall over on the ride back and the food spill out. At least, this way, she could keep an eye on them.

Before she could ask what he meant when he'd said she was doing well, he closed the door and walked around to get in the driver's side.

"Are you hearing anything we need to look into?" he asked with interest as he started the engine, and headed out of the restaurant parking lot. "Rogue immortals wandering the area, or anything of that nature?"

Stephanie licked her lips, took a deep breath, and then set to the task of opening herself to the voices in her head to sort through what she was picking up. A marital dispute here, a business negotiation there, someone grieving the loss of a loved one, someone bemoaning a breakup, a weeping child. She wasn't sure how long she'd been wading through the myriad voices in her head when Lucian said, "Stephanie?"

"No. There are no thoughts from rogues in my head," she said after a moment. "I don't think any of Dressler's men got away and are in the area."

"Good," he said. "So, about your engagement—"

"I'm not engaged," Stephanie protested wearily. "I—"

"Do you want to be?" Lucian asked.

"Well, of course," she said with exasperation, half of her attention on pushing the voices back again and reclosing the metaphorical bedroom door in her head. "He's my life mate, but while I know you don't think this thing with the voices in my head is a problem . . . What if it is?"

"It isn't," he said with certainty.

"You don't know that," she snapped, and scowled when Lucian glanced down at the instrument panel again. What was his fascination with the damned speedometer or whatever? she wondered impatiently, and gave him a sour look when he glanced her way almost expectantly.

He didn't say anything, or look away for a full minute despite being the one at the wheel, and Stephanie was about to comment on that when the voices in her head suddenly died.

"Gone?" Lucian asked mildly when she blinked in surprise.

"Yes," she breathed with relief, and then narrowed her gaze on him. "How did you know?"

"Because we are now five and a half miles from your house and Thorne," Lucian answered easily, his gaze back on the road ahead.

"What?" Stephanie asked with confusion and glanced around to see that they were approaching the post office in town. "What has that to do with anything?"

"Obviously, Thorne is the reason the voices go quiet," Lucian said with a shrug.

"No, he's not," she said with a laugh.

"I assure you he is," Lucian said firmly. "The voices started up again when we were precisely five and a half miles from the house. It was because you were out of range of Thorne. He is the one stopping the voices for you."

"No, he's not," Stephanie repeated with irritation. "I told you, the voices stopped a good hour before he arrived at the house the first time."

"Then he must have been somewhere in the area for that hour," Lucian said unconcerned.

"But—"

"Why do the nanos choose life mates?" he asked patiently.

Stephanie scowled impatiently at the question. "I don't know. I mean, do they really pick them? Or is it just that they recognize a certain energy in the other person that is complementary, or similar, to that of the person that is their host?"

"Is that how you recognize people who might be life mates?" Lucian asked.

"Basically, yes," she admitted.

"And what does having a life mate do for an immortal?" he asked, making her feel like she was in school, taking Immortal 101.

"You mean aside from hot monkey sex?" Stephanie asked dryly, and when he gave her a dour look, she sighed and said, "Usually a life mate gives their partner peace and companionship. They're someone they can live with without worrying about their mind being read, or their being controlled."

Lucian nodded. "I'd say that's certainly what Thorne gives you. In spades. He makes the voices in your head go silent. So, of course the nanos would consider him a good life mate for you."

"I told you, it can't be Thorne," Stephanie said wearily. "He was nowhere near me when the voices stopped the first time. And he was right there in the bedroom next to mine when they came back after the accident."

"He was in stasis when that happened," Lucian pointed out. "Perhaps whatever affects the voices in your head shuts down while he is in stasis. Sonar, perhaps," he added.

"Sonar?" she asked uncertainly.

"The ultrasound waves bats send out," he explained. "Perhaps that interferes with your ability to pick up other people's thoughts. He does have bat DNA."

"Yes, he does," Stephanie murmured quietly, and actually considered it for a minute before shaking her head. "But again, he was nowhere near the house the first time the voices stopped. It was just a fluke that the voices started again on this drive to Glencoe," she insisted.

Much to her amazement, Lucian suddenly pulled off the road into a driveway, brought them to an abrupt halt, then backed out onto the road and headed back the way they'd come.

"Where are we going?" she asked with surprise as he drove back toward Glencoe. "We were almost home. And the food will get cold."

Lucian didn't respond.

Stephanie scowled at him with exasperation as they drove through town, but despite not believing him, began to tense up as they left town and continued driving with Lucian constantly checking the instrument panel.

"Right now," he said suddenly, and Stephanie cried out as the voices returned, a hammering barrage of voices.

She was only vaguely aware when Lucian slowed and then pulled a U-turn, but a moment later the voices stopped again, leaving Stephanie gasping in the passenger seat.

"Now do you believe me?" he asked dryly.

Stephanie simply sat, trying to regain her equilibrium, but as her mind cleared, she began to think.

"Wait a minute," she said after a moment. "Do you mean to tell me you knew it was Thorne when the voices hit me again on the ride out to Glencoe and just kept driving?"

"Yes," he said simply.

"Well, why the hell didn't you turn back then and tell me this?" she asked with amazement.

"Because I'm hungry," he said. "Besides, you have

to learn to get control of the voices quickly when they come on you. Thorne won't be with you all the time."

"Yeah, right," she said with derision. "Now that I know he keeps the voices at bay, I'm not letting that man out of my sight. Or at least no more than five miles out of my sight."

"So, you'll keep him a prisoner to save you from the voices?" Lucian asked with interest.

Stephanie scowled at the choice of words. "No, of course not."

"And you do not wish to help with catching rogues anymore?" he asked next.

Stephanie bit her lip. She liked helping to catch rogues. It made her feel like she was contributing. It also gave her fodder for her books, which she needed to keep writing to make a living.

"Right," she sighed finally. "I have to learn to control the voices quickly."

Lucian gave an approving grunt and nodded.

They were both silent for a minute and then Stephanie began to smile.

"What?" Lucian asked, glancing at her out of the corner of his eye.

"I can marry Thorne," she said, her face breaking into a grin.

"Yes, you can," he agreed. "I give my approval."

"Yeah?" she asked with amusement. "Does that mean you'll play Daddy and walk me down the aisle with Victor?"

"You want both of us to walk you down the aisle?" he asked with surprise.

Stephanie considered it seriously, but not for long. While Victor had been her surrogate father since the turn, so had Lucian in his own way. She owed the woman she'd become to both of them and would really like both men to walk her down the aisle, so said, "Yes. I do."

Lucian was silent for a minute, and then said, "Stephanie, I've watched you grow from a gawky, sharp-tongued teenager into a beautiful, self-assured young woman. I've watched you help us with rogues, and make your own way in life, all while fighting your demons, and struggling to control the voices in your head. You've become a fine young woman. One I would have been proud to have for a daughter. I'd be honored to act as your father and join Victor to walk you down the aisle," he said solemnly.

Stephanie swallowed as a sudden rush of emotion welled up within her. Blinking her eyes against the tears suddenly glazing them, she turned her head toward the window so he wouldn't see, and whispered, "Thank you. For everything."

"My pleasure, little girl," he said as he reached up to push the button to open the gate at the house and slowed to pull into the driveway. As they waited for the gate to open, he said, "You'll want to tell Thorne the good news."

"Yes," she agreed, clearing her throat and sitting up in her seat as the gates opened up enough for him to drive through.

Lucian merely nodded as he drove down the driveway and along the grass path between the trees leading out to her house. But when her home came into view and they saw Thorne stepping off the porch to watch them approach, he said, "Well, be quick about it. I'm hungry."

Stephanie laughed at his curmudgeonly attitude and assured him, "I'll be quick."

"Sure you will," he said dryly.

"What does that mean?" she asked with amusement.

"It means I've lived a long time and seen a lot of life mates at their beginnings. You'll start out meaning to be quick, and the next thing you know, it'll be sex in the bushes, or on the lounge chair, or up against the house wall," he predicted as he brought the SUV to a halt, put it in park and shut it off. Turning to her then, he added, "I am not waiting for you two to return before eating, and I am not dragging your unconscious, naked asses into the house when you pass out afterward. I'll just leave you there for Thorne's mother to find."

Stephanie burst out laughing at the threat, and then shook her head and handed him bag after bag after bag of the food he'd dumped on her in Glencoe, as she assured him, "That won't happen. But if it does, I guarantee you will not find our unconscious, naked asses in a bush, on a lounge chair, or at the base of a wall."

"We'll see," was all he said as he got out of the car with the food.

Smiling, Stephanie watched him go, then opened her door and walked to meet Thorne as Lucian passed him, heading into the house.

"Are you okay?" Thorne asked at once, reaching for her as she approached.

"Yes," she assured him. "And I have good news. You're the reason the voices stop. At least I think you are," she added with uncertainty, and then asked, "Did you come straight to the house that first day? Or were you in the area for a while before arriving at the gate?"

"I came here," he said, and then frowned, and added, "Well, after I stopped at the reserve for coffee."

"You stopped at the reserve?" she asked sharply. The reserve was land held by one of the First Nations. It had a small town all its own with a couple of gas stations, stores, and a Tim Hortons coffee shop. It was also about the same distance away from her house as the post office. It was within the five-and-a-half-mile radius, she realized. Just in the opposite direction.

"Yes. Dani mentioned they have a Tim Hortons coffee shop there that opens at 6 A.M. It was close to that when I hit the area, and I knew there would be no cream for coffee at the house, so I went there, waited for them to open, and then had to wait for them to make the first pot of coffee, so I could buy a cup. Then I sat on the motorcycle in the parking lot and drank it while I called Marguerite's house to let them know I'd made the drive safely. We ended up chatting for a bit." He shrugged. "So, I was probably in the area for maybe forty-five minutes to an hour before I actually arrived at the house."

"So, it was you that first time too," she breathed, and then stilled and asked, "You went into a coffee shop?"

"No," he assured her. "If there'd been a drive-through I would have used that, but there isn't, so my options were limited. I did consider risking it and going in. I was wearing the duster you had me put on to go to town. It's why it was here. I wore it for the drive down to hide my wings on the road," he explained. "And I had my motorcycle helmet on, which hid my head, but I didn't think it would go over well if I wore the helmet into the shop, and wasn't sure someone might not see a flash of wing in the brightly lit store, so I asked the guy managing the gas pump to run in and buy it for me while the gas was pumping. I gave him a big tip, though," he added, and then tilted his head and asked, "Why are you smiling like that?"

"Because I think you were made for me, Thorne Salter," she sighed, sliding her arms around his waist under his wings.

"Yeah?" he asked, smiling now too and sliding his own arms around her. "Why is that?"

"Well, for one thing you are the reason the voices stop," she told him. "Lucian thinks it's something to do with sonar interfering with my ability to hear the voices."

His eyebrows rose at that. "Really?"

"Really," she assured him. "The voices started up again while you were in stasis and stopped again when your fever broke. And then when we drove to get breakfast, the voices started again once I was five and a half miles away from you, and then stopped on the way back when we got about five and a half miles away again. I'm pretty sure it's you. You give me peace."

"Just what every guy wants to hear from his girl," he said dryly, but was smiling.

"Oh, it's much more than that. I mean, that's pretty big. I love the silence in my head when I'm with you. I can actually hear you talk."

Thorne chuckled at that, but she continued. "And I do like talking to you. But you also understand the loneliness I've lived with, and feeling like a freak because you've felt like one too." She shrugged helplessly. "I think we could be very happy together."

"So, you'd maybe be willing to marry me?" he asked with interest.

Stephanie raised her eyebrows. "Is that a proposal?

Because I have to say, your mother already proposed to me."

Thorne groaned. "I heard. I'm sorry. I—"

"But the answer is yes," Stephanie interrupted him to say. She smiled and nodded when he paused and looked at her questioningly.

Thorne just stared at her for a minute, then bent his head and kissed her, a gentle nip of the lips before he breathed, "I like talking to you too." He kissed her again, his hands beginning to roam her body. "And you're right, I do know what it's like to feel like a freak, but I don't feel like a freak when I'm with you."

"Oh. I don't feel like one with you either," Stephanie moaned, arching against him as his hands smoothed down her back to her bottom, and cupped and squeezed her.

"I want to take you flying," he muttered, his mouth trailing across her cheek to her ear. "I want to strip you naked, hold you in my arms, and fly as high as I can and then—" His mouth covered hers as he ground against her.

Stephanie kissed him back excitedly, but when he began to pull her T-shirt out of her jean shorts, she broke their kiss on a gasp. "We have to go to the gazebo," she muttered, even as her hands now moved over his body through his clothes.

"Yes," he agreed, but gave up on her T-shirt to slide his hand between her legs and rub her through the cloth of her shorts as he muttered, "The gazebo."

Stephanie groaned at the caress, her hips moving into it, but then shook her head, and moaned, "I don't want your mother to find us naked and unconscious."

That seemed to make it through his passion, and Thorne scooped her up into his arms, his wings flapping as he half ran and half flew to the gazebo. Landing at the door, he let her work the latch to open it and carried her in, his wings folding away again. He then turned for her to pull the door closed before carrying her to the wicker couch against one wall.

"My mother wants the wedding to take place in June," he warned as he set her on the cushions and came down on top of her.

"Yes," Stephanie breathed, reaching around to undo the Velcro of his shirt to bare his chest. Sighing then with relief, she ran her hands over that expanse of beautiful skin rippling over muscle.

Thorne groaned at the caress, and then brushed her hands away and quickly tugged her T-shirt off over her head.

"I love that you don't wear a bra," he muttered, covering her breasts with his hands. "Where do you want to honeymoon?"

"The island," she gasped, arching under his caress.

"Really?" he asked with surprise.

Stephanie nodded and reached down to rub the bulge between his legs. "I want you to strip me naked and take me flying. I want you to hold me in your arms and take me as high as you can and then . . ." She squeezed his erection, moaning with him at the sensation it caused in her as well.

Pulling away from her abruptly, Thorne stood to quickly remove his jeans, then knelt between her legs and reached for the waistband of her jean shorts.

"I think I love you, Stephanie McGill," Thorne said solemnly as he unsnapped the button of her shorts and lowered the zipper.

"I think I love you too, Thorne Salter," she breathed,

lifting her hips so that he could pull her shorts off. "And I can't wait to start my life with you."

"You already have," he growled, lowering himself to lie on top of her. Easing into her then, he groaned, "And I can't wait to see what life has in store for us."

Stephanie merely gasped and rose up to meet him, unable to even say that she couldn't wait either. But it was true, and it was the first time in the thirteen years since she was turned that she'd looked forward to the future. With Thorne at her side, she knew it would be a good one.

Can't get enough of Lynsay Sands?
Turn the page for a sneak peek
of the historical romance

THE CHASE

Available Summer 2022

One

"What does she look like?"

Rolfe ignored the question as they crested the hill and Dunbar keep came into view. He sighed his relief. The castle symbolized an end to the sorry task he'd been burdened with, an end he would be happy to see. Though loyal to the king, he was beginning to think Richard II was going out of his mind. Rolfe Kenwick, Baron of Kenwickshire, was no cupid; and yet he had already been forced to arrange two weddings, was seeing to a third at the moment, and no doubt would have another to see to on returning to court. If he returned to court, he thought grimly. 'Twould serve Richard right if he did not. There were far better things he could spend his time on than arranging weddings and chasing after unwilling grooms. And this groom was definitely not eager.

It would have been smarter to simply send one of the king's messengers to Blake, ordering him to travel to

Dunbar. It certainly would have been easier. At least then he would not have been forced to listen to Blake's constant protestations or to suffer his many delays. He also would not have had to answer Blake's constant and repetitive questions as to the fairness and disposition of his soon-to-be-bride, or lied in the matter of both.

Grimacing, Rolfe raised a hand in signal to the two long rows of men-at-arms at their back. The king's banner was immediately raised higher to make it more visible to the men guarding the wall.

"What does she look like?" Blake repeated, his gaze moving anxiously over the castle on the horizon.

Rolfe finally turned to peer at the strong, blond warrior at his side. Blake Sherwell, the heir to the Earl of Sherwell, one of the wealthiest lords in the kingdom. He was called "the Angel" by the women at court. The name suited him. The man had been blessed with the appearance of an angel; not the sweet innocence of a cherub, but the hard, lean, pure looks of one of heaven's warriors. His eyes were as blue as the heavens themselves, his nose aquiline, his face sharp and hard and his fair hair hanging to his shoulders in long glistening golden locks. He was just over six feet in height, his shoulders wide and muscular, his waist narrow, and his legs long and hard from years of hugging a horse. Even Rolfe had to admit the other man's looks were stunning. Unfortunately, Blake had also been blessed with a tongue as sweet as syrup; honeyed words dripped from his mouth like rain drops off a rose petal, a skill he used to his advantage with the ladies. It was said he could have talked Saint Agnes into his bed had he lived in her time, which was why the men generally referred to him as "the devil's own." Too many of them had wives who had proven themselves susceptible to his charms.

"What does she look like?"

Rolfe put aside his thoughts at the repeated question. He opened his mouth to snap at Blake, then caught the expression on the face of the overlarge man riding a little behind the warrior.

Little George was the giant's name. A friend and knight, he had decided to accompany Blake on this journey. An odder pair could not be found; the two were as opposite as fire and water. Where Blake was blond, Little George was dark; where Blake was handsome, Little George had been cursed with the face of a bulldog. But what the man lacked in looks, he made up for in strength. The fellow was possessed of incredible height and bulk. He stood somewhere in the neighborhood of six-foot-eleven and measured a good three and a half feet across at the shoulders. He was a rock; silent, solid, and usually expressionless, which made the way he was now rolling his eyes and shaking his jowled face particularly funny. It seemed he, too, grew impatient with Blake's constant questioning on the appearance of his soon-to-be-bride.

Regaining some of his patience, Rolfe turned back to the man beside him. "You have asked—and I have answered—that question at least thirty times since leaving Castle Eberhart, Blake."

"And now I ask again," the fair-haired man said grimly.

An exasperated tsking drew Rolfe's attention to the bishop, who rode at his other side. The king had dragged the elderly prelate out of retirement to perform several weddings in the recent past. The marriage between Blake Sherwell and Seonaid Dunbar was the third he'd been called to officiate in as many months. If they ever got it done. Rolfe wasn't all that sure that they would. It had been nothing but trouble from the start.

Although the betrothal had been contracted some twenty years earlier, no one seemed to wish the wedding to take place.

While Seonaid's brother, Duncan, had forced the marriage with his demand that the king finally see it take place, he'd made it obvious he'd prefer to see the betrothal broken and his sister free to marry elsewhere. As for the father, Angus Dunbar had managed to avoid him for days, then made him talk until he was blue in the face before agreeing to the wedding. The moment he had, Rolfe had sent a message to the groom's father, the Earl of Sherwell, informing him of the upcoming nuptials and the necessity of attending, then he'd headed off to collect Blake. Rolfe could have simply sent a messenger to the son as well, but he'd needed the break from the Dunbars.

Damn. Rolfe had almost pitied the poor man for marrying into the cantankerous bunch—or at least he had at the outset of their journey. However, after the way the fellow had dillydallied using every excuse he could think of to delay on the journey here, then pestered Rolfe throughout the entire week of the trip with his repetitive questions about his betrothed's looks, intelligence, and nature, Rolfe was fair sick of the lot of them. He could not wait to show them his backside on accomplishing the deed.

"Well?" Blake growled, reminding Rolfe of his question.

Giving a long-suffering sigh, he answered, "As I have told you—at least fifty times since starting our journey—she is tall."

"How tall?"

"Mayhap a finger shorter than myself."

"And?"

"Lady Seonaid is well-formed, with long ebony hair, large blue eyes, a straight patrician nose, high cheekbones, and fair, nearly flawless skin. She *is* attractive . . ." He hesitated, debating whether it was time to warn the other man of the less than warm greeting he was about to receive.

"Do I hear a howbeit in there?" Blake asked, drawing Rolfe from his thoughts.

"Aye," he admitted, deciding if he were to warn him at all, the time was now.

"Howbeit what?" the warrior prompted, eyes narrowed in suspicion.

"She is a bit rough around the edges."

"Rough around the edges?" Blake echoed with alarm. "What mean you she is rough around the edges?"

"Well . . ." Rolfe glanced at the bishop for assistance. Bushy white eyebrows doing a little dance above gentle green eyes, Bishop Wykeham considered the question briefly, then leaned forward to peer past Rolfe's bulk at the groom. "Her mother died when she was young, leaving your betrothed to be raised by her father and older brother. I fear she is a bit lacking in some of the softer refinements," he said delicately.

Blake was not fooled. The bishop was a master of understatement. If he said she was lacking some softer refinements, she was most likely a barbarian. He turned on the younger man accusingly. "You did not mention this afore, Kenwick!"

"Well, nay," Rolfe allowed reluctantly. "Nay, I did not. I thought mayhap it would set you to fretting, and there was no sense in doing that."

"Damn!" Blake glared at Dunbar Castle as they approached. It appeared cold and unfriendly to him. The Scots had not exactly rolled out the welcome, but then he had not expected them to. They wanted the marriage no more than he did.

" 'Tis not so bad, son," the bishop soothed. "Seonaid is a bit rough and gruff, but rather like your friend Amaury is. In fact, I would say she is as near a female version of that fellow as 'tis possible to have."

Amaury de Aneford was Blake's best friend and had been since they'd squired together as children. They got on well and had even been business partners until Amaury's recent marriage and rise in station to duke had forced him out of the warring business. Bishop Wykeham thought he was offering a positive comparison to the young man. He thought wrong.

"B'gad," Blake muttered in horror. In his mind's eye he was lifting his bride's marriage veil and having to kiss a tall, black-haired version of his good friend. It was enough to near knock him off his horse.

Shaking the image away, Blake tossed a glare in Little George's direction as he burst out laughing—no doubt under the influence of a not dissimilar vision. When his glare had little effect, he slumped miserably in his saddle. He would dearly have loved to turn around and head straight back to England. However, it was not an option. The blasted betrothal had been negotiated when he was but a boy of ten and Lady Seonaid just four. His father—the earl—had regretted doing so almost before the ink had dried on the scroll. He and the Dunbar— once the best of friends—had suffered a falling out. They had not spoken to each other since two weeks after completing the betrothal, some twenty years ago. Both had been more than happy to forget all about the contract, but neither of them had been willing to break it and forfeit the properties and dower they had put up against it. Their reluctance had left the possibility of the king ordering the fulfillment of the contract if he so wished. Unfortunately, he wished.

Blake could not turn and head back to England. His future was set. By noon on the morrow, he would be a married man.

Life was a trial, and what little freedom a man enjoyed was short-lived. He forced himself to straighten in the saddle as he realized they were about to pass through the gates into the bailey of Dunbar keep. He would present a strong, confident front to these people. His pride insisted upon it.

Blake lifted his head and met the silent stares of the guards watching from the walls, but soon found it difficult to keep his face expressionless when the men began shouting to each other.

"Which one be he, diya think?" shouted one man.

"The poor wee blond one, I wager," answered another, an older soldier. "He be a fair copy of his faither."

There was a brief silence as every eye examined him more thoroughly, then someone commented, "A shame, that. I be thinkin' the dark braw one might have a chance, but the wee one'll no last a day."

"I say he'll no last half a day!" someone else shouted. "Whit diya wager?"

Blake's expression hardened as the betting began. Indignity rose in him on a wave. Never in his life had he been called *wee* before. He was damned big next to the average man, though he supposed he appeared smaller next to Little George. Still, he was of a size with Rolfe and by no means small. He also didn't appreciate the fact that they doubted his ability to handle one lone woman, taller than average or not. A glance at Rolfe and the bishop showed both men looking uncomfortable as they avoided his eyes. Little George, however, was looking a bit worried. It seemed he was letting the men on the wall unsettle him.

Well, Blake had no intention of doing so. Stiffening his back a bit more, he led his horse up to the keep's front steps. The absence of his bride, who should have been waiting on the stairs to greet him, was an added insult. 'Twas damned rude, and he would be sure to say so when he met the woman. He had just decided as much when the men in the bailey gave up all pretense of working and began to gather around their party to stare. Being the cynosure of all eyes was discomfiting, but their mocking smiles and open laughter were unbearable.

Blake was relieved at the distraction when one of the large doors of the keep creaked open. A young boy appeared at the top of the steps, turned to shout something back behind him, then bolted down the stairs.

"Thank you, son." Blake slid off his mount and smiled as the lad took reins of his mount. His smile faded, however, as he noted the mixture of pity and amusement on the boy's face. The child retrieved the reins of Rolfe, the bishop, and Little George's horses as well, then led them away.

Shifting uncomfortably, Blake raised an eyebrow in Rolfe's direction. The other man merely shrugged uncertainly, but worry crossed his features before he turned to give instructions to the soldiers escorting them.

Scowling, Blake turned to peer up the steps at the closed double doors of the keep. The upcoming meeting was becoming more intimidating every moment, and he took the time to mentally calm himself and gird his courage. Then he realized that he was allowing himself to be unsettled by a meeting with a mere female.

Blake paused and gave his head a shake. What the devil was he worried about? Women had always responded well to him. He was considered quite attractive by the opposite sex. He wouldn't be surprised if his soon-to-be-bride melted into a swoon at the very sight of him. Her gratitude at being lucky enough to marry him would know no bounds, and her apologies for not meeting him on his arrival would flow unending.

Being the Angel, he would gallantly forgive her; then they would be married. After which he would have done with the business and head home. There was no law and no line in the agreement stating he had to take her with him. Blake thought he would leave her here, making regular if infrequent visits, until he had a home where he could put her and forget her.

His usually high confidence restored, Blake smiled at an anxious Little George, then jogged jauntily up the front steps to the keep doors. He pushed them open with a flourish, then led his much slower and somewhat less confident companions into the keep. His steps slowed when he spied the men seated at the trestle tables in the great hall. They were wolfing down food and laughing with loud ribaldry. If he had thought the hundred or so men guarding the wall and going about their business in the bailey were all Laird Dunbar ruled, it seemed he had been sorely mistaken. There were at least as many men enjoying a rest and repast inside. 'Twas a lot of men for such a small keep.

Blake did a brief scan of those present, searching for the woman he was to marry and spend the rest of his life with, but there seemed to be none present. Other than a servant or two, the great hall was entirely inhabited by men. It mattered little, he reassured himself. He would meet her soon enough.

Blake moved toward the head table, slowly gaining the attention of man after man as they nudged each other and gestured toward him.

Ignoring their rude behavior, he moved up the center of the room until he stood before the grizzled old man he suspected was the laird, Angus Dunbar. The room had fallen to silence. A hundred eyes fixed on and bore into him from every angle and still the man did not look up. Blake was just becoming uncomfortable when Rolfe moved to his side and cleared his throat.

"Greetings again, Lord Dunbar."

Angus Dunbar was an old man with shoulders stooped under years of wear and worry. His hair was gray and wiry, seeming to stand up in all directions. He took his time about finishing the chicken leg he gnawed on, then tossed the bone over his shoulder and raised his head to peer, not at the man who had spoken—but at Blake himself. Blake immediately had to revise his first opinion. Had he thought the man old? Worn down by worry? Nay. Gray hair he might have, but his eyes spat life and intelligence as he speared Blake where he stood.

A brief flash of surprise shot across his face, then his

mouth set in grim lines and he sat back. "Soooo," he drawled. "For guid or ill ye finally shoo yersel'. Ye look like yer faither's whelp."

Blake took the time to translate the man's heavily accented words. Once he was sure he understood, he gave an uncertain nod.

"Weell, 'tis too late." His pleasure in making the announcement was obvious. "Clockin' time came an' went an' the lass done flew the chicken cavie, so I ken ye'll be thinkin' linkin'."

"Cavie? Thinkin' linkin'?" He turned to a frowning Rolfe in bewilderment.

"He said hatching time came and went and the girl flew the chicken coop, so he supposes you'll be tripping along," the other man explained, then turned to the laird, anger beginning to show itself. "What mean you the girl flew the cavie? Where is she gone?"

Dunbar shrugged a dismissal. "She dinna say."

"You did not ask?"

Angus shook his head. " 'Twas nigh on two weeks ago noo, the day after Lady Weeldwood arrived—"

"Lady Wildwood is here?" Rolfe's surprise was obvious. "She was to wait for us to fetch her back to court."

"Aye, weell, an' surely ye've taken yer time about it, have ye no? We expected ye back more than a week ago."

Rolfe tossed a dirty look at Blake, muttering, "We were unavoidably delayed."

"Weell, while ye were 'unavoidably delayed,' Lady Weeldwood was forced to flee fer her life."

"You do not mean Lady Margaret Wildwood?" Blake interrupted, and was surprised when the Scot nodded. He had met Lord Wildwood and his wife several times at court. Lady Margaret had been there often while the queen had still lived. From what he had seen and heard, the couple had been happily married for some twenty years. Lord Wildwood would never have hurt his wife when alive and certainly could not now he was dead. Blake knew the older man had died in Ireland but a few short months ago. "Lord Wildwood is dead," he spoke his thoughts aloud. "Who would threaten Lady Wildwood?"

Rolfe frowned and seemed to debate what to say, then sighed. "Know you Greenweld?"

Blake nodded at the mention of the Wildwood's neighbor. He was a greedy, immoral bastard, not well liked by anyone.

"He forced Lady Wildwood into marriage," Rolfe told him. "He separated her from her daughter, Lady Iliana, and used the girl's safety as a means to keep Lady Wildwood from protesting the marriage and to keep her in line."

Blake was stunned by the news. "Surely he didn't expect to get away with it?"

"But he did get away with it," Rolfe said. "Until Lady Wildwood managed to get a letter to the king through a faithful servant. The message recounted her predicament. Richard immediately arranged for Iliana to marry Duncan, Lord Angus's son," Rolfe explained, with a nod toward the seated laird. "Thereby removing her from Greenweld's grasp and threat. The king is even now seeking to annul the marriage Greenweld forced."

"Which is most like what got her beat," Angus commented grimly. "He wid see her dead ere givin' up Wildwood."

"Aye." Rolfe nodded. "That may be the case, if he caught wind of it." He considered the situation before glancing at Angus. "She headed here for protection, I presume? Why did she not head for court? The king would have protected her."

Angus shrugged. "I doona yet ken. She fled here with her maid an' the maid's son, but she fell under a fever along the way. She's been restin' since arrivin' an' I have no yet spoken to her."

"I see," Rolfe murmured, his expression tight with displeasure. "Is she well?"

The Dunbar pursed his lips. "Alive. Barely. He near knocked the life out o' her. 'Tis why she anticipated yer rescuin' her an' fled here to the safety we could offer as kin."

Rolfe and the bishop exchanged a glance, then the younger man asked, "Have you sent a messenger to the king with news of her presence here?"

"Nay. I thought to wait for ye to arrive. 'Twill be best to give him all the news at one time. He may wish ye to escort her back to court once she's recovered."

Rolfe nodded. "You are a wise man, Angus Dunbar."

The laird's lip curled. "An' yer a fair diplomat, lad. 'Tis why yer king sends ye out on such fool chores."

"Hmm." Rolfe's displeasure at being saddled with such chores was obvious as he peered at Blake. "We had best see to this one now."

Angus grimaced. "Aye. Weell now . . . that could be a problem. As I was tellin' ye, Seonaid took advantage of the uproar Lady Wildwood's arriving caused. The day after the lady arrived, the men an' I took to bowsin'. The chit waited until I was fou, then come gin nicht she flew the cavie."

"What?" Blake asked, with both confusion and frustration.

"He said she left the day after Lady Wildwood arrived—"

"I understood that part," Blake snapped irritably. "What the devil is gin nicht?"

"Nightfall. Laird Angus and his men were drinking and Lady Seonaid waited until he was drunk, then at nightfall she flew the—"

"Coop. Aye, I understood that." Turning back, he glared at the older man, who was eyeing him with open satisfaction. Blake liked to think of himself as something of a master of words. He used them often and well to gain his way in many things. It was the height of irritation for him to find himself unable to understand what was being said, and he suspected the Dunbar knew as much and was enjoying himself at his expense. "Am I to take it, then, that you are breaking the contract and are willing to forfeit her dower?" he asked.

Dunbar sat up in his seat like a spring. "When the devil sprouts flowers fer horns!" he spat, then suddenly went calm and smiled. "To me thinkin', 'tis ye who forfeit by neglectin' yer duty to collect yer bride."

"But I am arrived to collect her." He flashed a cold smile.

"The lass has seen twenty-four years," the Dunbar snarled. "Ye should have come for her some ten years back."

Blake opened his mouth to respond, but Rolfe touched his arm to stop him and murmured smoothly, "We have been through all this, Laird Angus. Been and back. You agreed to the wedding taking place here, and Lord Blake has come as requested to fulfill his part of the bargain." He frowned. "I do not understand why you are being difficult. You had agreed to the wedding by the time I left. Duncan agreed also. Only Seonaid was wont to argue the wedding taking place when last I was here, yet now you appear to be against it as well."

Angus shrugged, amusement plucking at his lined face. "Aye, I agreed to it. Howbeit, I dinna say I would be makin' it easy for the lad. He's tarried a mite long for me likin', an' 'tis an insult to every Dunbar."

There were murmurs and nods of agreement all around. Rolfe sighed. It seemed the laird would see the deed done, but not aid in the doing, which was not good enough in his opinion. "I understand your feelings, my lord, but I fear Lord Blake is right. By aiding your daughter in escaping her marriage, you are breaking the contract, her dower will be considered forfeit, and—"

Laird Angus silenced him with a wave of disgust. "Oh, save yer threats. I'd see the lass married soon as you would, 'tis well past time." He glared at Blake. " 'Sides, I'd have grandbabies from her, even if they are half-English." He paused to take a long draught of ale from his tankard, then slammed it down and announced, "She ran off to St. Simmian's."

"St. Simmian's?"

" 'Tis an abbey two days' ride from here," he explained with amusement. "She asked for sanctuary there an' they granted it. Though, I canna see the lass in there to save me soul."

"Damn," Rolfe snapped; then his gaze narrowed on the Scot. "I thought you knew not where she was."

"I said she dinna tell me," he corrected calmly. "I had one o' me lads hie after her when I realized she was gone. He followed her trail to Simmian's but had no luck in gettin' her out. Men're no' allowed inside, ye ken."

"Aye, I know," Rolfe muttered irritably.

Angus Dunbar turned his gaze back to Blake, his eyes narrowing on the small signs of relief he saw on the man's face and in his demeanor. "Well? Ye ken where she be now, lad, why do ye tarry? Go an' fetch 'er; she must be bored by now an' may e'en come out to ye."

Blake glanced at Rolfe. He had been thinking that he might have just slipped the noose they would place on his finger, but the expression on the other man's face and his would-be father-in-law's words told him he had thought wrong. They expected him to fetch her out of the abbey to wed. To his mind, it was rather like asking a man to dig his own grave, but it seemed he had little choice.

Sighing, he turned to lead the bishop and Lord Rolfe from the room, but at the door to the keep he paused and waved them on before he returned to face the Dunbar. "You say the abbey is two days' ride away?"

"Aye. Two days."

"Over lands friendly to you or not?"

Angus Dunbar's eyebrows rose in surprise. "Friendly to me. Though no always friendly to the King o' England," he added with amused pleasure. "So I wouldna be wavin' yer banner o'ermuch."

Blake nodded. He had suspected as much. It would no doubt please the Laird of Dunbar and his daughter no end if he died in the attempt, forfeiting the lands promised by his father should he fail to marry the wench. "I would have your plaid then, sir," he said with a predatory smile of his own.

Angus Dunbar blinked at him in surprise, then frowned. "Now, why would ye be wantin' me plaid?"

"If the lands we cross are friendly to you, I would wear your colors to prove we travel under your protection."

There was dead silence in the room and even a bit of confusion; then the men seated at the tables began to murmur amongst themselves, whispering something through the hall until it reached the man to the left of the bewildered laird. His bewilderment seemed to clear as soon as the man leaned to whisper into his ear. Whatever the fellow had said, Angus Dunbar found it vastly amusing. Throwing back his head, he roared with laughter, as did every other man in the room.

Still laughing, the grizzled old man stood, and with little more than a tug and a flick of the wrist, drew the plaid off. Left wearing only a long shirt reaching halfway to his knees, he tossed the brightly colored cloth across the tabletop.

His laughter slowed to a stop as Blake caught the plaid and grimaced at the stench rising off the blanket, then turned to leave again.

"Here!"

Blake paused and turned back. "Aye?"

"Would ye leave me standin' here in naught but me shirttails?" Laird Angus asked, his brows beetling above his eyes.

Blake stared. "What would you have of me?"

"Yer doublet and knickers there."

Blake glanced down at his gold doublet and braies with dismay. Both were new. He supposed he'd thought to impress his bride-to-be with the fine new outfit. " 'Tis a new doublet," he protested. " 'Tis but a few weeks old."

Angus Dunbar shrugged. " 'Tis a fair trade for me colors." He and the other men laughed again.

Sighing, Blake reluctantly handed the plaid to Little George, who had followed him back to the table, then began working at removing his clothes.

"He be bigger than he first looked," one of the men commented as Blake shrugged out of his doublet and tunic to stand bare-chested before them.

Glancing at the man, Blake recognized him as the older man on the wall who had said he favored his father in looks. It seemed some of the men who had lined the wall had followed them inside, though he had not noticed.

"Hmm," was all the Dunbar said. Taking the vestments from Blake, he handed them to one of the men to hold and quickly shrugged out of his own shirt. Tossing the stained and soiled top to his would-be son-in-law, he took the tunic back and tugged it on.

Blake caught the shirt and nearly groaned aloud at the smell coming from it. He would guess it had not been washed since being donned. Probably some three years ago, he guessed, then braced his shoulders and tugged the shirt on before turning his attention to removing the braies and hose he still wore.

"A mite tight, but no' a bad fit."

Blake glanced at Angus Dunbar as the older man finished doing up the doublet over the tunic. His eyes widened as he saw the truth of the words. It seemed his would-be father-in-law was of a size with himself.

"Quit yer gawkin' and give me the braies, lad. My arse is near freezin'."

Realizing he had been staring at the older man, Blake turned his attention back to removing the rest of his clothes. He gave them up to Laird Angus, then took the plaid back from Little George and began wrapping it about his waist.

"What the devil be ye doin'?"

Blake glanced up to see a mixture of dismay and disgust on Angus Dunbar's face.

"Ye doona wear a plaid like that, ye great gowkie! Ye insult me plaid in the wearin'." Finished tying the braies, he reached out and grabbed one end of the cloth. He tugged it from Blake's hold, then dropped it on the floor and knelt to fold it in pleats. Blake watched closely, amazed at the speed the man displayed in the action and wondering if he would be able to replicate it himself. Doubtful, but if he did, it certainly would not be with the same speed.

"There!" The Dunbar sat up straight and looked up at him. "Lay on it."

"Lay on it?" Blake asked with confusion.

"Aye. Lay on it."

Blake gaped. "Surely you jest?"

"Lay on the demn thing!" the older man roared impatiently.

Blake muttered under his breath and lowered himself to the ground to lay atop the pleated plaid. As soon as he had, the laird began tugging at the material. A mere second or so later, he stood and gestured for Blake to rise as well, then finished fitting the plaid about him.

"There." He peered over his handiwork, then shook his head. "I fear it doesna look as good on ye as it does on me," he announced, and there were mutters of agreement all around. "Ye look like a Sassenach atryin' to look like a Scot. Ah, well . . ." Shrugging, he glanced down at the new clothes he wore. "I daresay I suit your clothes much better. What diya be thinkin', lads?" Holding out his arms, he turned in a circle to model the outfit. "Think ye I'll be impressin' Lady Iliana's mother, the Lady Wildwood?"

There was a rumble of approval, then Angus Dunbar turned to take in Blake's sorrowful expression. "Doona fash yerself over it, Sassenach. Ye have enough on yer plate just now. Go fetch yer bride." He grinned, some of his grimness falling away as he added, "If ye can."

Blake stiffened, his face flushing at the chuckles the last three words caused. He was not used to being the butt of someone else's humor and did not care for it, but there was little he could do about it at that moment, so he whirled on his heel and strode toward the door, Little George at his back.

Angus Dunbar pursed his lips and watched Blake stride away. He waited until the men had left the keep, then moved back to his seat and took a long swallow of ale as he glanced around at his men. His gaze finally settled on Gavin, one of his finest fighters and most trustworthy of men. He called the soldier to his side.

"Aye, me laird?"

"Take two men and follow them, lad," he instructed. "The young Sherwell's just fool enough to get hisself killed, and then his fool English father and the English king would blame us. See he finds his way there without gettin' lost."

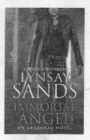
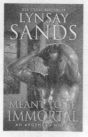